# I Knew I was Naked
# A Catholic Boyhood

# I Knew I was Naked
# A Catholic Boyhood

## Sean Lacey

Library of Congress Control Number:        2010904947
ISBN:            Hardcover            978-1-4500-7745-3
                 Softcover            978-1-4500-7744-6
                 Ebook               978-1-4500-7746-0

This book was printed in the United States of America.

Rev. date: 03/08/2013

**To order additional copies of this book, contact:**
Xlibris Corporation
1-888-795-4274
www.Xlibris.com
Orders@Xlibris.com
77788

# PROLOGUE

**M**odesty is good—they say.
But for me it was a big lead sinker.
I promised to tell my story.
"One day you'll see the humor of it," my brother said.
"Yes, I can laugh about it now, Bryan—most of it."
"What was the worst?"
"Altar boy."

# PART I

**6** years old.

I'm holding a white paper bag full of jelly sandwiches, waiting by the yellow station.

"Stand back from the tracks!"

The sound gets loud and fills my head. A giant sparkler lights me up as the wheels skid along the rails to a stop. I climb aboard, run to the first empty place, and slide across a slippery seat to sit by the window.

The car jerks twice before going smooth. The train makes a song: *I'm-in-a-rush! I'm-in-a-rush! I'm-in-a-rush!* All the people out the window can do is look at me whoosh by.

"One roundtrip, please."

"And the boy?"

"He's big for his age."

"Ain't they all."

The trainman looks like a policeman in his black cap. He tears two tickets off a roll, gets money from a shiny thing, and hands it to my mother with one of the tickets. He puts the other into his puncher, makes two clicks leaving jaggedy holes, and pushes it into a place on the back of the seat ahead.

At each stop he calls the name. At the last stop he calls, "End of the line! All change for the City!"

We get up and I turn to watch the trainman pull the seats on both sides of the car, making them go the other way.

The boat has an upstairs. I lead my mother to a seat on the high deck where the sun feels warm. I take out a jelly sandwich and tear some bread off. I walk to the rail
"Wait till I hold your hand!"
and throw the piece high in the air. A bird with grey wings and a white body does a dive, catches my throw before it hits the water
"Did you see!"
and drops it.
"Seagulls don't like bread," my mother says.

The opening's made of logs tied together. It's too small.
*We're going to crash*, I think . . . But we don't.
The boat's inside the opening. The salty-smelling water's the funny color of Mama's olive soap.
We're going to hit hard on this side . . . But we don't.
We're all the way in and almost stopped when we hit. Then there's the sound the logs make. Ropes as big around as me are thrown to tie the boat, and a wood road comes down making a bridge across the water.

We go fast through the big building, people all around, moving, shouting. I stop to watch the shoeshine boy snap his cloth, but my mother pulls me along.
A man's winding a toy monkey. He sets it down; the monkey jumps over backwards and falls kicking on its side. I squeeze my mother's hand and look up at her.
"You'd break that in two minutes!" she says, pulling me harder.
Outside we go up the steps of a streetcar. I drop our nickel into a box with a glass top. The carman takes a look and does something I don't see to let it fall into the bottom part.
We sit along the wall watching the seats fill up . . . People are standing in front of us hanging onto straps . . . It's our stop and we get off.

I pull out of my mother's hand and run ahead to the door that turns in a circle. Pushing hard I count my seven times around.
We go in the elevator. "Step to the rear, please!"
I'm shoved to the back. I hold my mother's dress with one hand and hold my nose with the other hand to stop the powder smells.

"Ladies' apparel!"

Everyone rushes out of the elevator and we go to a counter covered with pink things. My mother slides a door open underneath, "Sit in there with your bag of sandwiches and wait for me. Don't move till I get back!"

It's dark. I eat a sandwich. I hear noises from the counter. I hear talking. I hear ladies' heels hit the floor. I need to go. I don't know how long it's been. *I'll count to ten.* I eat a sandwich. *I'll count to ten again and my mother'll come.* I need to go bad. I slide the door open and get out. I look all the ways you can. My mother's nowhere in sight. I see a lady with a red book in her hand. I go up to her holding myself through the front of my pants. It feels warm. It's too late.

"Never mind," she smiles, "come with me."

I follow her to a phone, "Mr. Singer, we have a boy who needs dry pants. Do you think the store could donate a pair? . . . I'd say seven-years-old . . . He's wearing navy shorts, but anything will do . . . You have some that aren't selling? . . . You'll send a boy down? . . ."

"This is Manny," the lady says, "he's a great big high schooler. Go with him, and he'll take care of you. I'll wait here for your mother."

I follow Manny up some stairs. He gets a bag with little ropes for handles, stops at a counter, picks up something, and leads me into a tiny room with a big mirror on the wall.

He takes off my wet shorts and puts them in the bag. This gives him the talking to himself, "You're soaked. Looks like a major overhaul."

He does my sweater and shirt, then points to my wet BVDs, "You want to do those yourself? . . . Cat got your tongue?"

He starts unbuttoning, "You are a boy, aren't you? Well, Buster Brown, I'm about to find out . . . Ask a dumb question . . ."

I'm given back to my mother, a bag of wet clothes in one hand, the last of the jelly sandwiches in the other.

# CHAPTER 2

"**W**ho made the world? God made the world. Why did God make me? God made me to love him and serve his in this life and in the next.

"Hail Mary, full of grace. The Lord is with thee. Blessed art thou amongst women, and blessed is the fruit of thy womb, Jesus."

"Sister Angela," I asked the nun teaching Catechism, "what's a womb?"

"That is not a word we use."

"But, Sister, it's in the prayer."

"Hold out your hands!"

The wood pointer made a blur . . . I yelped like a puppy that had its paw stepped on.

"To help you remember the Catechism is to be memorized, not questioned. Will you remember that!"

She was a born teacher.

"How have you sinned?" came from the dark of the curtained box.

I couldn't think what to tell. I thought and thought, but couldn't think of anything bad enough.

"Three Our Father's and three Hail Mary's, just in case."

My stomach was making noises as the Monsignor put the white circle on my tongue, "Receive the body of Christ."

I gagged all the way to the wood seat, knelt in my first long-pantsed suit, and spit the bread into my handkerchief.

I knew I'd done bad.

The screen showed the big bellies of children in faraway places. That was God's punishment. I'd been let off—*so far*—but my sin wouldn't leave me be.

# CHAPTER 3

**7** years old.

I was in my nightie when a 12-year-old visiting across the street came in.

"Doesn't Sean get his bath this morning?"

"Usually," my mother said, "but I'm off to help Mrs. Flynn."

"I could give it to him—no charge."

"That's nice of you."

"Mama!"

"I'm sure Rose can manage. Have you done boys?"

"The mothers think I'm too young, but I want to learn."

"Well Sean will be a good place to start; he's all boy—you'll see what I mean."

"Mama!"

Mama was out the door.

Rose took me by the hand to the bathroom and started the tub.

"Let's see what your mother was talking about."

She came over and pulled my nightie off.

I hadn't learned to cover myself . . .

"Wasn't kidding, was she? . . . You're embarrassed about showing it, aren't you?"

Me standing in the tub, getting washed from the top down, past my belly button, "Ready for your—" she said, taking it in her fingers.

"Not supposed to touch it!"

"How can I wash it if I don't touch it?"

"M-Mama uses a cloth."

"No need for a cloth—stop complaining . . . He's a slippery fish—"

"Not a fish!"
"Ha, ha! He's a fish all right and I'm going to catch him . . ."
"Let go!"
"You want to get done? Then make him stop squirming."

I thought she'd never let go.

8 years old.
Saturday night my mother and Aunt Ellen went to play whist at the Church Hall, leaving my cousin with Dad and me. I'd had it with Mary, so I slipped out to join the kick-the-can game two streets over where she wouldn't find me.

When I got back to the house, Mr. Flynn was on the porch with my father, "Come in, John, while I get Sean ready for his bath."
They took a seat on the sofa, and my father lifted me onto his lap.
"Mary's already in the tub, so we better get moving," he said, starting on my shoes.
"I-I m taking a bath with M-Mary?"
"*Yes you are.*"
I knew that voice—it meant no more questions.
*He's going to undress me in front of Mr. Flynn.*
The shirt and pants came off. There was a knock on the screen door; my father put me on Mr. Flynn's lap, "Could you take his underwear off?"
*Dad!* I said inside me.
"Collection time, Mr. Lacey."
"Come in, Denny, get you in a minute."
He came in as my underwear came off.
"What do you think of him? . . . Take your hands away! Don't touch yourself there!"
"Think he'll do fine with the ladies," Mr. Flynn said.
"Bigger'n Herbie Miller, an' him 11."
"D-Dad . . ."
"What?"
"H-have to . . ."
"Well go to the bathroom."
"M-Mary's there."

"Denny, while I get your money, could you take him out back"

The boy took me in his arms, carried me to some dirt, and set me down, "Go ahead . . . What're you waitin' for?"

"C-could you c-close your eyes?"

"Don't be dumb; I ain't closin' for no 8-year-old . . . Fix it or I fix it."

Hot with shame I fixed it and splashed the dirt."

Once inside, I wiggled out of his arms, ran to the bathroom door, and opened it a crack.

"M-Mary?"

"Come in!"

"D-don't have any clothes on."

"Boys don't wear clothes in the bathtub. Come in!"

"Close your eyes! . . . Are they closed?"

"Yes! Come in!"

They weren't closed.

"Boys are so funny! Imagine having a thing like that between your legs—must be awful!"

Stepping into the water, I saw she was wearing white panties—*not fair—not fair at all.*

# CHAPTER 4

**W**hen I was nine my mother got fat.

The first stars were coming out.
"Take your night things and go next door to Miss Adams."
"Miss Adams! Why!"
"I'm driving your mother to the hospital. Nothing to worry about, Miss Adams knows about boys; she does part-time nursing. Move! Already phoned that you're coming."

My nightie was out—*Miss Adams might put it on me.* All I was wearing were Keds, button-up street shorts, and a pullover shirt. I thought about underwear, but the idea of me in my BVDs took care of that. *No, safest thing is to go as I am; with no nightie and no underwear, she'll have to let me keep my shorts on.*

So holding my toothbrush I knocked on the door. Two things happened: Miss Adams stood over me; my father rushed up from behind.
"Sean, you mind, hear? Miss Adams, I give you carte blanche to discipline him as you see fit."
"What about a bath?"
I held my breath . . . My father looked me up and down, "Doesn't need one," he answered, hurrying away.
I let my breath out.

Miss Adams reminded me of a crow. Her straight black hair pulled tight behind shined liked feathers; her thin nose was a beak.

"Through here. You can sleep with me."

"Not afraid to sleep in a room by myself."

"The other bed isn't made up, and who are you to question your betters? You know what I do to little boys who sass back? I take down their pants and spank their bottoms . . . Ha, ha!" she gave a laugh that made me jump, "When I was a girl, a boy took down his overalls in the cornfield to show me sights. Don't doubt you've shown Louise sights . . . Now let's get you ready for bed."

"My nightgown's in the wash," I lied.

"Then we'll have to do without it, won't we? Sit on the bed."

"Better brush my teeth first."

"*First*, we'll get you undressed," she said, pushing me down.

She pulled my Keds and shirt off, "Stand up, so I can unbutton you."

"You can't!"

"Why not, might I ask?"

"D-don't have any underwear on."

She went to a drawer and took out a pair of girls' black bloomers.

"You can wear these. Those are coming off. Stand up!"

"N-need to go to the bathroom."

"Wee?"

"Y-yes."

"Follow me."

Leaving the bloomers on the bed, she led the way to the bathroom and pulled me to the toilet.

"Seat up!"

I got that far. Couldn't take it out in front of her, so I tried squeezing my hand up the leg of my shorts, but the leg was too tight.

"Don't have to after all."

"Ha, ha!" she did her scary laugh, "You have to all right—admit it!"

She began tickling under my arms. Trying to get away, I ended on the floor . . . That made it easy for her. The more I laughed, the more she tickled . . . A dam broke . . .

"Those shorts will have to be washed."

She undid my bottom button and held up a thumb and finger, making a beak.

"A big bird came out of the sky to see what he could see," she pretended, diving toward the hole she'd made. "He stuck his bill in the ground, and said, *Just look what I've found!*"

Her fingers worked it out of the shorts.

"He's being doubly bad tonight. Is that the trick you show Louise?"

She ran some water in the sink and turned to finish me. After the shorts got hung on the curtain rod, she came at me with a soapy cloth.

"He'll have to be washed too. Take your hands away!"

. . . the soap burned . . .

The scrubbing over, she walked me back to the bed, laid me out, worked the bloomers on, and tucked me in.

I never brushed my teeth.

It was the middle of the night. I was sound asleep when she got me out from the covers; half asleep as she walked me to the bathroom and blinded me with light. "Not letting you wet the bed," she said, pulling the bloomers off . . . "Make wee!"

I couldn't. Out of the corner of my eye, I caught her looking away—ducked past her—down the hall—turned the door bolt—and ran naked into the dark. She didn't come after me. I went into our house through the back door with its broken lock.

I had a story ready—I couldn't sleep in her bed. But no one asked. I woke with my father looking at me with tears in his eyes.

"What's the matter, Dad?"

"Nothing, nothing for you to worry about. I'll go make breakfast."

When my mother came home, she came alone.

# CHAPTER 5

There was something that had to done before starting fourth grade, and that meant this week. I hadn't been to Communion since my sin, and it was burning a hole in me. The Fires of Hell were licking their chops for little Sean.

Without telling anyone, Saturday morning I went to Confession.
"How have you sinned?"
"N-need to be p-punished, Father."
"And why might that be?"
"R-rather tell the priest when it's time to p-punish me."
"If that's what you want. I have an older boy at 3 o'clock; I can take you then."

He'd told me where to show up. So jumpy as a flea—*you have to do it no matter what*—I went to the room. There was a big stuffed chair with high stuffed arms behind an open curtain. Outside it was a bench with an older boy sitting barefoot in undershorts, his clothes scattered across the floor. I sat down next to him.
"You want to go first or second?"
"S-second."
"Why the puss? Could be worse. When I was your age, every Monday they lined us up pants down before they took the wood to us, knowin' we must've sinned since the last time. But in this grand land they want you bare as an egg to have your backside beat. Let's get you down to your whites, an' the rest'll be like a slice with drippin's."
The boy was kneeling, already at work—*have to let him—*

"H-how do they d-do it?"

"Speakin' for him you see before you, it's my belief he'll be layin' me over one of those great stuffed arms wearin' not so much as the shirt me mither made for me. But whether club or whip or rod or hand, your guess is good as mine . . . Step out o' your bags."

And when a priest—a long way from thin—walked in, I was standing in my BVDs.

"How old are you, My Son?" he said.

"Nine, Father."

"So who'll be first?"

"You're lookin' at him, Father," the other boy said.

"Then take the lad across the hall and oblige me by passing water. I'm ready enough to do the Lord's work, but draw the line at getting peed on."

"Just had a go, Father, but I'll take the sprout."

"First pick up those clothes. Who brought you up to sweep the floor with them?"

The boy took me by the hand across the hall, through a door, and to one side of a toilet. "All right then, dig it out, not even St. Patrick could pee buttoned over."

I didn't move.

"There was this monk who'd lead us outside bare as trout in the dead o' winter, our weenies so cold we'd have to rub to get some blood in 'em. Is it the unbuttonin' you have no taste for?"

"U-u-u-h."

"O what a pumpkin head I've been! It's bashful you are. Lord help us, why didn't you say so? I'd show you mine but it'd break your heart an' they'd haul me off in the Paddy Wagon. I'll flush lest his ear be at the door, an' that'll be an end of it."

When we got back the priest was behind the curtain, "I'll take the older boy in here."

I heard it all but half was Polish.

"Self-abuse is it? Like Onan, you spilled your seed."

"If you want the truth, Father, my cousin spilled it."

"And where did this sin take place?"

"In the mornin' on the bed."

"And what did you wear to bed?"

"Not much, Father."

"Not much?"

"Well you see, the night before we'd taken a bath, the four of us together."

"Four?"

"Aye, Father, me'n my three cousins, with my uncle helpin' with the young'uns, an' tellin' me'n the oldest—he's 12—how to do ourselves."

"So you and the 12 slept together, is that it? And you weren't wearing much?"

"Well actually nothin' at all. You see, since we'd been naked together so long, it wouldn't be polite to cover ourselves like first-time strangers."

"Maybe it would've been better if you had been strangers. So what happened?"

"Well, when I pulled the cover back that mornin', he was asleep with it in an interestin' way—you know how that is, Father—an' I got to wondrin' whether he was old enough. Since someone'd been kind enough to show me, the least I could do I thought to myself was show him."

"Who showed you?"

"You wouldn't like if I said, Father."

"Tell me!"

"Without sayin' a name, it was a monk in low eighth. I'd used the toilet an' brought up the cow's tail in the changin' room. 'Wouldn't you like to take those off?' he said, pointin' to my playground shorts, which was all I had between him and me. 'Was thinkin' to do just that,' I said, slippin' out o' them. 'You're a fine broth of a boy,' he said. 'How long since you left Erin?' 'Three years,' I said. 'Then you'll not be bein' bashful,' he said. 'Never been thought to be that,' I said. 'In such a case I'd be doing God's work to teach you,' he said. An' he taught me."

"Lord help us! I'll look into that. So you taught your cousin?"

"Tried—came close, but he couldn't."

"But you could."

"Aye, Father, an' right at the top, my aunt walked in—'Stop!' she yelled—but all the Saints in Heaven couldn't've slowed it down. She

told my mother, my mother told I don't know who, an' that's how I'm in the way of enjyin' your company."

"What did your father say?"

"Lives in L.A. with my mother's youngest sister."

"Are they married?"

"Still married to my mother, Father. Just before their baby was born, he made us a visit, an' that first mornin' when I was on my way to the bowl, he came out of their bedroom naked—my mother still loves him you see—an' said, 'Let's take a whiz together,' so I dropped my pajamas to join him, an' the two of us had a fine one. Then he said, 'You have the boyo of a man now, but keep it buttoned tight 'round the women; for as you know well enough, the women've been the ruination of your da.'

"An' now them havin' a son, and me knowin' my fractions, Father, I'm wondrin' would he be my three-quarter brother?"

"God in Heaven!"

"Suppose you'll be wishin' everything off now, Father. Better tell you it's no small thing."

"If it's big as Cuchulainn's, I'll have to see it."

"Cuchulainn was a great hero; I'll not be matchin' his . . . What do you think, Father?"

"I'd say you're well-developed."

"That's what the Director at camp said—long on looks he was, an' too young to be your son—freckle-faced like a country boy."

"And he saw you?"

"Well it was this way, Father, some of the lads didn't have suits, so he had us swim in nothin' at all—all but him. He wore shorts with no buttons that showed a great lump, which bein' that way myself, I'm quick to notice.

"Will I be tellin' you more, Father?"

"Tell me everything."

"There were two 13s who wouldn't take their clothes off, so the Director asked me—bein' the biggest in every way you could wish—to see to it an' bring them to him when the deed was done so he could explain the sin of modesty. So four of us saw to it an' I brought them to him bare as you like. Then he explained that all boys are made the same an' what a boy has between the legs was nothin' to go on about an' as penance they must stay naked all that night an' he himself would roust them out for the mornin' pee. The

boys gone, he said, 'Silly to put up a fuss; I sleep in nothing at all. What about you?' 'Best way to share a bed,' I said.' He laughed an' said, 'Maybe we should share together.'

"For three days an' two nights I put my egg on that, tryin' to call up his mug as he said it. *Nothin' ventured nothin' gained*, chased around my bean. An' that very night I snuck into his bed naked. An' to leave off blabberin' like a housewife 'cross the fence, an' to put it in as few words as are proper to the occasion, an' as they say in this grand land, he didn't kick me out of bed, an' it was a lovely time we had."

"Father in Heaven!! And may He have mercy on your two souls! I doubt this will do a whit of good, but a priest can't give up a single soul as lost forever. I'll donate my good arm to whipping the Divil out o' you. Lay your sweet arse across the chair."

"Whack!!!"

"Aowwwwww!!!" came in a terrible scream.

"Do yuh feel the Divil coming out!"

"Aye, Father, that I do, Father!!"

"Whack!!!"

"Aowwwwww!!!"

"Do yuh feel the Divil coming out!"

"Aye, Father, that I do, Father!!"

"Whack!!!"

"Aowwwwww!!!"

"Do yuh feel the Divil coming out!!"

"Aye, Father, that I do, Father!!"

When the whacks got to 10, I thought he'd stop—*Holy Mary, he's going for 20!* What would he do to the likes o' little Sean who spit out the body of Christ?

I pulled on my clothes and ran.

I should've stayed and taken my punishment.

My father decided and my mother took me, "Can I do my errands or must I stay with him?" she asked the lady at the desk.

"Actually, we usually don't allow parents. Too many authority figures confuse the little darlin's. The doctors and nurses must have the only word. Your son will be with the 10s-and-under. Boys get undressed out here."

"Only boys?"

"Yes, boys that age think nothing of it—helps to have them ready. Ha, ha! Girls keep their panties on till a doctor orders them down. Why don't you get on with your shopping? I'll undress him."

"He's shy with strangers."

"We'll help him over it . . . Go ahead, I do it all the time."

My mother left.

The lady moved to do my BVDs . . . "C-Couldn't I keep my underwear on?"

"Ha, ha! By the time we've finished, you'll've forgotten you had underwear."

They were off. I used my hands.

"Stop! That's dirty! . . . Are you in the habit of touching yourself?"

She led me down a hall, "Let's get something clear, there'll be girls in the room and it wouldn't do for them to see a boy touch himself. Understand?"

"G-girls?"

"Girls and boys together in the 10's Room. So how are you to behave?"

"U-u-u-h."

"You're to keep your hands off yourself. See that you do!"

It was a small room with 5 chairs on one side and cupboards on the other side; over the cupboards was a picture of a tiger. There were no boys just two girls, one wearing peach panties, the other wearing pink panties. What seemed funny was they had three empty chairs separating them, The lady sat me smack in the middle.

"Remember about your hands!"

I never looked to either side, just stared at the tiger, but I could feel the girls looking at me. This went on till a lady in white came in, took a glass thing out of a cupboard, and handed it to me,

"Wee in this," and went away.

Both girls moved at the same time to take seats next to me. I got embarrassed and my weenie got embarrassed with me. Him an' me just sat there till the girl in peach said, "Are you gonna do it or not?"

I set the glass thing on the floor, jumped up, and did what I did best, ran like a rabbit.

The lady wasn't at the desk, and I was half dressed when she showed up,

"What are you doing!"

"D-Don't feel so good."

There was no way she was getting me back with those girls.

I waited outside for my mother. "I'll have to tell your father, and sooner or later there'll be another doctor's appointment."

I prayed it would be later.

But God wasn't through with me. Next Saturday on a hot afternoon, to keep me cool Mom dressed me in nothing but jersey shorts and sandals; then dropped me off to play croquet with Clare.

We gulped our ice tea; Mrs. Flynn sipped hers on the back porch while us two played croquet on the lawn. Me into the game—smacking Clare's ball away into the bushes—she hated that—I loved it—putting off the need to pee . . . again . . . and again . . . and again . . . telling myself it would go away—afraid her mother'd walk me to the bathroom and take my shorts down.

But in the end there was no help for it. Squeezing myself to shut things off—I went on the porch and whispered, "N-Need to wee."

Seeing what my hands were doing, "You'd never make it to the bathroom," Mrs. Flynn said, pulling my shorts onto my ankles, "Wee off the edge onto the grass."

Tripping on the way, I got to the edge before letting fly.

"O-o-o-o!" came from Clare. "Aim it high in the sky!"

I gave up croquet.

That night in the tub Mom said, "Wash that part yourself; you're getting too big for a mother bath."

# CHAPTER 6

**I** was 10, God'd spared me, and I took my own baths. Six weeks of smelling the clover. Nobody'd seen me in my underwear—let alone naked—and little Sean had no plans to change a speck of it. Nothing to worry about but our buckeye wars with the Kelly Gang across the tracks.

"Where'd'e go!"

The chase was on. I was the fox and I was Uncas, hunted by Magua and his Huron band. The foe was merciless—no place for the scaredy-cat rabbit. As the fox, I must sniff the breeze for the faintest scent; as the Indian brave, I must strain my ears for the snapping of the tiniest twig. There was plenty of cover, trees, bushes, and tall grass. I knew the land; it was part of my rounds due to the blackberries free for the taking. I was lying flat in a tire rut covered by thick oat straw, a good hiding place 'cause from a few feet away nothing showed. I wouldn't be spotted till they were set to trample me, but my heart pounded—each minute could be my last.

Across a small bridge stood my trusty bike. It was propped against a tree trunk by a dirt road that ran downhill. If I could get to the bike ahead of the war party, they'd eat my dust. I listened to their voices and raised my head; they were holding a powwow behind some bushes in the direction away from my bike. The rabbit was off and running . . .

"There he is!"

With bloodcurdling battle cries they took to the trail, but I was Br'er Rabbit after Br'er Fox flung him into the briar patch—*home free!* Except I hadn't counted on two scouts who hearing the yells

came from under the bridge. I tried to swerve and pitched into a spin on the dry summer grass . . . The two were on me . . . I was in the hands of the enemy . . .

"Thought you was pretty smart, didn't you?"
The trapped fox didn't move; the Indian brave didn't talk.
"What'll we do with him?"
"We could stake him out and leave him for the buzzards."
The leader, who would turn out to be Jim, looked in my face for fear.
"What buzzards?"
"We could make him walk the plank from off the bridge."
"There's no water."
"Maybe he'd like a bloody nose!"
The brave didn't blink.
"Five against one, and all of us bigger'n him?"
"Let's pants him!"
"Yeah! And when we're done, we'll leave him here in his shorts."
A mortal blow. Fear shot through the stone-faced Indian. I hadn't been promoted to boxers, I was still in BVDs. *What if I have to get home in them!*
Jim, about 12 and not much of a pirate, read me; something must've struck inside him.
"Leave him go!"
"Aw geez, Jim, that's no fun."
"Leave him go. You want some fun? We'll pants you."
"Can I just open him up and check his weenie?"
Black fear came down on me . . . Jim was deciding my fate . . . "Get going!"
"Th-thanks!"
"You waitin' for me to change my mind?"
I showed my heels. The rabbit sometimes lives to tell the tale.

I knew what a verb was, but I'd never heard *pants* used that way. In my brain, a meaning was made: *pants*—to take a boy's pants because you're bigger and leave him in his underwear. The way I saw it—some rule of chivalry I figured like they had at The Round Table—*pants* meant pants not underpants—and for sure Lancelot'd never open up his worst enemy's armor to check his weenie.

This kept my boyhood happy. Supposing I'd have some, I could picture me in front of other boys going down to my undershorts. Dropping the same never entered my head. This pipe dream was blown to Kingdom Come and a bit beyond when I brought up boxers to my mother.

"With your asthma!"

The time ahead didn't look bright. I was stuck with the hated BVDs in fair weather and the more-hated union suits when the wind blew foul.

A month after learning *pants*, there came a jolt—two boys with lipsticked faces were hitchhiking along the road wearing their underwear outside their clothes. A playmate was quick with the answer—these were high school freshmen, and this was their initiation.

"But how—?" I started to ask.

Wham! I didn't know Euclid from Euripides, but the geometry smacked me. Somewhere along the line these boys'd been bare of everything. Lucky for me, high school was in the far-off future . . .

# CHAPTER 7

**M**y parents had to go to a Boss party, and a 15-year-old high schooler was spending the night *in my bed*. We changed off between War and Slap Jack till he steered me to my room, "Get your clothes off."

I was worried, but Jeb let me slip the nightie on before I let the bottoms fall.

"Anything else?"

"Have to—"

"Me too, let's go."

He led the way to the bathroom and put the seat up.

"You first—better pull the nightie off . . . What's the problem?"

"U-u-u-h."

"Another Bashful Bertie. My last job had a heck of a time getting the kid into the tub. Lucky your mother didn't order a bath, or about now you'd be getting your weenie washed. Not good for you, but I'll let you off—just lift it a tad."

In a minute, him behind me, I went, embarrassed by the splash.

"Don't flush till I go."

Kind o' what you call spellbound, I watched him unbutton . . .

"It's no skin off my dick, but sure you want to see it?"

I turned and ran.

He shouted, "Going to take a shower; want to take it with me!"

I hopped into bed and pulled up the covers.

After 10 minutes Jeb came back in a towel, holding his clothes.

"Too easygoing—'less I mend my ways, I'll never wear the collar, which my mother wants more than gold and rubies. Ha, ha! Don't

suppose you'd let me practice on your bottom. More than once I presented mine at school. There was this monk—big and round he was—who couldn't get along without a bottom a day to his credit. Think he'd like to've mounted them on the wall to show as hunting trophies. His specialty was doing us double-weenie to make us blush. How about you lend me your bottom for an armload of good ones? I'd give it back. Here's a tip, if you're about to lose your pants, close your eyes and you won't mind so much."

The light off—I heard things drop—he crawled into bed.

In the morning the sound of footsteps made me look over to see Jeb sit up with his back to me, scramble to his feet, and face my father.

"Good morning, Sir, Sean's fine."

The bare backside embarrassed me, and I could tell the bare frontside embarrassed my father.

"Excuse me, Mr. Lacey, it gets this way in the morning. Do you think God's telling me something? About being a priest, I mean?"

My father picked up the towel and held it out, "I think He's telling you to cover yourself . . . Get Sean dressed."

My father gone, Jeb took hold of my nightie, "Your Dad's orders," and pulled it off.

I quick covered myself.

"Too late, I've already seen it."

I wasn't falling for that one.

"10-years-old? Who'd believe it? . . . Want some advice? Stay clear of Parochial School and don't go out for altar boy—they'd eat you for breakfast, lunch, and supper."

# CHAPTER 8

**M**om got a call that Grandma'd turned bad. My father was to drive her and come back the next day. They arranged for me to stay with a mother and son I'd never met. Knew I'd have to take my clothes off—was busy thinking up ways to keep things hidden. Jeb popped into my head—*goes around showing himself—thinks little Sean should do the same—well he has another think coming.*

Me up against sleeping in a strange house belonging to strange people. The night before leaving I had thoughts of a narrow cot to share with an idiot son—a pee-together like almost happened with Jeb—me chased naked by the Wicked Witch of the West. I got through the first part of my battle plan by taking a bath that morning.

Dad let me off at the curb. Carrying my paper sack up the steps I was nervous, and the tall blonde woman who opened the door looking strict as a nun was no comfort.

"You must be Sean; I'm Mrs. Zonar. Come in. I'll take your things to the bedroom you'll share with Stefan. Would you like to see it?"

"Yes Ma'am. Just want you to know there'll be no need to waste hot water on me—already had my bath."

I followed her. Not quite a cot—a single. *O Boy!*

"The bed is small, but the two of you can manage for one night. I'll put your things in this drawer. You won't need the nightgown; Stefan sleeps in the nude, so you will do the same."

*O God! . . . Have to keep my back turned.*

She must've seen my face, "Best thing in the world to keep a boy healthy. I trust you like peas and carrots; that's what we're having for dinner."

"What about dessert?"

"We don't eat dessert."

Stefan turned out to be seven. He had a Swedish mother, dark curly hair from a Greek father, and was smart as the old Greek with the Principle.

"Mrs. Zonar, my father gave me money for the movies. Can I treat Stefan?"

"We don't go to movies. To earn your keep you can do chores after supper."

The picture was a good one, plenty horses, plenty bad guys biting the dust. Two blocks from the house I took in a little park. Ever since not seeing Mary in the tub, I'd made it my life's work to solve the mystery. So when my eye caught the high bars where girls were doing skin-the-cats, I stopped to see what I could see. No luck—they had their dresses tucked tight into their bloomer legs.

On the way out I passed two older boys—probably 13s—going the other direction, and heard, "What d'yuh say we pants that kid?"

Lucky for me I got a head start 'cause they were burning my tail as I made the steps.

I never ate so many vegetables in my life. Supper over, I did the dishes and asked, "Anything else, Ma'am?"

"You said you've had yours, but you can give Stefan his bath for me."

"Y-you m-mean with his cl-clothes off?"

"Naturally. Be sure to wash under his foreskin; it's important to keep that part clean."

"H-how?"

"There's a glass by the tub. After you've uncovered his penis, pour warm water over it—don't use soap on that part. Stefan is in the backyard. Fetch him."

I found him sitting in a tree, "Time to go—you have to take a bath."

"Are you going to give it to me?"

"Yes."

"Do you know how?"

"Your mother told me how."

We walked through the living room where Mrs. Zonar was knitting.

"After the bath, both of you go straight to bed."

"It's not even 8 o'clock," I said.

"We go to sleep at eight, and there are still prayers to do."

My heart pounding—wasn't sure I could get through this—I took Stefan by the hand like he was two, led him to the bathroom, and shut the door. "We don't close the door."

"This time we do . . . Let's see, what comes first?"

"Run hot water in the tub, and while it's filling, undress me."

I started the water.

"Do you know how to undress a boy?"

"Sure."

"Have many boys have you undressed?"

"Dozens. Let's see, all boys are different—"

"I thought all boys were the same."

"Well, yeah, they are; I mean they come in different sizes."

"You start with my shoes and socks, and do my underwear last."

"That's what I usually do."

He was down to short pants.

"G-going to take them off—th-that OK?"

"Sure, it's OK."

His underwear was something like the panties Mary'd worn—these looked silky.

"Coming to the last part—"

"You better turn off the water."

"Just what I was about to do."

Plenty nervous I got back to Stefan, "OK, if I take th-these off?"

"You have to if you're going to wash my penis. I don't think you've ever undressed a boy. Have you ever seen another boy naked?"

"Uh, not lately."

"You mean not ever."

"Come to think of it, that's true."

"Neither have I; tonight will be my first time."

"What do you mean?"

"Mean I'm going to see you."

That stopped me; it took a while to come up with, "You might see my back, but you won't you see my front."

"Think I will."

This got my goat, "Well right now I'm going to see you!" I said, pulling his panties off.

He had everything. Couldn't remember when I looked like that.

"Well, is it the same as yours?"

"Not exactly."

I helped him into the tub.

"Best if you do my foreskin before the water gets soapy."

"Absolutely! Let's see . . ."

"It won't bite."

I got the glass and filled it.

"Maybe you should close your eyes," I said.

"Why? I want to see how you do it."

"W-warn you, I'm going to take it in my f-fingers."

"Naturally."

I took hold—very carefully—couldn't believe this was happening—

my mind wandered . . .

"What are you waiting for?"

"S-sure it won't bother you?"

"Of course I'm sure. My mother does it all the time."

It didn't bother him, but it bothered me.

The rest of the bath went pretty fast—him explaining these things are called testicles—me nervous about handling a naked boy—couldn't believe it didn't embarrass him.

"OK, I'm going to get my stuff. You use the toilet and brush your teeth."

"Why don't we urinate together?"

"Urinate?"

"That means pee. How about it?"

"Wouldn't be a good idea."

"Why not?"

"Because I say so—now do what you have to."

He was finishing brushing when I got back.

"All right, get in bed while I do what I have to."
He started to leave.
"Put a towel on!"
"Waste of time. We sleep naked."
I'd forgot about that.

In his room I flipped the switch, but moonlight lit the floor. He was on one side of the single—*Going to be tight*—I sat on the other side—pulled things off—throwing them toward the wall—did down to my pants—unbuttoned them and my BVDs—very slowly—the big moment—looked to see if he was where he ought to be—he was—pushed everything to the floor—gave it a quick toss—and backed under the covers.

It wasn't five minutes till Mrs. Zonar came and blasted us with light.

"Out from under the covers! Kneel down facing the foot of the bed!"

Stefan jumping—me grabbing a pillow to hide myself—forced to kneel next to him—squeezing the pillow between my legs—my hands together in prayer—Mrs. Zonar with palms on our heads—talking a language that might as well be Hottentot.

Stefan was wrong—*Thank you, God*—he saw only what I'd seen of Jeb.

# CHAPTER 9

"**Y**ou can have that nice boy you play chess with over for supper if you want; maybe you'd like him to spend the night."

"Supper, but not the night; Damon's shy, real shy."

"Look who's talking!"

Damon was my age, a boy from school who'd taught me chess. I liked him, maybe because he was bashful like me. Last year in 4th grade he'd been pantsed to his underwear behind the handball wall. The boys passed his pants around, teasing him, and Damon cried till he got them back. Underwear was fair game at our school, but more than that'd earn a trip to the Principal. Mr. Stillwater was famous for the rod; he'd thinned the seat of many a boy.

So Damon came to supper.

My father was talking, "Where did you get your first name?"

"My mother gave it to me. She wasn't Catholic."

"I understand Mrs. Harrington is your grandmother. I know her from Church, a very nice lady."

The following Saturday my father showed up in my room.

"Get ready to leave while I go for Damon—explain later—drink a full glass of water and meet us in the driveway."

I climbed into the back seat and whispered to Damon, "Where're we going?"

"Don't know, my grandmother said she'd arranged something with your father—made me drink a big glass of water," he whispered back.

We stopped at a building I didn't recognize and went inside.

"Turns out you both could use a doctor checkup, so Damon's grandmother and I thought you might like to go together."

*O Boy!* "Wh-what do we w-wear during the checkup?"

"I believe older boys wear pullover tops; doubt they worry much about younger boys."

*Is 10 young or old?*

We followed him to a room with chairs. A man had a small boy down to short pants on his lap; an older boy was in a sleeveless top that stopped at his knees.

"Go to those empty seats. I'll leave you now—this will take at least an hour."

"An hour? Why?"

"Better not to anticipate."

We went to the chairs. A lady nurse came and handed us tall paper cups. "No thank you, already had mine," I said.

"Drink!" She stood there till we did.

Another boy showed up, took a seat next to Damon, and fixed his skirt like girls do.

The lady nurse came back and motioned to the first boy, "Come with me!"

The same boy was back in a few minutes, followed soon by the nurse and the doctor, who looked around the room to size things up.

"Forgot to check something. Stand in front of me with your back to the room. Nurse, pull his gown up."

"Do you see that!" Damon whispered.

The doctor used his hands where we couldn't see, "Don't try to hold back . . . Good . . . How old did you say?"

"Th-thirteen."

"Right on target. You can put your clothes on."

He dressed with his back to us.

"Collect a specimen from the small boy, do his preliminaries, and bring him to me."

"I assume you want the usual for the two 10s—you haven't seen them before."

"Of course."

The nurse fetched a glass jar and came up to the man, "Sir, I have to do your son."

"He's ready."

The boy was sideways to us as she handed his shorts to his father.

"Help me, Grandma!" Damon whispered.

She put the jar under his weenie—*different from mine*, "Can you make wee for me?"

It made me realize how far ahead Stefan was.

"O-o-h!" Damon let out as the boy tinkled.

The nurse disappeared with the father and son and came right back.

"I assume you boys can undress yourselves."

She got that wrong.

"You undress him," she said to the boy sitting by Damon.

The next thing I knew my clothes were coming off . . . I felt the BVDs go—quick covered myself—"Take your hands away! . . . Foreskin . . . Does that one have a foreskin?"

"Tell you soon as I get his underwear off . . . Yes, Ma'am, he does."

I covered myself and looked next to me; Damon was naked with his back turned, hands at his sides.

"Damon! Cover yourself!"

He covered himself, we sat down, and the nurse took the older boy away.

"Sean, th-think I'm going to cry—so embarrassed! No stranger's ever seen me like that."

"Well there aren't a busload who've seen me. I'm just as embarrassed, but there's no use crying. All we can do is cover ourselves every chance we get. Let's think of a game; suppose we play 3-5-7 in our heads?"

Both hands in front of ourselves, we played game after game without keeping track.

The nurse showed up with a pad and pencil, "You should be ready. Follow me!"

Keeping things hidden, we followed her out of the room, took a sharp turn, and went through a door. Something seemed wrong; I looked up and saw sky.

"O my God! We're out in the open!"

"No swearing! You're not in the open. Don't you see the fence?"

There was a high wooden fence surrounding a small yard, but quick to spot trouble, I also saw that anyone standing next to the fence could look through the cracks.

"The two of you go up to that log. Stand just behind it, touching it with your toes."

She had us right where she wanted. Nothing for it but to do as she said, me tightening my grip to keep myself covered.

"See that piece of plywood painted black with numbered white stripes?"

It was hard to miss the big board, but I couldn't think what she was driving at.

"That's your target; the goal is to hit as high up as possible with your stream."

"Stream?"

"Pee, to use the term most boys understand."

She got that right.

"Prepare your foreskins—boys usually have trouble with this part."

Right again. Two out of two boys had trouble with it.

"You'll stand as long as needed."

A big glass and a tall paper cup kicked in and kicked in good.

"D-Damon, I-I can't h-hold out!"

I closed my eyes and fixed myself.

"Ready! Aim! Fire!"

I didn't look.

"Excellent!" the nurse let out as she wrote our scores down.

We were back inside still naked, the nurse forcing water into us. Me in a fog, staggering around with my eyes closed and my hands covering myself—not knowing what Damon was up to. The nurse doing things I paid no attention to—weighing—measuring—other stuff—"Open your eyes!"—she was holding a jar—Damon had his back to me, an older boy in front of him—the nurse saw my look—"He's helping your friend—I'll help you. Fix it!" She had me where she wanted—no getting away—so to save Damon seeing, I fixed it, took aim at the jar, finished before he turned around, closed my eyes, and covered myself.

Finally there was the doctor, "Take your hands away! . . . Take your hands away! . . . Nurse, hold them for me."

Back in the waiting room, Damon dressed, me in a gown too big, my father came with the nurse and the doctor, "Your son is slated for an early life change. Nurse, pull his gown off . . . Exceptionally well-developed for his age. Does it run in the family?"

"Uh . . . believe it does."

"There's a possible problem with his foreskin."

He took me in his hand and pushed things back—"Tight as you can see."

"A-a-a-h!"

"To satisfy my curiosity, I wonder if you'd submit to a brief examination?"

"Some other time."

"There'd be no charge."

"Thank you, Doctor, but we really must leave."

# CHAPTER 10

Sunday afternoon a call came that my grandmother was worse. I was building a mud house in the backyard with Louise. Her the work boss, clean as Snow White, ordering *do this, do that*—me barefoot in nothing but street shorts, showing more mud than skin.

My father came running, pulled my shorts off, and grabbed a hose.

"No time for a bath, Louise, do the faucet! . . . Step onto the grass!"

His thumb on the hose, he started at the top, "Hold your arms up!—She didn't close her eyes—"Turn around! . . . Face me again! . . . Keep your arms up!"

Me wanting to go potato bug and roll into a ball . . . Finally he dropped the hose.

"Turn it off!" he shouted to Louise as he carried me to the house.

He was drying me, "You're not showing yourself to Louise, are you?"

"No, Dad!"

I couldn't say it was him who showed me to Louise—every last inch of me.

"She's not Catholic, you know."

My best clothes were laid out on the bed, including a brand new pair of BVDs.

"Get dressed, bring your overnight things, and come out to the car—right away!"

I put on the new underwear with my Sunday outfit, grabbed my stuff, and ran to the car.

My father stopped at Stefan's, handed me a shiny fifty cent piece—most he'd ever given me—"Don't spend it all"—and took off as I climbed the steps.

Mrs. Zonar answered the door like before, "Stefan has gone to his piano lesson, and after that he will shop for us at the greengrocer's. You are free to do as you like until dinner; we're having watercress salad and rutabagas. You can have black bread and honeycomb for dessert. How does that sound?"

Sounded better than rutabagas.

"I expect you back in two hours—no later—and I don't accept excuses. It is only fair to warn you that your father has given me the authority to punish you as I would Stefan."

There was no place near the park to break the four bits—I'd hidden it in one of my shoes—all the time congratulating myself on being so smart. I ended up by the high bars—sometimes you get lucky—one of the girls was showing panties. I settled back to watch . . .

I must've catnapped because when I opened my eyes the girls were gone and two boys were standing over me. I knew right off they were tough—other side of the tracks for sure—and old—16 maybe 17—not a kind I'd had much to do with.

"Nice duds, Kid."

"Practically new," I said.

"Looks ta me they'd fit my little brother. Strip."

Wasn't one of my words.

"Wh-what do you mean?"

"Starkers."

"Starkers?"

"Bare balls."

"B-bare balls?"

"Jesus Christ! You some kinda dummy?"

He reached down and took hold of things, "Yuh feel what I'm feelin'? Those're balls. Strip means they got nothing round'em 'cept sky. Get the pitcher?"

"Y-you mean n-naked?"

"Yuh could put it that way."

Something told me he wasn't joking.

"M-maybe we could talk this over."

"What's ta talk?"

"G-got f-four bits in my sh-shoe. Y-you can have that."

"Jus' what I like ta hear, Kid; we'll take the dough an' the duds."

"Get the shoes, Charlie . . . Hand me the cash an' do the pants."

"Here's the pants, want the socks?"

"Sure, put'em in the shoes. I'll get his coat'n shirt."

. . . Clothes going fast . . . Down to my BVDs . . .

"What about the skivvies? Will your brother wear'em?"

"Look new. He'll wear'em or I'll whip his skinny ass."

"Please! Not my underwear! Please!!"

"Shut your yap! Think yur the only kid with balls to cover? Do a couple buttons and get his arms out . . . OK, hold'im while I pull'em off."

. . . I jerked my arms free and covered myself . . .

"Ha, ha! He's bashful. Make him show it good."

"Since when yuh into little boys?"

"Not into nothin', jus' what yuh call curious. Don't got no little brother like you."

"We done enough to'im. Can't yuh see the kid's scared shitless."

He got that right.

"Tell yuh what, help me wax Pa's car, an' while we're washin' it, yuh c'n hose Stevie down an' put the new duds on'im—he's 11—that suit yuh?"

"He let me?"

"Ain't got a bashful bone in his body—Ha, ha! Yuh c'n giv'em one."

"Yuh mean he—?"

"Sure. Don't yuh remember?"

"Not me, don't remember nothin' like that at 11. OK, 'sa deal—this I gotta see—c'n we do it right away?"

"If we get the hell gone."

Me naked and alone. 'Cept for a flash, hadn't had to show it, but time was chugging like a steam engine racing down hill. It was too light to try the street, so I hugged the leafy places and went toward the end of the park closest to the Zonar's, planning to lie low till the dark started.

My eyes were closed when I heard, "Let's do 'im in the bushes."

I opened to see the two 13s who'd chased me last time. They had hold of a boy wearing a swimsuit—probably 12. The three ended up on the other side of my bush—it was a big one—me flat on the ground—I shut my eyes, scared to breathe.

"Hey, you guys pantsed me two weeks ago! Had to go to Confession afterwards. Can't you find someone else?"

"Next time yuh c'n bring a friend—right now all we got is you. Take it off! . . . Hurry up!"

"Don't think it'll come off."

"Pull your dick out—that'll help."

"Not supposed to touch it 'cept to pee."

"Who tole yuh that?"

"A priest."

"We'll leave yuh pee."

"If I pee, will you let me go?"

"Did you pee for the priest?"

"Didn't actually pee."

"But yuh had your pants down, right?"

"Well yeah."

"OK, enough jabber. I'll work the suit off . . . Tight son-of-a bitch."

"Geez! Don't need it all the way off to pee."

"Yuh had it all the way off for the priest, I bet. If it's the one I'm thinking of, he had yuh mother, right?"

"Me'n Jimmy Murphy. He's older'n me—went big."

"How big?"

"Small banana big."

"OK, go ahead'n pee."

"I'm shy. Not the same as peeing next to someone like at school."

"Bet yuh look at what the other kid's got."

"Well the way it is crowded together, how can you help it?"

"Yuh c'n shut your eyes."

"All kids look. Got a look at Chuck's when we stood next to each other last week—gives it a hard shake afterwards."

"Next time I'll shake yours."

"Better not do it front of a monitor. You know that tall one who does the last half of lunchtime? He's 14—makes you nervous—stands right against the wall so he can see your dick. One time a new 7th grader was bashful about taking it out, so the monitor had him

pee bare. You know Proddies are bashful about showing it; that's why they have less babies. A bunch of us pantsed two Proddies by the hoop and made'em shoot baskets flop-dick—served'em right the little heathens—don't have foreskins like us Catholics."

"Not all Catholics have skins."

"Practically all the boys in Parochial School do—if you pee enough, you end up seeing most of 'em. Probably hav'em 'cause their fathers hav'em. My father an' his brothers hav'em; all my cousins hav'em.

"Even your girl cousins?"

"No way! They have—you know. A monk said it's a sin to change what God gave us."

"Shut up'n pee for Chris' sake!"

I heard the sound.

"Can I put my suit on now?"

"Yeah, but next time bring a friend."

I opened my eyes—it was dark. Crawfish-like and quiet as a spider, I worked my way backward through the bushes . . . got to the sidewalk . . . set a new record, knocked on the front door, and covered myself.

"You are late!" Mrs. Zonar shouted, not mentioning I was naked. "I'll get the hairbrush."

"Got robbed!"

"In that case there will be no spanking."

Stefan walked in dressed like me. "Both of you into the tub."

He took me by the hand, "Can Sean and I urinate together?"

"Stefan has always wanted a brother," his mother said.

He led me away. "This is going to be fun."

# CHAPTER 11

**I**'d managed to keep away from Damon, afraid he might bring up what happened at the doctor's.

But Thursday he caught up with me after school—I couldn't run away—and said, "Thought your father might want to know they took my grandmother to the hospital last night. I have two chocolate bars in my room. Why don't you come home with me? It's kind of lonely."

What could I say? Once there he handed me a Hershey. After gulping it, I asked what he'd like to do.

"You know what I'd really like to do?"

"What?"

"You won't get mad?"

"Why should I get mad?"

"You know I saw everything when they had your gown off."

"Y-you did?"

"Yes, clear as day. Stay there, I'll just be a minute."

He came back in a towel, "Let's play doctor—you examine me, I examine you."

I hopped on my fastest horse.

Damon's grandmother died early Friday morning, and Saturday afternoon my father brought him home. "Someone is coming to pick him up."

*An aunt or an uncle*, I figured.

After dinner Dad said, "You better get a bath, Damon, there's barely enough time—you can share with Sean."

"That's OK, he can take his own," I said.

"Waste of water, and you can soap each other."
*O Boy!*

We were in the bathroom in our BVDs . . .
Damon unbuttoned and let his fall . . . I turned my back . . .

My father stuck his head in. "Off! . . . Into the tub! And don't spare the soap!"

"Your peter's gotten bigger," Damon said.
"It's not polite to talk about what another boy has."
"Your father said I should wash you."
*"Touch my dick and you die."*

Damon had no aunts or uncles. He was taken to a Boys' Home, which was a fancy name for an orphanage.

# Chapter 12

You'd think after making it through what I'd been through, my modesty'd be all upslope, but come June it was all downslope. 1935 was a very bad year. It started with summer vacation; I was turning into an animal. I'd no sooner hit my 11th birthday than fur began to sprout. I was scared to death someone'd find out, and I'd be put in a cage naked so people could point at the monkey boy.

We were cutting bamboo for fishing in the patch behind Stu's house.

"Know the kid who moved into the old Thompson place? Know what he did?"

"What?"

"Guess."

"Can't. What'd he do?"

"Well a couple mornings ago he hollered from his bedroom window for me to come up and shoot cork guns with him. So I went up, and what d'you think he had on?"

"What?"

"Nothing."

"Nothing at all?"

"Bare as a banana slug. Got some look at his waterworks."

"Are older kids different?"

"It stuck out some."

"Was there anything around it?"

"Like what?"

"Oh, I don't know, like fur maybe."

"'Course not. You're talking gorilla—'member King Kong? Think she was naked on top when he held her in his fist?"

"Not sure—saw it twice and still couldn't tell. You know some people say we're related to gorillas. Think that could be true?"

"All I know is, you better not ask a priest stuff like that—a priest can send you to Hell."

"Speaking of which," I said, "I'm sweating a creek."

"You know seeing that older kid didn't embarrass me none; why don't you take your clothes off and I'll spritz the hose on you? Nobody around—how about it? Be fun. Look, if you're bashful you can hold your hands over your dick."

I glanced at my wrist to check Mickey, "O my gosh! Late! See you around!"

My mother'd given me a dollar for my birthday. I used 49 cents of it to buy a safety razor and a package of blades. *Have to keep the fur shaved.*

"Any 11-year-old kids around here?"

The boy was one of the 13-year-old twins who'd come to visit their grandparents.

"What do you want them for?" I asked.

"Just stuff. How old're you?"

"Thirteen."

"Ha, ha! Like I'm the King of France. That's for lying," he said, punching me in the stomach.

"U-u-u-h!"

"We knew you was 11 all the time . . . Tell him how we work, Kev."

"You give us stuff; we don't do stuff to you. Like how about we take your bike to our place so's we can use it when we want."

"I need my bike!"

"First let Dev tell the stuff we wasn't gonna do to you."

"Got the idea talking to your girlfriend," Dev said.

"She's not my girlfriend!"

"Oh, no? We don't get the bike, she's gonna know you better'n your ma. What we wasn't gonna do was pants you bare front o' Louise. What we wasn't gonna do was hold you down an' let her play with your weenie much as she wants. What we wasn't gonna do was stand you naked an' have her watch you pee. What—"

"T-take m-my b-bike."

That wasn't the end; every day they asked for more—my baseball, my glove, my bat—not my tennis racquet—said it was a girls' game. They liked scaring me as much as they liked the stuff.

The one they did most was, "When we got you naked front o' Louise, how long you think it's gonna take you to pee? Take too long an' we'll have her hold it for you."

There was no letup. One after another went my skates, my slingshot, my jackknife, my truck, my rubber-band gun, my mibs, my shooter, my taw, my kite, my killer tops, my sack of milk bottle caps. I stayed in the house, but they came in when my mother was at work. I bolted the front door, but they found out the back door was open 'cause the landlord wouldn't fix the lock.

I started on my Indian cards, a few at a time, not letting them know how many I had; my piggy bank was the last to feel it. I didn't tell my mother—I wouldn't've known how.

They never tired of putting the fear in me.

"That's enough stuff; let's drag him down to Louise's an' hav'im pee for her—'less he can come up with a nickel."

The pig coughed up five pennies.

I'd wake and go pee, thinking how it'd be with Louise watching.

A week before they'd leave, they trapped me in an empty lot.

"No shirt, no shoes, an' I'm bettin' nothin' underneath. Such easy pickin's I can't resist. We ain't seen what he's gonna show her. Let's have a look."

I tried to run, but they knocked me down.

"I'll hold his arms . . . pull his shorts off . . . Ha, ha! He don't like showin' it—that's the fun—they try to hide it and you pull their hands away. 'Member that 13-year-old sissy with the small dick—bawled like a baby—wiggle it good."

"Don't touch it!"

"Keep wigglin'."

"It's bigger'n ours!"

"Ha, ha! He likes it. Keep doin' im."

"A-a-a-a-h!"

"She's gonna love playin' with that! Wiggle it good!"

"A-a-a-a-a-a-a-h!

"An' wait'll she sees it pee!"

They fell over backwards squealing—"Let's go take a bath before Grandma gets home."

I jumped up—they didn't stop me—grabbed my shorts and ran.

They'd never let me off; wanted to watch Louise watch me pee. I could see it—they drag me to Louise's shed, pull everything off, her waiting to see me splash the dirt . . . I can't.

There was one last straw—only one I could think of—my girl cousin.

"Mom, Aunt Ellen asked me to come stay with Mary. I'd like to go."

"You realize you'll be sleeping in Mary's room?"

"Doesn't matter."

"You're sure?"

"Absolutely!"

"All right, I'll get a letter off."

"Mom, if I ask you a really big favor, would you do it?"

"If I can."

"Didn't you say Aunt Ellen got a phone? Phone her long distance and ask if I can come right now."

"Son, is something wrong?"

"No, just feel I've got to get away. Haven't you ever felt like that?"

"Many times! Well whatever's troubling you, I think the farm will be good medicine."

There'd still be Mary; last visit she said, "'Member the time we took a bath together?"

"No I don't!"

"You were naked as all getout."

That night my mother packed a suitcase. When she left I took out the BVDs—knew nothing'd be private from Aunt Ellen—but I didn't notice she hadn't put street shorts in.

# CHAPTER 13

The valley was hot.

Aunt Ellen held up my flannel nightshirt, "Tim!" she called to my uncle, "just look what he has to sleep in. What can Margaret have been thinking of?"

"He c'n sleep in his drawers."

"Doesn't seem to have any. Sean, do you have underwear on?"

"Unh-unh."

"There are socks, shirts, and an extra pair of corduroy pants like the ones he's wearing, nothing else."

"Cords are too hot; he c'n sleep bare."

"With Mary?"

"For God's sake, Woman, he's 11 years old. He's a boy, not a bull. He c'n sleep bare."

"He can't sleep bare with Mary. And mind, Timothy Duffy—I know you—don't go showing him how Ferdinand works."

"Farm boys know how a bull works by the time they're nine. And you c'n bet your last ha'penny Mary'll take him in at the pond where boys his age go skinny. Seen her watchin' behin' the reeds."

"You're talkin' the Blarney, aren't you?"

"She was lookin' all right."

"Well a girl better learn what's in store for her. Anyway Sean doesn't know what skinny means."

"Forgot you're a city slicker, Nephew; skinny means bare-ass."

"Timothy!"

"Excuse me, skinny means nekkid."

"If he goes swimming, we'll find him something to wear."

"Won't be wearin' it long; boys'll see to that—good thing too—don't want him endin' up a damn sissy."

I stayed clear of the pond and wore my cords all day in the valley heat. The worst things were the smell of the outhouse and watching my uncle grab a pair of roosters and cut off two heads with one chop. I'd get used to the smell, but said, "No thank you," when they passed the chicken platter.

So the first night I slept in the same bed as Mary, her some younger—not a sign of swelling—wearing white bloomers. Me in a ripped-out flour sack tied around my middle, one leg showing all the way up like Tarzan. The sack was too short to suit me—kept checking myself—and though in the morning the sheet was down with Mary's hand on my belly, I thanked God I wasn't naked in Louise's shed.

The third night I didn't sleep with Mary. Pedro was a 16-year-old Mexican who had a little room above the barn. There was no window—a single candle for light—and at night with the door closed, it would be black as the tomb.

My uncle'd offered me 25 cents to help Pedro turn over a vegetable patch. We broke for dinner; then back to work, shirtless, sweat pouring, me in Keds and cords, Pedro in sandals and shorts.

It was dark—I must've fallen asleep on my shovel—felt myself being lifted—carried up the steps—heard the door close—me laid on my back—the mattress hard—felt my Keds come off—a button of my cords open—"L-leave them on"—"Nino sleep—Pedro fix"—my pants down I felt a touch—"Ha, ha! Nino no es Nina"—the pants came off—the sheet covered me—I was gone.

I woke up—pitch black—*where am I?* Remembered—got my bearings—pushed back the sheet—naked—needed to pee—felt around for my pants—couldn't find them—reached my hand out—felt a bare bottom—Pedro naked too—"Pedro," I whispered—"Pedro!"

"Que quieres, Nino?"

"N-need to p-pee."

"Tienes que hacer pipi?"

Sounded right, "Si."

"Quieres candle?"

"No candle!"

"No like estar desnudo? Bueno, I get bucket."

He helped me stand up.

"I hold bucket—you pee. Want Pedro do pene?"

"No!"

"Ha, ha! No es nada—tengo dos hermanos pequenos y dos hermanos grandes."

*Thank God it's dark.*

"You pee."

I peed.

"You take bucket. I do Pedro's pene."

I heard him go.

"Ahora sleep."

He put the sheet back over us.

"Pedro, d-did you s-see m-me?"

"No luz. Manana see Nino, Nino see Pedro—cojones, pene, todos. Te gusta?"

"U-u-u-h."

It was early morning. I found my pants—put them on—opened the door to get some light—Pedro on his back—desnudo under the sheet—his pene outlined across a leg—me tempted to lift the sheet and check for fur—I couldn't.

At the end of the week some relatives of my Uncle stopped by and left their half-a-year-older daughter Amy to spend the night.

She had long blonde curls, and behind the barn she let me stretch out with my head in her lap. She stroked my hair . . . she stroked my chest . . . I was in love . . .

"I know about boys—I've seen my cousin—he's 12."

"Y-You have?"

"Without a stitch . . . Do you like me?"

"O yes!"

I looked up at the two small bumps under her top . . . *She's beautiful . . .*

"Is there something you'd like to do?"

"U-u-u-h."

"You know if a boy likes a girl, he lets her do things. I like to do buttons."

"Buttons?"

She slid her hand down my belly onto my fly . . . "Can I . . . ?"

I jumped up, "Have to wash for supper!"

All I could think about was bed . . . We'll sleep next to each other . . . Maybe she'll take her top off . . . Maybe she'll take everything off . . . Maybe I'll let her . . .

All worked up I couldn't wait for the night . . .

But when the time came, my aunt took charge, "You're sleeping with Pedro."

"I don't mind sleeping with the girls."

"You can't sleep with two girls—come with me."

This smashed my dreams, "Have to get my wrap."

"No need. You're both boys."

*O God!*

When we got to the barn room my aunt knocked at the door and called out, "Pedro!"

"Momento!" he called back.

When the door opened, the candle was lit and Pedro was wrapped in a flimsy piece of cheese cloth that gave a pretty good idea of what was underneath. My aunt smiled as she took things in—I was embarrassed for him—and broke into lingo too fast for me to catch the words.

But when he said, "Desnudo?" and she answered, "Si," I caught that.

He sat me on the bed, did my Keds, started on my shirt that I always put on for dinner. When he did the top button of my cords, my aunt, said, "I'll leave you to it," and went out the door.

The pants came off—I used my hands—he pulled them away—

"Que lindo pene."

"Don't look!"

"No es nada—somos amigos . . . Vamos hacer pipi."

He took me by the hand to where the hayloft doors were open a floor above the ground. It was cloudy and dark—*Thank God for that.*

He must've dropped his cloth because there was an outline of a pene hanging long against the black—*Big as mine*. We peed into empty space. When we got to the room his cloth was back in place.

He left the door open, "Mas luz. Go bed!"

I got under the sheet . . . He went to the other side, dropped his wrap with his back to me, gave a half-flash of himself—fur—a gob of dark fur—ducked under the sheet, and blew out the candle.

Blonde curls were in my head when slitted by the morning light my eyes saw the sheet pushed up like a tepee. Pedro already dressed came over and pulled it off laughing, "We fix."

I used my arms to cover myself—he pushed them away, "Es nada—somos amigos—vamos!"

Holding my hand he took me downstairs to a concrete slab with a barrel of water next to it. Taking a dipper off a nail, he kept filling it and pouring it over my peter.

The water warm from the valley heat hadn't helped when I heard, "Sean! Is that you!"

It was Amy. She ran in, took a long look—me a jumbo popsicle frozen solid—"You're gorgeous"—kissed me on the cheek, turned, and waved goodbye.

Mi amada was gone and a day later mi amigo was gone.

My uncle came from town with another boy. Franz, 17, quiet, blond, and muscled—lifted weights—read books. He'd saved his money to go to India the summer before—didn't eat them and animals loved him, came to get petted, lay down beside him.

One evening when he was finished for the day, I turned the corner of the barn and found him sitting naked with his legs folded like one of those snake charmers. A giant patch of black fur showed—made me gulp till I realized he had a cat in his lap.

He opened his eyes and said, "Take your clothes off and meditate with me; I'll lend you the cat."

"U-u-u-h."

"Bashful? To earn my supper I worked naked in the fields with the Nepalese. The girls brought us water—giggled at what they saw. Some of the boys—young as 13—were married to them. Understand you sleep with Mary; if that's embarrassing, you can share my bed."

*Another Jeb. I'll stick with Mary's hand on my belly.*

There was a job to do with moving alfalfa. I couldn't help because of my asthma, so a 13-year-old boy from a nearby farm was working with Franz.

My aunt sent me to call them for breakfast. When I got to the top landing, Sandy was naked with his back turned, splashing into the bucket.

"Come join him!" Franz shouted.

"Breakfast!" I yelled, taking the steps two at a time.

The day before going home, there was a close call. A pack of kids stopped Mary and me under some trees.

"Who's your boyfriend?"

"Not my boyfriend, he's my cousin."

"Guess you're kissing cousins."

"Are not."

"Let's see you kiss him."

"Not much for kissing."

"Either you kiss him or he goes home skinny."

"Wouldn't bother me none."

"Always wanted you to kiss me," I said.

"Really?"

"You bet!"

She gave me a slobbery smack, "You like that?"

I wanted to spit something fierce, but said, "How about another?"

She gave me another wet one.

"Reckon she's disappointed she ain't gonna see what he's got."

"Am not. I've seen it plenty."

The boys were laughing, me thinking, *She means when I was eight.*

But she came out with, "His is bigger'n Sandy's."

The blond boy blushed, the others screeched, I gulped.

And to prove her words, that last morning I woke early—my wrap gone—me naked as all getout the way Mary'd reminded me—her fingers curled around my bat like she was choosing up for baseball—her eyes shut tight.

"Thank God for that!" I whispered and slid myself out of her hand.

No sooner done than my uncle came in and picked me up, "Land o' Goshen! Didn't know you was that far along. Have to give you a bath—tub's ready in the pump house."

"C-can take my own b-bath."

"Won't allow it. Don't want her big sister sayin' she didn't send you home clean."

Outside, Sandy followed by Franz came up to us. *O No!*

"Too much for me," my uncle told him. "You take over his bath."

"Sure thing, Boss!" Franz said, lifting me like I was cotton candy.

"Hasn't peed."

"Ha, ha! In Nepal we lined up like birds on a wire—backs to the breeze of course."

He stood me on the chopping stump where the roosters'd lost their heads—"Be my guest."

. . . I was 8-years old again . . .

"Let it go, Boy," my uncle said.

I let it go . . .

"Force of a billy goat . . . She wants'im pecker-clean."

Me standing in a washtub . . . Sandy studying what I have.

"Strip off and I'll do you together."

"Think I better feed the chickens."

Sandy gone, I whispered, "Th-thank you."

"No need to be embarrassed; in Khatmandu they'd build a statue to it . . . Better take a deep breath; have to get you pecker-clean."

I took a deep breath, closed my eyes . . . and was running through the fields with my dead dog . . .

# Chapter 14

**T**wo long wonderful months before school'd start, playing baseball and tennis, riding bikes to explore new places, going house to house earning pennies from old ladies with grass to mow or weeds to pull. And there was always the creek—we never tired of it—with pollywogs and crawfish and minnows—and rocks to throw into drain pipes.

My razor blades were gone; Dev and Kev were gone, the summer of '35 was all but gone. It was afternoon recess, my third day of sixth grade, the highest grade in our small-town school.

We were breaking the rule, throwing rocks.

Stu said, "Bet you can't hit that pole."

"Bet I can."

The rock went past the pole and down through a window—*Please let me die!*

There was no use running.

"That was a wicked thing to do," Miss Galbraith said. "After school, report to Mr. Stillwater. Sit on his bench until he calls you in."

On the way, I ran into Clarence, the runt of our class who got picked last for every game.

"What do you think's going to happen, Sean?"

"Reckon I'll go home with the seat of my pants a mite thinner."

"You don't have to worry about that."

"How come?"

"You're in sixth grade now."

Didn't make sense, but that was Clarence.

"Suppose you wouldn't let me wait with you?"

"What's it to me?"

The two of us headed for the small building where the Principal had his office

The place was empty; we'd been sitting on the bench a good half hour.

"There he is," Clarence whispered.

Mr. Stillwater was tall with long arms like Abraham Lincoln.

"The guilty boy will follow me."

He took me into an office and through a door to a place lit by two high windows that let in the afternoon sun—the whispered *Punishment Room*. The door had a lock at the top that he reached up and bolted with one of his long arms; then from a group of three he chose a fat wood rod and gave me the once-over.

"A sixth-grader," he said, "are you afraid?"

"U-u-u-h."

He let out a smile—a small smile, not a make-you-feel-good smile.

I was pretty sure what he was smiling about wasn't going to make me laugh.

"You have reason to be. Stand by that chair and face me . . . You admit your guilt and accept your punishment?"

"Y-Yessir."

"Take your clothes off."

"Wh-what?"

"Put them on the chair."

"Wh-why?"

"Because the rule is—a rule I personally instituted—that sixth-grade boys may be punished bare. It is my experience that 10 strokes directly on a backside build more character than a year of Sunday sermons. Take your clothes off."

"Everyth-thing?"

"Everything," he said, letting out a bigger smile.

I couldn't get started.

"Very well, your friend can undress you."

He made a move to unbolt the door.

"Wait!"

I went to work on my shoes and socks—they were easy—did my shirt—slowly unbuttoned my BVD top—then, none too anxious to get to the pants, took one arm out. Deciding that was a loser, I started to put it back—

"Leave it! We are not going backwards."

Then with his biggest smile yet, "Unbutton your pants."

"N-need the—"

"You need the what?"

"B-bathroom."

"First do your pants."

"Please, Sir!"

"One more word, and I will march you down the hall naked as a newborn. Off!"

The pants on the chair, he opened the door and pushed me through into the hall. One arm in, one arm out, Clarence took in my half-unbuttoned BVDs.

"Your friend needs the bathroom," Mr. Stillwater told him.

"Me too. Can I come?"

"Never let it be said this school would deny a boy the opportunity to relieve himself."

Then turning to me, "It will save time if you unbutton on the way."

I did all but the bottom two—didn't want to show my fur. Mr. Stillwater took us to where there was a washstand and a toilet behind a swinging door.

"Both of you together. That will save time."

"T-tog-gether?" I let out.

"You are a male?" he asked Clarence.

"Yessir."

"And you are a male?"

"Y-yessir."

"Then you can go together—through the door!"

Inside I whispered, "We'll close our eyes, and if you peek, I'll show the girls your underwear."

"Look, they're already closed!" he whispered back.

I was getting my nerve up when I heard him hit water—mine came out with not a second to spare.

"Keep them shut till I tell you!" I whispered.

Finished, I stuffed it in, opened my eyes, and flushed.

"You can look now," I said, pushing the door open.

"Both of you wash your hands."

Me done first, Mr. Stillwater said, "Take your other arm out."

I took it out and holding tight raced like sixty up the hall before he got any more ideas.

On the way, I heard, "You wait in the school yard."

*Probably the nicest thing Mr. Stillwater'd done his whole life.*

He bolted the door, "Face me . . . Are you ready for punishment?"

Him smiling again—his small smile.

"Yessir, but it would hurt just as much through my underwear—honest!" I got out fast without a stammer.

"I will be the judge of that. I do not enjoy this; I do it for your soul."

Scared, flat-out scared, I felt myself shake—rock on my feet—my knees go weak—the smile gone big on his face—*He likes it.*

"Put your hands on your head . . . Now!"

I raised my arms, the BVDs fell, my insides with them.

He came over and touched my fur.

"You are 11 years old. What is the meaning of this?"

"U-u-u-h."

He picked up my penis.

"A-a-a-h!"

"And what is this Devil's instrument! . . . Your name?"

"S-S-Sean L-L-Lacey."

"Irish! And Catholic I'll be bound! Like all Irish, unable to keep it inside your pants! Abuser!"

. . . Blows came a hail storm—me a spinning top—the rod playing no favorites back or front . . .

I was still on my feet—"The man must have gone mad!"

I opened my eyes. *Miss Galbraith! I'm naked in front of Miss Galbraith!*

She rubbed salve on my backside, then came to the front.

*Embarrassed* is too short a word for it. I was still shaking—couldn't stop.

"N-not m-my—!"

"Needs it. Will it be all right if I just pat?"

"D-don't kn-know."

She took it in one hand and patted with the other, "How does that feel?"

"A-a-a-a-h!"

"You are very well-developed."

After that, every time my eyes met Miss Galbraith's, she'd smile and I'd blush.

# CHAPTER 15

**O**ur fathers'd ordered me'n Stu not to try for but *to be* altar boys.

"Take a bath tomorrow morning—I don't mean a lick and a promise—wash everything—I mean everything. It's a losing battle, but they go by the old ways and don't want boys who've been altered."

Didn't make sense—why wouldn't altar boys be altered?

"And put on the new BVDs your mother bought. The church wants altar boys to be dressed the same, so they supply special clothes. You'll have to try some on."

"Where?"

"They have a place. Listen, you behave yourself, and do exactly as you're told. Exactly! You're not too old to take my strap to— remember the last time?"

Did Captain Ahab remember the whale? Me nine, her a year older with blonde curls—for which I was known throughout the county to be a sucker for. Them visiting her grandparents. Our mothers— old friends from school—had gone shopping an'd left us alone in the house. To this day I don't know how she did it—must've been what you call an enchantress. Whatever she was—and however she worked it—she had me down to my BVDs, kneeling in front of her, licking peanut butter from one of her hands and currant jelly from the other . . .

And home from the office to pick up something, that's how my father found us.

"Taking your pants off for little girls, is that what you're into! On your bed and out of your underwear while I get the strap."

"Please, Dad!"

"Don't please—Dad me! Next time you'll keep your pants on."

She followed me, so I had to wiggle out of the BVDs face down without showing it.

Five swings and he left off, "Get some pants on!"

Him gone, I couldn't move.

She got on the bed and cuddled me in her arms—me wanting nothing more than to be on a rocket to Mars.

"Let me turn you over."

"Don't do that!"

"Has to be done."

She was strong. First her fingers underneath; then me flat on my back showing what she wanted to see.

"Can I touch it?"

"U-u-u-h."

She touched it.


"I don't want to hear about any trouble involving my son."

"You won't, Dad."

"I have a name to uphold in the Church. No excuses! And that goes for your friend Stuart; till this is over I'm responsible for him. Did you tell him to take a bath?"

He knows.


I took my bath—not everything—did it not long ago.

Stu showed up—me dressed except my coat and tie—*thank you very much.*

"Stuart, did you take a bath?" My father asked.

"Forgot."

"We have time. Help him with it."

Stu didn't look happy.

"Move! We don't have all day," my father said. "Best leave your Sunday clothes here—get started!"

Stu kept his pants and undershirt on.

"C'mon."

Him holding back—that talk in the bamboo about taking clothes off meant me not him.

"Can you close the door?"

"My mother's not here."

"You're here."

"I've given boys baths."

"Really?"

"Dozens. I'll run the tub—put your pants on that hanger."

Blushing, he followed orders . . . wearing boxers . . . me jealous.

He held out his undershirt—him skinny—real skinny. The boxers were too big—hung so low they'd like to've fallen off—showing his thin white belly all the way down—no fur in sight.

We stood looking at each other . . .

I shut off the water and turned back to him. He was still in his shorts.

"What about—?"

Stu's face went tomato, "I'm embarrassed."

*Pretend he's Stefan* . . . I couldn't.

"Dad!"

"What is it!"

"You have to do him!"

# CHAPTER 16

A young priest, a very young priest, told us, "Through that door and down to your underwear."

*Do exactly as you're told. Exactly!*

Some boys were ahead of us, all in boxers. Two of them on the floor, the boy on the bottom giggling, the boy on top with his hand up the leg of the giggler's undershorts.

"Felt like that when your father washed me," Stu whispered.

"Nothing to what'll you'll feel if we mess up—might have your dad's permission. Ever been whipped with a razor strap?" I whispered back.

"Can't be worse than a split bamboo pole."

The first priest came back with another priest—some older—who spotted the two on the floor.

"Take them to the small room and deal with them—the old-fashioned way—bare bottom."

"Not very good at that sort of thing, Father."

"Time you learned if you're to help with my work. Remember, boys are savages, pagans in need of the Cross, and not a jot better than we make them be."

The younger priest marched the two off.

The older priest turned to us, "Why are you in street clothes?"

We shed to our underwear—me embarrassed to be the only one in BVDs.

"Starting as of now, every altar boy takes a bath before showing up for duty; no getting into Church clothes unless you're clean. In the past we've had to deal with body lice, so there will be inspections. Anyone here hasn't had a bath this morning?"

One boy looked guilty.

"*You*? Have you or haven't you? . . . Well?"

"No, Father."

"All right, come with me. I'll give you a quick wash."

"Can't I do myself, Father?"

"A boy get himself clean? That I'd like to see. No, you can't."

"I'm bashful, Father."

"We'll soon scrub that out of you. *You*," he pointed to Stu, "Tell Father Arne to do the preliminaries."

"To do the—what did you call them?"

"Preliminaries."

He left, pushing the boy in front of him.

In a minute there was hollering from the other room, but being an old hand at such things, I could tell the two were putting on a show. Not like the time with the Irish boy—his screams made your skin crawl down your arms onto your legs.

The pair back, the tickler whispered, "Pushover, let us keep our shorts on."

It must've been 10 minutes before the blond priest showed up, "Did Father O'Connor say anything?"

"You're to do the preminaries."

The young priest turned pink.

"I was expecting him to do that . . . Let's see, what's the best way of going about this? . . . Get in line behind one another—and no looking at the boy in front of you—understand?"

Grabbing Stu's hand, I put me last and him next to last.

"I won't like this any better than you will. All right, you, take your member out."

The boy dropped his shorts.

"Not sure what you're after, Father, but take your pick."

Pink turned to red.

"Foreskin—you pass!—pull your shorts up and take a seat along the wall."

Just then the boy who'd gone for a bath came in.

"Take a place in line."

"He said I was to take a seat, Father."

"The other priest checked you?"

"Did he ever!"

"All right, take a seat."

"You're all to keep your underwear on. Next! . . . Do you know what your member is?"

"Yes, Father, you want my peter."

". . . Get dressed and go home."

"Thanks, Father!"

The third boy came out with, "Mine's like his—exactly the same— except bigger. Can I go please, Father?"

"Go!"

The fourth boy said, "This what you're after, Father?"

"Put it away, and take a seat."

The next boy took a seat too. I got alongside Stu, "His father was born in County Mayo, mine in Kilkenny. All of us love the Pope, good Catholics every one, and all with foreskins. Can we take a seat, Father?"

"Anything to get it over with."

I'd heard about County Mayo from his father, and I guessed about Stu, but I'd made up Kilkenny. My father was born back East, and I'd never seen his foreskin.

Stu whispered, "How'd you know about mine?"

Happy as a squirrel at not showing it, I said, "Betsy-you're-dipsy-for told me. She can see through pants."

"O my gosh!"


The other priest came back.

"I'll take over, Father, you see the altar clothes are in order."

The blond one left.

"Who wants to be first?"

"We do, Father!" Stu let out—me wanting to choke him.

"This way."

He took us to the small room and said to Stu, "You've had a bath?"

"Yes, Father."

"You're underweight; do you drink milk?"

"My father never buys it."

"Drop your underwear and I'll check your development."

"My what?"

"Your privates . . . Hurry up!"

"U-u-u-h, Sean's never seen me, Father."

"We'll soon fix that—off!"

They were small.

"Underdeveloped. No question you are behind your age. We have a free milk program for altar boys, one pint a day. Would you make use of that?"

"Does my father have to know? He's proud."

"No, I'll see to it . . . Now what about you?" he said to me.

"Big," I said, "drink milk all the time."

"Had your bath? Washed everything?"

"U-u-u-h."

"Not everything? We'll see to it."

"F-Father—" Stu started to say.

"Why are you holding yourself?"

"I'm embarrassed."

"You're more than that, you're hopping about."

"Can I put my shorts on?"

"No point in that till you pee."

The priest picked up Stu's shorts and hurried him away.

They didn't come back, but after a while the blond priest showed up.

"I won't like this any better than you will, but Father O'Connor insists."

He led me to a bathroom where the tub was less than a quarter full.

"Get in—just as you are."

I'd never had a bath in my BVDs, but I wasn't rocking any boats. I got in.

"Pull a leg of your drawers up."

"Wh-which leg?"

"Doesn't matter."

I pushed things to one side and pulled up the other side.

"No, I need your member exposed."

"Exp-posed?"

"Out in the open . . . Hurry up! Let's get this over with."

I agreed with him there. I pulled up the other side a little.

"Higher! I don't want to get your underwear wet."

I closed my eyes and followed orders.

"How old are you?"

"El-leven."

"Doesn't seem possible."

He was gentle . . . Hardly getting an "A-a-h!" from me . . . But by the time he'd finished I was pointing wrong.
"We can't leave you like that; get out of the tub."
I got out and played statue as he worked my underwear off. Me uncovered, for a long minute he took in my nakedness . . .
"God forgive me, but you're beautiful!" he whispered.
I looked at his face—it had a soft look.
The other priest came through the door.
"Everything all right? . . . Oh, I see . . . You better leave, Father."
The blond priest left.
"Did he do you?"
"U-u-u-h."
"Let me check."
He ran his hands down my body . . . I started to shake . . . till he got to things . . . He wasn't gentle as he checked . . . "A-a-a-a-h!" . . . "A-a-a-a-h!"
I looked at his face—it had a look I didn't know.
"Can you pee? . . . Try . . ."
I couldn't.
"All right, get in the tub and kneel facing the faucet."
Me weak in the legs, he turned the cold water on full . . .

"Get out and see if you can pee."
I was by the toilet.
"C-could you t-turn your b-back?"
"Don't be foolish; you've wasted enough of my time—pee!"
The chopping stump ran through me like a movie . . . I checked Father's face . . . It had that look . . . I turned my head and did what he wanted . . .
"Good boy," he said, patting my bottom.
He dried me, got me into my BVDs, left them unbuttoned, leaving my fur showing, and took me to a new room, "Stand with your back to that wall."

Alone—weak all over—afraid to button—I waited . . .
A new priest came and took a seat, the oldest so far but not grey. He must be shorter than he looked, since he was thin as asparagus,

drooping a butt long with ash from fingers stained brown. His eyes went over my BVDs—my hands moving this way and that, unable to stay put.

Finally he spoke, "You seem to be nervous about your underwear; it might be best if you take them off."

"T-take them off?"

"Yes, that will stop you fidgeting."

*Do exactly as you're told . . .*

The BVDs gone, I wanted to cover myself—bad.

"Stand like a Soldier of Christ with your hands at your sides."

*Look straight ahead—don't look down.*

"Are you frightened of me?"

"N-no, F-father."

"God gave you a beautiful body. I see intelligence. I wouldn't like you to be frightened. I want you to feel free to come to me with questions or problems. Do you think you could do that?"

"M-maybe, F-Father."

"I am going to tell you about The Church—first let me light a cigarette . . . There is only One Church, The Holy Roman Church, The Catholic Church. The Church is an army with God as the Supreme Ruler, the Pope His Commander-in-Chief on Earth, the Cardinals, Generals, the Archbishops, Colonels, the Bishops, Majors, the Monsignors, Captains, the Head Priests like myself, Lieutenants, and so on to the altar boys like yourself, drummers who carry the Banner of Christ. Does that excite you?"

"Th-think so, F-Father."

"The Church like an army operates on obedience. When the Bishop tells me to do something, I do it without question. And you as an altar boy will do what a priest tells you without question. Do you agree to that?"

"Y-yes, F-Father."

"The Church is a hard master, but the reward is eternal bliss seated at the feet of God. How about that?"

"C-can I play tennis sometimes?"

"You can play tennis on courts of gold."

"H-have to get used to the bounce."

"You will have plenty of time. Now swear you will be an obedient servant of The Church."

"Sw-swear I will be an obedient servant of The Church."

"I am going to bless you like when you were Christened—first let me put out the cigarette . . . Now come forward."

We were face to face.

"Kneel before me."

The priest knelt with me.

"Let me explain about your body."

He pointed to my penis . . . I felt it move . . .

"That is the gateway to Hell."

It wouldn't stop . . .

"Hell Fire! You understand!"

He wrapped his hand around it, "The Serpent has you in his power! . . . Get behind me Satan! . . . You would corrupt the other boys . . . Dismissed!"

I pulled away, grabbed my BVDs, and ran . . .

Father O'Connor had a naked boy in front of him—I kept going to the large room—scrambled into my clothes with my back turned—and went outside where Stu was waiting.

"I didn't make it—couldn't pee with him watching. You ever peed naked with a priest watching?"

"'Course not."

"I'm gonna get whipped."

"Want me to go home with you?"

"Rather go home with you."


"Messed up, didn't you! Stuart, help him out of his clothes."

This was double punishment—*Stu undress me? O God!*

But he'd said it too loud. My mother came out from the kitchen, "If you take your strap to him, there'll be no Saturday night for a month."

"Have it your way," my father said, "but he better shape up."


I didn't see how there could be no Saturday night for a month.


Stu asked me to go home with him. It was cold and there was no heat in the house. An empty glass and a half-empty bottle sat on the kitchen table.

"Mike called, tole me yuh screwed up—yuh know what to do," his father said.

I followed Stu to his bedroom . . . His dad came in holding a thick bamboo pole—the end split into a bunch of strips—and closed the door. Fear in his eyes, Stu pulled things off. Staring me straight in the face, he dropped the clothes off his skinny body. In front of his father he knew better than to cover himself . . .

"Looks like somethin' the cat dragged in—ever seen a prick that small?"

It was blue from cold. "He needs milk; it's cheaper than whiskey," I said.

"Yuh little bastard! I know yur to blame—he thinks yur God. Show'im what yuh've got!"

"Wh-what?"

"Strip tuh yur balls . . . Think I can't make yuh?"

I was pretty sure he could. His back was to the door, blocking the way out . . . I started undressing . . . Me shivering in my BVDs—I was cold and scared, "Show yurself!"

I unbuttoned and slow-like pushed them down.

"Gorilla!" Stu whispered.

"Tha's what I call a prick; why can't you look like that? . . . Both of yuh out the door intuh the yard."

"Y-yard?"

"Saves flushin'."

We were side by side facing a wire fence.

"Skin yur pricks."

"Th-there's a b-boy at the fence."

"So what? Got a prick ain't he? Twelve or more but the brain of a 6-year-old—skin'em! . . . Pee damn yuh!"

Stu started . . . I closed my eyes and was afraid not to . . .

We were back in the bedroom, This time he left the door open. "Side by side, lean forward with yur hands against the wall."

Shaking like our old washing machne, I leaned and saw down below was shaking too. I looked at Stu, everything was shaking. His father picked up the bamboo pole . . . I'd never been so scared . . .

"Now we'll see what kinda friend yuh got. Yur choice, Big Prick, yuh c'n take half his whippin' or yuh c'n pick up yur clothes an' run like a rat."

I scooped up my clothes and ran like a rat.

*You're a dirty yellow coward,* I thought to myself. As I made for the backyard I listened for screams but none came. Once outside I dropped my bundle . . .

"Big pee-pee," the boy at the fence said, "Wanna see mine?"

I turned my back and grabbed my BVDs.

I couldn't get the fear in Stu's eyes out of my head. Monday and Tuesday he didn't come to school. Wednesday I went to his house. There was a sign in the front yard, so I asked next door. They were behind in the rent, an'd left in the middle of the night.

I would never see Stu again.

# CHAPTER 17

**A**long with Damon and Stu, I had a buddy called Scooter, one of the youngest boys in sixth. Smudge was one of the oldest and hands down the nastiest. I never found out how he got the nickname, but I heard his real name was Beverly. What a choice— think I'd take Smudge. Maybe his mother loved him, but I never heard anyone rate him higher'n a weasel. And weasel didn't give too bad a picture of Smudge with his squeaky voice and dirty claws. I ignored him every whichway, but for some reason he'd settled on me as his patsy. Mostly I let the names he called me roll off like ducks do.

So as usual at lunchtime I was sitting by the high bars keeping the girls company when Smudge squeaked so everyone could hear, "Hey, Mick, is it true your father was an elephant and your mother was a whale?"

Somehow this didn't sit. In the first place my mother couldn't swim a lick. Scooter who had his own Smudge grudge motioned me behind the handball wall.

"Thinks he's the Bill Tilden of sixth grade. Wha'do yuh say we challenge him and Cameron to a doubles match?"

"Have you been practicing your backhand?"

"I'll play forehand and you take everything in between."

"You know Smudge calls balls on the line out."

"Not to worry, for every bad call Smudge makes, l'il ol' Scooter'll make two."

"It's all fixed for Saturday, but Smudge wants to play for something. You have a dime?"

"Spent all my money on Christmas presents. Think I have two pennies in my pig."

"I'm broke too, but I'll work something out."

"How?"

"Trust l'il ol' Scooter."

It was a cold grey drizzly Saturday morning, but not to be put off by a little drizzle, me in a pull-down hat and scarf my mother'd knit, the others bundled too, four of us met at the tennis court. Across the net with Smudge was the Class Monitor—a little too rich and a little too good for my taste—but it was hard to hold that against him.

No one else thought of it, but Cameron brought eight bananas and eight full-slice sandwiches of two kinds to share with classmates he figured were too poor or too dumb to feed themselves—the town gave us water. In the Great Depression kids looked at hunger like growing pains; an empty belly and a tightened belt were a part of things—you didn't see a lot of fat boys.

Setting out to play doubles, we never counted on less than 5 sets, and today we were playing 5 out of 9. We came for the long haul; food played no part in our plans. But when it turned up, we welcomed it like a strawberry patch in a dogless yard. Our opponents eked out the first set; we won the next two, and Smudge came out with, "Who wants to share a bush?"

"I'll pick the bush," Scooter answered, starting to walk.

"What about you two?"

"Hold water like a camel," I said.

"Cameron?"

"Not much for company."

"Ha, ha! Cameron don't like showin' it—come watch, Sean."

"Sure!" Scooter hollered, "Give you a thrill!"

"Three's a crowd," I said.

"Smudge'd let you take it out for 'im!"

"At least mine he'd be able to find."

We won the next two sets by big margins. I wasn't concerned much with Smudge, but because of the bananas, the sandwiches, and the look on Cameron's face, I felt sorry for him.

"Five sets is enough on a morning like this; would you consider stopping and calling it a draw?"

"You mean that?"

"If it's all right with the two of you."

"Oh, it's all right with us! And you know what? I'm treating the four of us to a movie this afternoon. I'll get there early and buy the tickets. It'll be a sellout because it's Mutiny on the Bounty with Clark Gable. The rest of you can come later to the candy store next door and pick out any two nickel bars you like. Did I say two? Heck, you can pick out four apiece. What do you say?"

What could we say?

It was hard to decide on all that candy. I chose a Love Nest, a Mounds, a Milky Way, and a nickel's worth of Licorice Whips.

First came the prevues, "Boy we gotta see that!" Next came the newsreel, usually stuff we didn't care about like some screaming German with a little mustache. But this time they had bathing beauties wearing swim suits.

Scooter came out with, "How'd yuh like to see that blonde without her suit?"

I'd like it fine, but I didn't know other boys thought about such things.

"You guys prob'ly never had a girl's panties down," Smudge said, "an' wouldn' know what to do if you did. Ever shown it to a girl, Sean? They like to play with'em, speakin' of which, I gotta piss."

"That all yuh do?" from Scooter.

"Guarantee I do more with it'n you. Anyway, don't cost nothin'."

Smudge left and was back fast, "Four 8th-graders're teasin' a 7th-grader about showin' it."

"Think they'll go all the way?" from Scooter.

"You can bet on it—kid's plenty scared, and that just feeds the fire. Ain't got a snowball's chance in Hell."

"Let's go, you guys!" Scooter let out. "Don't'cha wanna see a 7th-grade dick!"

"Seen plenty," I lied.

"Cameron?"

"Not taking any chances."

Smudge and Scooter took off.

They missed Mickey Mouse with all the hollering and foot stamping.

The two came back. "The works, but nothing special—less yu're hot to see a kid scared to his nuts," Scooter told us.
"Peter no bigger'n your average 6th grader's," Smudge put in.
"How big is that?" Cameron asked.
"Well you know."
I got the feeling he didn't know.
"Sean'll show yuh."

He was wrong about that.

We hated Captain Bligh—who wouldn't? I'd like to've seen it a second time, but there was only the one showing.

Going home a zigzag of lightning raised our hair—followed hard by a sharp crack of thunder. The skies opened wide as the Pearly Gates, and drops fell like marbles from a busted bag. Cameron peeled off toward the rich part of town; Smudge turned next. Scooter an' me made it to the railroad shed not far from our houses.
I had to ask, "What was the bet you came up with?"
Soon as I tell yuh, yuh'll see why Cameron was so generous—he'd like to've peed his pants when Smudge laid out the deal—'course Smudge told'im there was nothing to worry about 'cause they were a dead cert. But as you an' me know—"
"You going to tell me or not?"
"I'll paint a pitcher: Imagine pulling it out o' your pants; now imagine pulling it out for pimple-face Geraldine and letting fly."
"O my God! What if we'd lost!"
"Ha, ha! Not all that bad. Smudge wouldn't mind; shows it to Sylvia, yuh know."

. . . That got me thinking . . . *Prob'ly lets her play with it.* I knew babies came into it somehow. *Maybe a girl has to play with it to get a boy baby.* I tried to imagine my mother playing with my father's . . . Couldn't . . . . Thought about Amy at my uncle's ranch . . . Thought about her hand on me . . . Thought about when she'd seen me

naked . . . *Wouldn't mind marrying her, letting her do whatever girls have to do . . . Someday I'll know everything . . .*

Next week Cameron asked me to spend Saturday night with him.
*Wants to take a bath with me.*
"Chocolate éclairs for dessert."
It was hard to turn down chocolate éclairs.
"Why don't you ask Scooter?"

Monday Scooter said, "You must be crazy turning down chocolate éclairs. What's a dick between friends? Oh, and in case you're curious, Cameron's is just like mine. Care to sleep over Saturday?"
"Wouldn't want to come between you two."

# CHAPTER 18

**W**e'd have to move, and I wasn't looking forward to it. The landlord was giving our house to his son as a wedding present. We wondered if he'd finally fix the broken lock.

"You'd have to change schools in the fall anyway, so I've enrolled you at Saint Bartholomew's."

"Dad!"

"If you'd've made altar boy, it mightn't be necessary."

"Maybe if you talked to one of the priests?"

"Maybe you'll learn life is stingy with second chances."

It was a boys-only school. Brother Thomas was big in all directions—looked like he'd give Man Mountain Dean a run for his money—no way I'd cross him. If he said pink was blue, he'd get no argument out of me.

*Our Father, who art in heaven, hallowed be thy name . . .*

We spent the first five minutes on our knees; then moved to two-boy desks where my mate whispered in my ear, "You're gonna get it at lunchtime."

We got it but not lunch; the kids divvied what we'd brought—me'n another new boy—'mongst themselves. My desk mate one of a bunch howling for balls like those Romans howling for blood. But the biggest kid said underwear was far enough—the two of us down to bare feet, the other boy in BVDs, me in a union suit. A monk on patrol stopping to watch. It was cold and damp by the bay. They did us on a new-turned patch of dirt—black dirt—black

as coal and just as dirty. Us rolling over and over each other, the crowd egging us on with shouts and swats. And every time one of us got to his knees, a brogue in the behind sent him sprawling in the black dirt . . .

The shouting stopped . . .
"They've gone," the other boy said.
I looked around—no clothes.
"What're we going to do?".
"'Less you're packin' hooch, I'm gettin' out o' the cold. Don't suppose you'd swap underwear?"
I followed him to the door of our room where he stuck his head inside.
"Take your seat!"
We took our seats—the boys laughing—the teacher paying no attention to our underwear.
"Padraig Cleary!"
"Yes, Brother."
"This is your first time in Parochial School?"
"Yes, Brother."
"But you studied Catechism and made your First Holy Communion?"
"Yes, Brother."
"So you would be able to tell us what is meant by the Virgin Birth."
"Yes, Brother, that I would."
"You are certain?"
"Easy as fallin' down soaped stairs."
"Sean Lacey!"
"Yes, Brother."
"And you would be able to tell us what is meant by the Immaculate Conception?"
"Yes, Brother, since I understand the word conception, I'm sure I could."
"You are certain?"
"Absolutely!"
"So Cleary, what is your answer?"
"The Virgin Birth is when the Virgin Mary was born. That the hardest you got, Brother?"

"Think you'll find I have something harder. And Lacey, what is the answer to your question?"

"Well, conception means idea—I had a very smart teacher at my last school—and the only one who could have an immaculate idea— pretty sure I've got this right—would be God. So the Immaculate Conception would have to be the idea God had to make the world. Nothing else makes sense, does it, Brother?"

"Both of you are wrong. And I don't put up with public-school know-it-alls who are one step from heathens. To learn some Catholic humility, the two of you will report to me after the final bell—let me think a minute . . . [*You never been whipped till you been whipped by Brother Thomas—and after he's done, we'll take you to the gravel pit and make you pull dicks—you pull his, he pulls yours*, my desk mate whispered.] . . . My decision is to temporarily seat you in third grade—but I will see to you after the bell . . . Follow me!"

The third graders were giggling as Brother Thomas explained things to the nun in charge. She gave us a seat together.

"I'm Paddy. Think we'll get our clothes back?" he began the whispering.

"D-don't know."

"Your desk kid told you somethin', what?"

"U-u-u-h."

"We're gettin' it, ain't we? If they make us squeeze balls, don't squeeze hard, OK? 'Course we gotta put on a show screamin' our lungs out. Or maybe they'll have us pound dicks, you pound mine, I pound yours. You shy about stuff?"

I couldn't even say, "U-u-u-h."

From then on we sat like dunces till a young nun in a different head-thing and short sleeves came and announced, "Padraig Cleary and Sean Lacey!"

We stood up.

"Come with me!"

Marching up the hall alongside, she said, "It's lucky you are; Doctor O'Day—and him so young—just finished his year of training—he'll do you. He's dark and handsome as Rudolph Valentino. Ha, ha! There's more than one postulant who'd settle for Doctor O'Day as her bridegroom."

She took us into a room and I saw the bathtub . . . *Not again.*

"It'd be a sin for him to see you in such a state—black as chimney sweeps you are. Hurry up with you! Like most boys, expect you can't wait showing yourselves."

I watched Paddy drop his BVDs—bigger'n Stu's—no fur.

He let out, "You don't like showin' it to a skirt?"

The door opened and Brother Thomas came in, "Are they giving you any trouble?"

"That one's slow about getting out of his underwear."

"Off!"

I started to turn away.

"Don't give me your back!"

I faced him.

"Faster!"

I did it slow—Paddy coming around to watch.

"Out of them!"

I stepped out—and quick covered myself.

"Take your hands away!"

There's naked and naked-naked. With my hands at my sides and Brother Thomas taking me in, this was naked-naked . . .

Like Mr. Stillwater, he touched my fur . . .

"How old are you?"

"El-leven."

"You play with it, don't you?"

"Wh-what?"

"This!" he said, taking hold of my penis. "You can't fool me; I'll get the truth out of you after the bell. By the time I've finished, you'll show me just how you do it."

His smile was one I did understand—*He'll beat the bejesus out o' me.*

Brother Thomas gone—me pretending I wasn't naked—Paddy said, "You're wooly as my brother Gavin an' showin' more'n enough to tickle his steady an' her 17."

"In the tub with the pair o' you! . . . Do you want to do yourselves?"

"Yes, Sister!" I got out fast.

"Not good at doin' myself," from Paddy.

I washed with my eyes closed. Listening to them talk was like listening to John's Other Wife.

"Who does you at home?" she asked Paddy.

"Auntie. Does me and my sister together—Hannie just turned 10."

"Who does this part?"

"Auntie. Tickles my balls with soap, then a quick slide down my prick, so's not to stretch it front of Hannie who's too young to see it go long . . . That feels good, Sister."

*He'd worry about pulling my dick as much as he'd worry about pulling a carrot.*

"Looks like she never washes under here."

"She's afraid o' that part. My brother does it when we take a bath together—soaps it a pennyworth—but he don't like sharin' 'cept with a twist, so that's not often."

"Well, we'll give it a tuppenceworth this time."

She did us some rubs with a towel—taking too long between my legs—then knelt for our underwear and opened the door.

"Second to the left—same side of the hall."

"N-Naked?" I got out.

"An Irishman should do it in one great leap."

Our clothes were in a pile on a long bench.

"Sort out your things and stack your underwear with them, but don't put them on if you hope to reach Heaven without sore arses. See those rosaries hanging on that hook? I'll be back before you do five beads."

Paddy was talking, "My steady has a girlfriend startin' to swell. The three of us get naked together and have fun—how about you join us Saturday? They'll do anything you want, let you do anything you want. All you gotta bring is your dick. What d'you say?"

What I said was, "U-u-u-h."

The nun came with four boys. Me sitting covering myself; Paddy leaning back, legs spread, showing himself like he was doing the world a favor.

"Fifth and fourth graders," she said. "Younger ones done this morning; older ones tomorrow. Each of you undress a fifth; I'll do the fourths."

I saw the problem right off, mine'd be staring straight at my dick. The answer came quick—*sit him on my lap—bare though it might be—and do his buttons from behind.* He giggled so it worked fine. All four boys let it happen without a grumble. *Prob'ly have tons of brothers and sisters. How come I'm Catholic and have not a one?* In the end we were all lined up naked on the bench.

"Keep your hands off yourselves—they'd be an insult to the doctor."

Five uncovered foreskins in a row—mine covered—*So he'll be insulted*—the young ones comparing themselves.

"You'll be glad to see the back o' me," she said, leaving.

The head of Saint Bartholomew's came with a grownup, "We examine new pupils to check for health problems; then at the end of the school year we examine them all. That gives parents a chance to remedy things over the summer. All of you stand up! . . . Take your hands away! . . . You! Take your hands away!"

"He's well-developed, what grade is he?" the visitor asked.

"Keep your hands off yourself! . . . What grade are you?"

"U-u-u-h."

I saw the boy I'd undressed stretching his neck to see what he'd sat on.

"Sixth," Paddy said.

"Mine's seventh, and he's nothing like that."

They left . . . I took my seat and covered myself.

The doctor—*Can you get to be a doctor in a year?*—had shiny black hair parted down the middle. He was carrying a note pad. Rudolph Valentino was before my every-week movie-going, back when I couldn't read the words—*Mama! What does it say!* To me Doctor O'Day looked like George Raft slicked up for the Senior Ball.

"No girls, good—well maybe one," he smiled "We'll soon know."

I'd been smiled at before. I didn't smile back.

He looked at the pad and said, "Raise your hand as I call your name."

When he got to mine, I had to show fur, and he smiled again.

There was no weighing, no measuring, not even a chest-listener. But he looked everywhere, touched everything. After finishing the two 4t$^{h}$-graders, he set a bucket in the middle of the floor.

"Checking for urinary problems," and smiled as they peed.

*He likes it. O God, I can't!*

After marking a page, he told the 4$^{th}$-graders to dress and leave. The 5$^{th}$-graders came next.

*Even if I do, there'll be me'n Paddy getting our skin whipped off. And who knows what all Brother Thomas has up his sleeve?*

The two 5$^{th}$'s were peeing—the doctor was smiling.

*And after that us pantsed naked, doing things makes me sick to think of—best get whipped by Dad—even if it's a bad one—can't be worse than Brother Thomas who'll pound me bloody.*

They dressed and Paddy was called over.

*He wants me by myself!* Me taking off into my Secret Place.

I heard Paddy peeing.


"Over here!"

I opened my eyes—Paddy was gone. I went to the priest, covering myself.

"Take your hands away!"

I closed my eyes and showed myself.

"Well! See you're not a girl. We'll start with the testicles."

He took them in his fingers.

"A-a-a-h!"

"Checking your development . . . Could pass for a 9$^{th}$ grader . . . Any trouble with this part?"

My peter was in his hand.

"Don't touch it!"

"Quiet!."

"A-a-a-a-a-h!"

"Have to get everything out in the open . . ."

"A-a-a-a-h! . . . A-a-a-a-a-h! . . . A-a-a-a-a-a-h!"

"Definitely beyond your age."

After that I paid no attention to what he did . . .

"Open your eyes . . . Open your eyes! . . . I'll hold the bucket high for you; see if you can urinate."

I looked at myself—*Thank God Paddy's gone*—ran—grabbed my pile of clothes—pushed through the door—down the hall—outside the building into the cold—hurried into my clothes—without meeting so much as a sparrow.

One day at Saint Bartholomew's was enough. I'd rather die than go back.

Two weeks—it went on two weeks. Me off early in the morning, huddling cold behind a tree overlooking my old school, watching the kids at recess, crying my eyes sore. *I'll turn out stupid—prob'ly end up selling pencils on street corners.* I thought about riding the rails, stopping at farms to help with the milking. *Trouble is, I don't know how—doubt they'd feed me much for gathering eggs.*

# CHAPTER 19

**M**y father didn't whip me. I'd wish he had.

"I've spoken to Father O'Connor about altar boy [*O God!*]. You have an appointment for 10 o'clock Saturday morning. You do whatever the priest says, understand?"

"Y-Yes, Dad."

"You better not mess up!"

Saturday morning I was on a seat in the hall when four older kids came up to me. "Trying out?"

"Yes."

"Come with us; we give a debagging party for new boys—you like Delaware Punch?"

"My favorite."

I followed them to a small room. "Get his clothes off."

*Holy Mary help me!* One thing I knew about older boys, they had no mercy on younger boys. They'd strip you and do things it was better not to think about. I closed my eyes. There was laughing, lots of laughing.

"Cuff him!"

They forced my hands behind my back and locked some metal handcuffs around my wrists.

"Sully, tie a string around his dick . . . Father O'Connor's gonna have fun with that! . . . Take him outside!"

The boy led me to the entrance—"Not in the open!"

"Run him once around the building."

I fell on my knees, "Please!"

"Twice around."

I got up quick. The kid gave a yank and we took off.

We'd finished.
"One last thing, next time you see me, pull it out o' your pants . . . All right, uncuff him and take him to Father O'Connor."

They shoved me naked through a door.
The priest looked up from his desk, "Debagged?"
"Y-Yes."
"Take your hands away . . . Do I know you?"
"D-Don't think so."
"You must be the Lacey boy—through that door—we'll do your bath."
Inside he started the water and asked, "Can you pee?"
"D-Don't think so."
"All right get in the tub . . . Keep your hands off yourself . . ."

I'd had weenie washes, but none like this. Sometimes he'd stop and let me stand there shaking, "You're far along for your age."
Finally he said, "Come back next week, and we'll work on making you into a man. Now get out and pee."
"Whatever you say, Father . . ."

A janitor was sweeping the hall, "Looking for your clothes?"
"Yessir."
He took me to my stuff. "You're shaking; maybe I better dress you—all right?"
"Whatever you say."
"Have to take your arms away . . . I see boys all the time . . . But none like that . . ."

Outside I ran into the Head Boy talking to the priest who'd gone for 20 behind the curtain. "Well? . . . You looking for more times around?"
My fingers all thumbs, I started on the buttons—"Wait'll you see this, Father . . . Get it out!"
Shaking, I took it out . . . I started to put it back . . . "Leave it hang a while."
"You're a joker, Johnny O," the priest said.

"What happened?" my father asked."

"Debagged."

"All new boys get debagged. You're too sensitive; just do what the priests say, and everything will be fine."

The following Saturday as I went through the front door, a pint-size boy naked and cuffed was being pulled by a string toward me.

"You want to run him around the building?"

The look of fear I'd seen in Stu was in the boy's eyes. "Father O'Connor's expecting me."

I was low on sympathy, looking ahead to what was facing me. I made up my mind to let the priest do whatever he wanted while I went into my last tennis match, replaying the points.

"Lie down on the couch, and I'll undress you."

"Whatever you say, Father."

I couldn't stop shaking as he did the last button of my BVDS and pulled them off. His hand went down my leg, "You have a difficult body, but as a priest I can help you." He picked up my penis . . . "Some boys are sensitive in this part; I have medical training. Let me check it."

"Wh-Whatever you s-say, Father."

"Is it sensitive here?" . . . "Y-Yes, Father."

"Allow it to do what it wants." He pushed things back and held on.

"When I touch here, is that sensitive? . . . "A-a-a-a-a-h!" . . . "What about when I do this?" . . . "A-a-a-a-a-a-a-a-h! . . . Th-Think I h-have to p-pee."

He took me by the hand to the bathroom and didn't let go . . .

The third time instead of going to Father O'Connor, I went to Father Arne, "Could you give me a bath, Father?"

"Why do you ask for a bath?"

"Rather have one from you than from Father O'Connor."

"I see. Father O'Connor is my Superior, but I'll think of something. All right if that's what you want, take your clothes off."

I went over and lay down on his couch, "You're supposed to take them off, Father."

As he was doing my BVDs I felt his fingers shake as he touched below my belly button. "I'll leave the rest to you."
"You do it, Father."
He let me lie bare for a long minute . . . His face had a soft look.

I was in the tub being washed.
"Do you want to do that part yourself?"
"You have to do it, Father. He said I'll be a man soon. Is that how it happens? By a priest washing you there and making it grow?"
"God in Heaven!"

I looked at his face when he was holding it big . . . He was blushing.

While I was being dried, he said, "Suppose I suggest to your father it would best to forget about altar boy, that God has other plans for you."
I fell naked on my knees in front of him, "Thank you, Father! Thank you! And thank you for not making me pee."
"God help you! Let us kneel together and pray."

A giant weight was off my shoulders; I was done with Priests, done with altar boys, done with Monks, and done with Parochial School. My mother'd stood up for me an'd gone door to door till she'd found a rental coming up not far from the one we'd lived in as long as I could remember.
It was a time of wonder. It was the last of true childhood. It was Paradise with clothes on. But every now and then I'd look back and shudder: the look on Father O'Connor's face I didn't understand; the look on Brother Thomas's face I did understand.
As for the Virgin Birth and the Immaculate Conception, I stayed wrapped in ignorance.

# CHAPTER 20

Twelve years old. I knew it was hair—thicker and curlier—and everything else'd grown too. My father's cousin, a bachelor in his 30s, had at the war's end as a young soldier with nothing to do found his way to Africa looking for adventure. After 17 years on the Dark Continent, he came back to the States, and my parents invited him to stay with us while he hunted for a job. The new rental had a third bedroom so that was OK. Ted had neat stuff: a Massai shield, a blowgun, an elephant tusk, a rhino horn, a shrunken head kept in a little wooden chest, a big green crocodile covering one arm. He told me stories and I was glad he'd come.

"Nothing grand, a boys' school in a nearby county," was all Ted said about his new job. "I don't start till Monday, so you can do as you planned."

The Saturday trip was to visit Aunt Ellen and Cousin Mary. I grabbed the chance to stay home like a ripe pomegranate on a neighbor's bush.

"We'll be back on Sunday. Remember, Ted, lights out for Sean at 10 sharp, and he's to take his bath first."

"He'll be in the tub by 9:45. I'll see to it."

"Heck," I said, "I can take a bath in five minutes."

My parents were gone. "Jump in the jalopy, and we'll go for a ride," Ted said. "I packed lunch. Do you have a swimsuit?"

"Unh-unh."

We were on the highway.

"Where are we going?"

"Thought I'd like to see some ocean blue. You a good swimmer?"

"No, but I'm a good wader."

"Ha, ha! That's funny; I like a boy with a sense of humor."

We'd been on the road close to an hour when he pulled over.

"There's a restroom; care to share a bowl?"

"U-u-u-h."

"Ha, ha! Be back in a minute."

Soon as he left, I found a bush.

"We'll leave our shoes in the trunk so we can feel the sand in our toes. I'll bring the basket and things; you grab the jug. Head up the beach a ways where there are no people."

We walked half a mile before he stopped, "This is a good spot. You hungry?"

"I could eat.".

"Help yourself to sandwiches and lemonade. I didn't bring cups; mind sharing the jug?"

"Don't mind."

I ate three sandwiches and drank a quarter of the jug.

"Time to get ready for the water," he said.

Still sitting, he took his shirt off, showing his crocodile.

"Like it?" he asked, making his muscles move . . . Won't embarrass you seeing me naked, will it?"

It would be like seeing my father—or the Pope—the idea shocked me. He stood up and started to unbutton—I did a quick turn in the sand.

"Ha, ha! Hand me my suit; it's wrapped in one of the those towels."

I fished out the suit and dropped it behind my back.

"Last chance to see a Private First Class naked."

I didn't take it.

"Safe to look now. Stand up and turn around."

He had my shirt off before I got a word out.

"Wh-what are you doing?"

"Undressing you."

"Wait!"

"Take it easy! You don't need a suit; there's no one around. Anyway, they don't arrest 12-year-olds for going skinny. You're not bashful?"

"No, not bashful—it's because of my asthma—my mother always makes me keep covered," I got out fast.

"Forgot about your asthma—put your shirt on. Will you be OK if I leave you alone?"

"Sure, I'll take a nap."

A noise in the sand made me open my eyes. A boy in trunks was standing in front of me.

"Going to join him for a swim. Mind watching my stuff?"

"No trouble," I said.

"I'm Dory Callahan, sweet 14 and ready for love."

"Sean Lacey, and that's my Cousin Ted in the water."

I watched the two ride the waves for an hour before they ran back to me. Ted loaned the boy a towel.

"We're giving him a lift to town. Dory, is there a place we can shower and change, or don't you do that?"

"Yes, need to; these jeans are too tight to get over my trunks, and Ma always tells me to wash the salt off. I know a place that's hardly used. Show you from the car."

We packed up and left.

"So how do I get to this shower?"

"Just around that bend."

The place was open-air—wood partitions closing it in so it was private.

"You go first," Dory said.

"Don't tell me you're bashful?"

"Not if there's money in it."

"A teenager shouldn't be bashful. You any idea how many baths us Doughboys took together? Ha, ha! Most of them in a muddy creek that covered our ankles. Let's make you into a soldier. Shouldn't do this because it's for your own good, but I'll donate a quarter toward your education. What do you say?"

"A quarter? Sure, I'll do it for a quarter."

"Mind if Sean takes a shower with us?"

"I get extra?"

"No point in a shower," I said. "Got a date with a tub."

"Sit over there, Sean, where it's warm in the sun."

I found a place that let my toes wriggle in sand.

*They're naked*, I thought, after Dory's suit landed on top of a wall and Ted's followed.

*Thank God they're there, and I'm here.*


I must've nodded.

"You were asleep."

Dory was in jeans.

"Where's Ted?"

"Went for smokes. That was some shower. Next time I'll charge more."

"What happened?"

"Nothing that hasn't happened before—got a boner."

"Boner?"

"Peter went stiff. Maybe you don't know it, but your cousin has a hose, and having that in my face was no help. You ever seen a grown man naked? Let me tell you, it was scary—never knew dicks got that big—come in handy to dowse a campfire.

"So you don't know what a boner is? For a nickel I'll drop my jeans and show you. What do you say?"

"U-u-u-h."

A honk from Ted sent us hopping.

# Chapter 21

**S**upper over, I'd finished my radio programs and Ted was pouring a brandy . . . He quick went to a second.

"I'll play you some cribbage, but when the time comes you get into the tub pronto. Promise?"

"Promise."

"Don't think I told you about my nosedive in the Congo. I was trading upriver from Stanleyville with three boys—oldest no more'n 15. Hiking through the bush, I tripped on a vine and went head over heels down a bank onto a broken branch—ripped right through the khaki into my leg. Believe me, the Congo's the last place you want an open wound. If my helpers'd been shy, yours truly might've ended up feeding the lilies. But the boys wouldn't've known what to do with a fig leaf; they stripped me naked as themselves and pissed a pint apiece onto the bleeding gash—stopped any bugs in their tracks. What do you think of that?"

I didn't know what I thought about a grownup telling me such stuff. I went to get the cards and board.

"Oh, oh!" Ted said, checking his pocket watch at the end of a deal, "9:54."

He put one hand on the back of my neck, "OK, soldier, hay foot, straw foot," and marched me to the bathroom.

"I make it 30 seconds to get out of your clothes. I'll run the tub."

My feet grew roots.

"You made a promise."

I did my Keds and stuck my hand in the water.

"Pronto!"

I got my shirt off and stopped, hoping he'd leave.

"Don't know about your promises, but I'm keeping mine to your mother. *I'm seeing you into that tub. Comprendo?*"

I Comprendoed.

"Who'll do the pants, you or me?"

My back turned, I pulled the pants off and ended up with one of Dory's boners. Coming around to find out what was holding things up, he got a look at my pushed-out BVDs.

"Better see what's causing the trouble."

He started on the buttons—his fingers were close—I took off—him after me—grabbed me from behind—threw me face down on the living room rug—"By God, if it's the last thing I do, I'll skin you! Not bashful—you little liar! I should've stripped you on the beach and walked you to where those boys were playing ball. To think a cousin of mine would turn out dick-shy!"

Sitting on me, he pulled one arm after another out of the sleeves; turning around on my back, he shimmied the BVDs from my legs, and got off. In a voice that'd gone quiet again, he said, "Stay like that till your mother gets home; you can show her what you've got."

That got me going. The BVDs were still in his hand, so on my belly I snaked my way to the sofa, took a doily off one arm, and slid it under myself. All but naked, one hand free, one hand holding the thin lace bunched around my stiff, I got up—s-l-o-w-l-y. My inside told me anything fast would set him off.

"You're something! Really something!" he said. "Yessir, give me a white boy every time."

He poured himself a drink and sipped as he walked around my body.

"'Course, I have no complaints about black boys or brown boys either for that matter. In the Sudan, I'd go for weeks seeing no one but the two Arabs who did my chores, orphans who'd been taken in by Blacks. We'd started along the edge of this great desert—hottest place on earth—when Achmed came to my tent with a knife in his hand, wearing less than you.

"'It's past my time, please Master, make me into a man,' he said. He wanted me to circumcise him. I didn't do that, but I made him into a man all right. You don't know what I'm talking about, do you? Next morning we left for their village, where as it turned out the Witch Doctor'd just died. Three weeks later I held Achmed's

hand while the new man cut him, making a bloody mess. I told the butcher to get out, poured brandy on Achmed—must've hurt like hell—and bandaged him. When Mustafa's time came, I cut him myself."

My heart was hammering—I wasn't sure what'd been cut.

Ted turned back to my body, "You know, the cloth spoils things, but I kind o' go for the way your hair pokes out."

He felt in his pockets, "A dime for the doily," he said, holding it toward me.

I started to tremble.

"On the other hand, I could take it for free."

I went from trembling to shaking to my muscles gone haywire . . .

"Git, damn you!"

I broke toward the hall.

"In the tub! Don't make me put you in! And don't close the door!"

Me sitting naked in the tub, my boner out of the water, hiding it with my knees, he came with a glass of milk and handed it down.

"Make you sleep. Drink!"

I didn't like warm milk, but I drank.

"Wash yourself," he said, taking the glass and leaving.

I used some soap and splashed myself.

He showed up with a brandy, pulled the plug, and waited while the water ran out . . .

"Stand up," he said in a low voice . . . "Stand up," lower . . . I stood up . . . "Take your arms away," in a whisper.

I knew I had to . . . I let him see all of me . . .

He sipped, enjoying his drink and me. I never moved. It was ten minutes before he said anything.

"You sure you're 12? You'd make a 14-year-old like Dory cry. How long since your balls dropped? You know? Don't know much, do you? Don't even know what you've got. Stay like that—I need another drink."

I stayed like that. When he came back, he didn't talk, just stood there . . .

"I-I'm sleepy,"

"Don't you piss before you go to bed?"

"Y-yes."

"Piss in the tub—that way it won't go all over the damn floor—sure don't want to clean up after you. Then we'll see about sleep. Pull your skin back . . . For Christ's Sake! Think I never seen a boy piss? Pull your fucking skin back!"

The word hit me like a whip—I didn't know what it meant, but I knew it was the worst thing you could say. I'd never'd heard it said, but'd seen it on the station wall. They'd paint over it, and next time it'd be there again.

I pulled things back just a little—like my father'd taught me when I was seven—closed my eyes, and whispered under my breath,

"Please, God, help me!"

It didn't happen quick, but it happened.

"Open your eyes . . . Out of the tub . . . Brush your teeth."

I brushed and turned around.

"It's a change seeing it hang."

It stopped hanging.

"Ha-ha! Go to bed!"

I wrapped myself in a towel, ran, fell into bed, dragged a sheet over me, and went out like a light.

Sunday morning, I woke with my head funny and a dream fading—a man standing over me—the rest I couldn't pull up. I pushed back the sheet—naked—went through my bed, under it, all around. Looking up, I saw the towel neatly folded on top of my bureau. A shiver ran over me.

I got into clean pants and snuck out to the kitchen. There was a note on the table. Ted was gone.

I never told about that night.

Wednesday morning my mother came into my room early, "We have an appointment. I bought you some new jersey shorts; put them on with a pullover shirt. It's too hot for underwear or socks; wear your sandals."

Still sleepy, I dressed like she told me.

"Where are we?" I asked, as our tires banged the curb.

"Your father wants Dr. William to look at you. He's not like the other doctor you saw; he's our family physician now."

"So he wants to look at me? Where?"

"Your chest."

"Just my chest?"

"Well maybe your throat."

"Nothing else?"

"Eyes, nose, ears, basic things."

Far as I dared go—couldn't say *penis* to my mother.

"No nurse?"

"No nurse."

"I won't have to take my shorts off?"

"You won't have to take them off."

That explained why my mother had me skip the underwear; she knew I hated showing my BVD top.

The lady at the desk took us to a cubbyhole with nothing in it but a table and a clothes tree, not even a chair. For a door, it had a white curtain on rings.

"The doctor wants him ready."

The two of us alone, my mother pulled the curtain shut and smoothed the edges so they didn't leave a gap.

"Give me your shirt and sandals," she said.

I handed them over, and she pushed them under the curtain.

"Sean, look at me."

"You have your eyes closed," I said.

"And I'm going to keep them closed."

"Why?"

"Because the doctor wants *me* to take these off too," she said, pulling my shorts down . . . "I'll keep your clothes till he's finished."

Eyes shut, she took my shorts and fixed the curtain after herself.

I could feel it happening—just what I expected—me hopping from one foot to another like I was dancing on stove lids—any minute the doctor'd pull back the curtain . . .

I stuck my head outside, "Mom! Mom! Mom!"

"What's the matter?" she asked, running toward me.

I broke down crying, "Mama, please give me my clothes!"

"You have to see the doctor."

"Please, Mama! Give me my clothes! Please, Mama! Please!"

"What'll I tell the doctor?"

"Please, Mama! Please! Please! Please!"

She came with the clothes and went away.

I pulled the shorts on, held the rest out in front to hide myself, and ran barefoot to the car.

They wouldn't get me to the Doctor's anytime soon.

The next year and a half went smooth as penoche.

# PART II

## CHAPTER 22

**13** and a half. Everything was growing. The older I got, the more bashful I got; me still in little kids' underwear I'd rather die than show.

My mother put up the $6,000 left by her mother, and my father used it to buy a lot and have our own house built, doing the plans and some of the work himself. No palace, but my room had its own bathroom with a double-size shower that needed no curtain. The new house was only nine miles from our last rental, but it put us into a new town and me into my fourth school—counting the hours in Hell at Saint Bartholomew.

It was noon of my first day. It'd taken two minutes to finish what was left from morning recess in my beat-up black lunch box.

"You're the new kid," said a boy carrying a rope with a noose on the end.

"Yeah."

"Wanna play Cowboys and Indians?"

"Guess so."

"You gotta be an Indian."

"Don't mind being an Indian."

"Oh, yeah? Know what happens when you're an Indian and we capture you?"

"What?"

"Gotta do whatever we say, that's what. That's the rules. Still wanna be an Indian?"

"Guess so."

"Gotta swear to keep the rules. You swear?"

"Guess so."

"Gotta say, *I swear.*"

"*Okay, I swear!*"

There were no rules. We galloped around whooping and hollering riding our ponies, me shooting arrows, the others shooting guns, circling me like I was a wagon crossing the prairie. Finally, legs giving out, I slowed to a walk. Two cowboys came trotting up.

"Okay, Injun, you're our prisoner."

They led me to the others.

"Here's the Redskin, Joey. What'll we do with him?"

"Put this lasso round him and take him to the lavatory."

Six of them herded me into the boys' bathroom. My two captors shoved me to the far wall; three more stood guard between me and the door.

The lasso was slipped off by Joey who took charge, "You're our captive and you gotta do what we say. That's the rules. Remember, you swore! Okay, take your shoes and socks off. Indians go barefoot."

I got them off without thinking what might come next.

"Take off the sweater. Never seen an Injun wearing a sweater."

I dropped the sweater on the socks.

"You're doing great! Now the shirt."

Slowly I began unbuttoning my shirt, which was covering the top of the hated union suit I was wearing that January day.

"We ain't got all year!"

"My mom makes me wear union suits in cold weather."

"So? Let's have the shirt."

I got the shirt off, feeling 12 eyes on my long-sleeved underwear.

"Put that stuff by the door," Joey ordered one of his crew.

Then to me, "You know, had to wear those things when I was a baby, but's been so long, can't remember what the bottoms're like. Indians don't wear pants nohow, so take yours off and we'll all get to see."

This got snickers. My fingernails dug into the soft pine boards behind me to help my wobbly knees.

"You gonna break your word?"

"N-no."

"That's your 'nitiation. Anyway, what's the big deal taking your pants off? Easy as pie once you unbutton."

More snickers.

My fingers went to the top button—far as I got. No way I could take those pants off—I knew that for darn sure. A cornered rat, I lowered my head like a bull on Sunday and churned my legs. The kid in my way went to the floor with the wind knocked out.

"Get'im!"

. . . the world was all arms and legs and boy smells . . .

Bodies piled two-deep on me, I was gulping like a goldfish.

"He's pretty strong!"

"Okay, hold his hands and feet. I'll get the pants."

"What's the fight?"

Two newcomers'd shown up in the lavatory, which didn't get used much during lunch hour—better to raise a finger or two in class. There were maybe two dozen boys in our building and no men teachers. The cleanup was done by a lady janitor. Joey used the lavatory as his place of business; the oldest and biggest boy in school, he was top dog.

"We're just learnin' the new kid Injuns don't wear pants."

My fly came open. I could feel it go wide as he took hold of both sides and pulled his hands apart. I gave one last try, a quick twist of my hips that made him grab my union suit.

"Holy Cow!" came from Joey, his fingers doing a fast check.

"What's up?"

"Nothing, just having a little trouble getting them off . . . Okay, you guys grab the legs and pull."

The pants were off.

"You can leave him up now."

I wasn't about to stand and show my shape—I'd quick raised my knees. The crew stepped back, taking a break to enjoy their work.

Joey was lapping it up, "Look at the baby in his sleepers!"

This got a laugh.

"Maybe we should invite some girls in to take a gander."

Followed by giggles.

"Wonder if Miss Murgatroyd's ever seen a boy with his pants off? Prob'ly don't even know what boys go pee-pee with."

He had his audience in the palm of his hand.

"And she sure-as-shootin' don't know what else it's good for."

The laughter tailed off. Finally, the show pretty much over, Joey scooped up my pants.

"That's enough. Grab his stuff and let's head on out o' here."

Holding my britches high, he stopped at the door, "If you'd've kept your word, you'd've kept your pants."

Alone in my union suit . . . I looked around to make sure and tiptoed to the door to take a peek—in case he'd left my clothes in the hall. He hadn't. Some girls' voices chased me back inside. I went into the last of the three stalls and hooked the eye. Fifteen minutes never seemed so long . . .

"Sean, are you in here? It's me, Bobby. Where are you?"

Bobby was the only one I knew at my new school. Our mothers were friends, but we weren't. Bobby was bright, the first to wave an arm when Teacher asked a question.

"Last toilet. Got my pants?"

"Maybe. Come on out! Let's see what you look like."

"Heck no! Pass me the pants!"

"Want to know what happened? It was funny!"

"Just want my pants. Hand them over!"

"It was a scream. Got to tell you—or maybe you'd rather I just took the pants and vamoosed?"

I'd been around Bobby—you couldn't shut him up—I'd waste my breath arguing.

"No, don't do that! Tell me, but make it snappy."

"Well, Miss Murgatroyd started class after lunch, and noticing your desk was empty, asked where you were. Priscilla White said there was something in your seat, and when Miss Murgatroyd asked what, Priscilla said, 'His pants and things.' You can imagine how much everyone laughed, can't you?"

"Yeah, I can just imagine."

"Then Miss Murgatroyd said, 'But why would he remove his trousers and place them on his desk seat?'—you know how she talks. Someone came out with, 'Maybe he's become a nudist.' We all roared at that."

"I'll bet."

"Then Miss Murgatroyd said, 'Oh, that poor lad! Running around without his trousers!' And Joey said, 'If he's got the runs, he's probably in the lavatory.' The boys all laughed and the girls all blushed. Don't think Miss Murgatroyd caught on."

"He's got a dirty mind."

"When Miss Murgatroyd asked why he thought you'd be in the lavatory, Joey said, 'Well, that's where I sit when I have my pants down.' That really cracked us up."

"Some sense of humor."

"Well you'd've laughed too if it'd been someone else's pants."

"I doubt it."

"In the end Miss Murgatroyd told me to take your clothes and see if you were here. Open up, I'll give you your stuff."

"Put them by the door, thanks. I can reach them just fine."

He did. At last! A half hour out in your union suit is forever and a bunch of Sundays. I snatched the pants and pulled them on. What a difference a pair of pants can make. All at once the world took on its usual rosy look. I was careful to button my shirt before opening the door; I wasn't up to one more joke about my union suit. Bobby was welcome to watch me put on the rest of my things.

"You're too bashful. You know when we're in high school, bet I'll see you in your underwear, maybe naked."

"Maybe you'll see someone, but you won't see me, leastways not naked."

"Want to bet a million dollars?"

"Where's your million dollars? You just better get back to class."

"Aren't you coming?"

"Heck no! Think I'd walk in there right now, so everyone can have a good horselaugh? Don't know if I'll ever come back. You can tell Miss Murgatroyd for me."

# CHAPTER 23

**N**ext morning our 8th grade class ran like a new-oiled Singer. Yesterday wasn't mentioned by Miss Murgatroyd, a dainty old maid who'd rather reel off Longfellow than swing the rod. Our part of the school took in low 7th through high 8th. The building'd been done over from a house that'd been willed to the town. The size set the number of grades. Though my first school'd only gone through sixth, in our county grammar school went through eighth, and we wouldn't run up against physical education till we got to high school.

At lunchtime Joey stopped me, "No hard feelings, Sean, shake?"

I shook. I needed a friend more'n an enemy with Joey's clout. We were scuffing along, kicking rocks, and he took a path that went to some budding pussy willows.

"You got any brothers or sisters?"

"No."

"I got a brother, but he don't live with us—married and moved away. Wish I had a sister, so's I could see what a girl's cut looks like. You ever seen one?"

I must've looked blank.

"You know, what they take a leak from."

To spell out his meaning, he reached over and touched my fly.

"Ha, ha! Why're you so jumpy? 'Member yesterday when you made my hand land square on your dick? Felt that, didn't you?"

"Yeah."

"I never let on, but you could've knocked me over with a humming bird feather. Your dick felt like a 10-cent Butterfinger, 'cept nickel size's the biggest they come, and—ha, ha!—Butterfingers don't have nuts. Yours's even bigger'n mine. How old're you?"

"Thirteen and a half."

"Yeah, well, I'm a year older 'cause I lost a grade once. What say we go down the creek after school and feel each other? You know, like yesterday. How about it?"

"Can't—my dad'd kill me!" The first excuse that popped into my head.

"How could he find out?"

"Don't know, but I'm not taking any chances."

Joey tried again, "How about spending the night at my place? We'd pants each other."

"P-pants each other?"

"Sure, be fun, you do me, I do you."

*Never! if I can help it.* But I didn't want to cross him.

"Don't think my mom would let me, but I'll ask her sometime when she's in a good mood, and maybe she will."

"You're open!"

Joey'd done it with a swipe of his fingers. Then he was on me, tickling my sides, "Bet you're ticklish too!"

Very. He didn't let up. I was weak with laughing, but got strong fast when I felt a hand worming its way into my pants. "Oh, no!"

With a heave, I rolled onto my stomach. Joey tumbled off and lay there puffing.

"Hey! Don't be so touchy!"

The school bell rang, and I quick buttoned up. We got to our feet, and without brushing the dirt off, headed for class.

# CHAPTER 24

Looking back, I owe Peanuts. He sidetracked Joey's attention.

This was what Joey liked best, "We're 'nitiatin' the new kid today, so show up at lunchtime—no excuses!"

I'd stayed on Joey's good side enough so he'd left me alone since our wrassle by the willows; I daren't go against him openly. When I got to the lavatory, Joey was getting the kid to take off his undershirt. I was all for the boy, who turned out to be even younger than Bobby, but at least he wasn't wearing a union suit.

"Now, would you rather leave your pants on or take them off?"

Joey hadn't given me a choice; I wondered what he was cooking up.

The boy, whose name was George, squeaked out, "R-rather I-leave them on."

"Okay, I'm gonna learn you a game. If you play by the rules, you keep your pants on. If you don't play by the rules, we pants you, tie you up, and shove you into the girls' lavatory. How'd you like that?

"Listen, Kid, I don't chew my cabbage twice—asked how you'd like it."

"N-not m-much!"

"The first rule of the game is when I ask a question, you give a whole answer—sorta like Mother May I—then you say my name. You understand the first rule?"

"Th-think so."

"Wrong! The right answer's 'Yes, I understand the first rule, Joey.' Say it! Believe me, Kid, you can't afford too many mistakes."

"Yes, I understand the first rule, Joey."

Joey never missed a gangster movie, and for real-life heroes he had Dillinger, Baby Face Nelson, Pretty Boy Floyd, and Machine Gun Kelly.

"Let's try one more before I give you the second rule. Who am I?"

"Joey".

"Wrong! That's not a whole answer. Try again."

"You're Joey".

"Again."

"You're Joey, Joey."

"Know something? You're not as dumb as you look. Now the second rule. If my question is a suggestion like, 'Would you like me to comb your hair?' You answer, 'Yes, I would like you to comb my hair, Joey.'

"Try this one. Would you like to play the game now?"

"Yes, I would like to play the game now, Joey."

"You're a pretty smart kid. Here's your first real test—get it right! Would you like me to unbutton you?"

George couldn't get his mouth open.

"Look, I said you could keep your pants on if you play by the rules, so what're you worried about? But I can't give you all day. Gonna say the question once more, and if you don't answer by the rules, we start pantsing you. Here goes. Would you like me to unbutton you?"

"Y-yes, I would like you to unb-button m-me . . . Joey."

"Good answer."

George was leaning against the wall as Joey did his job. He let the top button stay put and made a game of the others. I was rerunning my own initiation.

"Well, now we've got you unbuttoned, what should we do next? Ha, ha! What do you do after you've unbuttoned yourself?"

There were chuckles around the room. I felt heat. George turned green.

"How'd you like me to put my hand inside and feel your dick through your underwear?"

George answered fast—he'd expected the worst, "Yes, I'd like you to put your hand inside and feel my d-d-dick through my underwear, Joey."

Joey looked at us like pudding wouldn't slide down his throat.

"Well, if that's what he wants—"

His hand disappeared, "Not very big, is it? . . . Said, it's not very big."

"Don't know—mean, no it's not very big, Joey."

"Would you like me to feel your nuts?"

"Yes, I would like you to feel my n-nuts, Joey."

Joey moved his hand around inside George's pants, then stopped to share, "Don't think he has any. Wait! There's something. God, they're peanuts!"

This got a laugh.

"Gives me an idea. How'd you like to be called Peanuts?"

"Yes, I'd like to be called Peanuts, Joey."

"Everyone got that? This is Peanuts. His dick and nuts are so small I'm having a hard time through his underwear. Would you like it better, Peanuts, if I put my hand inside your shorts?"

"Y-yes, I-I would like it better if you put your hand inside my sh-shorts, J-Joey."

I felt a tug below decks. I was sorry for Peanuts, but ever so thankful it wasn't my skin Joey was fingering.

"Feels soft and squishy like a frog. Don't it ever get stiff?"

"Th-think I'm too scared. Sometimes it gets s-sort of s-stiff, Joey."

This was a new idea—explained some times I'd been scared.

"Worried about you, Peanuts, you have a problem. Well, guess we'll just have to keep working on it. One last question: Would you like to play the game again sometime?"

"Yes, I would like to play the game again sometime, Joey."

For the rest of the term, Peanuts was Joey's.

During recess I'd spot Peanuts backed up against the building with Joey in front of him, and I knew he was at work inside Peanuts's pants.

One morning Joey an' me were out in the schoolyard with some girls close by. Joey called Peanuts over. Without so much as a *here-it-comes* he undid Peanuts's fly and slipped his hand through. The girls pretended not to look; Peanuts stood without a peep while Joey had his fill.

"He likes it," Joey whispered.

# Chapter 25

**I**'d come to the new school in January; now it was April, and there'd been no more problems with school or Joey. Life was one big Eskimo Pie and rattling off *Blessings on thee, little man, barefoot boy with cheek of tan.*

My mom came into my room, "We're having a guest; Bobby's spending a night with us."

"Bobby! Why!"

"His parents are going to see his grandfather who's scheduled for an operation. Ruth asked if we could have Bobby, and I said we'd be glad to have him. What else could I say?"

"You could say we'd hate to have him. You could say if we put on a Hit Parade of our least favorite druthers, having Bobby spend the night would make number one from here to Christmas. Besides, where's he going to sleep?"

"With you, of course. You've never had a friend overnight—I thought you'd enjoy it."

"You mean sleep in *my bed with me*?"

"What's wrong with that? You have a double bed."

"There's plenty wrong with it, Bobby for starters."

"You've known Bobby longer than any other boy—"

"You've known him, not me."

"Surely, you're too old to be embarrassed. It isn't that, is it?"

"No, it's not that," I lied, "just Bobby. We don't get along so hot."

"Tell you what, promise not to put up a fuss about Bobby, and I'll buy you some boxer shorts when the warm weather comes—you know how long you've been wanting them. Is that a bargain?"

*No more union suits or BVDs!* As for Bobby, I could undress in the bathroom. That might work.

"Can't you get them tomorrow?"

"I don't have the money to spare right now; they'll have to wait till the end of the month. Besides, I want to be sure the warm weather is here to stay so they won't be a shock to your system."

"When you do get them, we'll throw away the union suits and BVDs? Forever?"

"Well, maybe we should keep them just in case."

"No! I'll only have Bobby if we throw them away—or burn them!"

"I suppose you are getting a little old for them. If it will make you happy, we'll consider it settled. Bobby will be here Saturday night. It would be nice if you could think up something special for Sunday. Ruth said Bobby can miss Mass, so you can too."

"Dad let me?"

"I'll handle your father."

"Thanks Mom!"

"I'll pack lunches; maybe you could go on a hike somewhere."

"I know! We'll climb Horse Hill and have lunch in the old cabin down the other side."

*Might be fun. Too bad it's with Bobby.*

# CHAPTER 26

"Told you I'd see you in your underwear."

Bobby was talking. We were ready to turn in.

"Who says you'll see me in my underwear?"

"Well, you don't wear your pants to bed do you?"

"No, I wear my pajamas."

"What do you wear under your pajamas?"

"My skin. What's it to you?"

"You mean I'm going to see *everything?*"

"Are you crazy! I'm putting my pajamas on in the bathroom. You can put yours on out here."

I changed in the bathroom, burying my BVDs at the bottom of my laundry hamper.

"Ready to come out. Got your pajamas on?"

"Yes, come ahead. Anyway, I'm not goofy bashful like you. I wouldn't die just because somebody saw something. Want me to prove it and take my dick out?"

I'd only seen flashes of boys older'n 11 who weren't as careful as me. Using the lavatory wasn't easy; things were right next to each other with nothing in between. Usually if another boy was at it, I'd head for a booth. Not always though; sometimes I'd do battle with myself and press in enough to be hidden.

A couple months ago, the toilet in the movie theater was boarded over; that left the two wide-open bowls I'd never been brave enough to try. I thought I'd timed it, but soon as I got it out a high schooler slammed through the door. I had to pretend I was done, work it in my pants without showing it, and wait outside, hoping the coast'd

clear. But some other kids came along, and I couldn't hold out. I ended up peeing by the ashcan in the alley, and because the usher wouldn't let me back in I missed the end of Lonesome Rider.

I was curious as the next boy, but showing it wasn't my idea of how to be the life of the party. The only males I'd seen head on were on the young side. My father'd always kept himself covered around me, and after age 10 I'd managed the same around him.

"Don't care, just if you want to," I answered.

"I'll show you mine if you show me yours."

"Can't, my dad'd kill me."

The same move I'd used on Joey, but not said loud enough to fool Bobby.

"Sure, probably'd string you up on the big eucalyptus—have a priest come to cut your Purgatory time in half—could maybe get the Bishop and cut it in quarter. That's just an excuse; your dad wouldn't do a thing and you know it. It's 'cause you'd get so embarrassed you'd die. That's it, isn't it? Bet if you thought someone was going to see your penis, you'd quick get an erection."

"What?"

These were some of Bobby's dictionary words he liked to spring on me. Penis I knew from way back and I could make a pretty good guess at erection. I was stalling, having no comeback to what he'd said.

"What you've got there, right this second!" he shouted, pointing at my sticking-out pajamas.

I pushed them back against my belly and dove for the bed to get the covers over me.

"Ha, ha! Knew I was right. Tell you what, my mom gave me a whole dollar for staying home, and I'll let you have two-bits of it if you show it to me."

"Not for the whole dollar! Not for a hundred dollars! Not for a million dollars! You don't go around showing a thing like that. Anyway, it's getting late. I'm going to turn out the light. Just stay on your side of the bed."

Bobby wasn't ready to sign off, "How big is it?"

"What are you talking about?"

"You know what, the thing that was pushing out your pajamas. How big is it?"

"How should I know?"

"Well no one else is sure going to know if you won't let them see it."

I was half-asleep when Bobby came out with, "Have you any hair?"

"You wake me up for a dumb question like that? You know I do. What do you think I have a comb for?"

"Not between your ears, between your legs."

"I don't know what makes you think of these things, but I don't want to talk about them. I'm going to sleep. We've got to take off early for our climb."

"You could just let me feel what you've got, in the dark underneath the covers. That shouldn't kill you."

"You really are crazy. I'm warning you, *stay on your own side!*"

"Is your dick still stiff?"

"Don't know," I lied.

"How can you not know a thing like that? Bet it's bigger than before. How big does it get?"

"Look, I don't know how big, it's probably the same as yours. Good night!"

"Mine doesn't get anything like that. Tell you what—and this is a real good deal—I'll give you the two-bits if you just let me feel it through your pajamas."

"So help me Bobby, I'll smother you with my pillow if you don't shut up!"

"Okay! Okay! Good night!" he said.

"Thank goodness! *Good night!*"

# CHAPTER 27

"**D**on't forget to take your canteens. You each have a package of chocolate cupcakes, four oatmeal cookies, a ham sandwich, a baloney sandwich, and Sean's old favorite, a jelly sandwich."

"'T'was on the Isle of Capri that I met her . . . blue Italian skies above," went a song of the 30's. As the two of us set out, the sky was bluer than believing.

"Horse Hill looks like you could reach out and touch it!"

The morning was so warm my mother let me go without a sweater. We took knapsacks to hold our lunches and canteens, and I brought a rope, which could come in handy for climbing stuff.

The hill was steep, so we weaved back and forth. Halfway to the top we reached the shade of a stunted acacia tree, unpacked the knapsacks to get a drink from our canteens, and sat down to polish off the cupcakes.

"It's hotter than Hades. I'm going to stick my shirt and undershirt in my knapsack. How about you?" Bobby asked.

"Rather keep mine on."

"Look, I already know you wear a union suit. So what's the difference if I see the top?"

"Who said I wear a union suit?"

"Joey told me."

"Joey's got a big mouth. Anyway, I'm wearing BVDs—won't have to after this month. My mother said so."

"Don't be dumb and die from the heat. You can tuck the top in your pants, and it won't even show. Go behind a bush if you want."

"What's it to me if you see some old buttons? I'll prove I'm not bashful as you say—but you better not make any cracks!"

Like I did it all the time, I took my shirt off, unbuttoned the BVD top, slipped my arms out, and pushed it inside my pants. The BVDs were made of lightweight cotton. The reason my mother thought they were warm was they had half-sleeves—undershirts had straps. T-shirts weren't invented.

Bobby lifted an arm and pointed underneath, "You've got hair there."

"So?"

"So I think that answers my question about whether you've got hair someplace else."

"Let's just change the subject, okay?"

"You pretend you don't want to talk about these things, but I bet you'd like to know how babies are made."

"I already know. They grow in the mother's stomach."

"Yeah, but how do they get started?"

"The mother makes a seed, like a tree or something."

"But what does the father have to do with it?"

Bobby's question'd bothered me for months. We'd never heard of sex education; sex was what you wrote *male* next to. Once I went to my mother feeling very grownup, saying naturally I understood how the baby got the mother's blood, but I didn't see how the baby could get the father's blood. She got flustered and said I'd have to ask my father. 'Course, I never did.

"I used to think a girl had to play with your p-penis, but I don't see how that can work."

"Not exactly play with; the father puts it inside the place between the mother's legs and pushes the seed into her."

A bombshell! But it fit in with some stuff I'd heard but hadn't understood.

"I think the seed comes out during an erection like you had last night. Ever have anything come out of yours when it's like that?"

"Don't think so."

I wasn't sure. I was a sound sleeper—my mother always said I'd sleep through a buffalo stampede. Some mornings I'd find sticky

spots on my pajama bottoms that'd come during the night. But these couldn't be baby seeds, which had to be big as avocado pits.

"You're probably not old enough," Bobby said. "I've seen dogs do it."

I remembered the time our Samoyed was back-to-back with a male and I ran to my father to get him to pull them apart. He turned the hose on the male, but they stayed stuck together and my father said it was too late. I never thought that had anything to do with babies.

"You mean to make a baby, a girl has to take it inside her when it's all stiff like that? No way I'm going to be a father!"

"I think you do it in bed in the dark. That's why married people sleep together."

"I wonder if she holds it in her hands. Can't believe my mother'd do that."

"Ha, ha! You wouldn't be here if she hadn't. Even Mrs. Roosevelt does it."

Bobby's eye-opener was all I could handle for one sitting; I got up to push on.

At the top we watched some toy automobiles crawl along the silver ribbon at the bottom. Then we went on to the old cabin halfway down the other side of the hill. The small building was in the middle of four good-sized pine trees which must've been planted years ago. The cabin meant adventure, and with the temperature in the sun over a hundred, we were glad for its shade. Our lunches down to crumbs, we put our heads on our knapsacks and let our eyelids droop.

# CHAPTER 28

"Look at the sleeping beauties! Hope you kids saved some grub for us."

We were stirred from our snooze by four older boys who were standing inside the cabin.

"Sorry, finished everything up. There's water if you want it," I said.

"Got our own. Mind if I see your rope?"

One of the boys who looked familiar picked up the rope and signaled me, "Com'ere a minute! Want to try something I saw in a movie. Won't hurt you."

I had my doubts, but went to where the boy'd made a slip knot on the rope. He looped this around one of my wrists, pulled it tight, and threw the loose end over a log that ran across the inside of the cabin.

"Just like Tom Mix. Okay, what I want you to do is put both arms in the air."

None too happy, I did. He held the rope against the top of my hand and tightened a second noose over my other wrist.

"There, try that. Can you get out of it?"

I pulled on the rope with no luck.

"Good, it works," he said. "Dan, don't you recognize this kid? He's the one you were hot to pants a few summers back."

"By gosh, you're right, Jim; I remember you were too softhearted to go through with it."

I recognized Jim as my pants-saver, and let out a groan.

"Hear that? He's looking forward to it. You'll see how softhearted I am. He was too small then, but he's plenty big now. A good pantsing's just the ticket at his age. How about it, Kid, you ever been pantsed?"

I was using all my will power to keep cool. Bobby chipped in, "He got pantsed at school earlier this term."

"Ha, ha! Whereabouts?"

Bobby answered, "In the boys' lavatory."

"Heck, that wasn't so bad. Did you like it?"

Jim was doing my Keds.

"Asked whether you liked it?" He did my socks too.

Bobby never kept a secret in his life, "He was wearing a union suit."

"See your point, Kid. Well, you're not wearing one now, so you won't mind this time."

Bobby spilled the rest of the beans, "He's wearing BVDs; has the top stuck down in his pants."

"You're a little old for BVDs. Sorry, Kid, we'll just have a look-see—haven't run across BVDs lately—anyone wearing 'em in the locker room'd be run out naked on a fence rail. By the way, go a lot easier on you if you don't try any funny stuff."

I didn't try. Hands tied above my head, no way I'd come in higher'n last. I was busy with a new fear that'd wiggled itself in—my loose BVD bottoms.

"I'll unbutton him. Dan gets to pull his pants down. There—two buttons should do it. Give a tug, Dan."

I could feel my pants and BVDs slipping, and what was left of my cool with them.

"Holy Toledo, Jim! His drawers've fallen a ways, and he's getting some kind of bone on!"

"Hold it! Let's have a look. Getting? As of this second, I make it official; he's got one on. Check yourself, Kid; at your age you ought to be ashamed. Hasn't your mother told you that's a no-no?"

I looked down and saw the top of my pole.

"So that's why you don't like getting pantsed; you're ashamed to show your big boner."

Turning to Bobby, Jim said, "Ever seen his stiff?"

"N-no."

"Come 'round and take a look."

"Don't think I'd better."

"Why not?"

"Don't think he'd want me to."

"Oh, he won't mind. A boy likes to share these things with his pals. I mean it, come see."

"Holy mackerel!"

"My sentiments exactly. And 'less I miss my guess, that's just the tip of the iceberg. Kid, doesn't it embarrass you like that? Want me to fix it so it isn't showing part way? . . . Want me to fix it or not?"

"F-fix it, please."

"You want me to fix it so it isn't part way out?"

"Y-yes."

"Then how about all the way out? . . . Hot damn!" came from Jim, as he saw what he'd uncovered.

Naked.

It was my worst times come back; ever since Ted, I'd had nightmares about it. I was plucked clean from tip to toe; the pants and BVDs'd been tossed aside. Wanting to cover myself was like having an itch I couldn't reach. Bobby was bug-eyed.

Jim turned to him, giving up on getting me to answer, "How old is he?"

"13."

"Jesus! Whoever looked like that at 13? Know you've never seen a dong like his. Who has? Can tell you for a fact it puts everyone's here to shame, and I'd stake my Dick Tracy badge nothing at school'd give it a run for the money. You'd never keep that baby undercover in our locker room, and once word leaked out, the news'd spread like prairie fire . . . Ha, ha! Say, Dan, how'd you like to take yours out to compare?"

"No thanks. Anyways, Jim, yours's bigger'n mine, so if someone's going to compare, better be you."

The other boys were looking nervous. One of them said, "Oughtn't we let him go now, Jim?"

"No, don't want Dan saying I was softhearted. Besides, wouldn't be polite to leave his wanger all het up like that. Let's take him to the big horse trough and water his pony. I'm sure he'll thank us for it."

Jim undid one of my hands, pulled the rope from the log, and tied my wrists together behind my back.

"Just leave his clothes'n everything." Then to Bobby, "You wait here and guard his stuff."

*In the open!* That got some words out.

"C-can't g-go like th-this."

"Why not?"

"Wh-what if we m-meet someone?"

Jim picked up one of my socks and tossed it to Dan.

"Put this on him . . . Pull it down far as you can."

"What about his balls?"

"Leav'em hang. There you are, Kid, snug as a bug in a rug. And if you want to get into your BVDs sometime soon, you better not put up any more arguments."

Jim took hold of the rope, gave it a snap, and giddyapped me outside. We marched for 10 minutes, my sock bouncing in time. The trough was downhill from the cabin, near a big oak. Longer than wide, it was made of stones cemented together and was deeper on one side. Going to it was a metal pipe with water from a spring. The trough was full, with a trickle flowing over one end.

We were almost there when two boys who'd been squatting under the little waterfall popped up. They looked about 11 and had trunks on, one in the usual navy, one in bright yellow, a color I'd never seen in a swimsuit.

"Why's he dressed like that?" asked the small fry in navy who did all the talking.

"He's bashful about showing his dick."

"That's his dick!"

"Ha, ha! Guess you've never seen an older kid with a boner, leastwise not a beaut like his. Going to join you for a little swim so's he can cool it off. Undress him, Dan."

"Not my sock!"

Dan had no mercy.

Four young eyes on me, I felt like Frankenstein's Monster.

"Mean mine's going to get like that!"

"You should live so long. If the girls found out you had one like that, they'd pester you purple. But let's make sure; Dr. Dan'll check you out."

Dan wiggled a finger, "Come to Dr. Dan."

"What're you gonna do?"

"Today's your lucky day; you get a free physical."

"What's a physical?"

"That's when the doctor plays pool with your balls."

The boy looked at the grinning faces and knew he was for it, "Hey, Doctor, don't you have an office or something?"

"You're a likeable little rascal. OK, we'll go to my private tree," Dan said, taking the boy behind the big oak.

"All right, Young Man, drop your suit and I'll give you my professional opinion," came from the tree.

"Can Harold see me?"

"Nobody can."

"You can."

"The doctor has to. Quit stalling or I'll call Harold over . . . That's better. How old're you?"

"Eleven."

"How old's Harold?"

"Thirteen."

"He doesn't look any older than you do."

"He's small for his age."

"You're scared aren't you? Know how I can tell?"

"N-no."

"Look at your dick. Ever seen it like that?"

"N-never noticed."

"Called a half-bone. OK, let's go."

"Wh-What about my trunks?"

"You've got nothing worth hiding."

Big or small, Dan had no mercy. He brought the boy back naked and took him up to everybody including his friend to show his weenie.

"Ha, ha! Hasn't a thing to worry about."

"What about the other kid?"

"Sure," Dan said, going up to the quiet one, "I'll check him too."

"Look, Harold, I'm not walking back to the tree for another inch-and-a-halfer, so if you'll just step out o' your suit I'll do you right here."

The terror on the boy's face brought back old times, and though I had no right to feel sorry for anyone, I felt sorry for this 13-year-old who looked 11.

"I'll help you," Dan said, reaching toward the yellow.

The boy started to shake, and ended like me the time Ted took out a dime for my doily.

"Back off, Dan!" Jim ordered. "It's okay, Harold, no one's going to pants you. Hit the water, it'll calm you down . . . Give the other kid his trunks."

Jim got around to me, "Your turn, Kid, got a bad case of swelling. Get in and we'll see what we can do about it."

He didn't take the rope off, so I had to sit on the edge and lift one leg at a time into the trough.

"Move over into the deep part and hunker down."

We waited a few minutes, Jim never letting up on gab.

"Move back over, and we'll have a look."

All I had to do was stand . . .

"You may never get rid of that thing, Kid. Afraid we can't stick around. You stay here; we'll leave your sock at the cabin—come when you're ready. Ha, ha! Don't take too long getting there or some tramp might make off with your clothes. Shouldn't walk along the road the way you are—cause too many crashes."

Then to the small boys, "Don't untie him, or you'll end up like him with your weenies roasting in the sun."

They left. I crouched in the water and cut my mind loose . . . Coming out of a bad daydream, I was in a haze—for some reason I had to get back to the cabin. I lifted myself out of the trough—

"Hey, it's part way down!"

The two boys were still with me. My dream was bad all right, but it was no dream.

"Holy smokes, it's going up again!"

Stumbling to my knees, I started to run. All the way to the cabin, my eyes stayed locked on the ground, the rope dragging behind. Inside I saw only Bobby. Saying nothing, I went to my knapsack, and lay down with my head on the khaki. Bobby said nothing, knelt beside me, and worked on the rope. When he had it off, I rubbed my wrists and stretched out, eyes closed. I felt the BVDs slip onto my legs, and raised myself so he could pull them up. He did the same with the pants, buttoning them all the way. I opened my eyes.

"Bobby?"

"Yes, Sean?"

"You won't tell?"

"No, Sean."

"Cross your heart?"

"Cross my heart, hope to die, and promise to spit on my mother's grave the day she's buried."

# CHAPTER 29

**I**t was Saturday; I was going to play tennis with Janet. Last summer, her just 13, she won the Tri-County Championship for girls 16 and under; she could clobber any girl around, and time after time she took it out on me. Janet was the most boy-crazy girl I knew; and though I'd never've admitted it to her, she could shock me without half trying.

"Janet, you can listen to the radio while I go change."

I went to my room, an'd finished taking my shoes off when I saw her in the doorway.

"Holy cats, Janet! I was about to take my pants off!"

"Well don't mind me."

"Boys don't go around taking their pants off in front of girls."

"That's all you know. I'll tell you a joke. We had hot dogs at our school picnic; the boys brought the weenies; the girls brought the buns. Get it?"

"Girls shouldn't tell jokes like that to boys."

"Says who? I'll tell you the rest of the joke. At the picnic a boy named Snow and a girl named June went off together into the bushes. It must've been a cold summer 'cause there was six inches of Snow in the middle of June. You're probably too innocent to get that part. 'Course, six inches is an exaggeration to make the joke better."

I could feel my cheeks burn. A week ago, I wouldn't've gotten the joke. Anyway Janet didn't know everything—she was wrong as liver about the six inches—if mine'd been a flopping trout, nobody'd throw it back in.

"Seeing a boy with his pants off wouldn't be anything new to me," she went on. "I've seen my dad in his underwear and my brother in his skin."

"Jackie was probably five when you saw him."

"He turned 12 two months ago, and I saw him last weekend. I'll tell you about it to prove how dopey boys are. My parents were at a party and Doris was spending the night. Around ten o'clock Jackie came out in his pajama bottoms complaining his head felt hot. Doris—she wants to be a nurse, you know—suggested he take a cool shower, but Jackie put his hands over his ears and went in the kitchen to get a drink.

"Doris said, 'He really ought to take a shower.' I said, 'Okay, we'll give him one.'"

"You didn't!"

"It was for his own good, but he kicked and squealed like some wild animal—you wouldn't believe the fight he put up to keep his pajamas on [I believed it]. Finally we got him on his back—Doris all excited, yelling, 'Get his thing out!'—her sitting on him, I pulled his pants off."

"You pantsed your own brother? In front of another girl? To the skin?"

"Ha, ha! Bare as a worm. Doris got her first glimpse and giggled, 'It's showing!' When Jackie realized everything was out in the open, he got so embarrassed his dingus went straight up in the air and stood there like a peeled pink Crayola."

"The poor kid!"

"Doris allowed as how it was the cutest thing she'd ever seen. She has two younger sisters and no brothers, and I know she'd never laid eyes on a naked boy old as Jackie. 'Course she looks at the pictures in The Geographic, but they always show little boys. I wish they'd show some 16-year olds."

"You would!"

"After we got off, Jackie just stayed there with his hands over himself, but I put a stop to that foolishness."

"You made him take his hands away?"

"Well hadn't we seen everything there was to see? What was the point in covering himself now? Besides, I could tell Doris wanted to look some more, and I thought, her having no brother, it was only

fair I share Jackie. So I warned him if he didn't quit acting like a baby, we'd scrub what he was hiding with a bar of soap.

"That scared the pants off him. Ha, ha! 'Course I don't mean pants—I'd thrown them into the hall—I mean it scared the hands off him. But not till I reminded him how much the soap would tickle. When his tip peeped above his thumbs, Doris started giggling again. That closed him fast as a clam, but I'd had enough; I reached down, gave him a hard slap, and pulled his arms away. After that he pretty much resigned himself to having his thing where Doris could look to her heart's content.

"We made him stand in the shower 10 minutes. He screamed when the cold spray hit him, so we let him off easy with warm. At the start he sneakily tried to turn his back, but Big Sister wasn't letting him get away with it—nosiree! I reached in and gave him a sharp whack on the bottom. Believe me, he didn't try that again! I think it's ridiculous the way boys make such a big fuss over such a little thing—four inches at the outside. Tell the truth, Sean, would you get embarrassed like Jackie if I saw yours?"

A question I wasn't about to answer.

"Janet, it's not the same; Jackie's 12 and your brother; I'm 14 and not your brother—"

"You won't be 14 till Decoration Day. I bet with nothing on you wouldn't look any different than Jackie."

"Well you're not about to find out."

"What if we got married? You'd have to let me see you then, wouldn't you?"

"We're not going to get married."

"But just suppose we were, would you show yourself then? Would you?"

I had a hunch that in this back-and-forth with Janet, I'd come off as damp behind the ears, so I made a stab at righting things, "Well sure, you've got to when you're married. Your wife gets to see you lots of times."

"Like when?"

I was winging it all the way, "Well, like when you take a shower and there's no towel. You call her, and she brings you one; maybe she dries you herself."

"I can hardly wait till I get married," Janet sighed.

"You won't even get to play tennis if you don't go away and let me change. I'm sure not going to do it while you're standing there."

"You spoil all the fun!"

She flounced back to the living room, and I closed my bedroom door.

It was six days after Horse Hill. The weather'd stayed hot, and today'd started even hotter. My mother hadn't bought the boxers yet, so I had nothing to wear but my BVDs. I couldn't face wearing BVDs in such heat because they'd make me keep my shirt on, no matter how boiling it got. So I took my chances with a hand-me-down pair of long baggy shorts and nothing underneath.

# CHAPTER 30

**W**e were the only ones at the high school courts, where I'd never played—it was new territory—Janet wanted to get a head start for the fall semester. She won the first set 6-3; I pulled out the second 7-5. I was rarin' to get on with the third because this would be my first-ever chance to win 2-out-of-3 from her. But Janet'd been grumbling about the heat, and at the end of the second set stomped off the court, refusing to play another point till we could find some water. It was blistering on the black asphalt, and we knew about cramps. Not sure where to find a drinking fountain, we headed for the High School Gym.

As we rounded a corner of the building a boy was holding a door open and shouting back inside, "Make sure you lock up when you're through!"

When he turned, blue-green eyes jumped at me—I'd never seen their like. They went with white-white skin and a mess of dark curls.

"Sure and methinks it's Helen Wills herself! And what can I be doin' for the loikes of two such foine-looking racquet-swingers?"

Janet, like she owned me, gave a brush to the wet hair hanging down my forehead. That got a grin from the boy and a blush from me.

"As you've already guessed," I said, "we've been playing tennis, and it's hot as blue blazes on the courts. Any chance of getting a drink around here?"

Taking in my dripping face and sopping shirt, he dropped his brogue,

"How about a shower to go with it? You look like you could use one."

"And how!" I went along with him, "I'll take one of those too, thanks."

"Would you now? Sure and what about the lovely young lady?"

"I'll take the drink, thanks, and watch Sean take the shower."

"Don't mind Janet," I said. "She likes to shock you."

"Let's see, Janet and Sean and I'm Bryan. There's a drinking fountain in the locker room. Give me a minute to make sure everyone's presentable."

He went inside.

"Wait till I tell Doris I was in the boys' locker room! She'll turn green with envy. Isn't Bryan a dream!"

It was more than a minute before he put his head out, "Sorry, had to take care of something. Come in! They're all respectable; nary a spalpeen romping in the raw."

"Just my luck!" Janet said.

"Ha, ha! I bet if Janet saw a boy in the buff, she'd faint dead away."

"I most certainly would not!"

"No, she'd love it," I said.

"Well, we may not be able to offer Janet a naked boy, but we do have an initiation scheduled in a few minutes. It'll be good clean fun, and you're both welcome to stay."

"We have to finish our tennis match," I put in.

"It's too hot for tennis, Sean. Thank you, Bryan, we'll stay for the fun."

*Initiation* gave me the jeebies, even though it would be someone else's. I didn't want any part of it, but I knew Janet would get her way.

"How many are going to be initiated?" I asked.

"Just one. Makes it more special."

Like Janet, I'd never been in a boys' locker room, and as we followed Bryan past dented metal lockers and wooden benches with initials carved all over them, I saw myself undressing at those benches in front of a roomful of boys, something set to take place sooner than I wanted to think about. Horse Hill flashed back to me, and my shorts moved.

A row of tile showers came next, white and cold, and the shower heads set so close together you'd have to keep your elbows in. They stood open to everything, no curtains, nothing between them, not even tucked out of the way somewhere. My imagination went to

myself standing naked in those showers for everyone to take in. The problem in my shorts was keeping up with my thoughts, and though choosing my baggiest pair was a winner, there was nothing for it but to put my hands in my pockets and do the usual fix.

"We've got the bucket of mud." Four boys'd come around a corner.

"Is the kid we're going to initiate here?" Bryan asked.

"He'll be ready when you want him."

"Sean, you can take your drink; Janet's finished hers."

I hardly stopped to breathe.

"Put your tennis things down and take a seat. Let me tell you about the entertainment we've got planned. Nothing fancy. A bucket of nice thick mud that's to be poured over the guest of honor; then we'll enjoy the show as he cleans himself up in the showers. Ha, ha! Just as I said, good clean fun. Not too awful. Taking a shower on a day hot as this should be a breeze. You were saying as much earlier, right Sean?"

I wasn't sure what was going to happen, and this talk of showers did nothing for the trouble in my shorts, but I kept up the game, "Right! No one would mind a shower in this heat."

"We have to decide something though," Bryan said. "What's the guest of honor going to wear while the mud's being poured over him? Before we decide, let's ask our lady visitor something. Janet, tell us honestly, would it embarrass you to see a boy in his underwear?"

"Why should that embarrass me? I wouldn't mind seeing him in nothing at all."

This brought whoops from the high schoolers.

"Ha, ha! Well, the boy might feel a little different about it. Let's have Sean decide. What do you say, Sean, undershorts on or undershorts off?"

"Keep them on, absolutely!"

"A lad with the wisdom of Solomon—though I fear he disappoints Janet. Now let me introduce the guest of honor. Sean, take a bow."

I'd half suspected. My brain went numb, I went dumb.

"Fred and Lou, help Sean off with his shoes and socks. Cal, give him a hand with his shirt."

I was still sitting.

"Sean, if you'll stand up, Marty'll do your tennis shorts."

A hand came toward me . . . *No way out!*

I jumped up on the bench, ripped the shorts open, jerked them free, and threw them back over my shoulder past the tops of the lockers.

"There! Got my hands away! Take a good look! That's what you want, isn't it! Hope you're satisfied now!"

"Holy Mother of God!" came from Bryan.

"Jesus Christ!" from one of the others.

"It's so big!" from Janet.

Bryan took charge, "Okay, you guys take Janet and clear out. Push the lock and don't come back. I'll calm him down. Hurry up! Get going!"

The boys got going; they pulled her to her feet, grabbed her racquet, and hauled her away, Janet's eyes all the time stuck on my swollen pole.

"So big! Never thought it'd be so big!"

# CHAPTER 31

**C**hrist, I'm sorry, Sean!—didn't realize—never suspected—sit down a minute—everything'll be all right," Bryan said.

It dawned on me he was undressing.

"Y-you're taking your clothes off."

"You and I are going to slip into a nice cool shower together. Nothing like a cool shower on a hot day; it'll relax you."

He was undoing his pants, "Don't mind if I take them off, do you?"

"No, it's just . . ."

"Just what?"

"Just that you're facing me."

"So what's the problem?"

"N-never seen an older boy naked from the front."

"You're kidding me!"

"No, honest! Just from the back—well once from the side, but it was dark."

"Ye gods and little fishes!"

"Actually, once from the front, but he was wearing a cat."

"Sure, and you're havin' me on!"

"No, he was sitting with his legs crossed like a Swami and had a black cat in his lap."

"Ha, ha! You have the Irish in you. Well, let's get the show on the road, off come the pants."

I couldn't help comparing his neat white boxers to my droopy BVDs.

"The O'Neills were Kings of Ireland, and you're about to see what they've passed down from father to son for a hundred generations. Ready for this?"

"G-guess so."

"Tra-da-a-a!"

He stepped out of his shorts.

"See, there's nothing to it; anyone can do it. Hope I live up to your expectations."

Bryan wore his skin like most people wear their dress-ups. The dark jungle on his head matched a black forest below, which made him look white as a statue and made me blush.

"Before we have our shower, I need to pee. Come on! If you pee, you'll get rid of that boner you've got. Say, did you catch the look on Janet's face when she saw it?"

I must've turned beet red, and things started jiggling worse than ever.

"Sorry! That was dumb of me. Wasn't thinking. That's my weakness; can never pass up a chance for a joke. Now don't go getting' yourself all in an uproar. Sure and you can't be blamin' me for marvelin' at the wondrous weapon you bear so proudly. I'm thinkin' one day the colleens'll be scratchin' one another's eyes out for their love of you."

"Please don't! Can't you tell I'm dying of shame!"

"Sure and it doesn't matter to me that you've got it on with a tally-whacker grander than me own, which—begorra!—bein' an O'Neill's, is no small thing. Sure here and now, I'm thinkin', we'll be after shakin' hands. If I'd had a brother, he'd've been Sean. If you'll be havin' me, we'll be two brothers against the world. With the O'Neills, that means for as long as ever we live. Would that be playsin' you? Would you be shakin' on it?"

"You're just poking fun; you don't even know me."

"It's not what I know that counts with me; it's what I feel. When I saw Sean leap onto that bench, yank those shorts off, launch them high in the air, and cry to the heavens with his wigwag all red and wavin', I thought, 'Bryan O'Neill, sure and there's the brother you never had!'

"Sean, I give you my word, and the day Bryan O'Neill breaks his word that very night the Banshee'll be wailin' over his cold carcass. You and I have the blood of Ireland in our veins, and many's the Irish

friendship that's started with a good donnybrook. Shake hands and be my friend?"

"I would like us to be friends," I said.

We shook hands.

"By the blood of Christ, you do have it on! Now let's take that pee."

I followed him around a corner to a long trough set the short way against the wall so boys could line up on both sides and pee facing each other.

"Come on me lad! Step right up and see what you can do!"

I walked elbow to elbow with Bryan; without holding on, he pressed forward and let out a stream.

"C-can't g-go like th-this," I said. "Don't you get embarrassed with someone watching?"

"I don't, but some kids do. I've stood next to boys who got it on while they were trying to pee. Let me tell you something that happened last semester. There was this kid who was a new freshman—you could tell he was a greenhorn—me in my first flush as a sophomore, feeling high and mighty as the King of Siam. It was after school, the opening day of classes. We were walking alongside each other in the main building—practically no one left in the halls—and he turned into the Boys' room. Quick as you could spell Michaeleen McGillicuddy, I turned with him. He waited to see what I would do, so I went over and wet my hands. With his back to me he made for the ditch, so wanting to be sociable, I waltzed over and parked next to him before he'd gotten it out. He just stood there without moving, while I slowly unbuttoned, took my time fishing around inside, finally hooked something, and hauled it into the air. His fly was open, but he couldn't reach in and take it out. I said, 'Turn around.' He said, 'Wh-what?' I said, 'Turn around!' He turned toward me, and I toward him with my meat dangling and said, 'You're a freshman aren't you? You need some help.' I reached over, put my hand inside his fly, felt around for the opening in his shorts, pushed on through, grabbed his peter, and pulled it out. He was so scared, he didn't say anything. I said, 'Okay, I'll hold, you pee.'"

"Holy Cats, Bryan! You didn't!"

"So help me, I did—told you I can't resist a joke. Anyway, of course he couldn't pee, and his peter went stiff in my fist. I said, 'Here, watch the way I do it,' and holding his bone in one hand and

my meat in the other, I went ahead and peed. Still holding him tight, I put away my pride and joy and buttoned up one-handed. 'Still have to pee?' said I. He just shook his head. I stuffed his maypole into his pants without bothering to get it inside his shorts, did him up myself, and said, 'Okay, let's go then.' We walked together to the street where I said, 'Better luck next time!'"

"Good Lord! How could you do it?"

"Sure, it did him no harm. Besides, he can't go through life not taking it out when he has to pee."

"Bryan, don't you ever—" I looked down at myself.

"Don't I get it on? And wouldn't I want it a steel pipe if I was naked with a pretty girl? Besides, some days nature is just too strong; I wake up in the morning so hot and bothered I can't help myself—have to—well you know all about that—as they say, boys will be boys. Anyway, I have a confession to make. As far as I recall—and I've a pretty good memory for these things—no one's seen me naked with it on. I'm not sure Bryan wouldn't get just as discombooberated as Sean."

"I wouldn't think anything could throw you."

"Anyhow, now that we're friends you'll be sleeping over, and sooner or later you'll find out for yourself. You can't keep a good man down, I always say."

"About staying at your house, I'd like to try if you'll stay at mine sometime. I've always been too bashful to spend the night at another boy's, but I guess it couldn't be any more embarrassing than right this second."

We took a long shower. I came out still up but less swollen and shared a towel from his locker.

"Bryan, can I ask you something sort of personal?"

"Told you, I'm your friend. Ask me anything you want."

"Yours is different from mine—on the end."

"Oh, I've been circumcised—"

"That's circumcised!"

"Sure, what did you think?"

"Oh, nothing."

"Ha, ha! I've never counted, but I'd say 80% of the kids at Pineapple've been circumcised—just the opposite at Parochial School—monks favor the old ways. The doctor does it soon after you're born. He cuts that skin you have around yours away."

"Doesn't it hurt?"

"I think when you're a baby you don't know the difference—at least you don't remember. Probably if you had it done now, it would hurt like Billy O. Anyway, you're lucky; supposed to be more fun doing you-know-what with a girl when you haven't been circumcised."

"That's supposed to be fun?"

"It's what I dream about every night and pray to the Virgin Mary for every morning."

"You pray to the Virgin Mary for *that*?"

"And why not? Sort of one virgin to another."

"You mean boys can be virgins too?"

"Alas, 'tis true, too true! You see before you the worst-off of all God's creatures, a 15-year-old male virgin halfway to becoming a 16-year-old male virgin."

"But, Bryan, what've you done that makes you a virgin?"

"It's not what I've done; it's what I haven't done. I haven't done it with a girl. You do know what *it* is."

"Oh, sure!"

"Oh, sure, my Aunt Mathilda! Little Brother, I see I'll have to educate you. First lesson: women. Every last one's convinced God made males for the sole purpose of slobbering after females. As long as she's playing bashful Juliet to your calf-sick Romeo, a girl can't do enough for you. The minute you break out in a wee rash around some new tomato, she'd as leave cut your heart out as spare you the time o' day.

"That's the sermon for the week. If I keep blathering about women, I'll end up with a poker hot as the one you showed Janet. Sorry! Not supposed to mention that. Let's go find your shorts. Whatever possessed you to throw them away like that?"

"Don't know, but sure hope I never do it again."

# CHAPTER 32

The May Day celebration in Red Square that morning could've been no louder than my own; the kewpie dolls on my bureau were covered with new sets of underwear. The boxers weren't white like Bryan's; they were all bright plaids. I had my doubts about the patterns and colors, but pushed them away. It was one of life's important moments; I was no longer a child.

The new underwear came none too soon. I found out from Bobby, who was always up on everything, that the District Nurse was coming to check us for tuberculosis.

"Thought you'd like to know because we'll have to take our shirts off."

"Just our shirts?"

"She doesn't do teenage nuts."

Since Horse Hill my feelings toward Bobby were kinder; I could see he was telling me out of friendship.

"Look!" I said, pulling out my shirttails to show my undershirt.

"Congratulations!"

"Thanks!"

Thursday afternoon there were a dozen of us 8th-grade boys shuffling down the hall to the room where we'd be examined. Joey had the ears of his mob, "Bet I can get the nurse all fussed. Anyone wanna bet?"

"How're you gonna do it, Joey?"

"Jus' wait'n see."

We took our shoes off like we'd been told, leaving them lined up along the wall so our heights could be measured.

"Is there a boy here named Bobby?" the nurse asked.

Bobby stepped forward.

"Miss Murgatroyd chose you as one of my assistants."

"She would!" piped up Joey, who, nudging the boy next to him and nodding toward the nurse, went on in a loud voice, "Not a bad looker. Bet she's a pretty hot number."

To us the nurse wasn't young, but in 1938 you didn't see Jean Harlow hair every day.

She faced Joey, "We'll begin with you—look like the oldest—can set an example for the others. Take off your shirt and undershirt! Put them on the chair! Get on the table!"

There was no *please* in the nurse; she barked orders.

"Sure you don't want my pants off?"

"That may not be necessary."

Joey turned toward us and smirked as he sat on the table.

The nurse listened to his chest.

"Lie on your back!"

She went lower, poking his middle next to the top of his pants.

"Hmm! Have you had your appendix out?"

"N-no, is there something the matter?"

"Don't know yet. Bobby, help out here! Unbutton his pants!"

"You don't have to do that, do you?"

"Yes, it's necessary. You're not bashful are you? You offered to take them off, remember?"

"Well I . . ."

"That's fine Bobby, pull them down! Good! On second thought, pull them off!"

Bobby couldn't keep back a smile as he got Joey's pants all the way off, leaving him in shorts and socks. Joey gave Bobby a dirty look. Right then a girl from our class came into the room with a pad in her hand.

"Miss Murgatroyd said I was to take notes."

Joey tried to get up, "Not in front of her!"

The nurse was strong; she held him down with both hands.

"You must be Doris. Understand you're the best speller in the school and you want to be a nurse some day. Stand next to me and print each boy's name as I work on him; then write what I tell you. Right now put under his name: *checking for appendicitis.*"

Joey looked downright miserable. Doris made no bones about what interested her; she went over his striped underwear like she was studying for a test. I was up front and could see Joey's shorts stayed flat. I wondered if I was the only boy who never missed out on that.

The nurse felt Joey's side.

"Hmm! Have to check more closely. Bobby, loosen his shorts!"

"O my God! You're not going to take *them* off!"

"We'll just push them down a bit, but if I were you, I'd be more worried about my appendix than about my shorts."

Bobby was grinning ear to ear as he undid a button.

"Fine, push them as far as you can without uncovering his you-know-what—we wouldn't want to embarrass Doris."

Doris's mouth dropped with the shorts. Bobby kept going till brown hair showed up.

"Stop! That's too far!"

"Yes, that's enough." The nurse used her weight to keep Joey down.

"Jesus Christ!" he let out.

"There's no call for swearing."

Meanwhile, Doris'd ducked her head even with Joey's belly, trying to see the part under cotton.

"What's she doing? She don't have to do that!"

"Yes, Doris, we may be curious, but we mustn't be obvious about it," the nurse said, working Joey over. "Good news! Doris, write: *Diagnosis negative.*"

It hit Joey what'd happened as he watched boy after boy get nothing but his chest examined.

# CHAPTER 33

**B**obby was sweet on a girl. She was three months younger, a year behind him in school, pretty, and just plain nice. I met them coming out of the Saturday matinee. Bobby looked sheepish.

"Sean, you know Patsy. Want to walk with us?"

I didn't, but I skipped into step. Bobby chattered while Patsy beamed. He was talking about the weekly serial we'd just watched.

"Wait and see next time; I bet Buck jumped off the train just before the dynamite went off."

Like always, we cut across the baseball field near our school. When we reached the hut players used, Joey popped out, all smiles.

"Hi! Wanna see something cute, Patsy? You like newborn kittens?"

The three of us followed Joey inside.

"Where are they?" Bobby asked.

"Where are what?"

"The kittens."

"Who said there was kittens?"

I looked around and saw Joey's bunch blocking the doorway.

"You did."

"No I didn't. Just asked Patsy if she liked kittens."

"Well, you asked if she wanted to see something cute. What did you mean?"

"Oh, *that*! Thought she'd like to see her boyfriend in his undershorts. Ought to be pretty cute, don't you think? Patsy, how'd you like to see Bobby in his undershorts?"

Patsy couldn't answer. Bobby took in the crowded opening, and slumped, "O Geez!"

"You'd like that wouldn't you, Patsy?"

"D-don't think so."

"Why not? Never seen him in his shorts, have you?"

"N-no."

"Well let's get going!"

"Wait!" Bobby shouted. "Look, Joey, what happened with the nurse wasn't my fault!"

"Maybe not, but you had a loud enough hee-haw all right. Time's awastin'—shoes, shirts, pants. Ha, ha! You can keep your socks on."

"Joey, I'll make you a deal. I'll give you a whole dollar if you don't let Patsy see me in my shorts."

"Fork it over!"

"It's at home, but I promise you'll get it."

"Don't know if I can trust you."

"I swear to God!"

"What do you say, Sean? Can I trust him?"

"You can trust him."

"Let's get this straight—Sean'll be a witness—I promise Patsy don't see you in your shorts; you promise to give me a buck. Honor bound?"

"Honor bound!"

"Okay, Bill and Mac, take Patsy outside, but keep her there till I'm done with him."

"I'll go too," I said.

"No, you stay'n see I keep the bargain. Don't want him having any excuse for not paying up."

"It's OK, Sean," Bobby said.

"Well, get going!"

Bobby got going.

"Drop'em!"

He dropped them.

"Kick'em away!"

He kicked them away.

"Peanuts, hand me my rope."

Joey must've seen the same movie as Jim of Horse Hill because he tied Bobby's hands over his head like Jim'd tied mine.

"Peanuts, open his top button."

"You're not going to take my shorts off!"

"No, just let'em fall a ways," Joey chuckled, "sorta like you and the nurse did for me."

Peanuts did his job. Bobby's shorts fell a ways.

"Now, let's see you hula."

"Wh-what?"

"You heard me—wiggle your hips."

Bobby wiggled, but stopped when he felt things slip. The shorts were low as they could go and still do any good—no hair. Bobby'd turned 13 in February.

"Well that's as far down as mine when that dame tried to sneak a peek. How do yuh like it?"

"My shorts feel like they're about to go!"

"Too bad. Now let's have some more hula."

"They'll fall off!"

"If I was you, I'd worry more about Patsy than about my shorts. Take your choice, hula or Patsy."

He wiggled.

"O God!" Bobby cried, looking down at himself.

The socks didn't go with his nakedness. He was like Bryan, but smooth all over—I wanted to cover him.

"He's got more than Peanuts, but nothing like what Sean's got. Sean, be sure and tell me what period you sign up for Gym. I wanna take it with you."

I'd been sharing Bobby's trouble, but Joey switched me to another track.

"Aren't you f-finished?" Bobby asked.

"Almost. Peanuts, stuff his shorts in his pants; then tell Bill and Mac to bring Patsy in."

"You can't! You wouldn't! You promised!"

"I promised she wouldn't see you in your shorts. Ha, ha! She's gonna see you in your socks."

"N-o-o-o-o!"

That blast lifted Bobby's tube, but it couldn't get past level. I had my own worries—Gym—

Two days ago I let my guard down, and Joey got me alone during the lunch hour. He went right to work, began to tickle and quick sat on my chest. With one hand he tickled under my arm, with the other my stomach. This time he didn't pull my fly open; with me laughing, he jammed a hand under the waist of my cords. His strength surprised me—I couldn't buck him off. He was outside my shorts,

but nothing else was good. He gave off something new to me—his fingers ran up and down—his breathing got heavy—his strength left him—I gave one big buck, rolled myself out from under, and took off, leaving him moaning on the ground.

Gym—it was made real to me—Gym with Joey—*Please, God, not that!*

"Let's go! We'll leave the two lovebirds get together in private. Tell Patsy he'll stay here all night if she don't help him out," Joey said, and turned to Bobby, "Patsy can untie you—if she don't swoon when she sees her boyfriend's dick sticking out like Pinocchio's nose. If you know what's good for you, bring my rope to school Monday and the buck you owe me."

I didn't ask—and Bobby didn't say—how Patsy took his nakedness. She did untie him. Monday at lunchtime Joey waved the dollar.

# Chapter 34

No more pencils, No more books

No more teachers' dirty looks

School was out, and the long, long summer'd begun. The summer went to a time so far off I couldn't imagine it ending.

The book I'd been looking at for 15 minutes in the secondhand store was called "Your Speech is Your Fortune." 25 cents was written inside the cover.
"Want to buy that book?" the man who owned the place asked.
"Do you ever have a sale?"
"How much've you got?"
I took two nickels and three pennies out of my pocket.
He picked up a pencil, crossed off 25, and wrote 13.
"Thanks!"
"At that price you don't get a bag."

To me, Bryan was a soaring hawk; everything was easy for him. I knew I could never be like him, but maybe I could learn to use words like him, so I bought the book and I studied it hard.

It was the second week of summer vacation. I hadn't spent a night at Bryan's, but I'd been to his house. In Bryan's bedroom was a bookcase full of books, all to do with Ireland: Irish history, Irish fairy tales, Irish Mother Goose, Irish poetry, Irish plays, Irish short stories, Irish novels. Some of these he'd bought himself, and some'd

been sent by his grandmother, who'd lived her life in the town of Waterford.

But Bryan'd never been to Ireland; he got some of his brogue at the movies, and some he flat made up. He didn't have a father; he had his father's Irish name.

"I'm Bryan O'Neill!" he'd say to one and all.

Here's what I found out: Bryan's father was born in Ireland; came by himself as a boy to live with his uncle in Boston; earned his way through college, going out for ROTC; was sent to France when the war started; made captain; was stationed in Paris after the war; met Bryan's mother there; married her in this country; before Bryan was born, his father was killed in a truck crash during a training run. Bryan and his mother lived on an army pension and Mrs. O'Neill's job at the town library.

I was taken with her from the start. I wouldn't've known how to say it, but she made me feel my maleness. Bryan had eyes that surprised you; his mother had eyes that held you. They were large and soft, not blue-green like Bryan's, but deep blue. To set off the eyes, she had pale skin and dark hair. She'd married at 17; now twice that age, she was the most beautiful woman I'd seen up close. Her accent made anything she said different; right then I decided my foreign language would be French.

When Bryan introduced me, I said, "How do you do, Mrs. O'Neill, I'm very pleased to meet you."

"I will not be made into an old woman! Do you think I look like an old woman?"

"Oh, no! I think you're beautiful!"

"Charmant! Bryan, we should have this young man over often." Then to me, "You must always call me Jeanne. Do you promise to do that? Always! You understand?"

I wasn't used to calling grownups by their first names, "I'll try, J-Jeanne," I said, doing my best to copy her.

"Good! I think we will be fine friends, you and I. Is it not interesting that we sound the same? You are Shawn and I am Zhawn."

Bryan was good at everything, but though he'd once traded a week's yard work for a used racquet, he'd never played tennis. He wanted to try his hand, so today we were going to hit a few at the

high school courts. With butterflies in my stomach, I looked ahead to the night, which'd be the first I'd spend at his house.

Unlike that other time at the high school, today I was wearing boxers under unbaggy shorts—a big boost to my confidence—but it fell like a rock as the playing area came in sight and I saw Janet. I'd kept out of her way since the afternoon in the boys' locker room.

"Oh, no, it's Janet! Let's go to the other courts," I said.

"Too far—besides, you can't duck her forever. Just act like nothing happened."

"Yeah, but you don't know Janet; she'll have something to say—you can bet on it."

"Anyhoo me bucko, are you after imaginin' you're the first bonny lad whose willie's been seen in its Sunday best by a fair lass?" said Bryan, who wasn't above mixing a little Scotch with his Irish.

"By now she's certain to've whispered your dark secret into the ears of her best girlfriends, and they'll be after going insane with their love o' you."

"Please, Bryan, it isn't funny! You don't really think she'd talk about it?"

"Sure and I doubt she's talked about much of anything else—sorry! can't help myself. No, I'm positive she wouldn't mention it—but then again you never know—she might just talk about it in her sleep when she has a chum over to spend the night. Sure and I can hear her moanin' now, 'It's so big! Never thought it'd be so big!'"

There were three courts, and I went to the one that left an open space between Janet's, where she was playing with one of her girl partners, and ours. When Janet saw us, she motioned with her arm to come over, but I just waved back, hoping that would end it.

The two of us tried to get a rally going. It wasn't easy because Bryan hit the ball as hard as he could, and it kept sailing over the fence. He saw no reason a home run shouldn't be as good on the tennis court as on the baseball field. For once I had a chance to make a joke on him.

"I guess you don't understand why they put those white lines on the court."

"No piddling dab of paint can hold an O'Neill to the ground, but to oblige an earthling like yourself, I'll curb my mighty blows and knock the ball within your puny reach."

Bryan's nimbleness was something to watch. Once he set his mind to it, he hit the ball over the net and into the court enough to test me. I shut out everything but my strokes.

"Hello, Bryan! Hello, Sean!"

Janet'd come over, leaving her friend to pick up their practice balls. Bryan jumped in and saved me from answering.

"Let's see now, is it Janet? Or is it Helen Wills? Or is it a fairy princess? Whoever it is, begorra! how she blinds us mortals with her terrible beauty!"

"Bryan, you're such a card! Had any initiations lately?"

"Not lately."

"Too bad. Aren't you hot in those shorts, Sean?"

I could feel a flush begin at the top of my head and bounce off the bottoms of my feet.

As she started to leave, Janet fired the other barrel, "I've been wanting to ask you to play tennis, but I haven't seen much of you lately. 'Course last time I saw an awful lot of you."

A naked pink blob—that's how I felt. I'd been turned into raspberry junket, and Janet's look as she sashayed away left no doubt she knew it.

# CHAPTER 35

**W**e'd finished our self-made sandwiches, peanut butter slapped between two slices of bread.

"Where should we take our shower? Suppose you're set on the Gym?"

"The G-Gym?"

"Ha, ha! You should see your face. Just kidding; we'll go to my place."

On the way we stopped at a house with two cherry plum trees. The fruit wasn't a favorite of grownups, and dozens messed up the lawn. Cherry plums ripened early, and boys were glad enough for them—sure beat a growling stomach. Two apiece and we were off for greener pastures.

"I know where we can get some real cherries. You game?" Bryan asked.

"What do we have to do?"

"Not much. Climb a fence, climb a tree—I'll climb the tree while you keep a lookout."

"Keep a lookout for what?"

"Oh, just in case Old Man Clayton shows up."

"What would he do?"

"Not much, he's on the wrong side of 50. Probably cuss us though."

I'd been cussed before, "Okay, if you think it'll work."

Bryan was taking me across an empty field.

"We'll hide our tennis stuff under a bush and get it on the way back."

As we made our way over the open ground, I could see an old shack up ahead.

"Hope you're not afraid of dogs—"

Dogs—except for two gentle females we owned at different times—made my childhood a misery. There were no dog laws. Until one bit you—bad—it was free to scare the daylights out o' you.

On one side of our house there was a police dog that'd been hit by the train and patched up with one eye and half a tail. The dog didn't turn into Beautiful Joe; it turned on every boy and cat. I hated this animal after it streaked up onto our back porch and snatched our 10-year-old calico in its jaws. My mother ran after the dog, swatting it with a broom, but my longtime pet already had a broken back. The look in Kitty's eyes before she died is still in my head. Some weeks later the German Shepherd chased me up that same porch and into the house—in my hurry I'd left the door unlatched behind me. Once inside I relaxed, but got going fast at the sight of the charging killer. I made it to the bathroom and slammed the door on yellow teeth.

Later that year when I was walking on the sidewalk past its house, the animal broke through the front screen door and sprang at my throat. I was knocked to the pavement and ended up with bloody teeth marks on my shoulder, which I'd hunched up to protect myself. Lucky for me, the owner came out to pull off his dog.

I remember the owner's wife, who was a Christian Practitioner, comforting my parents, "I know most people would worry, but if I were you, I would simply put it out of my mind."

Not until a three-year old girl got bitten on the face by this Hound from Hell was some kind of warning given the owners. Rather than part with their pet, they decided to sell their house and build a new one up in the hills. Meanwhile, off their back porch they made a pen, sealed on top, out of 2x4s and steel wire.

That German Shepherd moved out of my life, but for all the years of my childhood, trudging back and forth to school, I'd walk blocks and blocks out of my way to keep clear of dogs—

"What kind of dogs?" I asked.

"See that shanty coming up? A mean old chow lives there. Probably jump out and bark at us. If he does, ignore him; keep walking straight ahead. Whatever you do, don't run."

We were almost to the edge of the lot—I could see the place was a homemade junkyard.

"Let me walk on the side he'll come from; I've been by here plenty times."

We'd just passed what was left of a picket fence with an opening where a gate was lying flat on the ground.

"Growf! Growf! Growf!"

It was the deep bark of a red chow with a black tongue and a bushy tail curled over his back. *Mean* was dead on; he looked mean, he sounded mean. The barker circled round to my side of the path—he knew right off which was the weak link. I looked at Bryan.

"Sure and you're doin' foine, me boy."

Circling wasn't enough for the chow; he began darting toward me and backing off. I was ready to crack when on one of his dashes teeth nipped the heel of my Ked. "O God!"

That did it for the rabbit—it was an all-out race—I couldn't see behind me, but after twenty yards, I felt a tug. "Yip!"

The tugging stopped. I must've gone another forty yards before pulling up winded. What happened was that when I started running, the dog hesitated, then took off. Bryan joined in after grabbing a doorknob lying in the junk. About the time the chow got his teeth into my shorts, Bryan let go, scoring a direct hit on the animal, which hightailed it back to its lair.

We sized up the damage, a small tear in the right leg of my tennis shorts, not enough to bother even me. I counted myself lucky to've gotten off so easy; though I knew I'd be wearing those mended shorts for the rest of the summer.

Half a mile further we came to a high board fence with rusty nail heads sticking out all over.

"I'll climb up and check for booty," Bryan said.

He reached the top with his fingers, and by using his rubber soles, raised himself to where he could sit.

"The coast is clear, and I see tons of cherries aching to be popped."

"What about dogs?"

"Old Man Clayton doesn't have a dog. Come on up! I'm going in."

I had to tiptoe to catch the top of the fence, and my feet slipped twice before I made it. There were two large cherry trees on the other side, along with half a dozen more fruit trees. Beyond was a brown shingled cottage. I lowered myself into the yard and made my way to where Bryan was swinging himself into one of the cherries. They were something with their smooth red bark, big green leaves, and shiny dark fruit. He worked his way along a branch, picked a pair, threw one down to me, and tossed the other into his mouth.

"How do you like that? A little better than plain old cherry plums, don't you think?"

"They're delicious!"

Spitting out the pit, something moved in the corner of my eye.

"Holy God! He's coming!"

Bryan landed hard on the ground, did a full somersault, ended up on both feet, and cried, "Head for the hills!"

We made for the fence. "Pop!"

"O Jesus, he's shooting!" I yelled.

Bryan was up and over, me still pawing against the boards. "Splat!"

It was a BB hitting wood, how close I'd never know. That sound took the fighting spirit right out of me. I was ready to throw my arms up in surrender when somehow Bryan was back behind, shoving my rear end with the palms of his hands. Just what was needed to get me to the top.

"Splat!" I let go and fell down the other side.

On the way to the ground, I heard: "R-r-rip!"

Next thing I knew, Bryan was pulling me to my feet. He didn't have to tell me to run; that came naturally . . . "Stop! He's not coming."

I looked around; there was a smiling Bryan, walking slow like he was taking in the scenery. He held up two cherries, "Have one! I shoved these into my pocket before I jumped from the tree."

I began to laugh. Bryan began to laugh. We rolled over and over on the wild oat straw near the path, grabbing our stomachs. Finally Bryan pulled himself together, "Faith and I doff my hat to a lad who can enjoy a good belly hugger when his bare behind is hanging out for all the world to admire."

This hit me like a shovel in the face. I turned my head and felt with my hand. On the right where the chow'd made the tear, a patch 6 to 8 inches square'd been ripped from both pairs of shorts. I'd

heard a sound when I was falling, but it'd been pushed away in the excitement. A nail head must've hooked me on my way to the ground. Sure enough looking back toward the fence, I could see the missing pieces hanging on the nail.

"Oh, no! I can't walk to your place like this. Even if I hold my hand over it, it'll show."

"Take your shorts off."

"Right here?"

"There's no one around. Anyway, I mean just your tennis shorts."

Bryan stepped out of his shorts and held them out to me, "Care to trade?"

"Are you sure it's all right?"

"Be fine; my white boxers'll hardly show at all."

Holding my breath, I dropped my shorts and traded for his—a small thing, but I was pleased as Punch with myself.

On the way back, I tried talking Bryan into a loop to miss the chow, but he'd have none of it. He searched around for two good-sized rocks, "These should do the trick."

We went past the picket fence as before; the dog ran out with the same low bark—one well-aimed throw—and the barker turned tail. That was that.

Bryan wore my shorts with a square missing all the way home, passing in different places two ladies, four boys, and three high school girls. Seeing our racquets, they must've wondered what'd happened on the tennis court to tear Bryan's seat out. I couldn't help turning each time to see the ladies raise their eyebrows, the boys grin, and the girls whisper, but Bryan looking straight ahead walked like a prince in velvet.

# CHAPTER 36

**M**rs. O'Neill was at the library, so the house belonged to us. We went back to Bryan's room where he pulled off his shirt, shoes, socks, and my torn shorts, "Wonder what your mother'll do when she sees these?"

"I'll get a lecture about how clothes cost money and about how money doesn't grow on trees. One good thing though, she won't be able to mend them."

Bryan dropped his undershorts and stretched out faceup on the bed with his hands behind his head, as much at home out of his clothes as in. His nakedness embarrassed me. It'd been a month since the locker room. In the meantime I'd seen Bobby, but Bobby naked and Bryan naked were like white and black. I turned to his bookcase and pulled out a blue leather book with gold-edged pages. The cover said SHAKESPEARE.

"Bryan, wasn't Shakespeare English?"

"Never! Only a son of Erin could've written like that. It's my theory he was stolen from his cradle by gypsies and sold across the sea— not all the water in the rough rude sea can wash the poetry from an anointed Irishman. Or mayhap Calliope put the wild waters in a roar, and Mrs. Shakespeare was seduced by a wandering Irish minstrel cast up by the tempest onto rocky English shores. Or possibly— listen," he interrupted himself, "if we're to hit Jerry's so you can get your ears lowered, we better grab a shower. Aren't you going to take your things off?"

I'd run through this a dozen times, but in the tryouts, it was just a matter of getting into my pajamas before turning in. I'd imagined

sitting on the edge of the bed with my back to Bryan, then slipping out of pants and undershorts in one move and into my bottoms. This was different. Broad daylight, Bryan lying like he'd never worn clothes, expecting me to undress out in the open and walk side by side with him to the bathroom. It was too much.

I laid the book down and slowly got my shoes and socks off, but the end was never in doubt; trouble was already knocking. I stalled half bent over . . .

"Sure, and if you don't call to mind Father Arne. You know who he is?"

"He's the priest who looks like a high school student," not to mention he was old friends with my body.

"The time I have in mind, you could've taken him for an eighth-grader. It was the week of my 13th birthday, and he didn't look much older than myself—doubt he'd ever touched a razor to his chin. I want to tell you what happened, so you'll know you're not alone in the world.

"The church had this program where a priest would celebrate a birthday with a boy who had no dad. I was to knock on Father Arne's door at eight in the morning, but I got there at six instead."

"Why so early?"

"Curiosity. And to win a small wager. Billy Dolan stated to me as a certain fact that when you become a priest they lop your knackers off. I bet him a nickel it wasn't true—"

"Knackers? You mean—Lord! He wasn't right was he?"

"You're an impatient lad, you are. Would you be lettin' me tell my story?

"After rappin' half a dozen times, Father Arne, rubbin' his eyes, still in his pajamas, stuck his gold mop out the door, and said I'd have to wait downstairs. With the cheek of a brass monkey, I pushed my way inside. 'Rather wait in here if it's all the same to you, Father,' I said.

"He didn't pull his pajamas off as I'd hoped; just gathered up the clothes he was gonna wear and made for the bathroom, sayin' he had to shower. Think I was bested? Not a bit of it. I whipped off my own clothes—I'm pretty fast at it—"

"I've noticed!"

"And opened the bathroom door. He was naked, sideways to me, his knackers in plain sight, but I was sorely disappointed."

"Why disappointed?"

"Well there was I, 13, just comin' into my hair, inquisitive you might say as to what a grown man would look like naked, expectin' to see I didn't know what, when up turns this fellow with fewer hairs to his name than myself—and those so pale as to hardly show at all—not to mention a radish I'd've been ashamed to call my own. Anyway, there he was with the seat up, about to pee. 'Mind if I join you, Father?' I asked ever so politely.

"He twirled around to see me naked as himself and turned blotchy all over. His stream never got going 'cause his Saint Peter rose straight toward heaven. 'Forgive me, Lord!' he cried, 'for I have sinned!' Then he fell to his knees with his elbows on the bowl and did his first Hail Mary."

"God! What did you do?"

"Sure and I did the mannerly thing—exactly what I'm gonna to do for you—I left him alone."

Bryan got up, stepped into the hall, and came back with a towel. Then he went over to the overnight bag I'd brought that morning and took out my clean boxers.

"Go get your shower. Come back when you're ready in these jazzy shorts of yours. First we'll make you at home in your skivvies; then one fine day when the birds are singing and the bees are buzzing and the girls are hot for our bods, we'll try your Sunday suit."

I did as I was told. Knowing I wouldn't go to the bedroom naked made all the difference. After a cold shower I was ready for company, so face flushed I marched back to Bryan in my boxers.

"Faith, you're such a handsome Divil in your Highland plaids even Janet mightn't want you to take them off."

# Chapter 37

**O**n our two-mile tramp to town, we took the railroad tracks. Seeing no reason to hurry from one moment into the next, we stopped along the way to check any rock whose color or shape caught our eyes. Soapstone or flint went in our pockets; others got used for target practice on nearby telephone poles. Walking on the outer rail to keep ourselves from the high voltage, we used our arms like wings. I'd fall off after 20 steps or so, but Bryan'd get to a hundred and run to end it.

The tracks rumbled with a coming train, and we got ready to hug the board fence, which'd put a few feet between us and the speeding cars. We waved wildly at the engineer before covering our ears—he shook his fist hard in return. The wind whipped our pant legs like wash on the line; we hallooed at the tops of our lungs, unable to hear ourselves—the pair of us together in our own small world. When the train'd passed, we chuckled, tickled with our tiny adventure.

"Just trim the back and sides, please, nothing off the top."
Jerry knew what my mother wanted for my first haircut of the summer. When he'd finished I was mowed on top and shaved on the sides.
"Ha, ha! You won't have to comb it for a while."
"Just leave it dry, please."
"This'll make you smell good. The girls love it."
Jerry doused me with a bottle of green stuff that'd empty a church, and followed with a choking cloud of powder slapped from

a dirty brush. I handed him the silver dollar my mother'd given me, and got a fifty-cent piece and a quarter. He expected no tip from a boy, for if he had, he'd've made sure I had a nickel.

"What about you?" he asked Bryan. "Wouldn't you like to get rid of those hot curls for the summer?"

"Sure and I swore to my poor old mother—God rest her soul!—I'd never cut them off. She'd whirl in her grave like a Dervish if I broke my oath."

My father'd given instructions to stand Bryan, as my host for the night, a treat. Next to Jerry's was the ice cream parlor with its marble counter and wooden stools you could twirl on by pushing against the counter. Chocolate, strawberry, and vanilla—those were the flavors. Macadamia nut-passion fruit-bubble gum-ripple would've seemed as far in the future as Buck Rogers's flying belt.

There was Coke. The Coca Cola patent had run out, and a flood of new bottled colas hit the market, most of them going belly up before you got a chance to learn their names. Coke was still king. Fountain Coke, which bottled Coke took a back seat to, was made by taking a curved glass marked *Coca Cola*, shoveling in a scoop of crushed ice, holding the glass under the syrup spout, squirting just the right amount, putting the glass under the soda spigot, filling close to the brim, and giving one stir with a long spoon—perfect!

There were root beer floats, ice cream sodas, milk shakes, and sundaes. I was going to treat Bryan to a sundae. The usual sundae with two scoops of ice cream piled on top of each other in a high dish, syrup, whipped cream, chopped walnuts, and a maraschino cherry cost 15 cents; but bent on playing the big spender, I insisted Bryan order a 20-cent sundae, which came in a flat dish. Bryan wisely picked hot fudge. Me showing off my know-how by ordering a Black and White—I liked the name—which had a big-size scoop of vanilla ice cream covered with chocolate sauce alongside a big-size scoop of chocolate ice cream covered with marshmallow sauce, plus a double portion of trimmings. The combination of chocolate ice cream and marshmallow sauce would sicken a bee, but that didn't stop me Jack Spratting the dish clean, making sure my last spoonful had a good-sized gob of whipped cream and a maraschino cherry.

When we got to the library, Bryan went up to the counter, leaned over, and kissed his mother full on the lips. I couldn't remember the last time I kissed my mother on the lips.

"Hello, Sean," she whispered.

"Hello, Mrs.—"

"Who?"

"Hello, J-Jeanne."

"Good! But now you must be like two small mice. Do you see that?" She pointed to a sign saying QUIET!

I never thought the library had to do with entertainment; I saw it as dark and dusty, a hangout for fussy old maids and cross old men. Bryan took me to a table with a viewer and half a dozen brown-colored slides. We passed the time looking at 3-dimensional shots of the Pyramids.

"It's like you're right there!" I whispered.

"Used to have a half-naked woman without arms, but someone stole it," Bryan whispered back. "Com'ere! Want to show you something."

He led me to a wooden stand holding a big one-volume dictionary that'd been printed when hoop skirts were in. We read the definitions of *coitus, copulation, and intercourse*—they went around in a circle. At the end I knew what I knew at the beginning—not much.

Before we left the library, Bryan's mother handed me Rafael Sabatini's "The Sea Hawk," which she'd checked out for me. When the film starring Errol Flynn came to town two years later, I got my reward.

"The movie was good, but the book was better."

# Chapter 38

"**B**efore cooking, I am going to slip off my shoes and sip un petit Dubonnet while we listen to the dinner concert. You boys cannot be hungry after eating all that ice cream and syrup."

"I'll get your slippers, Maman, and fix your Dubonnet. Can Sean and I have one too?"

"And when the police wagon carries me off for being a bad mother? You would like seeing me through the bars, I suppose. If you and Sean will shell the peas without eating them all, you can each have a glass of ginger ale . . . Do you like music, Sean?"

"Do you mean classical music?"

"But of course! When I say music, I do not mean boop boop a doop."

"Well to tell the truth I haven't listened to much classical music. You'll probably laugh at me for this—"

"Absolutely no! I promise I will not laugh."

"Well, I've always thought people who say they like classical music are just pretending, and don't really like it at all—especially opera!"

"Ha, ha! No, I do not laugh at you, Mon Cher; there is justice in what you say. You have hit on a truth, but it is not all of the truth. Shall I explain?"

I was getting a crush on Bryan's mother, but besides that I felt here was a grownup who wouldn't treat me like a child.

"Yes please!"

"Of course, you are right that there are those who claim to admire something not because they do, but because they wish to impress others. However, do you not see that if none of these others liked it

either, this kind of pretense would wither and die? Does that make sense to you, Sean?"

"I suppose it's like the Emperor's clothes—the make-believe couldn't go on forever."

"How clever of you to think of that." Jeanne went on, "And opera lends itself to such a thing because there is so much glitter surrounding operatic productions: the prima donnas, the costumes, the first nights with the ladies in their expensive gowns and jewels, and so on. I confess I do not like opera as much as some other music, but we must remember that opera is not just music; it is also drama and spectacle. Still, the best operas contain some beautiful music; that is what makes them the best."

"But what makes music beautiful? Is it because it describes something beautiful? Or is it because it tells a beautiful story?" I sensed Jeanne had the answer to a mystery that baffled me.

"Ah! I see you have the searching mind. Malheureusement, I am not Socrates, but I will do my best. First let me say there is a type of music called program music, which may describe something or tell a story, but all that is a red herring. The best music does neither; it is just music. Tell me, Sean, you very much like to play tennis, do you not?"

"Yes, I do."

"And what if I should say to you—which I do not—that you only pretend to like tennis so people will admire you? Would there be any truth in that?"

"N-no—at least I don't think so—you see I really like the way it feels when the ball hits the strings; and when I watch it go off my racquet and land almost on the spot I'd planned, it's as if I'd made a beautiful bird inside me that flew out of my mouth to take up its life in the outside world." I reddened at my fancy words.

"But that is prettily said. Still, I put it to you that if I want to learn wherein the true beauty of tennis lies, I cannot do so by hearing your words. I must go out on the court and swing the racquet. You agree?"

"Yes, certainly."

"And could I swing just once and create a beautiful bird? Would it not be an ugly crow?"

Bryan, who like a wise old master had been following the talk between two pupils, put in, "Right, Maman, crow after crow flew out of me today, while Sean was sending forth flights of bluebirds."

We laughed.

"But how is music like tennis?" I asked.

"Well only in this way, just as the experience of tennis requires playing, so the experience of music requires listening. The first step is to listen and listen and listen, until the brain begins to make sense of the sounds the ear is receiving. In the beginning the progress is slow, but after a while we recognize pieces we have heard before, and it is then we long to hear one we know. At the next stage, we remember the music well enough to hum it or play it in our head. In the end, we can listen to works where many things are happening at once, and the brain is able to sort them all out and appreciate the whole. That is when we cannot help thinking, *How beautiful!* That is when the bluebird flies out of the composer's mouth."

It was the first of many evenings I'd spend listening with Jeanne. I was ashamed—the sound didn't mean anything—I made up my mind—I'd listen till my ears ached.

# CHAPTER 39

**D**inner was simple, but with that touch Jeanne gave to things: small heads of butter lettuce; olive oil and wine vinegar in cut-glass bottles; French lamb chops, one apiece, with ruffled paper leggings; baby peas, sugar sweet; new potatoes boiled whole in their thin red jackets; garlic bread made with sourdough bread—I couldn't get enough; that dessert of the '30s we never tired of, strawberry Jell-O capped with swirls of whipped cream; hand-ground black coffee served in tiny cups.

When it was time to go to bed, Bryan kissed his mother on the lips while I watched.

Jeanne caught my look, "Bryan likes to think himself Irish, but his French blood is too warm to be denied. Am I not right, Sean, in thinking the Irish do not show their affection easily?"

She came up to me, "I think you are too shy to kiss me, so I will kiss you."

She kissed me on the corner of my mouth.

Back in Bryan's room after using the bathroom, I went to my bag for pajamas.

"Too hot for pajamas. Let's sleep in our undershorts. That okay with you?"

"Guess so, if it's what you want."

"Ha, ha! 'Course we can take the shorts off and sleep in our skin if you'd rather."

"No, that's OK! In our shorts will be fine!"

He was done fast. I had everything off but my pants, and my back to Bryan, he commanded:

"Just a sec! You need a lesson in the way to take your pants off in front of someone. Doesn't matter whether you're taking them off in front of a boy or in front of a girl. Never turn your back; they'll think you've got something to hide. Look them straight in the face, better yet right in the eye. Okay, try it. Turn around and look me in the eye!"

I turned toward Bryan.

"Stand up straight!"

I straightened up.

"Now, look me in the eye!"

I looked him in the eye—for a second.

"No! Keep looking! Good! Now start unbuttoning! Remember, I'm watching everything you do!"

"I know!" I said. "That's just the trouble!"

"Don't linger over each button. Just go from one to the next at a good steady pace without hurrying. Okay, you can peel'em off now."

"It's not going to work," I said.

"Of course it's going to work. Why shouldn't it work? Just pull them down!"

"Do I have to?"

"Yes, you have to! Pull them down!"

I pushed my pants to the floor and stepped out of them, still leaning over.

"Good! Now stand up straight and look me in the eye!"

I stood up straight and looked him in the chest.

"Well, back to the drawing board," Bryan said, noticing my pointed boxers.

"Okay, you were right, I was wrong. Get in bed. It'll probably go away in a week."

We were lying side by side. "I don't understand; there's no reason at all. This afternoon you came out in your shorts, and there was no problem. What happened?"

"It's just that you made me so self-conscious. Once I get like that, I'm hopeless. I might be OK if I could forget what I'm doing."

Neither of us said anything for a minute.

"Bryan?"

"Yes, Sean?"

"I never thanked you for coming back when Old Man Clayton was shooting at us. That was a brave thing to do."

"You think I want my best friend full of holes?"

"Do you mean that? Am I your best friend?"

"Well now you mention it, I guess you are. If you want the truth, I don't think I've ever had a really good friend. I've known lots of kids, but never thought of any of them as a best friend."

"Funny, that's the same with me. Bryan, I want to say something—if I can find the right words. I may not always be able to do what you expect of me—you're so much better at most things than I am—but I want to make you a promise. If you ever say to me, 'Sean, I'm asking you as my best friend to do this,' I'll do it, no matter what it is, no matter how hard it is."

"I swear that's the noblest thing I've ever heard. I'll make the same pledge to you, but let's agree we'll never use those special words unless the thing we ask is as important as . . . as important as our friendship! Agreed?"

"Agreed."

I woke in the morning to the bedroom door opening. Bryan was coming from the bathroom.

"Holy mackerel, Bryan! You're naked!"

"Well, I'm usually naked when I get out of the shower."

"I mean, what if you ran into your mother?"

"Ha, ha! Maman!"

He stepped into the hall, "Maman!"

"What is it, Bryan?"

"Can you come? It's important!"

"All right, just let me slip into my robe."

Jeanne in the room, Bryan took hold of her hands and kissed her.

"It was so important that you should kiss me before you dressed?"

"No, it's so funny! Sean was afraid it would shock you if you saw me with nothing on."

"Pauvre Sean, he cannot understand the French. Still, he has reason. Look at you, Bryan! You are no longer a little boy; you are a grown man. What would people say? What am I to do with you? Sean, you must help me civilize him. Is that all you wanted? May I go now?"

I was lying on my stomach under a sheet.

"Wait, Maman! I want to show you something."

Like a magician, Bryan pulled the sheet off, "Isn't Sean good-looking in his plaid boxers?"

I buried my face.

"But yes, Sean is truly handsome and his underwear is très chic, but Bryan, you are embarrassing him. Not everyone is without shame like you. You must be more considerate of people's feelings."

"But I was being considerate; before I pulled the sheet off, I made sure Sean was lying on his stomach."

# CHAPTER 40

It was the Fourth of July; Bryan would spend his first night at my house. True to form, he had all on his own mapped out a jam-packed day for us, "Oh, maybe I forgot to mention it; I entered us in the Park Doubles they always have on The Fourth. That's why I had us practice."

"What! You think we're good enough to play in a tournament?"

"And why not? I checked; you'll be the best player there."

"Bryan, have you ever played doubles?"

"No, but I figure you can show me the ropes. Anyway, it should be duck soup; you get to use all the lines don't you? They made us the second seed."

"And how did you work that?"

"Sure and wasn't it my bounden duty to let the director know about the case of trophies you've won and about how much we've been practicing together?"

"I've never won a trophy, just two playground tournaments where the Director gave me a pat on the head, and the day before yesterday was the second time we ever hit together."

"Well maybe I laid it on a bit, but it was in a most deserving cause. Besides, the Director's name is Mahoney; he has the lilt of County Cork on his tongue, and when I tried my brogue on him, he took to me like a long-lost son."

It was a 16-draw tournament. We had no bye, so we'd have to play four matches in one day if we somehow lived up to our seed. Most of the players'd never been in a tournament, and our first round we faced beginners, giving Bryan a chance to get his feet wet. He

was improving by leaps and bounds, and though our second-round opponents weren't bad, we won handily.

We reached my house with Bryan bubbling over, "Sean, me boy, the gift of prophesy I inherited from my Irish grandmother is whisperin' to me now: *Sure as the sun sets o'er Galway Bay, Lacey and O'Neill will win the day.*"

"Bryan, me bucko, have you heard the one that goes: *There's many a slip twixt the egg and the chick*—or something like that?"

My mother wasn't home, but lunch was set out for us and we made short work of it. Back in my room, which Bryan had yet to check out, it took him three seconds to find the bathroom.

"Didn't know you were a Vanderbilt, as you surely must be, having your own private watering hole."

At a time when a Saturday night bath was the rule, Bryan was a Water Baby. He straightaway asked for a shower, and didn't coax when I mumbled an excuse for not joining him. He was bare in nothing flat, a habit of his that made me look for something to stare at; his nakedness rattled me almost as much as my own. I showed him his towel and left him alone.

A few minutes passed before I glanced up from my place on the bed.

"Where's your friend? I'd like to meet him," it was my father coming up to me.

"Who's that?" Bryan asked through a crack in the bathroom door.

"My dad. Wants to meet you when you're decent."

"Daycent? I'm always daycent," Bryan said, walking naked toward my father with his hand out. "Pleased to meet you Mr. Lacey, I'm Bryan O'Neill."

I don't know who gulped louder, my father or me. He shook Bryan's hand, reddening.

"Yes, Bryan, glad to meet you too, but mustn't intrude on you boys."

He backed out the door.

"I don't think he likes me," Bryan said.

"That's not it. I think you . . . shocked him."

"Shocked him? I hardly said a word."

I motioned toward his body.

"You're telling me seeing me naked shocked him? That doesn't make sense because, pardon my saying so, I'm sure it's a lot more shocking seeing you than seeing me."

"He's never seen me."

"What! That's impossible! How could a father living in the same house never have seen his son?"

"Well I didn't quite mean never; I meant he hasn't seen me with hair."

"Excuse me, but what a family! I suppose you've never seen your father either?"

"Not that I remember."

"Jesus, Mary, and Joseph! I'd want to see my dad's just to find out how big mine was going to get. Have you ever thought that big as yours is, it might get bigger? I bet it's still growing."

"O God, Bryan! I wish you hadn't said that. I'd rather die than have it get bigger!"

"Steady on, Sean. Some day you may change your mind. You don't know how lucky you are."

"Lucky! You call it lucky having everyone gawk at you like a carnival freak?"

"Sure and it would depend on who's doing the gawking. Now if it were a gorgeous girl—"

"A girl! What could be worse! That reminds me, Bryan, you won't pop out naked in front of my mother?"

"You think she'd be shocked?"

"I *know* she'd be shocked. Please, Bryan! Promise me!"

"Ha, ha! Of course I wouldn't gallivant naked in front of your mother—think I don't know my Emily Post? All the same, I also know the female of the species is not only deadlier than the male, she's thicker skinned to boot. Men shock more easily than women—take it from Father O'Neill."

In our semifinal match, I broke Bryan in on net play. He reached over it once and hit it with his racquet another time, making us concede both points. Still, getting him over his fear of going to net paid off. These were the best players we'd faced, but we won 3 and 2. The final was another story. Both opponents had good groundies, and they hit to Bryan every chance they got. He was buffaloed by the power of their shots and stayed stuck behind the baseline where

his strokes crumbled. Trounced by a score of 6-1, we sat down on the bench between sets.

"We're going to lose; I feel it in my bones."

"Bryan, we've still got a chance, but we have to change our strategy."

"Won't make any difference, but I'll do whatever you want. Just tell me what to do."

"Okay, I see only one hope for us. You've got to stay at net whenever I'm serving or whenever I'm receiving. Just stand as close to the net as you can without reaching over it or touching it and hit anything—you understand, anything—you can get to. Can you do that?"

"I'll make myself do it. What else?"

"After you serve or after you receive, don't stay back. Just run as fast as you can up to the net—don't worry if you miss a few. Do you think you can handle that?"

"If it's what you want, I'll handle it."

In spite of what I'd just told him, Bryan couldn't force himself forward every point. We were behind 2-1 when we sat down at a changeover.

"Bryan, whenever you've gotten to net we've done great. You've just got to make yourself go there every time. Can you do it?"

"I swear by the blood of the O'Neills I'll do it!"

He did. He raced around knocking off everything he could get to. When our opponents sent up a couple of lobs, which they hadn't tried all day, they were short. Bryan jumped two feet off the ground and bashed them, bouncing them all the way over the fence. His form wasn't book, but his results were—they never tried another lob. They stayed away from Bryan and zeroed in on me; we rallied and won the set 6-4. By the end of the second set, our foes'd lost their nerve and their strokes with it. We won the third set 6-0. Each of us was handed a small silver cup.

"Never expected to take home one of these, did you?"

"Sean, me boy, you have so little faith. Myself, I never doubted—not for a single second! You must learn to trust the gift of my Irish grandmother."

You'd think four tennis matches in one day would be enough, but Bryan squeezed in the free-throw-shooting contest which he won

in a romp—I lost in the first round. He added the 50-yard dash—my rabbit blood brought me in second—and the high jump—I dug my heels in and sat it out. He finished off the day hopping us left-footed to victory in the bag race, where he had his right leg and I had my left leg tied into the same burlap bag. He'd've entered more events, except our tennis matches got in the way. For these contests we were handed ribbons instead of cups.

At dinner Bryan blarneyed permission from my mother for the two of us to stay out till midnight, something I'd never've dreamed asking on my own.

"Never fear, Mrs. Lacey, I'll guard your bairn with my life and my honor."

# Chapter 41

The town park on the Fourth of July made our summer. Just after dark there was a tiny fireworks shoot that got *ohs* and *ahs*. There were booths where you could bring home the bacon betting the wheel, or you could try your luck at the dice. And you could pick your poison throwing darts at balloons, knocking down bottles with baseballs, or pitching pennies into saucers. It was all for charity, with the usual spread of hot dogs, peanuts, soda pop, and beer.

Fourth of July, except for Christmas, was the holiday I liked best. From the beginning of the year, I squirreled away nickels, dimes, and pennies to splurge on one lovely binge. Afterwards I'd start hoarding all over again to buy Christmas presents. This year I wanted to win enough prize tickets to stamp my brand on two special kewpie dolls, Alice the Goon and the Sea Hag. I already owned Popeye, Olive Oyl, Wimpy, Swee'pea, and Bluto; these two would round out the Popeye characters decorating my bureau. The dolls were only painted chalk, but on that day of my life they were my heart's desire.

Bryan wanted to play dice where you were paid off in coins, the only time of the year this was legal. He loved the ups and downs of gambling and preferred cash to kewpies. I left him at the Chuck-a-Luck cage and made my way to the baseballs and bottles. The ten wooden milk bottles were stacked in a triangle on a platform. You not only had to knock them down, you had to knock them off the platform. You got three balls. If you knocked them off using three balls, you earned one prize ticket; if you knocked them off using two balls, three tickets; and if you knocked them off using one ball, five tickets, something I was never able to do.

I must've played two hours, switching off with other throwers, before I ran out of money. Fighting my disappointment, I turned in a good part of my tickets for the Sea Hag and left to round up Bryan. Not wanting to disturb him, I watched him study the fall of the dice, trying to dope out a winning strategy.

"How'd you do?" he asked when he finally noticed me.

"OK I guess, got the Sea Hag. Have some tickets left over, but not enough for Alice the Goon."

"Thought you wanted Alice the most. Why'd you get the Hag?"

"Well, she cost less tickets."

"So what? Why not get what you want?"

"Don't know, just thought it was better to be left with more tickets."

"Sean, are you sure you're Irish? An Irishman would never think like that. Anyway, how many more tickets do you need for Alice?"

"Five."

"I've got four nickels left. Where's this shell game of yours?"

"No, Bryan! You want to play Chuck-a-Luck."

"Doesn't matter; in a few spins, I'd lose them all anyway. It's finally sunk in that the odds are rigged in the House's favor. Let's stake the O'Neill fortune on your bottles."

On his first try, Bryan knocked them off in three balls—a good start—earning one ticket. His second try—same thing—two tickets in all, two nickels left.

"Have to do better than that. I'll pretend Lou Gehrig's at the plate and give him a taste of the O'Neill fast ball."

The bottles splattered like they'd been blasted by a bowling ball—all off with one throw.

"Ha, ha! The luck o' the Irish! You have two extra tickets, and I still have a nickel."

I murmured my bashful thanks as I smiled at Alice the Goon, to my eyes a most lovable monster.

"Spit on this nickel for me and I'll play it on the dice. Know what I'll do when I win?"

I spit. "So what will you do *if* you win?"

"So little faith! I'll buy us each a beer."

I'd never'd tasted beer in my life, and was pretty sure I didn't want to start.

"Bryan, no way they'll sell you beer!"

"Don't worry, I'll get it *after* I win."

He lost.

"Can't win'em all! Have an idea; I know how we can get free beer. Nothing to it! You game for a little adventure?"

"Will it be anything like the idea you had for getting cherries from Old Man Clayton's orchard?"

"Sean, you really disappoint me with your gloomy outlook on life. I tell you this'll be like falling off a log."

"Just so it's not like falling off a fence," I said. "Well, you were right about winning Alice. What do we have to do?"

"You know the big Shepherd place at the top of Moneybags Lane? The rest of the family go to the mountains for the summer, and last Fourth of July Tom Shepherd gave a secret beer bust for a bunch of his buddies. 'Course, it was strictly illegal 'cause Tom was only 19, but the Shepherds have so much pull the peelers wouldn't dare lay a glove on him. I heard there's going to be another shindig tonight. They'll be roaring drunk, so they'll never notice us. Anyway, no one'll care; they'll be passing out beer by the bucketful. I wouldn't be surprised if they fill the pool with suds, so let's crash the party, and I'll rustle a keg or two. Are you with me?"

I knew who Tom Shepherd was. When he was in town he sped about in an ivory Cord roadster honking at the girls, the envy of every male in the county. At a time when a kid would walk a mile barefoot to spend a penny, the Shepherds had millions to strut with.

I could see Bryan was set on his scheme, "I don't like it, but I'm with you."

"Sean, I swear I'll look after you."

Bryan pointed to a distant glimmer, "That's the place."

We found some shrubs to stow Alice and the Sea Hag, and by the light of a slice of moon going down too fast to suit me, turned onto a narrow road. It wasn't a hike I'd have taken on my own. There were tall trees hanging over the pavement from both sides, making black moving shadows that kept me looking over my shoulder. As we went along, the houses got bigger and further apart. After two miles on the curving lane, we came alongside a high hedge that bordered the Shepherd property. We followed the hedge till things came to a dead end; to our left was a driveway leading to grounds that covered a low hill.

I thought Bryan would scout the layout before pushing ahead, but he marched straight up the drive like a conquering general.

"Just act like you own the dump, and if you sight the enemy, sing out with the mating call of the wild gobbler."

"Br-y-y-y-an!"

"Whoa, Boy!"

There was a small building off to one side.

"It's a playhouse that has an honest-to-goodness kitchen with its own electric stove and Frigidaire, everything child-size. They built it for their little girl Barbara as a birthday present."

The place had white plaster walls, a roof of Spanish tile, and a lighted courtyard. But for real excitement there was a merry-go-round with eight horses painted in rainbow colors.

"Does it work?"

"Sure! It has an electric motor, and it plays music when it goes around."

"Golly!"

"The party'll be at the pool on the other side of the house."

We were hidden in shadow as things came into sight. I'd never seen a pool lit from underneath, and the lighted blue water made me catch my breath, "It's beautiful!" I whispered.

The pool looked enormous. At one end was not only a springboard but a diving platform, so high up it gave my stomach conniptions.

"Don't tell me anyone jumps off that thing!"

"Tom Shepherd's a diver; he plans to try out for the Olympics."

Keeping to the cover of bushes, Bryan led us close to the action and up against a high iron fence with sharp points on top. Through the bars I could see young men in swimsuits standing around a table laid out with food and tubs heaped with ice. As we watched, one of the partiers pulled two bottles from a tub, and popped the caps with an opener.

"Yum, yum!" came from Bryan.

We moved along, passing a gate that was chained and padlocked.

"There's no way to get in. We sure don't want to climb that metal stockade. Even if we didn't get speared going over, we'd be trapped inside with no chance to make a quick getaway," I said.

"Follow me! There's more than one way to skin a skunk."

We went to where the fence met a small building near the mansion the Shepherds called home.

"See that door? It leads to the dressing rooms."

"What if it's locked?"

"It will be locked, but there's a key—at least I hope it's still there."

"Bryan, how do you know so much about this place?"

"Oh, my aunt was Barbara's nursemaid—my father sent for her before I was born. Many's the happy hour I've whiled away on these grounds, but it's two years since Aunt Annie pulled out her savings to live the life of Riley on the Old Sod—Barbara got too big for a nursemaid.

"My last visit I was 11, Barbara was 10. Ha, ha! Just remembered something. I came into her room as Barbara was getting up, and she wouldn't take her bath unless I took it with her—my aunt saw no harm in it. So that morning Barbara and I were sitting opposite each other in her mother's big marble tub."

"You took a bath with a *girl*?—guess she wore panties."

"No, I saw her sweet place."

"You looked?"

"Naturally. Anyway, why shouldn't I take a bath with her? My intentions were pure as the driven snow—oh my gosh! Just realized I lied to you the first time we met."

"How do you mean?"

"I told you no one'd ever seen me naked with it on. Well I must have had it on all right—as much as I could at 11—because Barbara was playing pat-a-cake with it, batting it back and forth under the water. I was too dumb to know what was happening to me. When the tip surfaced, she really got exercised; the higher it stuck out, the harder she'd slap—all the time giggling like an old maid on her wedding night. It was red as a lobster and just as sore when her mother walked in."

"Lord, Bryan! What did she do?"

"Hooked me by the ear, reeled me out of the tub, and towed me to the kitchen where my aunt was talking to the cook, and where Tom Shepherd was lolling in orange silk pajamas eating cake and ice cream for breakfast. What a grip that woman had! I was putty in her hands. She swung me around to give everyone a ringside seat and said, 'Just look what your nephew's been up to!'"

"God!"

"That was the last time I was invited over. Anyway, if I lied, I apologize, but I don't think having it on counts when you're a year

and a half from hair number one. Besides, this is the first time I realized it was a boner—now getting back to business."

Bryan went to a bank piled with rocks, worked one free, uncovered a rusty metal box, opened it, and took out a key, "Eureka! Bet everyone's forgotten about this."

He unlocked the door, tested the knob, and put the key back in the rocks.

"I'll case the joint. You wait here. If things turn sour, take off."

"You mean leave you here and go home by myself?"

"Sure!"

"No, Bryan! If you're not back in 15 minutes, I'm coming after you."

I didn't know what all could happen, but it had to be better than running—I sure wouldn't be walking—along that dark deserted road.

# Chapter 42

**I**n 10 minutes, back came a smiling Bryan decked out in bright red swim trunks.

"They'll never notice me in these. Come on! I found a swell place where you can keep an eye on my rags while I stick some bubbly through the bars."

I started to say something, but the happiness on Bryan's face made me swallow it. He led us into a hall that cut the building in half. At the far end was a glass door opening onto a patio separating the swimming pool from the main house. Part way down were two doors facing each other; one said, "Ladies," the other, "Gentlemen." Bryan started to open the Ladies' door.

"Bryan, that's the girls' room!" I whispered.

"I know! That's why it's such a good hiding place; there are no girls at the party."

We were inside. Bryan hadn't turned any lights on, but there was a bulb over the door that must've been kept burning day and night. "You didn't find that suit in here?"

"No, the other side. They keep them for guests. Want me to get you one? You could take a dip."

It was just like Bryan to think I might take him up on it. I didn't give all my reasons, "I don't know how to swim. Closest I've come is wading at the beach with my pant legs rolled up. My mother would never let me go to the pool because of my asthma."

"No wonder you're so shy—haven't had any practice taking your pants off in public. Going to be tougher than I figured getting you over your grudge against dropping your drawers. But don't worry; we'll do some drill work on it. Right?"

"Say, where are your things?" I quick changed the subject.

"Behind the couch. Did you notice how fancy it is? That's in case a girl's having one of her days and has to get off her feet. The boys rate iron benches to sit on. Okay, I'm going into the enemy camp now. You stay here and hold the fort. Don't panic. It'll take a while 'cause long as I'm at it I'll try for an armload—might as well be hanged for a sheep as a goat, I always say."

"But Bryan, they'll know you're not one of them!"

"Tom Shepherd's the only one who'd know for sure, and I'm going to dodge him. Besides, they'll all be pie-eyed."

Bryan gone, I looked the place over. There were polished wooden lockers with hangers inside; there was a stack of light green towels with a dark green S; there was a deep drawer full of ladies' swimsuits; there was a mirrored dressing table laid out with a silver hairbrush set and all the stuff ladies smear on their faces; there was a glassed-in shower. There was a closed-in purple toilet; on a shelf over the toilet was a blue box with big white letters—KOTEX—like my mother kept hidden under the silk step-ins in her bottom bureau drawer. I once heard Joey say about another boy, "He thinks girls use Kotex to stop nose bleeds." I'd have to ask Bryan what it was really for. I decided not to let the toilet go to waste, flushed it, and wished I could take it back, afraid the sound would give me away. Making my way to the sofa, I sank into its softness. My eyes closed . . .

"'S'a kid!"

I woke to the beery breath of a face pushed into mine. By the door stood three more youths, the one in the middle held up by the other two.

"Pull'm off an' hold'm whil'we pu'Ben t'bed."

"What're'yuh doin'ere, Kid?"

"I . . ."

"Let's tak'm t'Tom!"


Tom Shepherd was feeling good, but he wasn't drunk. "You say he was snoozing on the couch? Doesn't sound like a safecracker. How'd you get here?"

"He's with me!"

It was Bryan striding toward us.

"What's going on around here! Who the hell are you! Wait a minute, you look familiar. Didn't you know Barbara? I remember,

you were related to Annie. Well a fine kettle of fish when servants crash my parties."

"I'm nobody's servant, I'm Bryan O'Neill! And I'll have you know the O'Neills were ruling Ireland while the Shepherds were ramming sheep and milking rams."

"Tsk, tsk! A nice-looking boy like you shouldn't talk like that, especially in your predicament. In your place, I'd have enough sense to keep a civil tongue. If I had any doubts, you've just taken care of them. I say these kids have to pay a penalty. What do the rest of you say?"

"Damn right!"

"Y'betcha, Tom!"

"My friend had nothing to do with this. I'll pay the penalties for both of us. Tom, I know the Shepherds are men of honor. Will you make a gentlemen's agreement it's all on my head?"

"Ha, ha! So now we're men of honor. A minute ago we were hard-up sheepherders."

"It's my terrible Irish temper. I humbly beg your pardon."

"Well at least you're loyal to your friend, and you seem to have some guts. Take your medicine like a man—no sniveling!—and we'll see. But don't think you're getting off easy!"

Tom turned to one of his pals, "In a few minutes we'll hold the drawing for the door prize I'm putting up. Mel, will you go to the study and get a pencil, a ruler, and some paper, so I can make tickets. Also a bowl or something to pull them out of. By the way, where's Rembrandt? He'd want to take a look at this kid. Someone go find him."

Mel came back with the things, and a bearded male made his way to Tom's side.

"Oh, there you are, Rembrandt. Where were you?"

"Behind the rhododendrons reading Richard the Second. These parties get deadly dull when you don't drink."

"I want you to watch this kid. He's going to show us how to dive. Isn't that right, Bryan O'Neill? We're waiting for your first performance."

Bryan walked toward the springboard.

"No, not from the springboard! We'd rather see you take off from the platform."

Bryan turned, went to the ladder, glanced up—"Your Majesty's not afraid of a little height?"—took a breath, and began to climb.

Looking at that landing over 30 feet in the air, I hollered, "Don't do it, Bryan! I don't care what happens, but don't do it!"

"It's all right, Sean! What a Shepherd can do, need cause an O'Neill no concern!"

He reached the landing, stepped to the edge, looked down on us—"If you'd rather squawk like a chicken, you can call it off!"—and lofted himself up and out.

I'd never seen diving except in newsreels, but to my eye Bryan did a perfect swan dive, turned down with everything together, and went in with hardly a splash.

Blotto as they were, the audience let out cheers. "Atta boy!" "That's showin'em!"

Bryan got out of the pool and came back to Tom and the bearded Rembrandt.

"Well, Rembrandt, what do you think of our Irish monarch?"

"Yet looks he like a king! Lord, he's beautiful. I'd love to paint—"

"I'll be a son of a sea cook!" Tom broke in. "I just remembered something about this kid, and it gives me a red-hot idea on how to hold the drawing for the prize. It's one of those new army radios—can't buy 'em in a store—great for a camping trip."

"Baby, that's f'me!" came from one of his buddies.

Tom used the ruler to tear off strips of paper, marked each strip, folded it, and put it in the bowl.

"There. That covers the nine of you, including young Ben lying passed out in the girls' john. Sorry, party crashers don't get one, but neither do I. For his next trick, Bryan O'Neill's going to pick the winning number. Everyone take a slip from the bowl. Last one left is for Ben."

"What'sis? 'sa funny nummer," one of the ticket holders said.

"Everyone's got a number, most with fractions. Don't tell what it is yet. Just hold on to it . . . Rembrandt, if you were going to paint Bryan, what would you have him wear?"

"With a body like his? Nothing but a crown of laurel."

"Well, tonight you get your wish. Bryan, before you absentmindedly walk off with them, would you mind handing over those trunks?"

Like he'd been asked to pass the bread, Bryan stepped out of his suit and held it out.

"Hmm! You've grown a tad since I last saw you," Tom said, taking the trunks.

"Ods bodkins!" Rembrandt let out. "He's not an Irish king, he's a Greek God."

"Get it on, please!" Tom ordered.

"You want me to put the suit back on?"

"A smart kid who knows about ramming sheep and milking rams, and who takes baths with little girls, ought to know what I mean."

It was the only time I ever saw Bryan blush, "Oh! You want *that*!"

"It's entirely up to you. We can use your friend instead."

"No! This was all my bright idea."

"As I remember, you can get it up. Do you want Rembrandt's help? He's experienced at posing models."

"I'll manage."

"Christ! I don't know if I can watch this," Rembrandt said.

Bryan started running without going anywhere, flopping himself against his belly. Then keeping his legs stiff, he jumped up and down, turning his shaft into a whirling propeller.

"Ha, ha! That's a good stunt. Well, Rembrandt, how do you like your Greek God now?"

"Jesus! He's not only beautiful, he's potent. He's a Roman faun in full rut."

"I may've underestimated this Bryan O'Neill. Wouldn't Barbara love to climb into the tub with him now!"

"You're a better man than I am, Gunga Din!" put in Rembrandt.

"Ha, ha! Never let it be said this drawing wasn't strictly on the up-and-up. The length of his royal rod to the nearest quarter of an inch will pick the winner of the radio. Rembrandt, take the ruler and measure from the belly on up. I'll check by sighting . . . I make it . . . 7 . . . and . . . 1/2—Curses! Foiled again! That's more than I allowed for . . . The drawing's off. Seven's the biggest number I wrote down. I'll have to think of something else."

"'S'one helluva ram y've got there, Tom. Ain'cha gonna milk'im?"

I was watching Bryan's face. Something went across it. I wondered what.

"I know Bryan O'Neill puts nothing past us Shepherds, but I'm not partial to hot milk."

# CHAPTER 43

**B**ryan was dressed. We'd been let go and were by ourselves outside the fence.

"Now for the beer!"

"I wouldn't think you'd even want to mention beer after what you went through."

"Sure and where would lie the profit in keeping myself all roiled up?"

"But, Bryan, you must've been embarrassed!"

"Maybe for a minute, but I've always known it could happen. Sean, my boy, let me give you some words of wisdom. In this vale of tears we call the world, it's pants or be pantsed. There's only one question: Is yo' gwine to be the pantser, or is yo' gwine to be the pantsee?" Bryan said, switching to Amos'n Andy.

"Mind now, you should always aim to be the pantser; but if Lady Luck gives a yank to your drawstring, and it's your own bags that fall to the ground, you may as well enjoy the joke, even though it's yourself it's on. Anyway, it's water over the dam. Next time, I won't even blush. As you saw, I got off easy. It could've been worse."

I didn't see how it could've been worse, but I had no chance to ask. We'd come to the place where Bryan'd stashed the beer.

"Look! Six bottles and an opener. Let's sample some right now!"

Bryan swigged his. I took one sip of mine. "Ugh! I Can't drink it. Do you want the rest?"

"It'd be a mortal sin to water the grass with it. Father Donovan would tell you the same."

He guzzled mine and opened another for along the way. I carried two of the bottles; he tucked one under an arm while working on

the fourth. Bryan was in high spirits, so I got my nerve up to ask him something I'd been wondering about, "You looked sort of funny when that drunk said you were a ram and Tom should milk you. They don't really milk rams do they? I know you said shepherds do. I figured it was some kind of joke, but I didn't get it."

"Ha, ha! Sean, you're a sly one! You're pulling my leg!"

"No, honest!"

"Holy Mither! I think he means it!"

"Of course I mean it! I just want to know what it was all about."

"Did you understand when Tom mentioned hot milk?"

"I think so. He doesn't like to drink it. I don't like it either; I don't even like warm milk. If I drink it at all, I drink it cold."

"Jesus help us! Afraid I already know the answer, but don't you ever get it off?"

"Get what off?"

"Let me put it this way, you know what it means to get it on, don't you?"

"You know I do! I wish I didn't!"

"But when you do have it on, doesn't it ever drive you kind of . . . crazy?"

"I don't know about crazy, but it makes me awfully uncomfortable."

"But don't you want to get rid of it?"

"Sure! But what can I do? I just wait, and after awhile it behaves itself. Bryan, if there's a way to make it go away sooner, I wish you'd tell me."

"The lad knows not whereof he asks! But my best friend can ask what he will of me. Faith, it won't be aisy—who could deny it's a most ticklish proposition? But I'll make a knightly vow: If by summer's sad close thou hast not tasted of The Tree, I'll instruct thee in the way to eat of The Fruit. And may the Lord have mercy on my soul! Now I'll drink a toast to Innocence! And no more on this we'll say, till fair September holds full her sway!"

We plodded along, me puzzling over his words, Bryan into his drinking. By the time we reached the kewpie dolls, he was starting his fifth bottle. "Glad's'not much further," he said, as legs spread he unbuttoned and hosed the pavement. "Not sure could make't."

Except for the small bulb over the front porch, the lights were out when we reached my house, for which I thanked my lucky stars. I

set the kewpies down, with one arm around his waist walked Bryan to my room in the dark, closed the door, and got him to the bed where he plopped like a sack of potatoes. I groped my way to the bathroom and clicked the switch to get a sliver of light. Though Bryan looked out cold, I felt him as I pared to my shorts.

"Sean, gotta 'ndress me!" Bryan's eyes were closed; only his lips moved.

I did him part way, "You can sleep in your pants."

"Tak'm off!"

I waited, hoping he'd black out again.

"Tak'm off!!"

"Sh-h-h!"

After unbuttoning him, I started his pants down over his shorts, glad to find them slipping so easy. But halfway through, a pink jack-in-the-box jumped out the leg of his boxers. Trying not to look, I pulled the pants off.

"Shortstoo!"

"No, Bryan, we'll sleep in our shorts."

"Shortstoo!!"

"Sh-h-h! My parents are asleep."

"Don' want shorts!!!"

Swallowing hard, I turned to Bryan, and unbuttoned him. I saw that his rod, held pointing straight toward the ceiling by his drawers, would be bent backwards if I pulled the shorts off.

"Bryan, they won't come off," I whispered. "Your . . . your . . . won't let them."

Bryan pawed around with his eyes closed and found the trouble, "Mus'n be 'fraid o' Johnnie. Would'n hurt a fly. Shorts off!!"

I swallowed harder, took hold of his pole, and worked it up through the leg opening. That done, I finished him, all the while dripping from my armpits. The bedspread was on a chair, so I only had to get Bryan under the sheet, which was enough for the Fourth of July. That done, I flipped the bathroom switch and climbed in beside him.

"Sean, y'undressed?"

"Yes, Bryan, I'm undressed."

"All th'way?"

"I've got my shorts on."

"'rwe bes' frien's?"

"Yes, Bryan, best friends."

"Shortsoff!! Noshorts, bes' frien's!!"

"Shhh! Not so loud! You'll wake my parents!"

"Shortsoff!!"

"Okay! Okay! I'll take them off!"

Pouring more sweat, I lay on my back and slipped out of the shorts.

"Theyoff?"

"Yes, they're off."

"Mak'sure!"

I felt Bryan's hand land smack on me and go slack.

"Bes' frien . . ." and he was gone.

# Chapter 44

**B**ryan was shaking me hard. "Come in!" he said.

We were under the sheet as my mother put her head through the doorway.

"You sleepyheads better get up if you want breakfast; it's past ten o'clock. I'm glad to see you covered for a change."

"Covered?"

"When I looked in earlier the sheet was off the bed."

"The sh-sheet was off?".

"I put it back," Bryan said.

"All the way off?"

"Yes, lying on the floor. Why don't you boys wear your pajamas?"

I was sorry as soon as I said it, but strong in my mind, it slipped out.

"Were we on our stomachs?"

"No, flat on your backs, and let me tell you, the two of you together made a pretty picture!" my mother said, closing the door.

"Ha, ha! So your mother would be shocked would she? Was I right about women or was I right about women?"

With that, Bryan bounced onto the floor and pointed to his boner, "Ha, ha! Wonder if I was like this when she saw me?"

Under the sheet I was his twin, but I wasn't laughing, I was picturing us through my mother's eyes, *Were we or weren't we?*

I waited till Bryan was in the shower to ease out from under the sheet. By the time we got ourselves together and breakfast finished, the morning was over.

"If things go according to plan, this afternoon will be the start of a whole new career for you," Bryan said.

After marching us a mile at double-time he was leading me Indian file, darting from tree trunk to tree trunk along the top of the creek bank on a very hot 5th of July.

"By plan, you mean your plan, naturally."

"Naturally. As I was saying, what you do today may go down in history as on a par with the time Seabiscuit broke his maiden."

"Broke his maiden?"

"Won his first race. Sean, my boy, I am sometimes shocked at the extent to which your education has been neglected. But let us keep to the point. You know that kid called Boomer?"

"Never had anything to do with him, but I know who he is all right, next King of the Hill at dear old Red Dirt. Boomer's only a month younger than me."

"Well, I've had my eye on him lately, and he's a nasty piece of goods. I wouldn't be surprised if he pans out worse than Joey."

"Bryan, me lad, never underestimate Joey. He's in a class by himself."

"As I was about to tell you, when it's hot like this, Boomer and his sidekick hang out at the Deep Hole and pick on the younger kids. If they do it today, the Lone Ranger and Tonto will step in."

"Me Tonto, naturally."

"Naturally."

"What we do, Kemo Sabe?"

"Squat in these bushes and await developments."

We could barely see the deserted Deep Hole—a 4-foot-deep pool, the best the creek had to offer during the summer—but we had a good view of the path leading down to it. First to come were three boys in the 10-12 range. They were followed by a 13-year-old girl named Harriet, who like Boomer was a year behind me in school. She was with another girl of about the same age.

"Shh!" Bryan warned.

Three boys in bathing trunks'd come into sight. I recognized Boomer and his lieutenant, Cooky. The two were leading the third boy, Toby, an 11-year-old from my neighborhood.

"You know what we do to stool pigeons?"

"Wh-what?"

"You'll find out!"

As the three went down the path, I pulled on Bryan's sleeve and pleaded dumb-style with my hands and face. He shook his head.

"Let the punishment fit the crime," he whispered. "We don't know what the crime is yet. Besides, we can't come between that kid and his destiny. Probably deserves whatever he gets. But never fear! Vengeance will be ours!"

Bryan motioned for me to follow to a new bush, so we could see what was happening below. Cooky was holding Toby's arms behind his back.

"Harriet! Wanna see what happens to squealers? Bring your friend over!" Boomer called out.

The girls didn't need to be asked twice. The three younger boys who'd come before them didn't need to be asked at all.

"They get their little weenies shown," Boomer said, jerking Toby's trunks down and off.

The legs went wild, thrashing every whichway, but Boomer waded in, grabbed one ankle then the other, and with Cooky's help, stretched the struggling boy so the girls could drink him in.

"OK, Tonto, that's all the evidence we need. You take the sidekick, I'll take Boomer," Bryan whispered before starting his gallop down the path.

Five yards from pay dirt he did his Lone Ranger, "Hi-ho, Silver!"

Bryan was all over Boomer. I made a lunge for Cooky, but he took off up the bank.

"Never mind him; we've got the one we want."

I looked for Toby; he was trying to get into his trunks and run at the same time.

"One more kick, and I'll break your neck!" Bryan threatened, tightening the full nelson he held on his prisoner.

"Uncle!" howled Boomer.

"You girls want to see what happens to bullies?" Bryan asked. "They get their big weenies shown."

"Quick, Harriet, run!" Boomer screamed.

"What for?"

"So you don't have to see!"

"I don't mind seeing."

These words took the starch out of Boomer. His body wilted like a zucchini plant on an afternoon in August.

"OK, Seabiscuit, this is where you break your maiden. Pull his trunks off!"

"Bryan, I can't!"

"You admit he deserves it?"

"Oh, he deserves it all right, but I can't!"

"No stomach for it, eh? OK, my boy, you needn't be a party to the deed. I'll meet you on top by the grove of bay trees."

I charged up the path, happy to get away, but wondering how Bryan was going to bring it off.

In a few minutes he showed up looking like a judge, "Justice has been done! And guess what? He has a small one. Harriet laughed when she saw it."

"Really! She actually laughed—but how did you—?"

"I didn't. Harriet had none of your scruples."

"You mean she—?"

"Sean, my boy, when are you going to learn about women?"

# CHAPTER 45

**O**f course I should've known better, but Bryan was at camp piling up merit badges, and I didn't know what to do with myself. Joey and Peanuts were on the curb across the boulevard.

"Sean, come with us! We're on our way to shoot baskets!" Joey called out.

"Well, maybe for a little while!" I called back.

"Great!" Joey said, as I joined them, "We'll go by my place to pick up the ball."

"Come on in, Ma's gone for the afternoon," he said, as we came to his house.

"That's OK, I'll wait outside."

"I gotta change these clothes or Ma'll smack me. You'n Peanuts can look at my Indian cards."

Joey was said to have the best collection of Indian cards around. I'd heard he had real pictures of Cochise and Geronimo, and I wanted to see these famous warriors I knew from the movies. I suspected most of Joey's cards'd come his way like Bobby's dollar. When we got to the living room there was an ordinary pack on an end table. "You like poker, don't you Sean? Let's play a few hands."

Joey'd hit on my weakness; it wasn't in me to turn down a chance to play cards, any kind of cards. We spread out on the wood floor, and Joey dealt a hand of Spit in the Ocean.

"Four ladies," I said softly, not wanting to rub it in, as I fanned the winning hand, which after the draw included a pair of queens and a card to match the Spit.

"Okay, Peanuts, me an' you lose. We each gotta take a shoe off."

"What for?" I asked.

"Well we got no dough so we'll play Strip Poker. It's no fun when you got nothing to lose."

Joey's idea of fun gave me the shivers. I took my last chance to back out, "Heck, that'll take too long. I want to get some basketball practice in before I go home."

I thought Joey would argue, but he smiled, "You're the boss, Sean. Let me get the Indian cards. You can look'em over while I change."

He settled me in a heavy wood armchair with a big box of Indian cards on my lap and Peanuts off to one side. In a minute he was back on my other side, "Let me show you the one I like best."

Out of the corner of my eye, I saw he was down to his undershorts. Joey, me, and undressing made my teeth go funny, but I tried not to show it.

"Which one?"

He leaned over from behind, "This one!"

I felt the lasso squeeze my arms against the back of the chair.

"Ha, ha! Haven't played cowboys and Indians since school," he said, looping more rope around me.

It was too late to fight, and my inside voice said, *Don't give Joey an excuse to put you in the wrong.*

"What am I supposed to do?" I asked, pretending it was a game.

"Just be a good little Indian while I tie you to the bottom of the chair . . . Peanuts, take the box."

Caught. Walked right into Joey's web. My outsides were OK, but my insides were running through some old feelings. Joey glanced up—our eyes met—that look! Made my heart sink. A scene from weeks ago played in my head: Joey stalking a fly at recess; with one swoop trapping it in his fist; plucking it out; with a thumb and finger on each wing, giving a quick jerk; the unlucky insect falling to the ground wingless; Joey turning toward me—his eyes with that look . . .

I couldn't figure why it pleasured him so, but I knew his fingers were itching to play me like a sweet potato. His face said it all; this time there'd be no cotton between him and my skin. I had no doubt, everything out in the open with Peanuts looking on. There'd be no running away, no bell, no rescue; Joey gloating over my shame. A

shudder as all this ran through my head was music to his ears, "How do yuh feel?" he grinned.

"Fine."

I'd been taught you always answered, "Fine," when someone asked how you felt.

"Nobody's interested in hearing a body recite his miseries," my grandmother used to tell me.

Besides more than anything, I wanted to be wrong—Joey mightn't be all bad. So I kept a flicker alive he'd remember I was his guest.

"You're gonna feel much better. We're gonna have some real fun. Peanuts, call Bozo in."

Bozo was a large, slow, brown and black hound, who at Joey's command rolled onto his back.

"How d'yuh like them balls?" Joey asked as he held Bozo's plums in his hand. "Ha, ha! Peanuts'd give anything for a pair like that. Watch this!"

Joey took hold of the dog's thing; the unhappy pooch tried to pull away. Joey commanded him back into place and worked red out of him, "How does that make you feel, Sean?"

Weak.

"Peanuts, go feel the front of his pants and see if he's stiff yet."

I was ever so grateful when Peanuts answered, "Don't want to!"

"He's all tied up, so what're yuh scared of? . . . Never mind, ha, ha! Sean likes it best when I do it."

As soon as Joey turned to me, Bozo scrambled to his feet, clanking his nails against the wood floor, dashed faster than you'd expect to the screen door, pushing it open with his nose, and raced to freedom—*lucky dog!*

My nerve caved in like a sand tunnel as Joey bore down on me. I strained and twisted, but the rope put an end to that.

"Ha, ha! Just pretend I'm that blonde nurse and you won't mind at all. Tell me, Young Man," he said, imitating a female voice, "do you have a problem with that thing between your legs swelling up?"

It was touch and go whether I'd break down and beg for a scrap of mercy that'd have as much chance as the oysters with the walrus, but my pride won out. Joey grunted as his fingers worked along my

pants, and when he reached the end, he pinched so hard I had to fight back tears.

"See you do, Naughty Boy! Well lucky for you I know how to cure it—don't even need bad-tasting medicine." Then switching to his own voice, "He's stiff all right, and big! Peanuts, I guarantee you never seen one big as his."

"Seen yours—"

"Shut up! Now, Sean, let me give you a prevue of coming attractions—just like at the movies. In a little while I'm gonna open you up wide, so's we can all enjoy that big banana. You don't mind sharing it, do you? Been waiting a long time for this, but I can wait another couple minutes just so's you have a chance to look forward to the swell time you're gonna have. Ha, ha! Let's make a bet. I bet by the time I pull it out, it's already drooling. What'll we bet? Ha, ha! I know: If you win I'll do you three times; if I win you only get done twice. 'Course if you said, 'Pretty please with sugar on it,' maybe I'd do you three times anyway."

He was the spider. I was the fly. And this young fly didn't savvy spider talk.

"You know the first thing I'll do when I've got it out? Peel it like I did Bozo. Ha, ha! Don't think I don't know you've got skin over the juicy part. Then I'll show you how to make bananas into bananas and cream. Geez, I'm going to love seeing you squirt!"

My brain was a block of ice, and I could only half follow what Joey was saying. *Squirt* got through to me; I took it like a nickname he'd decided on.

"Peanuts if you're real good I'll let you pull his dick out. You'd like that, wouldn't you?"

"Not me!"

"Oh, no? Just for that you can help me warm him up a touch more. I'd hate to lose my bet. Take your clothes off and show Sean how I've trained it to stand up like a tin soldier."

"Aw, Joey, not in front of someone!"

"Off!"

He undressed to his boxers.

"Please, Joey! I'll do like you want tonight."

"Then go get the jerking lotion."

He came back with a bottle that said *Jergen's Lotion.*

"Gotta take a crap, and by the time I'm done one of you better be ready."

Peanuts was alongside me, "Sorry, Sean."

"Wh-what're you going to do?"

He started on my top button . . .

"You don't want to do that!"

"Feels terrible what he does to me."

"Please don't!"

"It's OK, I'm used to seeing peters. Joey an' the gang're pantsing all the kids going into eighth grade. Three together yesterday—every kid skin-naked. Joey always gets them stiff-weenie; you'd've laughed watching them reach for the sky like bad guys in the movies."

He'd finished the buttons, showing my stretching boxers.

"Gotta get it out."

"Please, Peanuts!!"

"You'll see what I mean after he's done it to you."

He put his hand in and took hold.

"A-a-a-a-h!"

It was out in the air—me halfway to Planet Mongo.

"You have a big one. They did Boomer and Cooky a couple days ago—Boomer has a small one—tried to hide it. Joey'll want your nuts too—gotta get everything out in the open."

The shorts were unbuttoned all the way and pushed down my legs as far as the rope would let them.

"You're hairier than Joey."

He picked up the lotion, poured, kept pouring, had it running down my pole like it was a banana special turned on end—me one pool of slop . . .

A loud sound got through—"What's that!"

"Garage door—probably his mother."

"Do something! . . . Please do something!! . . . Do something!!!"

"She's seen me in my underwear."

"She hasn't seen me! Do something!!!!"

"Maybe I better."

He'd left my underwear down—me wet with lotion inside—*thank God my pants are buttoned—hope she doesn't spot the stretching.*

"Land sakes, Peanuts, don't tell me he has you-all playing Cowboys and Indians again? I declare, big as he is, Joey's still a little boy at heart."

"How do you do, Mrs. Hairgrove?" I said, remembering my manners.

# Chapter 46

**B**ryan was still away, and nobody asked me. If they had, I'd've put it in a nutshell: *Let sleeping Joeys lie.*

The axman was Bobby's cousin Lloyd—going into his senior year at high school—helped by two classmates. The brain was Bobby. Though only a quarter Italian, Bobby wasn't named Salone for nothing; ever since Patsy and his dollar, he'd been plotting his Sicilian revenge.

He wouldn't take my excuses, so I made my way to the ballplayers' clubhouse, wondering what it was about. Bobby met me outside; in a few minutes along came Janet and Doris—which didn't make my day.

"No point in waiting for Peanuts," Bobby said. "Knew he wouldn't show. Let's go in."

*Peanuts?* I thought, *Why Peanuts?*

"Right this way, Ladies and Gentlemen!"

It was dark at first. I made out the pitchman wearing an old-fashioned straw boater cocked over one eye. It was Lloyd twirling a cane.

"It is my privilege to present to you for the very first time in the United States of America a genuine Mexican Hairless dressed in his native costume consisting of a white linen handkerchief held up by a single cotton strand. Ha, ha! You could say his fate is hanging by a thread. Ladies and Gentlemen, gaze and be amazed!"

We turned to the thing being poked by the cane. It took a while to recognize Joey. His arms were stretched between two posts by ropes, making him into a cross; red and black war paint streaked his

face and chest. But what made him really hard to pick out was his head; it was white as an egg and just as smooth. Joey made a good savage.

"You are glad to have visitors, aren't you?"

"No!"

"That's not the right answer. I have to explain something to you, Ladies and Gentlemen. This Redskin and I have been playing a little game, but he's having a hard time remembering the rules; which is odd because he's the one who made them up. Now then, Bald Eagle, would you like to try again, or do we go to plan B?"

"Yeah, I'm glad to have visitors, Lloyd," Joey scowled through his paint.

"If the ladies will step around to the rear, they'll notice that what we have here is no Hollywood Indian. You'd never see a backside that bare in the movies."

"Hee, hee!" Doris tittered.

"Now, ladies and gentlemen, I want to prove to you beyond a shadow of a doubt that this is a genuine Mexican Hairless. Note the head—no hair. Check under the arms—no hair. Not convinced? All right then, would you mind helping us out, Young Lady?" Lloyd asked, pointing his cane at Doris.

"We'd like you to play a new version of an old game; it's called Lift the Handkerchief."

"Hee, hee! You want me to lift his handkerchief?"

"Keep her away from me!" Joey screamed, twisting his hips.

His thread snapped—the handkerchief fell. Joey'd been shaved clean, as smooth as Bobby two months before in this same place.

"Help!" shrieked Joey.

"Ladies, I direct your attention to the decoration the males of this tribe wear under their handkerchief."

The girls didn't need help; they'd found it on their own. Joey's growing pole looked like the one outside Jerry's barber shop—red and white stripes with a solid red cap.

"My goodness, it's big!" came from Doris.

"I've seen bigger," from Janet.

"Me too," said Bobby.

Quietly, I backed my way to the door . . .

# CHAPTER 47

"**Y**our father wants you to see a doctor; you won't even have to take your shirt off," my mother tacked on fast.

"What for?"

"To test for allergies, things that might give you asthma. This first time you'll be tested against animal dust—tame animals like dogs, cats, horses, cows, chickens, and so forth. This is a new field of medicine, and this man's a specialist in it.

So two days later we were in the City at a doctor's office. Mom was right; all I had to do was roll a sleeve up. On a tray were 10 little brown bottles with droppers in them. For each test, he made a scratch on my arm with a sharp knife and put a drop on it from the next bottle in line. He never got to the last bottle—

"Hold him!" the doctor shouted. "He's going into shock. I'll give him an injection of adrenaline."

I woke up in a strange bed. I remembered being at the doctor's office and something scary happening, but I had no idea how long ago that was, nor how I'd gotten into this bed. I was foggy about where and foggy about when. I was all mixed up, but otherwise all right—no asthma. Checking things out, I lifted the covers and saw what I'd just as soon not. Looking around the room, there were no clothes in sight.

"Feeling fine this morning, are we?"

She wore a white hat and uniform. *Must be a nurse, a young nurse.*

"Think I'm OK. Am I at the doctor's?"

"You're at the hospital. Now that you're feeling all right, we're going to make you feel even better by letting you have a nice bath before breakfast. Ha, ha! Did you know a bath's the first thing most boys ask for?"

"Don't seem to have any pajamas; I'll need something to wear if I'm getting up."

"I'll fetch you a gown after a while. The doctor doesn't want you up yet, so I'm giving you a bath in bed. Be right back; didn't bring my cart because I wasn't sure you'd be awake."

I was clamping my jaws, tightening my legs, trying to hold back—it didn't work. The only thing I could think of was to roll onto my stomach.

The nurse wheeled in a cart that had a basin and stuff.

"You can just leave that. I'll wash myself if you don't mind."

"Ha, ha! I can tell you're the bashful type; they're the most fun. Don't worry, I've done hundreds of boys and never lost a one."

My covers came away in her hand. "I forgot to ask, do you want to urinate? I'll get a bedpan."

"No thanks!"

I wondered whether the nurse would've watched me go. That moved things along.

"Now then, shall we turn over?"

"C-can't you do this side?"

"All right, but sooner or later you'll have to introduce me to your little brother—if you get what I mean."

"Anything you need, Beautiful? Anything special?" A young man had his head in the doorway.

"You can bring some sheets and a gown if you want."

"Not what I had in mind, but your wish is my command," the helper said, letting the door close behind him.

The nurse washed my neck, shoulders, arms, and back. I flinched as she got to my bottom, and when she put her soapy hand between the backs of my legs, I'd like to've catapulted off the bed.

"Here're your sheets and gown, Gorgeous. Anything else I can do for you?"

The worker was in the room, and the last thing I wanted was an audience.

"You can help me roll him over. He's a bit jumpy, and I don't think he'll want to be turned."

"You can turn me anytime you want, Darlin'. What's the matter, Sport? Not every day you get a beautiful girl to run her hands over you. I've been trying to get her to do that to me for a month. Some guys don't know when they've got it good."

He stepped toward me—

"W-w-wait! . . . I-I'll do it!"

He waited . . .

"A-alone," I murmured.

"Alone?" came from the nurse.

"Don't you get it, Doll? He wants to be alone with you. Can't say I blame him. Okay, Sport, you don't have to hit me on the head with a sledge hammer; two's company and three's a crowd."

". . . Well, he's gone," the nurse said. "Not going to have to call him back, am I?"

Hot all over, I got both arms under me and rolled onto my back. The nurse smiled, reached out, took hold of my wrists, picked up my arms, and laid them at my sides, leaving my bone bare as Mother Hubbard's cupboard.

"That's better. Mustn't be shy, must we? Thought I was going to meet your little brother, but now I see he's Great Big Billy Goat Gruff."

She brought a clean bowl of water from the sink and washed my face and chest.

"Gets in the way, doesn't he?" she said, as she swabbed my belly button.

Taking the bar of soap, she worked up a lather to suds between my legs, setting off feelings I'd never been introduced to. I shut my eyes to take my mind off what was happening. That no sooner done, she said, "You realize this is a Jewish hospital, so we don't get many patients who haven't been circumcised; just the same I know it's proper hygiene to wash under a boy's foreskin."

But when she took my pole in one hand and pushed the skin back with her other hand, she got every bit of my attention—"A-a-a-a-a-a-h!"—I stiffened my back and clutched the bottom sheet, holding on for dear life—my secret self wasn't a secret any more. The skin was tight, but she got everything into the open. My knob swelled like red bubble gum as she washed it with warm water. For

the first time I got an idea of what Bryan meant by fun; her fingers on my raw place made feelings so strong I cried out, "O-o-o-o-o-h! Please stop!"

"Sorry! Not used to washing uncircumcised boys."

It couldn't be happening—no way I could be handled like this and live—I tried wishing myself home to my own bed where it would end up a dream.

"Now let's get the sheath back over the glans," she said, teaching me some new words.

"It won't come!—I can't do it!—have to get some help!—don't move!—I'll be right back!"

I lay like a turned turtle, my bulb lit to welcome visitors. At first I couldn't move, but fixing on that swaying red poppy convinced me there was no time to lose. I'd no sooner flipped onto my stomach when the young nurse came with an old nurse.

"This is the Matron; she wants to have a look."

I shook my head.

"Boys!" said the new one. "See if you can get Dr. Stein; he's on floor duty."

The young one came back with a grey-haired doctor.

"Well, well, hear you've been frightening our nurses. You ought to be ashamed, a boy your age. How are you feeling?"

"F-fine."

"Can you turn over for me?"

My eyes rolled from the old female to the young female.

"He's shy," my washer said.

"No chance of fazing our nurses; they're frontline veterans of the battle of the sexes. Seems every time I walk into a room, one of them's bent over some red-faced male in the state of Adam. I'm continually amazed at the stories nurses come up with to separate a chap from his undies."

"Really, Dr. Stein! You shouldn't go on like that in front of a youngster. He'll believe you."

"I say only what is true. Now then, shall we take a look?"

"D-do we need . . . th-them?" I stammered, still eyeing the nurses.

"Ah! There you have touched on a deep question: Do males need females? Too deep for me. Matron, I'll take over here. If you'll send the orderly with some ice, that's all I'll require."

The nurses gone, the doctor asked, "Are you always this embarrassed about being seen?"

I nodded.

"Perhaps I've forgotten what it's like to be young. How old are you?"

"Fourteen."

"Fourteen . . . yes, I remember . . . or do I? Enough of that! Shall we get on with it?"

"C-couldn't we wait till after he's brought the ice?"

The easy-going helper came with a bowl of ice cubes. With the doctor there, he didn't say a word, just set the bowl down and stood by the bed.

The doctor looked at me, then at the orderly, "Don't you have some other duties?"

The young man made a beeline for the hall.

"I take it you also get embarrassed at being seen by other males?"

I nodded.

"Both young and old?"

I nodded.

"Well, include me out. Dare say I've seen more male organs than you've seen bull elephants."

This pulled a smile from me, "Not sure I've ever seen a bull elephant."

"Therefore, my statement is patently true. Getting back to my credentials on the male organ, I've examined white ones, black ones, brown ones, yellow ones, red ones, pink ones, blue-from-cold ones, and purple-green-from-infection ones. And now you've got my curiosity up. Shall I add you to my butterfly collection?"

He put both hands under me and flapjacked me onto my back.

"Remarkable! Fourteen, you say? Quite remarkable! The foreskin is tight—no two ways about that. Let's try some ice."

After getting me good and numb, he put things where they belonged.

"I know an excellent man at the Children's Clinic who specializes in adolescents. I'll tell him your problem and arrange an interview. He's a psychoanalyst as well as a practicing MD; he'll deal with the psychological aspects before deciding whether you should be circumcised."

# CHAPTER 48

It's hard to believe, but in the '30s the doctor came to your house.

"How in tarnation can they expect a body to get up from a sick bed and go out into all kinds of weather without catching his death?" An old-timer would've asked.

Our family had two doctors, a husband and wife who saw each other's patients. When you phoned the Palmerstons, you never knew who'd show up. I was in bed with my pajama top open as Dr. Beatrice Palmerston listened to my chest, "Not too serious, but I shall leave some potassium iodide drops to foster expectoration," she said to my mother in her high-toned talk.

I'd noticed from an earlier visit that while Dr. Bea talked like a duchess, her sense of humor would've been right at home in a barnyard.

"I believe there was something else your husband had in mind, but he did not elaborate."

My mother answered with a flush, "Doctor, would you please come into the living room."

Once they'd gone, I tiptoed into the hall to listen to what I knew had to be about me.

"You see, I think my husband expected Dr. William would come— since Sean is now 14—"

"Ha! I thought so! It is true I normally do not attend boys past the age of 12—William's idea—but I think it stuff and nonsense. I am quite familiar with the—ha, ha!—salient features of male anatomy. Among other things, I have served as a harem-of-one for 22 years.

I presume we are dealing with a below-the-waist problem. What exactly?"

"Well, Sean has this foreskin—"

"Humph! William has a foreskin—although I am not at all certain he would appreciate me describing it to our female patients—and I assume since Sean has one, his father has one. Am I correct?"

"I . . . think so."

"You do not know what a foreskin looks like?"

"I've never . . . the fact is, Doctor, my husband is extremely modest."

"Never! My dear girl! I do not shock easily, but you have succeeded in shocking me. As your personal physician I insist we have a session concerning the facts of life. But for the moment let us deal with Sean. What exactly is the problem with his foreskin?"

"I believe it's rather . . . tight."

"It is too much to hope that you know the exact stage of his development—for example, whether he has morning erections."

"Oh, yes! I've seen—"

*O God!*

"Ha, ha!! You have seen your son's but not your husband's!"

"It was quite by accident. For some reason—maybe it's a new fad—Sean and a friend were sleeping in the altogether. I came to wake them—they didn't hear me knock—I opened the door and the sheet was on the floor. They were both . . . in that condition."

"Ha, ha! That must have been worth a second look. Would you say Sean is well-developed?"

"Yes, I'm sure of it. I think he's inherited his father's size."

"I thought you had never—but—ha, ha!—a wife does not necessarily have to *see*, does she? In any case it certainly will do no harm to take a peek at Sean. Indeed I am quite enthusiastic; it may broaden my background in comparative anatomy."

I'd heard more than I bargained for, way more—*my father bashful!* I tore back to my room, grabbed some clothes, and ducked out my bedroom window. *No lady doctor for that, thank you!*

# CHAPTER 49

**M**y father laid the law down. They didn't tell me why, but I put two and two together. All the way to the Clinic, I was in a stew. *Everything off or just unbutton?* I couldn't decide which'd be worse. In some ways being naked might be better than reaching in and pulling it out; it would be some excuse for what I'd show.

When the first thing Dr. Reiter said was, "Today you and I are going to talk—no examination, only talk." I felt like this prisoner in a movie I'd seen who gets pardoned by the Governor just as the straps of the electric chair are being fastened around his ankles.

I was studying Dr. Reiter's beard—bushy like the ones on the cough drop box—when his phone rang . . . "I must check a patient in the ward. Please wait. I will be back in 20 minutes."

I'd been sitting for no more than five minutes when a giant nurse came up to me. The picture of her carrying a boy under each arm flashed through my head, and I missed what she said.

"What did you say?"

"I said, 'You're a new patient. Have you had your lab work?'"

"What's that?"

"Just routine. Come with me."

"But Dr. Reiter told me to wait. Said he'd be back in 20 minutes."

"Ha, ha! With Dr. Reiter 20 minutes can be 2 hours. This won't take long; I'll see you're rushed through. What Dr. Reiter says is one thing; the rules of the Clinic are another. Come with me!" she said in a voice that got its way.

I followed her to where she picked up a paper, "I'll hand this in for you. Name and date of birth?"

"Sean Lacey, S-E-A-N L-A-C-E-Y, May thirtieth, nineteen twenty-four."

"Putting Standard Entrance Exam. Take about 15 minutes."

She stopped next to a door marked 121, "This is where you come back to when you're ready."

"121," I said.

She led me around a corner, down a hall, around another corner, where we met a lady who didn't look old enough to be what she was.

"I don't know what they've done with my son Harold. Have you seen a 13-year-old with blond hair?"

"Can't keep track of them all," the nurse answered.

The visitor smiled at me and said, "It's a little frightening for you boys, isn't it?"

"Yes Ma'am."

We went to a door marked 143, "Here's where you undress; then you go back to 121."

"U-undress? U-undress how far?"

"Ha, ha! Just to your toes."

"You mean n-naked? And walk through the halls?"

"Ha, ha! There are towels and baskets. Put your clothes in a basket and yourself in a towel."

Better than nothing. If I could keep hold of the towel, and if I was left by myself to get into it, I might see another sunset.

"I'll go ahead and arrange priority, so don't dawdle!"

Like it was Dracula's house at midnight, I inched 143 open. Inside was a closet with two benches. But what caught my eye was the naked boy—you could tell he was oriental—who stood up and made a low bow. I took him to be older than me, though he was shorter, thinner, and less grownup in other ways. After finishing his bow, he picked up a pile with slipper-shoes on top and held it out . . . "Basket! Put them in a basket."

He smiled and pushed his clothes at me again. I took the pile, looked around, and dropped it into a wire basket, "Basket!" I said.

The boy smiled, made another bow, opened the door, and stepped out.

"Wait!" I shouted, grabbing a towel off a stack and rushing after him.

He was standing in the middle of the hall where he'd stopped. I quick put the towel around him, "Towel! Important wear towel!"

He got the idea because he tucked the towel in good before smiling, bowing, and going on his way. Back inside, I was jumpy. What'd just happened was a bad sign, but I knew what to do. The important thing as I saw it was to get into a towel before the nurse's next victim came through the door. Using a tip from Bryan, I started on the multiplication table to take my mind off what was happening, "7 times 9 is 63," and there I was wrapped in white.

Getting into the towel without a hitch helped, and the trip through the halls didn't turn up much, but my heart was in my mouth as I opened 121. Straight across was a second door with no number; the walls were a dirty peeling grey. No window. No air. What light there was came from a flickering bulb hanging from a cord in the ceiling. Two walls were lined with chairs, all but one filled with boys. I picked out the friendly Oriental, who gave me a smile and pointed to his towel. Of the others, the oldest looked about 13. I was on my way to the empty chair when a man in white came out of the inside door with a glass jar in his hand.

"Lacey! Who's Lacey?"

"Me," I said in a low voice.

"Yo' don't look so special."

"S-special?"

"Seems yo're a rush job. They took away my help today and only own one pair o' hands. Do what I can. Meantime, ain't had my mornin' tea yet. I'd take it kindly if yo'd fill this," he said, handing me the jar.

"There's no drinking fountain."

"Just a country boy, take it straight from the hose."

"The hose?"

He made a fist down low and stuck out his thumb, "Pssss!" he grinned.

My legs turned to custard, and I dove for the back of the chair to save myself.

"Wh-wh-wh-where?"

"Suit yo'self!" he said, waving his arm around the dirty walls.

I turned a full circle, looking for something . . . anything . . . I didn't find it.

Putting me down as simpleminded, the medic called the 13-year-old.

"Yo' there! Come here!"

He took the jar and gave it to the boy, "Make damn shore he don't spill! Understan?"

The boy did some fast head bobs, "Yessir!"

"I'll keep this for yo'," the medic said, whipping my towel off and disappearing with it into the inner room.

It didn't happen right away, it took a while to dawn. Like this soldier in no-man's land who keeps reaching for the leg that's been blown to smithereens, I kept pawing at myself for the cloth. When it sank in that the towel'n me had parted company, blood began rushing everywhere. Some sounds that went up and down like a singer practicing made it into my head. It was the oriental boy watching the 13-year-old track my stalk. When I got straight up, the tracker got fuddled; he ended with the jar pointing down, ready to hang on a peg. Deciding that was no good, he flipped the glass and moved it to where he figured it'd catch something. No saying how long this would've gone on if the twittering of the younger boys hadn't gotten through to me. Life oozed back in . . .

"My tow-ow-ow-el!" bounced off the walls.

Fast as a cat could wink her eye, I was being wrapped by my friend who was naked again. He smiled and gave a low bow. I doubt I did a smile, but clutching the towel, I made a bow. Though there'd've been pretty good agreement I was in no shape to stroll the halls, I had just one thought: 143. There was only one answer: speed. I opened 121 and checked the hall: empty. The rabbit took off . . .

Rounding the first corner, I didn't spot Harold's mother in time. She must've seen me because she reached out to save herself. At the last fraction of a second, I zagged, going by with just a brush, but enough for her hand to hunt for something to hang onto and come away with a towel. In no mood to chat about the change in the weather, I didn't brake for repairs. "Pardon me!" came out over my shoulder as I stepped on the gas and raced toward my target . . .

Hitting the final curve naked, I was on the lookout for anything that moved. I spotted a boy-in-towel halfway out of 143, head

turned, testing the water. I let out all the stops, giving it everything I had. The boy worked up enough courage to take the plunge. He took two steps into the hall before sighting me bearing down like a charging rhinoceros . . .

"O Jesus!" he let out as I thundered past. "That's how they send you back!"

# Chapter 50

**M**aking my way to Dr. Reiter's I was a Mohawk scout, sneaking around each bend, going over the ground of a recent raid, afraid of coming face-to-face with Harold's mother.

*What would we have to say to each other?*

I got to his office 15 minutes ahead of Dr. Reiter, who began by telling me he was a Freudian. I'd never heard of the place, so that was no help. Like I'd know what they meant, he threw in a bunch of doctor words: neurosis, psychosis, some kind of complex, ego, superego, and a little word *id* I remembered to look up, but couldn't make any sense of.

Then following a hint given him by Dr. Stein, he put his nose to the same trail as Bryan.

"So-o-o!" he said, drumming his fingertips together, "Your father has not seen you naked since you were a small boy. And what about you, have you seen your father naked?"

"N-not that I remember."

"Interesting! And you have no curiosity? You have never wondered what your father might look like naked?"

I blushed as Bryan's words came to me: *I'd want to see my dad's just to find out how big mine was going to get.*

"D-don't think so."

"But you are not certain, yes? Some things we do not admit, even to ourselves; however, all that will come out in good time. We will have your father bring you for your next appointment; I want to ask him some questions. So often it turns out that heredity plays a decisive role in these cases."

Next, pouncing on each mumbled word, he dragged my hospital morning out of me, then stopped to make a phone call.

"This is Dr. Reiter. Could you send that new trainee to my office? Yes, in about twenty minutes."

We worked backward to the high school locker room and Horse Hill. I didn't mention 121, the night with Ted I couldn't talk about, I left out the priests, but there was enough to get Dr. Reiter nodding his head and rubbing his hands.

In a deep voice he came out with, "Acute neurotic modesty. Quite probably we could trace its origins to infantile narcissism. We must accustom you to the nakedness of both other males and yourself. Herr Professor Freud might not agree with me, but I believe in confronting the patient with progressively stronger doses of precisely those situations he is most anxious to avoid. A harsh but—"

We were interrupted by a dream in white—*what every girl should look like.* She had to be new-16—red-gold hair hanging long, high cheek bones, green eyes. With her was a cute enough bobbed blonde probably two years older.

"You wanted to see one of us, Dr. Reiter? I'm Phyllis in my second week at the Clinic. This is Elizabeth; she's in her first week."

"Please meet Sean. I had not realized there were two of you. Thank you both for coming, but it is Elizabeth for whom I have a question."

"Anytime, Dr. Reiter, I'll be getting back then. Be seeing you, Sean!" Phyllis said. "Bound to come my way sooner or later—they all do."

The blonde gone, the doctor turned to the dream girl, "I was hoping you could convince Sean that not all nurses are the dragons he thinks they are."

"With two years of high school to finish, I'm lucky to be an aide. What do you have against nurses? Is it something they've done to you personally?"

I went red to the roots of my hair.

"It seems one of them gave him a sponge bath. She may have been a trifle overzealous."

"I can sympathize. I had to help a ward patient with a tub bath this morning, an 11-year-old who'd been in bed a week."

"How did it turn out?"

"Embarrassing."

"For the patient or for you?"

"Both. He was speechless at being naked in front of a girl for 20 minutes. I was embarrassed because . . ." A pink flush showed up her cheek bones. ". . . well I didn't think boys his age—I didn't know they got that way. I'm afraid I wasn't his idea of a mother substitute."

"Not many males would cast you in that role. How would you feel about working with older boys? Suppose, for example, you were assigned the disagreeable duty of undressing Sean?"

I sank low in the chair, my face on fire. I knew Dr. Reiter meant to be funny, but I didn't think much of his joke. Elizabeth gave me a smile and I turned three shades redder.

"Well, since I want to learn nursing, I guess I'd do my duty."

She put her face in front of mine, inviting me to dive into her cool green eyes, "I promise you, Sean, I'd be ever so gentle."

I had to grab the arms of my chair to keep from melting onto the floor.

"Thank you for coming, Elizabeth. For the sake of all male patients, I hope you do become a nurse," Dr. Reiter said with a nod.

". . . Now there goes a beautiful girl. You are probably wondering why I had her come. I want her to be the leading lady in a little drama you and I are going to compose. Let me explain: Sometimes in cases like yours, where the patient finds certain realities too difficult to cope with, we bridge the gap with a substitute reality. Look through that door. See the examining table? Study it closely. I want you to imagine yourself lying faceup on that table with that lovely girl beside you. You hear me, the doctor, say, 'Nurse, prepare the patient for examination.' What do you think she will do? . . . I am asking you, what will she do?"

"T-take off some of my cl-clothes?"

"How many clothes?"

"I guess that would depend on the kind of doctor."

"But who is the doctor? I already told you that."

"Oh! You're the doctor."

"Exactly! Remember—no need to be embarrassed—this is make-believe. How many clothes will she be taking off?"

Gulping, I got out, "All my clothes?"

"Excellent. You are grasping the idea. She is going to take off all your clothes. I want you to build a picture in your head of how it

would be, how you would react, how you would feel as she takes off each item of clothing. I gather from what you have told me that if we were discussing reality, somewhere in the process you would experience a problem. Tell me at what point you believe that would happen."

"When she starts untying my first shoelace."

"I see! Well after all, that is the reason for the exercise. I want you in the drama to practice self-control. Run the scene through your head and observe how long you can remain composed. The goal, if I may put it somewhat poetically, is to see yourself fully exposed, relaxed and free of tension, as she warms you with her smile. We could set further goals, but no need to anticipate. For now, I would like you to run through your reality substitute several times a day, adding more detail each performance: how she undoes your buttons, her method of working your trousers off, how she executes the coup de grace with your undershorts, the feel of her fingers—"

"Soft and cool—"

"Just so! That is what you must do; enter into the spirit of things! We are going to declare war on your modesty. I want you to think of it as *The Enemy*. As one of the first skirmishes in our campaign, I shall arrange with your mother to have a younger boy stay with you a few days. That will place you in a position of dominance. You will be the older brother. I want you to forget your modesty—more, I want you to challenge it to a duel! Will you make that effort for me?"

"I-I'll try."

"I have your word on it?"

"You have my word."

"Then here are some things you must do . . ."

The trip to the City had its reward. As a treat, my mother took me to the Merry-Go-Round restaurant for lunch. The booths were laid out around a revolving belt inside a glass case. Dish after dish of mouth-watering desserts sailed by. You only had to lift the glass door and latch onto whatever took your fancy. The bill depended on the number of plates left on your table. I wondered whether anyone ate the dessert and slipped the empty dish back onto the belt.

All through my hot roast beef sandwich and mashed potatoes pooled with gravy, I was wrestling with what to choose. I couldn't decide, old-fashioned strawberry shortcake or chocolate pie, both piled high with whipped cream so thick it was almost yellow.

My mother guessed what was going on, "I'm too full for dessert. Could you do me a favor and eat mine?"

At times like that I realized how much I loved her.

# CHAPTER 51

They called them coffin nails. There were four big brands: Camels, Lucky Strikes, Philip Morris, and Chesterfields. There were also little brands like Wings—10 cents a pack—and Marlboros— red tips so a lady's lipstick wouldn't show. In the '30s the hands in Marlboro Country wore dresses. For real cowboys and tightwads there was Bull Durham. A nickel bought you a sack of tobacco with a pull string and a pack of papers. Some stores threw in matches.

"One Bull Durham, please," I said in my deepest voice.
"For your father?"
"Yessir, for my father."
"That'll be five cents."
"Do matches come with it?"
He reached under the counter and tossed me a book, "How're you fixed for spit?"

I was carrying out Dr. Reiter's instructions, playing big brother to my cousin, the son of my father's sister. That afternoon, two weeks before his 13th birthday, Davy'd come by bus. Soon as we were alone, he sent me to buy smokes, "'Less you're scared to!"
He handed over the Indian Head nickel from a Chinese puzzle box whose secret place was stuffed with do-re-mi. I wasn't about to admit to this whippersnapper cousin I'd never so much as taken a puff. I went along hook, line, and sinker, leading him bent over to the center of a drain pipe that ran under the railroad tracks to the creek.

With one arm in a sling, I'd seen a movie cowboy roll his own, and I was sure I could do the same. But using two hands neither Davy nor me could get the hang of keeping the tobacco inside the paper. Finally with the pouch half empty, I sucked in enough smoke to make me sick as a dog.

Sheepish about the smoking, Davy ran for more ammunition from the Chinese box. When he got back we headed for the candy store by the railway station, where he handed me my first-ever 10-cent bar, a U-No by Cardinet. For all my stomach, the creamy chocolate really did melt in my mouth. *This must be how the other half lives.*

Dr. Reiter'd told me exactly what to do this first night. Before putting my pajamas on, I was to stand naked a few seconds, "providing your little brother a full front view." This "in as casual a manner as possible."

Bryan was off on his second week of camp, and I missed his advice. For though I knew Dr. Reiter was a smart man, he was a grownup talking about boy stuff. Still, I'd given my word, so I made up my mind to steer the course till the first torpedo struck hard amidships and it was every kid for himself. My heart beating like a tom-tom, I said to Davy, "About time to slip off the duds and give the old skin a breath of air."

"What do you mean, skin?"

"Mean it's time to get into our pj's. Ha, ha! Can't very well do that without showing a little skin."

"I'm not showing any skin! I'm changing in the bathroom! And that's another thing, there's no lock on the door. How do I know you won't walk in on me?"

I grabbed this bolt from the blue like a life preserver in the China Sea. I'd promised to play by the rules, but if Davy wouldn't go along, Dr. Reiter'd have to put it down as a case of that's-the-way-the-ball-bounces. After all, he knew I was no boy of steel.

"We'll make a pact; when one of us is in the bathroom, the other doesn't go in. Furthermore, I don't undress in front of you, and you don't undress in front of me. OK?"

"Guess it'll have to be, but one more thing, I'm sleeping on the rug."

"God help us, what a family! You sleep in the bed; I'll take the rug."

It was the last day of Davy's visit; he'd be leaving by bus the next morning. We'd never gone back to being the pals of our first hours together. I went my way, and he went his—usually to the store for sweets. I'd seen him take off bright and early in his spotless white ducks, which he was peacock-proud of, and which I knew he meant to wear on his trip home. I guessed he wanted to show off to the lady owner who'd taken a fancy to this well-dressed nickel machine. On the spur of the moment I decided on a little spy work to check if my hunch was right. But Davy'd been gone longer'n I thought. I was almost to the old green bridge when I saw some boys taking the footpath on the far side, one of them wearing white pants. I ran out onto the wood planks and looked down at the creek bed below to see a scared Davy in the middle of Joey and his bunch.

"What're you doing with my cousin!"

"Ha, ha! Don't tell me this pretty boy's your cousin? You know what he went and did? Threw a perfectly good ice-cream cone into this here mud hole," Joey answered.

"Why would he do that?"

"We made him give us each a lick, and after we was done he just tossed it away. Now that wasn't very considerate was it? If he was all done, he should've let us have it. You know me, Sean, I'm fair as you can get, but he'll have to pay for that little insult. Ha, ha! Reckon he'll end up joining that cone in the mud."

"Christ, Joey! You'll ruin his good pants!"

"You know me better'n that, Sean; he won't be wearing pants. Think I'd pass up a chance to see if big salamis run in the family?"

In the middle of this—at *pants*—Joey stuck his hand over Davy's mouth to gag his squeal, and—at *salamis*—there was big-time goings-on in my belly.

"Tell you what, Sean, make you a deal; if you wanna pay the price for him, we'll leave him go. 'Course in your case the price'd be a mite stiffer. Bill and Mac, why don't you help Sean down?"

I had no say—the rabbit took charge—started to run—no stopping till we got to my room.

I was shaking like a leaf in November, lying on the rug, my face buried in my hands, feeling yellow as a buttercup . . . The time ticked by . . . Trembling, I went to the bathroom, took my clothes off, and stepped into the shower to calm myself. As I turned off the spray, I

heard the front door open. Dripping, I tied a towel around my waist and went to the bedroom.

"You've got to help him—you may never in your life play another big brother. You have to make this an Academy-Award performance—pretend you're Bryan."

Davy came in holding a ball of clothes, barefoot and bare on top, muddy all over except his white ducks, which were stained by mud coming through from the inside.

"Sure and you're a sight for sore eyes; I'm that glad to see you. Let me take that stuff off your hands," I said, lifting his bundle.

He was too out of it to notice my words or my towel.

"So what happened?" I asked.

No answer.

"Let's see if I can reconstruct the crime. They took off your shoes and socks; they took off your shirt. What about the pants? Since you're muddy on the outside, and they're muddy on the inside, they took them off too—how'm I doing?"

No answer.

"Now we come to the heart of the matter; what about your undershorts? Ah! Here they are in the pile of clothes. Therefore, they had you naked as the day you practiced your first scream, and you were embarrassed something turrible, right?"

"Y-y-yes!" Davy blubbered.

I pulled him down beside me on the floor and put his head against my chest.

"Now you have to give old Sherlock a clue. What did they do next?"

"T-tied my hands behind my b-back with my shoe laces."

"Go on!" I said, hugging him closer. "Then what?"

The words spilled out, "The big short-haired kid practiced on me with his lasso—they were all laughing—it was awful! His rope caught me, an' he pulled it tight. Then he started running, making me follow along like a circus pony."

"He had his rope around your neck?"

"Not my neck. It was around my . . ."

"I see it all! He had his rope around that railroad spike you keep inside your pants."

"You know about it?"

"Those spikes are the family curse; crop up every time a male descendant of Grandpa Lacey is pantsed naked."

"Have you been pantsed naked?"

"Aye, me boy, that I have, and on more than one occasion."

"Golly!"

"Should've guessed right off about the Lacey spike, but I wasn't sure you were old enough."

"I'm old enough all right; I've got some hairs!"

"So was that the end, being led around like a horse?"

"Mostly. They took turns pulling me with the rope—it hurt—making fun of my . . . Anyway they finally got tired. Before they left, they untied my shoe laces and dumped me in the mud."

I felt to blame, and I was worried. Not sure how to put it, I used Bobby's word, "What about your penis? Did the rope cut through the skin?"

"My what? Oh!" he said, "Not sure—feels sore."

I stood up and pulled him to his feet, "Slip your pants off."

"Hey, nothing doing!"

"OK, my mother'll examine you."

That made him think.

"Look," I coaxed, "I've given boys baths—"

"You have?"

"Dozens. You've just been seen by half the town, and I'm you're cousin. Which'll it be, my mother or me?"

"You, I guess, but afterwards you have to do something."

"Sure, if I can."

He did some fiddling, pushed his pants to the floor, and stayed bent over.

"It's OK," I said, "Straighten up in memory of Grandpa."

Davy showed his Lacey blood, but it took a while to spot the hairs he'd bragged on.

"The skin's been rubbed, but it'll heal. I'll get you some salve."

As he pulled his pants up, I asked, "Now what did you want me to do?"

"Show me yours."

"Certainly not!"

"Why not?"

"Wouldn't be right."

"Why?"

"Because I'm older and—well you know—more . . . developed."

"You mean hairier?"

"Yes, and . . ."

"And what?"

". . . Bigger."

"You promised. You've seen mine; it's fair I see yours. Unless you show me, I'll tell on you."

"Tell on me? I didn't do anything."

"You ran away and left me."

That hit a sore spot. I remembered my word to Dr. Reiter and braced myself to bite the bullet. I closed my eyes . . . undid the knot . . . let go . . . felt the towel fall . . . felt myself snap to attention . . . heard, "Criminey!" . . . and scrambled for the towel . . .

"Davy wants to take a shower with you," my father told me.

"I'm not—"

"*Yes you are.*"

# CHAPTER 52

**I**n a family meeting it was decided I'd go to the Clinic by myself. This made me feel terribly grownup, but I wondered if I could do the two streetcar transfers that'd get me a block from the door. It would be my last ride on the passenger ferry. The auto ferry had already closed its docks, killed by the opening of the Bridge. On that day our school let out, and we hurrahed as we danced along the pavement, little knowing we were celebrating the end of our county's country ways.

Aboard the ferry, looking toward the two towers, I saw a white fog rolling like a river of cotton wide as the Mississippi into the Bay. By afternoon the heavy mist blanketed the water, and homeward bound the ferry's foghorn boomed to warn other boats. Halfway across, our sister ship coming from the north joined in. Bells rang and whistles blew; the two boats almost touched as they passed fully lit in fog so thick neither could see the other.

Dr. Reiter'd no sooner pulled Davy out of me when—eyes closed, stretched out on his table—"Nurse, prepare the patient for examination!"—he put me through my dream.

After getting me all worked up, he came out with, "Go upstairs to room 218. When Elizabeth is finished with you, come back here." I didn't like the sound of *finished with you*.

Room 218 was a small room with nothing much in it but a bathtub. "God! She's going to give me a bath!"

Just then a barefoot boy in a nightgown came through the door pushed along by Elizabeth looking like a strawberry soda, "Sean, this is Billy. Dr. Reiter wants you to observe his bath."

Probably wasn't the news Billy was waiting to hear, but I could've danced a jig. *Better him than me.*

"Tell Sean how old you are."

Billy wasn't talking.

"He's 12," she said, closing the door.

Elizabeth started the water running and turned to me, "You can take his nightgown off."

I looked at Billy; he wasn't smiling.

"I don't think he wants me to."

She walked over, "How silly! You're a boy, he's a boy. Why would he mind? Raise your arms, Billy," she said, pulling his nightie off. "They don't get hair till their teens," she taught me.

A skinny kid, we had something in common—he wasn't circumcised either. But Billy behaved himself.

*If only I could be like that.*

Elizabeth sat him in the tub and started shampooing the hair he did have.

"We're supposed to do every part twice."

Then she stood him with his back to us and started soaping; when she got to his bottom, my trouble started. It seemed like she did more stroking than scrubbing—all at once I was in my dream, and I was the one being stroked . . . next thing I knew, she had him turned around with his soft weenie in her soapy hand . . .

". . . Sean! . . . Sean! . . . Sean! . . ."

". . . What?"

"Fill that pitcher with warm water, please . . . When I pull back his foreskin, pour it over him."

She stretched things—Billy quit behaving himself—and his button red as a berry, I poured.

"You're not used to seeing uncircumcised boys, are you? They're not much different; it's just that they slide back and forth, like so," she said, showing me.

*O Jesus!* I did a turn and grabbed myself—I wasn't staying for the second soaping—don't know what I did with the pitcher.

"Have to get back to Dr. Reiter!" I called over my shoulder.

I raced into the restroom next door, pulled everything down, and ran cold water over myself.

Dr. Reiter was full of surprises.

"I have arranged for you to go through your entrance examination in the company of an older boy who is also my patient."

"You mean put on a towel in 143?"

"You know about Room 143?"

"A nurse showed me."

"Fine, you will be able to take him there. The boy you will be with is 16. He and his mother live alone without companions on a large isolated estate—she acted in silent films. Years ago she purchased the property, but now there is barely enough income to keep the two of them—not a single servant to help with the place, and she tutors her son at home. Of course, she could sell off some of the land, but she refuses to do that; though I believe she occasionally parts with a piece of jewelry. For years she has been a recluse."

"Recluse?"

"A hermit, and she has made her son a hermit with her . . . Ah! Here he is. Sean, meet Robert."

I was facing a slender, good-looking boy with dark red hair, darker than I'd ever seen.

"Here are your forms; take them along. Robert, Sean will show you where to go and what to do. You can rely on him to help in any way he can. Am I correct, Sean?"

"Absolutely!"

Walking down the hall Robert never said a word.

"See, that's room 121, the place we come back to."

When we got to 143, I opened the door, "We sit on those benches to take our clothes off; then we put a towel on."

"Tog-gether?"

It dawned why Dr. Reiter'd teamed us up—*this kid has it worse than me*. Though right then I was just as antsy. I'd gotten my dream to where I was down to my pants without an alarm clanging, but soon as Elizabeth touched the first button . . . That topped off by Billy's bath made it a lead-pipe cinch I couldn't get into a towel without disgracing Clan Lacey.

"I'll wait in the hall till you've got your towel on."

I was about to stick my head in when Robert stuck his out.

"What ab-bout our clothes?"

"I'll take care of them. Would you sort of keep watch outside while I change?"

"Emb-barrassed. Can I stay? I'll sit with my b-back turned."

What could I say? After I got my towel on and put our clothes into baskets, I said, "Come on, let's get it over with."

Walking toward 121, I began to worry. I didn't want to borrow trouble, but I had to warn Robert.

"There's this doctor, medic, something like that; he might ask us to drop our towels for a minute," I said, breaking it gently.

"Y-you don't mind?"

"I do mind! May as well warn you; when I'm naked in front of someone—just about anyone—my . . . my . . . you know—swells up."

"Y-you mean—?"

"I mean the thing between my legs—you do have one?"

No answer, he just fixed his towel tighter.

Dirty walls pressed in on us as I led Robert to a chair in 121 across from two younger boys. A pair of towels came out the unmarked door making for the hall, followed by the Southern medic.

I was carrying the forms, which he ran his eyes over.

"Which one's 16?"

"He is."

"Don't say! Take you-all right away!"

"Those boys were here first," I said.

"They're used to waitin'. Don't get older boys to come here much, so we give them special consideration. When yo're sweet sixteen, yo' get the red-carpet treatment."

He turned to Robert, "Listen, Boy, going to tell yo' and tell yo' just once. Got me a young nurse in there, and all the time yo're in that room, I want yo'r Johnson pointing straight toward the floor. Yo' understand what I'm saying, Boy?"

"J-Johnson?"

"Every boy's best friend—your pisser."

I could only guess how Robert felt, but I was feeling sickish as we entered the inner room. And when a blonde nurse said, "We meet again, Sean—don't say I didn't warn you!" and I recognized Phyllis, the 18-year-old summer trainee, I felt sicker.

The medic was doing something with a microscope; Phyllis was handling things. She sat us down and stuck thermometers in our

mouths, then took two jars and marked them in black with our names.

"These are for your specimens. When it's time, you'll take them through the red door, fill them, and leave them on the table."

Robert shot me a look, and I shot right back. I didn't know what was behind the red door, but at least we wouldn't pee in front of Phyllis.

Our temperatures were written down, then our heart beats and blood pressures—without telling us what any of them were.

As we made for the scale, I had the panicky thought, *Maybe they want your weight so accurate you have to take your towel off.*

False alarm.

"Anything else you want done at this point, Doctor?" Phyllis asked, buttering her boss who was no doctor.

"Check the redhead's chart. See anything unusual?"

"He's 16, that's unusual."

"You know the policy when they're 16?"

I noticed when talking to Phyllis the medic had no drawl.

"Guess not; we haven't had one that old since I've been assigned to you."

"16s and 17s get an old-fashioned short-arm inspection."

"Short arm? Oh! You mean for VD!"

"VD's what we're after, but long as we're at it, we check for anything abnormal. You haven't done one of these. Take care of the towel, and I'll tell you what to do."

Phyllis turned, "You'll have to put your towel on that chair."

Robert sat down in the chair.

The medic got up, "On your feet!"

Robert standing, the medic shouted, "She wants this off!"—reached out, gave a yank, and threw the towel in the direction of the chair.

The boy's knees buckled and I knew how he felt—like he'd been hit with a frying pan. I noticed he didn't look down—*prob'ly telling himself the towel's still there.*

Phyllis did a once-over of Robert's body—a thick patch of dark curly red and a penis hanging long.

"What do I do, Doctor?"

"Visual and tactile examination of the genitalia. Check for lumps, bumps, cysts, welts, sores. Go over everything with a fine-tooth

comb, and by the look of him you have a fair amount to cover," he said, grinning.

"Start with the scrotum; feel for any lumpy places."

Phyllis hesitated. The medic went into his talk, "The red don't come off. Ha, ha! If yo' get anything on yo'r hands, most likely be white."

Robert sucked air as Phyllis took his pair in her hands. She rolled them between her fingers, bugging his eyes wide.

"They seem normal. The penis next, I presume?" Phyllis asked, making like an old-timer.

Robert's Adam's apple bobbed up and down; water stood on his forehead—he never changed the spot he was looking at.

"On the penis, check for chancres, any kind of sore. Start at the base, and work down."

Phyllis put a thumb and two fingers on him and turned them side to side. A shiver ran through Robert, bumping his knees together as it went by.

"Cold, Boy?" the medic asked.

No answer.

The nurse worked her hand along in her back-and-forth way. Robert's body was wet all over.

"Couldn't find anything, Doctor."

"Listen, Boy, coming to the last part. Keep hold o' yo'self! Yo' hear?"

Something about the medic's face hit me. I wasn't clear about why, but I knew he wanted Robert to go big in front of Phyllis.

"All right, Nurse, take hold of the end of the penis . . ."

Robert jerked as Phyllis took him in her hands.

"Check for any kind of discharge . . ."

Every muscle on Robert was trembling.

"Roll the foreskin back so the glans is exposed . . . Run your fingers over the surface and around the circumference . . . Feel for any abnormalities."

Robert was shaking so hard the floor boards creaked. Sweat was streaming down his belly onto his privates, dripping off the end like a leaky faucet. Obviously, he didn't get boners. *Are redheads different?* I wondered. How else could he stay down with Phyllis's fingers touching his most sensitive part?

"Seems perfectly smooth all over," she said, still holding on.

The medic, deciding there'd be no 16-year-old erection to embarrass the young nurse, commanded, "Go make water!"

Without waiting for Phyllis to let loose, Robert took off toward the red door, pulling himself out of her hand. I started too, but was blocked by the medic's arm.

"The jars, Boy!"

I reached out.

"Check for rupture when you-all get back. Yo' won't need this." No doubt about it, the man was a snatcher.

I saw the start of Phyllis's smile, but didn't wait to see the end. My back was turned—*Thank God*—as things began to mushroom.

On the other side of the red door, a dazed Robert faced me. He was sitting on the front of a table that stood against the wall, his hands squeezing the edge. He was shaking so hard, his 7-incher swung back and forth like one of those things on a piano.

"Are you all right?"

No good asking—he wasn't there.

I knew I couldn't pee, and figured he couldn't either. Behind him was a row of jars in different shades of yellow. I filled our empties with a mixture of boys.

On one wall was a second door—*must lead into the hall*—I unlocked it and looked out—*pretty sure this is the same hall as 143.*

"Do you want to go back in there and face that nurse again? . . . no sign of life . . . Come on, let's go."

I got him to his feet and led him out the door—couldn't get him to run so we walked, not meeting anyone. 143 was empty. I sat Robert down, dropped a towel on him, dressed myself, then helped him into his boxers.

# Chapter 53

**O**nce I let it slip I'd met a movie star's son, it didn't take long for Bryan to drag the story out of me. Nothing less than a full report would satisfy him. Whenever I tried skipping something, he pulled me up short, "I'm not letting you off the hook, Me Lad."

Bryan kept up his grilling till he'd gotten a blow-by-blow of Phyllis's examination of Robert.

"Sweet Mary, mother of God! I'd swap dear old Granny's Sunday corset to have an 18-year-old blonde hold it in her hand."

"How was CYO camp?" I asked before he could start on me.

"You'd've loved it. Dropping your skivvies and hopping into a cold shower packed in with a dozen squealing boys, the Pope's idea of how to damp the appetites of teenage males."

"You mean they don't give you enough to eat?"

A pitying look was all I got for an answer.

"Father Arne had to set an example, but he used a shower on the other side of the wall. We invited him to join us, but talk about shy; we never saw him in the morning till everyone was dressed, and whenever we'd start changing for swimming or whatever, he'd take off like Jesse Owens. 'Course you realize that was waving a red flag at a bull."

"Bryan! What did you do?"

"The first thing I did was bet Tito Lucca a dime that before the week was up we'd see Father naked. I might've lost my bet if it hadn't been for your pal Salone."

"You mean Bobby was at camp and took showers with you?"

"Aye, that he did. And took a ragging as well; he was the only kid there without a hair to his name. Got teased something fierce

about it. The fourth morning, think it was, we were standing outside the showers all in our skin except Bobby who'd gone gun-shy. Two 14-year-olds took him down, pulled his shorts off, and started rubbing where it would do the most good, saying that was a sure way to grow hair. Your chum got an honest-to-goodness bone on—frankly, I didn't think he had it in him—and that gave me an idea . . . 'Want to see Father naked? Then everyone kneel around that pole like you're praying to it. And as for you, Salone, don't go soft on me!' I yelled, starting off around the wall.

"A bare heinie stared at me. There were no clothes outside the stall, just a towel. I grabbed that, reached in, and turned off the water. 'Father!' I shouted. 'Something real bad's happened to Salone. Come quick!'

"'Hand me the towel!' he called over his shoulder.

"'Don't worry about the towel, Father, I've got it,' I said, breaking into a trot. 'Hurry! You may have to give him last rites.'

"With that he took off naked after me. When he got there, he couldn't see till he'd cleared away some of the kneeling kids.

"'Is it catching, Father?' asked Neddie Foley, a bright lad quick on the uptake.

"Father stared at Bobby, who with all the attention he was drawing had lost none of his starch, and went blotchy.

"'Must be catching,' Neddie said, "cause you're getting it, Father.'

"I thought Father would run, but he didn't; he knelt down beside Bobby in his own bone and said, 'It's God's daily trial to test the faith of boys and men. Let us pray together that God will lend us the strength to endure that trial.'"

I was to spend the night at Bryan's, and we'd set off from his place with our knapsacks on some kind of hike he'd planned.

"Where're we going?"

"'Tis a curious kitty-cat you are. I'm thinking you'll be getting a little of that curiosity satisfied this fine day. Ever wonder what retired race horses do to earn their oats?"

"I saw Man o' War in the newsreel once," I answered. "He didn't have to pull a plow or anything; was just nibbling grass in this great big pasture he had all to himself."

"Well, if he'd stayed to himself there wouldn't've been any War Admiral. You have heard of War Admiral?"

"Didn't he win some race?"

"Some race! Just the Triple Crown, that's all! Anyway, one brisk morn they led Man o' War into the barn and introduced him to War Admiral's mother. And what do you think happened?"

"I don't know—did they like each other?"

"Enough so War Admiral was born a year later. Does that give you a clue as to what kind of monkeyshines Man o' War was up to at the ripe old age of 16?"

"Well, I suppose . . . O God! You mean he . . . ?"

"Even as you and I were we presented with a beautiful young bride with no clothes, eager to receive the thrust of our manhood into the secret place beneath her smooth white belly."

"Please, Bryan! I'm feeling sick!"

"Easy, Lad! It's part of growing up. It's the Dance of Life. It's what makes the World Go Round. Though it's late in the year, they're rebreeding a mare who lost her foal. We'll be Johnny-on-the-spot when Sir Beneville stands at stud. He's new at the game, so I'm sure he'll be full of fire."

"You mean watch him . . . *do it?*"

"Aye, watch him plant his seed, wishing all the while it were ourselves in his place."

"I wouldn't want to be in his place—especially with someone watching!"

"Horses don't mind. Naturally, if you and I are ever lucky enough to have our innings, no one'll be watching."

"But, Bryan, she'd be watching!"

"And wouldn't it be lovely!"

We walked along thinking our thoughts. Bryan was the first to talk.

"Haven't been to this place since it reopened, but got some info about the guy running it. Calls himself Indian Jake—not really an Indian, just pretends he is. The word is *don't mess with Jake*. He's big and dumb and doesn't know his own strength; there's a story he killed a man with his bare hands."

"Bryan, maybe we should get our tennis stuff and hit the courts."

"Sean, my boy, there's more to life than swatting a white ball. Some day you'll think fondly on your initiation into The Great Mystery . . . Look! the main barn's straight ahead."

As if I didn't have enough on my plate, who should be leading a horse toward us but Joey. He came up, smiling, "Well, well! What's this? Big-Brother-Shows-Little-Brother-the-Facts-of-Life Day? You've come to the right place 'cause in a little while Sweet Senorita here's gonna get all she can choke down. Ha, ha! You won't believe this, Bryan, but Big Ben's got a clapper longer than Sean's. Let me put the mare in a stall and I'll show you around. I'm the only help Jake's got right now—how about a job? I can fix it for you."

I was fuddled, and even Bryan kept his peace. There could be no doubt as to who the next horse handler was as he came from the other side of the barn. I'd never seen such a giraffe; he must've been six-ten and 300 pounds. This monster was bare-chested and had shoulder-length black hair trapped out by a wampum band circling his forehead.

"Hi, Jake!" Bryan called.

Jake stopped.

"Back! Big fella smell mare."

Even I could tell the animal meant business. I'd seen horses in the field with their things dangling, but this one was pumping up and down like an arm swinging at the elbow.

"You know Indian Jake?"

"Not know, heard about. You're famous in these parts. Okay if we stick around?"

"Joey say," Jake answered.

The past few minutes'd been too much: facing Joey and a giant; having my Elizabeth dream set off by a jumpy stallion; and to top things off, the barn smell was making me wheeze.

"Bryan, I'm starting to get asthma—I better leave."

"Why not go back to the shade of the water tank where we ate lunch. Wait for me there—unless you want me to come now."

"No, that's OK, take as long as you want; the rest will do me good."

Drawing a deep breath, I headed out with slow steps as Joey came to fetch Bryan.

With a gulp from my canteen, I swallowed the ephedrine capsule I'd taken to carrying in my watch pocket since the allergy tests . . . I rested . . . I felt well enough to try a short walk down to a wooded place . . . I rested . . . I came back to the tank . . . I fell asleep . . .

"Sean . . ." I found myself looking into blue-green eyes that had no sparkle.

". . . Should've gone with you—how do you feel?"

"Better. I took my asthma pill. You look worried—is something wrong?"

"No, nothing."

"Bryan, do you smell fish?"

"I was handling some at the barn. Know what I wish? Wish I had a nice clean lake to jump into."

I wondered about the fish, but could tell Bryan was in no mood to answer questions.

"There's a small open tank down among those trees fed from this one. I think it's for cows, but it looks clean. Shall we check it out?" I asked.

"You better stay here,"

"No, that's OK, I'll come along."

"I'm going to take my clothes off."

"Ha, ha! I'm pretty used to that!"

"I suppose it would never occur to you that someone else might be modest for a change."

"Gosh, Bryan, I'm sorry! I'll stay right here; I won't even look that way."

"Sean, I didn't mean to bite your head off; it's just I'd rather be alone. I won't be long. You're not sore at me?"

"What's there to be sore about?"

But I was worried.

# CHAPTER 54

It was almost suppertime when we got back to Bryan's. Jeanne was working late at the library, and she'd left a note telling us what to fix. The dishes finished, Bryan picked up a book of poems and I picked up "Tracking the Leprechaun."

I wasn't sorry when at nine o'clock he said, "Let's go to bed early."

We were in our undershorts; there'd been no talk about the happenings of the day.

"Might as well get this over with; think it's going to take a while to heal," Bryan said.

He jumped up on the bed, pulled his shorts off, threw them over his shoulder laughing, "Ha, ha! Got my hands away! Take a good look! That's what you all want, isn't it?"

It looked like it'd been boiled.

"God, Bryan! What happened?"

"Joey happened—thought it was his Christmas toy—off and on for an hour—lost track of time—couldn't get enough—wouldn't stop—thought every layer of skin was rubbed off—couldn't move—tied down with ropes—hate being tied—Indian Jake watching like a big ugly toad—and the cats—that was the worst . . ."

Bryan fell to his knees and broke into sobs. I sprang up, eased him into a sitting position, and held him in my arms, his head against my shoulder. It was Cousin Davy all over again but ten times worse . . . the sobbing made tears . . . then there was only our breathing . . .

I heard the front door open. "It's Jeanne—have to tell her—you may need a doctor."

"Don't let her see me! Don't mention Jake!"

I skidded to a stop halfway into the living room.

"Sean, what is it?"

"Nothing to worry about, but I have to tell you something."

"Then let us sit on the sofa while you tell me."

"Bryan's in his room. Everything's OK, but he doesn't want you to go back there tonight."

"Fine, I will not intrude. Is that all?"

"Well, today some . . . boys . . . captured Bryan . . ."

"Mon Dieu, how I dislike that! And what happened?"

"They made his skin all red and sore—looks awful!"

"His face?"

What I had to say was too much for me. "Th-the skin on his . . . on his . . . p-penis."

"Naturellement! Where else? Tell me, Sean, is that all you boys think about?"

I couldn't even try to answer . . .

"Forgive me. That was unjust. Wait, I shall only be a minute."

Jeanne came with a blue jar and a roll of white gauze, "Here is what I suggest. Tonight pat Bryan with cold cream and tie a bandage on him. He will not object since it is you. Tomorrow morning when he has finished in the bathroom, do it once more. Can you manage that?"

"I-I'll try."

She kissed me on the lips, "Sean, you are a fine friend."

When I got back to Bryan, he was still naked, lying faceup on the bed, hands behind his head, looking as though he hadn't a care in the world.

"Sorry to cave in like that. Did Maman comment on your attire?"

"My attire?" I looked at myself. "O God! I was talking to her in my undershorts!"

"Just out of curiosity, were you sitting down?"

"We were side by side on the sofa."

"Aha! Hercule Poirot will now reenact the scene as it took place in the living room. Get rid of that stuff and sit next to me."

I followed orders.

"Just so! Once again the little grey cells do not fail me. From my front row seat I have a fine view of the Lacey family treasure. Look at your lap."

I looked down, bounced to my feet, and suffered.

"Ha, ha! That missing button makes for a fine window. Do you realize this is the first time I've been able to inspect your equipment when it wasn't primed for action? *Well-hung* is I believe the expression. I wonder how Maman would say it in French?"

"O Lord! You don't really think—?"

"What big eyes she has!"

"She never let on."

"Maman is a lady. By the way, what instructions did she give you?"

"I'm supposed to pat on cold cream and tie a bandage around it, tonight and tomorrow morning."

"Are you waiting for a formal invitation?"

"Y-you wouldn't rather do yourself?"

"Mother knows best! Ha, ha! I'll be interested to compare your technique with Joey's."

"Bryan! How can you joke about it?"

"Humor, my boy, is all that makes some things bearable. Believe me, a lot of milk was spilt today, but I've done crying over it—"

*Someone fed the cats milk, somebody spilled it, and Bryan fed the cats fish,* I thought to myself, *but what was so bad about that?*

"All I have to decide now is whether to kill Joey or just cut his head off."

"Bryan, don't say such things!—even as a joke. Do you want to talk about what happened?"

"Know what makes me the maddest? Bryan O'Neill a prize chump, an unsuspecting lamb led to the slaughter. Would you believe I was actually dumb enough to take my own clothes off? Are you going to do anything with that cold cream or just stare at it? Incidentally, if you're worried about getting a rise out of Johnnie, I guarantee it's a medical impossibility."

"Here g-goes. Tell me if it hurts."

"Oooo! That feels cool! What soft hands you have, Grandma!"

Next morning, Bryan was shaking me, "It's late. I've had my shower and want to get dressed, but first you have to fix my new bandage. Here's the stuff."

"What?" I asked sleepily.

"The cold cream!"

"Okay, but I'm not awake. Oops! Didn't mean to use such a big gob."

"The better to rub me with. Never fear, Johnnie will be meek as a mouse."

He was lying back with his eyes closed as I nervously did my job. "Bryan . . ."

"Don't disturb me! I'm imagining your dream girl at the Clinic. It feels wonderful!"

"But Bryan . . ."

He opened his eyes and took things in, "Thanks be to God! I was afraid Johnnie'd never stand again. Wrap him up, tie a bow on him, and we'll pretend it's my birthday."

# CHAPTER 55

Joey was smart enough to realize he could lose an arm and a leg or a few front teeth. So till things cooled down, he spent days and nights at the stable with Indian Jake. When news made the rounds that Joey'd been spotted in the neighborhood, I expected Bryan to go on the attack, but a week passed without him saying a word about it. It was Monday morning; Bryan was leading the way.

"Joey's back in form; came out of the Saturday matinee waving a pair of undershorts. During the movie his gang took them off a kid from the City. Just as I expected, he's as cocky as ever—think it's time the Lone Ranger and Tonto tracked him down."

"He's never alone," I warned.

"He will be. At the first sign of danger that pack of Joey's'll desert faster than rats from a scuttled garbage scow. Anyway all I want to do now is get a fix on his routine; if we keep low and put our ears to the ground, we may be able to figure out where and when he's going to strike next. If we're lucky, we might catch him in the act. My idea is to split up. Easier to keep out of sight, and we can cover more territory. I'll do the playground and the clubhouse, then take the creek far as the Deep Hole. You know Joey best. Any suggestions?"

"How about Outlaw Trail?"

"Come again?"

"That's a name I made up—a while back of course."

"Of course!"

"I mean the shortcut through the brush just beyond the old green bridge. Kids over my way use it to go to the candy store. The Trail's where Joey held up my cousin Davy."

"Mais c'est admirable, ca! Hastings, you have outdone yourself! Is there a way in Joey wouldn't use?"

"Sure, the railroad tracks go past it on the far side; he'd never come from that direction. I can sneak in and get almost to the path without being noticed—there're plenty bushes."

"Then away! Cry, *God for Harry! England and Saint George!* We'll rendezvous in a cozy clump of bushes beside your Outlaw Trail."

"But, Bryan, how will you find me?"

"Tribe not call me Eagle Eyes for nothing."

Taking my place in a patch of poison oak—I was allergic to everything, but immune to poison oak—a ways off the path was child's play. No one in sight, I stretched out in my leafy tent.

I woke realizing I'd been asleep. Boomer and Cooky were eyeing some red-striped apples high up a giant of a tree whose lower branches'd been picked clean. I sank back into my hiding place . . .

"Either give us both a piece, or we both give you ten socks on the arms."

"How hard?" a small voice asked.

"Ready, Cooky? . . . This hard!" Boomer said, as he and Cooky punched opposite shoulders.

"Ooow!" wailed the small boy, who looked no more than seven.

"Only have three left."

"So what'cha complainin' about? That leaves you a piece, don't it? That's all we get."

The idea of playing Robin Hood came into my head, but I just watched the child go on his way looking sad at the piece of candy in his hand. I shut my eyes . . .

"Let's get out o' here!" It was Boomer again.

"Don't'cha want some apples?"

"Don't'cha want some pants?"

My question at the pair's take-off was answered by the sight of Joey and two of his gang. With a shiver, I bunched myself into a ball.

"What're we gonna do, Joey, climb for apples?"

"Maybe—pretty high up. First we sit down and see what falls in our laps—bound to be some kids coming back from the store."

Another of the crew who'd been posted as a lookout came running.

"Guess what's up the path, Joey? Janet's brother, Jackie, and Doris's sister, Becky, and get this, they're holding hands!"

"Ha, ha! I owe those two dames something. This'll be rich; watch me scare Janet's kid brother bowlegged. How old are the two turtledoves?"

"He's twelve and a half. She just turned eleven."

"That's cradle snatching! I'd say it's high time Little Red Riding Hood found out what the wolf's got up his pant leg."

"You gonna pants him, Joey?"

"Who me? 'Course if he wants to show off to her, who am I to interfere? Quiet!"

Into themselves, Jackie and Becky got to the tree without noticing they had company.

"Ha, ha!" Joey laughed, "Didn't know sisters held hands."

Jackie quick let go, "We're not sisters!"

"Got a nickel says you're sisters, wanna bet?"

"Sure, I'll bet."

"No backing out or welshing?"

"What for? I can't lose."

"Got the nickel on you?"

"Not on me, but I won't need it."

"Just in case you'd foolishly consider it, gonna show you what happens to welshers. Mac, get rid of the kid's shoes and socks."

"What are you doing that for?" Jackie asked.

"Just wanna play a game of This Little Pig. See this jackknife? What I do to welshers is take each foot and cut off the pig that went to market, the pig that ate roast beef, and this here pig," Joey said, wiggling Jackie's little toe, "the one that cried *wee! wee! wee!* all the way home. But you wouldn't think of welshing, would you?"

"No, Joey, scout's honor!"

"The last kid that welshed on me has a heck of a time finding shoes that fit. I say you're sisters—you better be able to prove you're not."

"That's easy. A boy and a girl can't be sisters."

"Which one's the boy?"

"Me, of course. Look at my haircut! Look at my pants!"

"Girls can get short haircuts; girls can wear pants. Bet you got girls' boobies."

All mixed up, Jackie worked himself out of his shirt, "Look, Joey! They're not girls'!"

"Just means you're too young to swell. So far you've proved exactly nothing, but one thing about me, I've always been a square shooter. What're you wearin' under your pants?"

"Boys' boxers, honest!"

"Might be proof, but can't be sure without seeing the evidence."

"You mean take my pants off? Right here front of Becky?"

"Don't matter none to me. Just as leave have the toes."

Jackie started to unbutton, "See! You can tell by the top."

"All the way off!"

Jackie stepped out of his pants, "Kind of embarrassing, but that proves it—right Joey?"

"Mac, hold the arms from behind. Just thought of something. Why couldn't a girl put on boys' underwear? Like I said, there's no way to prove this kid's not a girl. Bill, hold the toes. If they move while I'm cuttin', the blood spurts all over. We'll start with the pig that went to market; that's always the messiest. Kid, helps if you clamp your jaws—don't hurt so much. Ready?"

"Wait!"

"You thought of some proof?"

"U-under my sh-shorts . . ."

"Don't let go o' the arms, Mac. Might try to get away. Seems there's something under the shorts. 'Course they'll have to come off, but I'm not gonna pull down a girl's drawers—Becky'll have to do it. Kid, if that's what you want, ask her; otherwise we start on the toes—ask her!"

"T-take them . . . o-off . . ."

"'Cept in pictures, I've never seen a boy's . . . Are you sure?"

"He's sure he don't want to lose his toes—tak'em off!"

"Oh!" Becky let out, as the shorts fell.

"Pick those up, Bill. He won't be needin'em for a while. Now ain't that cute, it even begs. Don't worry, Becky, it might grow up in time for your honeymoon. If I was you, I'd burn rubber before I was asked to prove I wasn't a boy."

She took one last look, then took Joey's advice.

"Well, Jackie, seems you win the bet, but—ha, ha!—a nickel's too much; a penny an inch's my limit. Let's say four cents, and at that price you're robbing me blind. Trouble is, you're gonna have to help me earn the dough. Don't worry, you won't need to lift a finger—ha, ha! leastways, not another. Figure all we gotta do is wait for enough girls to come by. They ought to cough up a penny apiece easy to see a kid in your shape. Might even fork out double to feel the merchandise. Ha, ha! 'Course we'll have to keep it in fighting trim."

Joey rubbed the boy's button, pulled his weenie-stick down, and let go to test the spring. As for Jackie—I knew the look—he was in another world.

"Mac, get him to some cover. We're not givin' free samples; till they pay, he stays outa sight."

Mac gave him a shove, "Find some bushes!"

Jackie stumbled in my direction. All that skin came toward my poison patch . . . almost there . . .

"Stop!" I yelled, throwing myself at the white, bringing it to the ground.

"Get him!"

Mac came first . . . then the mob . . . I rolled over and over . . . I rolled no more . . . me pinned on my back . . . staring into those eyes . . . that look!

"Gonna give you just what I gave your friend Bryan. Ha, ha! Too bad we got no fish to draw some cats."

I wasn't sure all I was in for, but I was sure I'd do battle till my last breath.

"You guys get his shirt. I'll take the pants."

I wasn't making it easy for them; kicking, turning, twisting, squirming, I was being pulled in two directions. The shirt was caught on my shoulders; Joey had my pants inside out, almost off, but they were stuck at my ankles where the Keds stopped them. R-r-rip! The shirt gave way. Behind me I could see the three at my head lose their balance and end up in a pile. Joey kept pulling, and with nothing on the other end, I was sledding over the slick dry grass in and around stuff. As Joey slowed to make a sharp turn past a bush, I reached for a branch to brake myself. One after another, the Keds and pants came off. Joey kept his balance and I got ready to meet his attack when, wonder of wonders, still holding my pants he turned and ran. Something streaked by and my heart sang—*Bryan!*

Thinking to guard the rear, I found my legs and went back to a place where there was a clear opening to the spot we'd come from. No Jackie. No mob. As I'd learn later, Bryan's take on Joey's troop was right-on; one bleeding lip drove off all three. Also, Bryan's face must've played a part; flying past he looked like Zeus about to hurl a thunderbolt.

I took up the chase. My first glimpse was of Bryan making a flying tackle and bringing Joey down by the ankles . . . *whether to kill* . . . The words beat in my head, and my legs pumped faster. I could see Joey on his back with Bryan riding him, slapping his face from side to side. Blood was coming out of Joey's nose. "Stop, Bryan!" I shouted.

He put his hands around Joey's neck . . . "Bryan!" I screamed.

Joey didn't look so good . . . "Bryan! I'm asking you as my best friend! Best friend, Bryan!"

"Best friend . . ." he whispered, and took his hands away.

I got into my pants while Joey got his breath.

"If you ever touch me or Sean or any relative of ours again, I'll kill you. Repeat it. Repeat it in your own words."

"If I ever touch you or Sean . . . or any relative of yours again . . . you'll . . . you'll k-kill me . . ."

"Though I should need to come from halfway round the world, this I swear on my honor as an O'Neill! . . . OK I'm going to get off, and you're going to lie there and strip . . . Jump to it—we don't have all day."

Bryan picked up Joey's clothes as they came free.

"On your feet . . . Start running."

"Where!"

"Anywhere you like, so long as it's out o' my sight" . . . Scat! . . . I'll drop your clothes in the creek!"

# CHAPTER 56

## Journey to a Day I'd Never Forget

A favorite game of mine when we were on a trip was to call out the make and year of every car we met along the road. Of course, except for the Rolls Royce and Daimler which you saw about as often as mule teams, they were all American-made. But there were many more American makes in the '20s and '30s than there are today. There was the Pierce Arrow, the rich people's limousine, easy to recognize by the way its headlights flowed into its fenders. There was the Duesenberg with its bullet body, the Cord with its chrome superchargers, and that favorite of the gangsters, the Packard. There were La Salles, Lincoln Zephyrs, Studebakers, Nashes, De Sotos, Hudsons, Auburns, Hupmobiles, Austens, Terreplanes, Reos, and Rocknes.

We were setting out for the City and Dr. Reiter in our two-toned green Pontiac, which shined like a mirror though it was 10 years old. I almost never did anything alone with my father, so this would be a day to remember. We stopped at a gas station. While the attendant was servicing our car, I went inside and looked over a claw machine to study the prizes. My father came alongside and held out a nickel. This was a surprise; he never wasted money.

"Thanks, Dad!"

"What are you going to try for?"

There was a pearl-handled automatic that looked real to me but was probably a fake. I pointed to it.

"They just put that there for a come-on; no one ever wins it," he said.

The machine had a claw that you steered with two wheels after putting in a nickel; then the claw lowered, clamped onto whatever was in its jaws, and moved to an opening where it dropped its load into a chute to the outside. I put in the nickel and worked both wheels. When I let go, the claw started down right over the gun . . . took hold . . . and began lifting the prize in its jaws . . .

"Look, Dad!"

The pearl handle twinkled as the gun slipped from the smooth teeth to fall back into place.

"What did I tell you?"

It had to be Blue-Green gas whenever we set off on a trip because that company gave out free folders with funny jingles to sing along the way. The chorus went: "Blue-Green Gas, Blue-Green Gas, there's no one on the highway you can't pass, unless they're using Blue-Green too."

We traveled the winding unlined road through the village railroad stops. Each town was different, and I tried to picture as we passed its houses what my life would be like if I lived in one of them. Our way curved in and around a small stand of giant trees whose great height and deep shade got me pretending—dwarfs, dragons, and pots of gold. We went into the tunnel; I didn't relax till we made it back to open air. Then onto the Bridge, which for all its steel and concrete seemed too close to the tides below.

My father dropped me at the Clinic and took off on his own. He was to pick me up for lunch; Dr. Reiter'd said he wanted me there for indoctrination. I wasn't sure what that meant, but anything with "doc" in it didn't sound good. I sat down outside his office and was joined by a boy who dumped a pair of pajamas and a toothbrush out of a box into my lap.

"Sorry! Haven't seen this doctor, but my father—actually he's my stepfather—fixed it for me to stay over—some birthday present—I was 14 yesterday. You been here before?"

"Oh, yes."

"Can I ask you something sort of embarrassing?"

"Sure."

A high-schooler on my street—likes to scare me—said they make you stand in front of other kids without a stitch on and . . . fill a bottle—you know what I mean. I couldn't do it—I'd die. That can't be true can it? You ever done that?"

"No."

"That's a relief."

Elizabeth ended our talk—*God she's beautiful*—"Hello, Sean, Dr. Reiter wants you."

He waved me into his office. "This morning you will be bathing a group of boys who are being admitted to the ward. What do you think of that?"

What I thought was, *It's going to be a bad day at the Circle L.* What I answered was, "Aagh."

"Please understand, this is not standard procedure, and I had to get Dr. Hauptmann's approval. However, when I explained my reasons he made no objection. Here, take off your shirt and put on this smock; it will give you official status. You will be completely on your own, but I know you can handle it. Remember, my reputation is at stake. That is all for now. Report to the main office; the nurse will show you where to go and what to do. Good luck!"

The nurse in the office was the one who belonged in Jack and the Beanstalk. She took me up some stairs and landed me in a room that had a hippopotamus-size tub, "You will have four boys, all to be bathed at the same time. The first thing to remember is you do everything—that's important—some boys can't do themselves, and they mustn't be made to feel different. Secondly, you explain as little as possible—they feel more secure that way. For example, if you're starting to undress a boy, and he asks what you're doing, say you're taking his shoes off. Get the idea?"

"Aagh."

"Furthermore, once you start undressing a boy, it's best to finish him. Ha, ha! Put them out of their misery fast is my motto. You're to take urine specimens. Those jars have their names on them. Get the specimens as soon as they're undressed. I assume you know boys sometimes have trouble producing. Make them drink water. Don't ask if they want a drink; just fill glasses from the sink and hold them to their lips. If you forget that step you might be in for a long wait. Two glasses, three if you can get them down. The urinal there is for emergencies. Now let's suppose you have them undressed and the specimens are out of the way; then get them into the tub together. The four you will have can stand, but you can seat them if you wish.

Use the shower to wet and rinse. Do the hair first; soap their heads and rinse them; later soap and rinse again. Soap their bodies—and I mean all over. Understand?"

I couldn't even say, "Aagh."

"You're the doctor—you don't ask permission. Everyone gets a soaping, a rinse, another soaping, and a final rinse. Then you get them into hospital gowns, which will be brought to you. Any questions? . . . Good. Two of your boys are across the hall. The one in the wheelchair is Paul, the little one's Jerome. While I'm collecting the others, you can bring in the first pair and get started."

I had a notion I'd be working with small boys, so I gulped when Paul looked Bryan's age. I took hold of his chair and motioned for Jerome, who was no more than nine, to follow; I wheeled Paul in and shut the door after the two of them. Without saying a word—I was afraid of blowing it right at the start—I got a glass of water and held it to Jerome's lips, "Drink!"

While the nine-year-old was drinking, Paul spoke up, "I need to take a leak right now, and if it's all the same to you, I'd like to get it over with before that nurse comes back."

"Absolutely!" I said, not a little fussed at being thrown into the thick of things so soon.

I started on his shoelaces. "Look," Paul said, "I know you have your orders, but I've been stuck in this chair since sunup. This is no time for shoelaces; *I need to go now.*"

Picking up the jar with his name, I held it out for him to take. "My legs work some, but my arms don't work at all—polio—you have to do everything."

That stopped me, but for Paul's sake, I had to get going. I set the jar down—Bryan's story about the greenhorn freshman came into my head. Giving myself no more time to think, I opened his fly—he didn't say a word. I took a breath and plunged my hand through the gap in his boxers, which'd been left unbuttoned. I hit hair on my first try—pushed south and reached a penis whose softness made me ashamed—mine wouldn't've been soft. I took another breath and pulled. It was Bryan-size, but uncircumcised. I let go and put the jar under him.

"You have to fix me."

I expected trouble, but it didn't happen.

"Better hold on, or I'll pee all over myself."

Jerome who was taking it in said, "Are you going to hold mine?"

"Everyone gets treated the same."

Paul filled the best part of his jar; I put it on a shelf and moved to stuff him inside his pants. "No point in that, might as well undress me."

"Wouldn't you rather wait till the nurse has gone for good?"

"What's the use? This place can turn into Grand Central at the drop of a hat. Look, you can lay one of those towels on me when you're done."

". . . Golly!" Jerome yelped, as I uncovered a dark bush.

"Half Italian, half Spanish," Paul said.

I laid a towel over him, just as the nurse came with three boys.

"Brought you an extra. That's Tim, age 13. This is Bret, age 11, and the blond is Harold, going on 14. All right, Sean is in charge. If he says drink, you drink. Sean, you're on your own.".

I swallowed hard . . . *Pretend you're Bryan* . . . and sized up the newcomers. All three looked like pea soup . . . *I'm Bryan O'Neill, and like it or not, me Buckos, I'm pantsing the lot o' you.*

I started the water treatment, got a glass into each of them, and stopped when one asked, "Wh-where's the bathroom?"

Paul'd been easy, but I knew the hard part started with this almost-14-year-old. I went over and kneeled to untie his shoelaces.

"Wh-what are you doing?"

"Taking your shoes off."

Without a letup, I did his shirt, got his pants open, and saw yellow.

I recognized the swimsuit before I recognized Harold from Horse Hill—he'd grown taller and slimmer. I had him down to his trunks and reached for them. He didn't waste time trembling; he started right in shaking. Me gone to mush inside, I knew the only way to get through was to act tough.

"Why the heck are you wearing trunks?"

"W-was afraid the doctor might take my pants off in front of a nurse."

*You poor fish, as Bryan would tell you, flashing those trunks at a doctor would be like waving a yellow flag at a bull* . . . I changed my plan.

"Jerome, pick up your jar and come here. I'm going to demonstrate what each of you will go through—*exactly*—there'll be no exceptions—OK?"

While I was doing Jerome's shirt, he whispered in my ear, "I'm wearing BVDs."

I whispered back, "I wore BVDs when I was 13."

Even so, I could feel the 9-year-old's embarrassment as he stood in those BVDs, watching me unbutton him—I pulled them off fast and fixed the jar.

"You're supposed to hold me," he said.

"That's right," I said, grabbing his stub.

"O Boy!" let out Bret. "O Brother!" from Tim. Harold went white. Jerome did his job.

As I turned from putting his jar on the shelf, Jerome asked, "Can I get dressed now?"

"Everyone stays undressed till we're through, and that may take an hour."

Bret went pale as Harold. "O Mama!" from Tim.

"Whoever's ready to pee, raise your hand."

No takers. Deciding to do them by age, I said, "Com'ere, Bret."

He couldn't move, so I went to him—I knew what was behind that young face. When I had his shirt off, he whispered, "Never been pantsed before."

"Nobody's pantsing you," I said, pantsing him.

"Boy, I'd've given my eyeteeth to've had a snazzy pair of boxers like that at your age."

"Harold's got his hand up!" Jerome yelled.

I deserted Bret and turned to Harold, "Put your arms around my neck and hold on."

He took me in a death grip. By feel I worked his trunks down far as I could, "Let go of my neck for a second."

I got my hand inside, pulled his bone out, and finished the trunks. Except Paul, the boys were gathered round, taking in the uncircumcised five-incher.

"Can you pee?"

He shook his head.

"Soon as you can, raise your hand again."

It slipped my mind I hadn't finished Bret, so I started on Tim.

"Bet Tim's been pantsed before," Paul put in.

"L-last month. At the lake. I was with this girl, and some older kids pulled my suit down. Sh-she got a real good look."

I glanced over. Bret was holding onto the front of his shorts, shifting from one foot to the other. *Better hurry or I'll have a flood on my hands*; I rushed over to him, "You're ready, aren't you?"

"Unh-unh!"

"Like heck you're not!"

I undid his buttons and pulled his shorts free of his weenie, which stuck out in a half-bone. He hid it with his hands. I lifted his jar, "Wow!" I said, "Did my eyes deceive me or did I see what I think I saw? Mine could never get like that when I was 11. Can I see? . . . Please?"

Shyly, he uncovered himself.

"That's amazing!" I said, taking hold and pointing him toward the jar.

"OK, I'll aim, you pee."

He let go to the tune of 3/4 full.

"Harold's got his hand up!" Jerome shouted.

I raced over, took his jar, and grabbed him. He started to spritz, so I shut him off and fixed it. I was afraid that might foul things up, but with me holding on, he let loose. I could feel him soften, and that was all to the good, but the jar went past the 3/4 mark with no slowdown. I panicked, clamped it tight and pulled him to the bowl where he emptied himself.

I turned to Tim—he'd had too much time to think about the girl at the lake—and fetched another glass of water.

"Don't think I can," he said.

"Drink!" I said, handing him the glass and pulling his clothes off fast as I could.

"Holy Moly!" Bret said, spotting hair.

Facing Tim's stiff, I ran for more water, "Drink!"

"Please! I already have to go bad, but I can't!"

Paul came out with, "See that bottle of rubbing alcohol on the shelf? Pour that over his peter. I had a nurse do that to me once."

There was a knock at the door.

"Jerome, stick your head out and see who that is."

"It's a boy. He has a jar and says Dr. Reiter sent him to join Sean's group."

"Let him in," I said, getting Tim over the drain and pouring a half-bottle of alcohol on him.

That and three other naked boys were the newcomer's first look at my group.

"Do you next," I greeted him without glancing up. "We're running late, so go ahead and take your own clothes off."

I got back to the job, put Tim's jar on the floor, had him kneel in front of it, and took a grip. Out of the corner of my eye, I saw the new boy hadn't moved.

"Jerome, give him water, lots of water, and get his shoes and socks off."

The alcohol worked like magic. In a second Tim let go. The jar past the 3/4 mark, I pulled it away and let him pee down the drain. I turned to the newcomer and saw Gary. *In shock* described Harold, but it would take Dr. Reiter to come up with a word for this 14-year-old. I gave his jar to Jerome, got him bare to the waist, did some buttons inside and out, and remembering what he'd said about having to fill a bottle without a stitch, I asked, "Rather pee with your pants on?"

For answer an uncircumcised 6-incher shot into the open. Jerome took this in stride, but Bret acted like he'd been belted.

"There's no more alcohol; we'll just have to go ahead with the bath," I said, letting everything fall to the floor.

"He's hairier than Tim!" Bret squeaked.

Without much hope, I said, "When you can pee, let me know."

I took stock of the rest of my group and saw yellow; Harold had his trunks back on. Done in, I jerked the trunks so hard they split. Everything showing, Harold started to cry—I wrapped him in my arms.

"For God's sake, don't cry! Did I cry that time Dan pulled my sock off?"

"That was you!"

"That was me—sorry about your trunks."

I finished part one by taking Paul's towel and helping him into the tub. Paul was the perfect patient; he never complained and wasn't bashful. But his bush caused Bret a blink. The boys in place, I took my smock off, laid it on a shelf, and wet the six under the shower.

*So beautiful! Wonder if she'd let me buy her a soda?*

"Well, Sean, I hear you're trying to steal my job," she said, laying down some gowns.

Bare-chested, I was as embarrassed as if I'd been in the tub. But half a dozen naked boys didn't flap Elizabeth; this late in the summer she'd seen 16-year-olds, 6-year olds, and everything in between. I looked at my bunch; Paul was outdoing Gary, proving he was normal with an inch to spare, and the others were trying for new bests. Even Jerome's peenie was giving its all.

"Gary and Harold stay undressed," she said. "Soon as you're through, Harold goes on the examining table across the hall for Dr. Hauptmann; after that, Dr. Reiter will take Gary. I see three are uncircumcised—half, that's a lot. Remember what to do about it?"

"D-do about it?"

"Foreskins are retracted before you rinse—like so."

Elizabeth pulled back Harold, then Paul, then Gary, who took in the dream handling him and peed straight up in the air—Elizabeth jumped back with an "Eek!".

Afterwards, I kicked myself for not catching some, but in the excitement I just stood there watching him spout. The amazing thing was Gary's heavy pee made no dent in his bone.

Not having peed in front of a girl lately, I ignored it and got out, "But they haven't been soaped yet."

"No problem. I'll just put them back in place," she said, making the circle again.

"Remember, retract before you rinse. By the way, Sean, don't we have a date?"

If it was a joke, I didn't get it. Looking at my six and thinking of the soaping, scrubbing, and rinsing ahead, I wanted to call her back, but settled for clenching my teeth. I started nervous, bit by bit forgot myself, and by the second soaping, was as quick to tackle a dick as a neck. I think I even remembered to retract before the final rinse.

At last I had four in gowns and two in towels. The giant nurse came, loaded Paul's clothes onto his lap, had the other gowns pick up their stuff, and led the four away. I took Harold across the hall and got him onto the table.

A doctor came with a lady. *Harold's mother!* I thought, making the connection.

"Don't leave me!" he pleaded, grabbing my hand.

"Haven't we met?" his mother asked.

"Don't think so," I lied, watching her flinch as the doctor got rid of the towel.

Dr. Hauptmann held up Harold's peewees, "Note that both testicles have fully descended. Furthermore, the penis is now a respectable size."

The doctor rubbed his fingers around things, "No pubes yet, but that will come. The glans used to be markedly underdeveloped," he said, peeling Harold, "but I am quite proud of this one. Of course I will circumcise it—every boy should be circumcised. What do you think of him?"

"N-not sure. How does he compare with other boys?"

"I can show you," Dr. Hauptmann said, coming toward bare-chested me.

*Go ahead, stand there like a dummy and do nothing. This crazy doctor'll skin you front of Harold's mother—that'll jog her memory about how we met.*

"I don't think you should!" she let out.

"I assure you, Dr. Reiter would have no objection; we do each other's patients all the time," he answered, setting his sights on my buttons.

"Wait!" I yelled, "I'm too old, but I have a boy across the hall, Harold's age to the day."

"That would be better," the doctor said, "bring him here."

Gary was standing in his towel.

"You're wanted in the examining room," I said, feeling like the snake I was.

"D-Dr. Reiter's ready for me?" he asked, his first words since joining my group.

"The doctor's ready."

"There isn't a n-nurse, is there?"

"No nurse."

He pointed to the pole under his towel.

"You're worried about crossing the hall? Believe me it's been done before and without a towel. But hold on, I think I saw a supply closet next door."

I left the room, came back with a bottle of rubbing alcohol—he blushed when I took his towel off—him raw as a soup bone—"Nothing to be embarrassed about," I lied.

I led him to the drain—let the liquid splash down his pole—watched it collapse and shrink—filed it away in my head as something to use on myself in case of emergency. The bottle empty, I rewrapped him, and walked him next door.

"Excellent!" the doctor said. "Remove the towel, please."

It took Gary ten seconds to size things up and give me the look Jesus gave Judas. Ten seconds too long for Doctor Hauptmann, who was no slouch as a snatcher. It took Gary five seconds to waste a quart of alcohol while Harold's mother steadied herself against the examining table.

"Dr. Reiter wants me!" I cried, making for the hall.

Having passed a good part of the morning watching boys pee, I had to myself. I was about to look for a restroom when I remembered my smock and the empty jar.

*Why not kill two birds with one stone? That's the least I can do for him.*

I went back to the tub room and filled Gary's jar.

"Thank God this morning's over!" I said out loud, going down the hall.

But it wasn't. Dr. Reiter had other ideas. I was in his office starting to take my smock off when he stopped me, "Keep it on. Phyllis is alone in 121 and needs assistance. Go help her. Then you can leave for lunch."

"What do you want me to do?" I asked.

"There's a group of boys from a private school in the office—rich kids."

"So you want them in towels?"

"Waste of time, and there are too many—ha, ha!—round them up, shear them in the waiting room, and we'll run them through like sheep. You can be Boy Blue, I'll be Bo Peep."

I stopped counting at 20, ages 11 to 13, I figured, maybe a couple turned 14. *You have to be tough,* I said to myself.

"Line up at the water fountain and take a drink—a long drink!" I was thinking ahead.

"Through that door!"

There was a boy-in-towel sitting on a chair.

"Stand up! We'll run you through with this bunch," I said, doing a snatch that'd've made Dr. Hauptmann proud.

I turned to my flock, "Everyone exactly like him!"

One of the boys giggled, "Excuse me, Sir, mine doesn't get that big."

I looked behind me; the kid had a six-incher.

Clothes came off—real close quarters—skin bumping skin—maybe 30 boys—so much white made me think—*O Jesus!*—*Gym class like Bryan'd told me, You'll probably get Coach Alexander—has no truck with modesty—the first day he has the class line up naked on both sides of the trough.*

Then back to the Clinic—boys laughing—grabbing at weenies—me yelling, "Stop! . . . Stop!"

I pointed to the first kid, "Pick up your forms and make a line, a curving line behind him! . . . All right, through that door!"

"What's behind the door?"

"A nurse, a young nurse."

"Y-you mean a girl?"

"Good-looking blonde—through the door!"

She did the temps and pressures and hearts—me the heights and weights—most of the older boys covering themselves with their hands, most of the younger ones showing their weenies.

"Take your hands away! . . . Take your hands away!"

Me marking their forms for circumcision and hair. Her pushing up testicles—one, then the other—"Cough!" she'd order.

Both of us marking jars. Boys peeing everywhere—paying no mind it was in front of a girl—scooting the holdouts naked across the hall—them none to anxious to make the trip—"Go! I'll hold the door for you!"—to give them the cold water treatment.

Finally they were dressed and gone.

"Ever thought of becoming a doctor?" Phyllis asked.

"Think I'd rather dig ditches."

# CHAPTER 57

The time before our afternoon appointment was spent in the Park. I smiled at the tiny sea horses, laughed as the seals did their act, and shivered at the great sharks. My father was in a holiday mood, and he gave in to my choice of the Tea Garden for lunch. The happiness of that hour has stayed with me throughout the years: the setting, the costumes, the meal served so politely, but most important, the tie with my father at its closest—by day's end it would plop like a mud ball. We were walking to the car.

"Sean, I'd like to discuss something, something that will affect you, your mother, and myself, perhaps in drastic ways. You know times have been hard—"

"Sure, Dad, I know that."

"Any idea how long it's been since I've had a raise?"

"Gee, Dad, I don't."

"It's been five years. The owners think employees—even professionals—should be grateful just to keep their jobs and not take a cut."

"Why not find another job?"

"Easier said than done, but that's what we need to talk about; I have been offered a job, one with an extremely handsome increase in salary plus an allowance for expenses."

"Swell, Dad!"

"The job's in Arabia."

"Arabia! That's nothing but sand!"

"But underneath the sand there's oil. It wouldn't be forever, five years, maybe ten—"

"Ten years! I'll be ancient! What would I do there?"

"That's the main thing I want to talk about. There are no educational facilities where we'd live; you'd have to go away to school. Seems to me you'd be better off staying here. Your mother and I would come back to visit in two or three years."

"Can't Mom stay too?"

"Wives belong with husbands—how can I explain? Some subjects aren't meant to be discussed outside the Confessional, but perhaps you're old enough to be told the basis for marriage. A man has certain . . . needs, needs which can be properly satisfied only by a wife. Therefore, it would be wrong for him to be separated from her for long periods of time. Does that make things clear?"

"Oh, sure!"

"I was wondering, since you seem to like them so much, how you'd feel about living with the O'Neills? Would you prefer that to boarding school?"

"Absolutely!—if they'd have me."

"I've already spoken to Mrs. O'Neill, and since you agree, we can take it as definite. Actually, they'll be moving in with you. Our house is new and larger, and they'll save paying rent. Of course, there are only the two bedrooms, but as I pointed out to Mrs. O'Neill, they're oversized and each has its private bath. Would you mind sharing your room with Bryan? It should be a little like having a brother. I've often thought it would've been good if I'd had a brother."

"How, Dad?"

"No way really—just a crazy idea."

"Anyway, Bryan's better than a brother; he's my best friend."

I got ready for what I thought'd be a long wait as my father went into Dr. Reiter's office, but he was back in five minutes. "Let's go!" he said, making for the front entrance.

"We're leaving already?"

"We're going swimming. Dr. Reiter's arranged for us to be guests at the Sparta Club; he thinks every boy should get a swimming lesson from his father. We're to come back here afterwards."

I had no trouble recognizing Dr. Reiter's heavy hand. I pulled up something from my first visit: *So your father has not seen you naked since you were a small boy? And what about you—?*

"We'll need suits—there will be suits?"

"Of course. Dr. Reiter said the club supplies grey trunks that have *SPARTA* written across them in blue letters."

"Boys get them too?"

"Men and boys alike."

*Thank God for that.*

"Guess there're benches for changing."

"They have private cubicles where you leave your clothes and valuables."

Something was rotten and not in Denmark. I was positive Dr. Reiter had only one reason for sending us swimming together, so I kept on,

"One for the two of us?"

"Naturally we'll take turns."

*Bet Dr. Reiter wasn't counting on that.*

It was an all-male club in a big building with Greek columns out front. We followed an arrow with *POOL* over it. This was a quiet time of day; there were no swimmers in the water. A lone grownup was stretched out on a canvas lounge, *SPARTA* in blue down one side of his grey trunks. The sleeper had a belly, and I was proud to compare my father with him.

We went past the pool to a door with a sign saying *NO ONE UNDER 21 UNLESS ACCOMPANIED BY AN ADULT.* Just inside there was a man sitting at a desk next to some cabinets; on the wall beside him was a board full of keys hanging on nails. My father handed over the guest pass Dr. Reiter'd given him and got a key, "Number six, down that aisle. Showers straight across."

In full sight of the desk was an open line of showers.

"I understand you supply the suits," my father said.

"Sure thing. One men's medium, one men's small. Towels too."

"Where do we get the suits and towels?"

"Right here. Pick them up after you shower. That's how we enforce the rule."

He pointed to a sign over the door.

NUDE SHOWERS REQUIRED BEFORE SWIMMING—SOAP PROVIDED—USE IT!

"I see . . ."

Jaw muscles showed my father's feelings, but he started down the aisle.

*God! It's really going to happen!*

Halfway, my father muttered and turned—"You wait by number six."

I could hear talking, but couldn't make out the words. He came back with a new plan.

"No need for me to go in the water—I can teach you from the edge. I'll wait by the pool. Come out when you've suited up."

He handed over the key and took off.

. . . me feeling like one of those babies who's been tossed from a sleigh to slow down the wolves . . .

Inside number six, I said to myself, "Look, you've spent the morning with boys showing the works, and no one died. This guy sees dicks all day long. So what if he sees yours?"

I almost convinced myself—almost—till I argued, "But the dicks he sees point down."

Everything off but my pants, I opened the door and went up the aisle to the attendant.

"Excuse me, Sir, is there a rule against getting your towel before you shower?"

"Never heard of it."

"Can I have a towel, please?"

He handed me one.

I went down to number six, got into the towel, and hurried to the nearest shower. Keeping my back to the desk the whole time, I let the towel drop, felt myself boing, stepped in, turned on the water, soaped, rinsed, turned off the water, and took two steps backwards to pick up the towel. I didn't dry myself; didn't even wrap myself, just bunched the towel around myself—way better than a doily—and walked to the man.

"My suit, please," I said without looking at his face.

"You leave the towel here."

"L-Leave the towel here?"

"Yes,"

"Y-You want me to give you the towel?"

"That's the rule."

I let it slip off . . .

There was one of those long pauses like when I was 11 . . . That over, he helped what would fit of me into the suit.

"Ice," he said, pointing to a brown chest.

I chipped off two big pieces, went back to number six, pulled off the suit, packed myself in ice till my blood turned blue, put the suit back on, and went out to my father.

As soon as I got to the pool area, the man with the belly left for the locker room. In a few minutes he came back a policeman.

*That was close*, I thought to myself—*He'd've put me in jail.*

The swimming lesson was hardly a starter; I learned just enough to want to try again.

In the locker room, I raced past the desk looking at the floor. "Hey! You're suppose to leave the suit!"

"Be right back!"

Me dressed, waiting for my father to finish his cigarette, a boy came running towards us trailed by a grownup.

"Hurry up, Pop! Last one in the shower's a rotten egg!"

We turned our heads together, meeting each other's eyes . . . Dad flushed and looked away . . .

I would never see my father naked.

# CHAPTER 58

**I**'d finished bringing things up to date, and eyes closed lay on the examining table ready to act out my Elizabeth dream. His own interview over, my father'd stepped out for a coffee and smoke.

"Nurse, prepare the patient for examination!"

"Now she's untying my left shoelace—" I said out loud.

Someone was untying my shoelace! *Dr. Reiter?—my date with Elizabeth!* I opened my eyes and there she was, red-gold hair, high cheekbones, green eyes.

"God, you're beautiful!"

She smiled, "I was afraid you'd stand me up."

My feelings were all jumbled—scared to death and excited like crazy. The thought of her hands on me! There was no holding back; she watched it fight my pants till it had nowhere to go.

"Now lie still and let me do my job."

The first touch on my skin as she slipped off a sock wasn't soft and cool as I'd once supposed, but soft and warm—she was slow and gentle with the shirt, scarcely causing me to move while she eased it off—as she undid the first button of my pants, her fingers touched my belly—she warmed me with a smile—Bryan's words roared in my head, "Eager to receive the thrust . . ."

My manhood exploded through my boxer fly, past the top of my pants, brushing her fingers . . .

. . . my body left to carry on the battle . . . my mind off in a place of its own . . .

. . . sounds leaked in . . . "Dr. Reiter!" she called, "I think you should see this!"

"A problem?" he asked.

"No problem, just checking everything is as you expected."

"Perhaps more than I expected, but continue. I shall stand by."

"Doctor, am I right in thinking he's abnormal?"

"On the tail of the distribution curve to be sure—extraordinarily well-developed for a Caucasian. Even among naked tribes, he would hold his own . . . There is a history of a tight foreskin; if you will retract it, we can judge the matter."

I gasped as Elizabeth's fingers brought me down to the table, turning me into a slab of beef on a butcher block . . .

"Tight without doubt. Now we observe full florescence. I assure you a glans this size is not an everyday sight. Let us determine whether the foreskin can be manually restored to its original position. While you are attempting that, I will go for his father."

*My father!* The glob of grey cells back in working order dove into a rabbit hole.

My brain was cut off again, but Elizabeth's sausage-stuffing jumped the gap . . . my legs went weak . . . pins-and-needles moved across my body . . . the light faded . . . a cloud of dark filled the room . . . I was falling down an elevator shaft . . . the shaft went on and on . . . I reached out . . . the shaft flew by faster . . . I knew when I hit bottom I'd die . . . I raced toward death . . . I let myself go . . . I welcomed death . . . faster and faster . . . I longed for death . . . the falling was unbearable . . . I begged for death . . . "Take me, Lord!" I cried . . .

"My God!"

My father's voice came down the shaft . . . I grabbed for the sound . . . too late . . . I hit bottom . . . splattered into a million pieces . . . opened my eyes . . . expecting to see my Maker . . . I saw a Roman Candle shooting into the air . . . shooting white . . . shooting hot milk . . . the pieces of the puzzle fell into place . . . I'd eaten of The Tree . . .

. . . I saw my father . . . his face all twisted . . . my insides came out . . . gushing vomit mixed with squirting milk . . .

. . . the storm died . . .

Elizabeth and my father were gone.

Dr. Reiter spoke, "Behind you is a wash basin and some towels. I will leave you to clean yourself, but do not dress; a nurse will bring a gown. Tomorrow morning Dr. Hauptmann will circumcise you."

I'd washed and was reliving Elizabeth . . . The door opened . . .
"O my God! Excuse me! Looking for Dr. Reiter . . . What did they do to you!"
Gary shook his head and backed out.

Next through the door was my father, "For the love of Christ, cover yourself!"
I looked down . . . "Cover yourself!"
. . . and willed my arms in front of me . . .
"Get dressed!"
"Dr. Reiter—"
"Forget Dr. Reiter! Get dressed!"
He closed the door as he left.

My father was waiting in the hall; we avoided each other's eyes. He didn't speak, just motioned for me to follow. We walked from the Clinic to the car and drove away. In a few minutes he pulled over to the curb, pointed to a neon sign, and made for an eatery called Bar and Grill. I tagged along. Inside the building, he led the way to a booth, saying nothing till a waiter with a small white towel over one arm showed up.
"First things first, a bourbon and soda, please."
The drink came on a round tray. My father downed half of it in two swallows; then spoke, more to himself than to me, "God knows, I'm entitled to this after what happened."
He finished his drink, called the waiter over, and placed an order, which like so many things from that day stays sharp in my memory: *two hamburger steaks with shoestring potatoes, one coffee, one milk, and one piece of banana cream pie.*

The Great Mystery had shaken me to my deeps. I thirsted for my father's forgiveness, hungered to hear I was still part of the family.
I heard: "Swear you will never use your hands on yourself—swear you will save your body for marriage. Swear on your immortal soul! Swear on the immortal soul of your mother!"

"I swear on my immortal soul! I swear on the immortal soul of my mother!"

"As soon as you're settled with the O'Neills, I want you to go to Confession and take Holy Communion."

It was too easy—it wasn't enough. I'd have sworn to anything—been glad of any punishment—and keeping to what I'd sworn wouldn't even be hard. The Fruit was too strong for boy flesh, and that one would choose such dirtiness, I couldn't believe.

"Remember! It would be a sin against yourself, a sin against your mother, a sin against your future wife, and a sin against God."

# PART III

## CHAPTER 59

**A**t the end of goodbye my father said, "Every Catholic family wants one of their own as a priest, so I've taken steps to get you into City Seminary after you finish high school."

"B-but I thought you wanted a grandson."

"A priest-son will do nicely—and you better not mess up like you did altar boy."

*Me a priest? Bad as a doctor.*

But that was far in the future; I had other things to worry about. The war against my modesty was back to square one. Even down to my undershorts in front of Bryan was too much. I was afraid of my body, afraid of its power, afraid of what it could do. The past two weeks had turned me inside out; changing my Elizabeth dream into the real thing; waving goodbye to my mother till the train faded into the distance, wondering if I'd ever see her again; learning everyday living with my new family.

Bryan was tuned to me—he knew there was something, but asked no questions—told me to change in the bathroom till I got used to having a roommate—said it was a good month to switch to pajamas—suggested no brotherly showers.

But Bryan couldn't help me now; staring me hard in the face was the day I'd prayed would never come, my first day of high school and my first day of gym class. Freshmen who didn't go out for a sport

had only two choices, straight out of the box in the morning or right after lunch. I let it slip to Bobby that come frost-on-the-pumpkin time no way you'd find me greeting the dawn in an icy locker room. Knowing Bobby was a walking newspaper, I hoped this flash would travel the grapevine and throw Joey off the scent. If only he weren't in the class, maybe—*Please, God!*—I could get through it.

I showed up 15 minutes early and took a bench in the farthest corner. Boys slowly straggled in, one or two at a time, three from my small graduating class, most strangers from around the county. There wasn't much talk; the mood would've been just what the director ordered for a Jimmy Cagney-Pat O'Brien scene set on death row. I was counting off the seconds when Joey sauntered in and swaggered over.

"Well if it isn't Sean; heard you was taking the afternoon class, but I don't believe everything I hear. This oughta be nice'n cozy; sure I can fix it so we get next-door lockers. Don't worry, you'll have nothing to squeal to Bryan about—I won't touch, just look."

Dirty! Dirty all over—that's how Joey made me feel.

Two muscled youths wearing yellow sweaters with four red sleeve stripes showed up.

"Are you pip-squeaks in the right place? This isn't Kiddiegarden, you know."

One of them went over to the smallest boy in class, "Sure this is the school you want? You weren't looking for Dumbbell Elementary?"

"Yessir—I mean nosir—I was looking for Pineapple High."

"You do know this is *Boys'* Gym?"

"Yessir."

"And that to get in you need a dick?"

"Y-yessir."

"Well, let's see it."

"Y-you mean—?"

"I mean."

The boy had trouble digging inside.

"You're keeping us all in suspense."

Circumcised and small. "Jesus! That should've been drowned at birth. Put it away! Okay, let's get the introductions over with, I'm Bob, he's Rob. You can call me *Sir*—ha, ha!—you can call him *Hey You*. I'm sure you've all heard of the Bob and Rob Show. In last year's game against the Cats, I threw a perfect pass for the winning

touchdown; all Rob had to do was stand there and watch it fall into his big mitts. Did a repeat performance against the Dogs. As a reward, Coach has given us two weeks to whip you mamas' boys into shape. If one of us says *Squat!* you squat. Is that clear? . . . I didn't hear anything. Let me give you a clue, the right comeback's *That's clear, Sir!* Let's hear it!"

"That's clear, Sir!"

"Didn't hear you."

"That's clear, Sir!!"

"Better. You'll end up a lot healthier if you learn right off I'm a ramrod. Show proper respect, break no rules, volunteer every time you're asked, and you might not taste what Rob's got behind his back. Show'em Rob!"

Rob held up a very large, very thick, polished wooden paddle.

"Rock maple. Ain't she a doozy? We call her Big Bertha. Any kid who earns Bertha meets her crawling mother-naked across the locker room floor while Rob tails along scoring bull's-eyes. Sorry to say, Rob doesn't know his own strength; the last kid he zeroed in on couldn't sit for a month. Questions?"

"No questions, Sir!!!"

"Better. Incidentally, a minor legal point, hazing has been outlawed by the Principal, so what happens in this class is between you, me, Rob, and the lamppost. Rat, and you go for a swim in the Bay wearing concrete boots and a necklace of teeth—your teeth. That clear?"

"That's clear, Sir!!!"

"We'll start off this morning with a history lesson about your new alma mater. You know we're Pineapples. Anyone know why? . . . No one?

"All right, Small Balls, listen up while I'll tell you the school legend."

In the beginning, there was a boy and a girl.

Girl say, 'Boy tall like tree. Me call him Pine.'

Boy say, 'Girl full like fruit. Me call her Apple.'

Girl ask, 'What boy have between legs?'

Boy answer, 'Him called Dick.'

'Boohoo!' girl cry, 'me no have Dick.'

'No cry,' boy say, 'Pine stick Dick in Apple.'

And nine months later the first Pineapple was born.

Not a snicker was to be heard, not even from Joey; nobody was in a laughing mood.

"Ha, ha!" Rob put in, "they don't get it."

"Too subtle, but they better get this: no copying Pine in the locker room. Any kid who gets it on around here meets Bertha. Questions?"

"No questions, Sir!!!"

"One more thing, next time I tell a joke, there better be a few chuckles . . . Which brings us to the subject of gym outfits. Here we have a fashionable top done in prison grey, followed by stylish grey shorts to match, coordinating grey socks, and Keds in your choice of white. This contraption is called a jockstrap—a supporter to your grandmother—it's not to keep your chin warm. When the nice old lady at the gym store asks what size, don't do like Rob as a freshman and say *six inches*."

This got a small laugh.

"Now, one of the things we try to do in this class is bring good friends close together. All here who have a good friend in class raise your hands."

Eight hands went up.

"Rob, pick out two who qualify."

Rob went around whispering, "This one should do—name's O'Toole."

"All right, O'Toole, step over here. And I want O'Toole's friend to stand with him as a friend should. Come forward, Friend . . . Name?"

"Bancroft, Sir."

"So you two are buddies and've never seen each other where it counts. Why is that? What happens when you sleep over?"

"We keep our backs turned."

"That's not very friendly—you won't have to turn them next time. All right, face each other and strip to the skin . . . Now!"

. . . O'Toole had hair—Bancroft didn't.

"Like what you see, Bancroft?"

"Yessir—nosir—I don't know, Sir."

"It'll grow on you. OK, you two, see that door? Straight across the hall's the Nurse's office. Tell the senior girl at the desk you want the deluxe job—actually you'll get the deluxe job whether you want it or not. Take the grade-schooler with you. He'll be the comedy act . . . Out!"

"L-like th-this!"

"Rob, get them into their undershirts . . . That make you feel better? Nothing to be bashful about; that dame'll end up seeing more dicks than she can count to—'course she'll always look back on you three as her first. Go! Or down on the floor for Bertha. Skedaddle! . . . The lot o' you!"

They skedaddled, the friends trying to hide themselves.

"Should warm up her first day. Fair's fair. That's what they did to me and a pal—whose name I won't mention—when we were freshmen. All the girl helpers are dick-crazy—why else volunteer?—and believe me, there're plenty volunteers—no undershorts when an assistant weighs you—no sooner through the door than you're showing balls—some kids think they can make it in a jockstrap—fat chance.

"What I'm going to tell you now is considered unmentionable—innocents better cover their ears—more than one boy's gone off in front of an assistant. The powers that be call it an accident of nature—happens mostly to freshmen—some of them first-timers. I know a first-timer who passed out—senior in this room."

"That's a lie! I didn't pass all the way out."

"Like heck you didn't—I was there, remember? And I suppose it wasn't your first time?"

"Everyone has a first time."

"Yeah, but usually before they're going on 15—my brother did me the day I turned 13—*Happy Birthday! Take your clothes off!*—'course I was a prodigy. Enough of that—we come now to swimming. Anyone here doesn't know how to swim? If you're not champing at the bit to be thrown off the deep end into 14 feet of water, better raise your hand."

I thought about my chances—*14 feet?*—*my father kept me in the shallow end where I could touch bottom*—*I'd drown for sure.* With a sinking feeling, I put my hand in the air—the only one who did.

"Over here! On the bench!"

"The bench?"

"That's what I said. Stand on the bench so everyone can get a good look at you. What's your name?"

"Lacey, Sir."

"So you're our only beginner. Imagine a big kid like you not knowing how to swim. But I can tell you're dying to learn. Why else

wear your beginner's suit under your clothes? I bet someone told you we'd want you to model it for the class."

"Honest, Sir, nobody told me anything about swimming. I don't have a suit on."

"I say you do. Rob, tell him what frosh wear for swimming."

"Their birthday suit."

"We're waiting, Lacey! Model your suit or prepare to taste maple, and I don't mean syrup. Either way you'll end up across the hall in the hands of the assistant—unless of course you're dead from Bertha."

This was what you call Hobson's Choice. One of the sea of faces stood out—Joey's. *That look!* Leaning on my old one-foot-off-the-gutter days, I took my only shot, hit the floor, broke through the bodies, made the door, and kept running till the school grounds disappeared behind a rise.

# CHAPTER 60

**I** stopped. I had no plans for the next hour, the next day, the next week. I wondered how long it took to hitchhike to Arabia. *My asthma!—a doctor's excuse—there must be such a thing—why can't Dr. William write me an excuse?* It was three miles to his office, but the morning was mine.

"An excuse for asthma? I couldn't say; you'll have to ask the doctor," came from the lady at the desk. "There's an examining room open if you'll follow me."

It was a few steps down the hall.

"In here. The doctor shouldn't be long. In the meantime, undress completely."

"I-It's just my chest."

"Dr. William's standard procedure for boys. I'm sure Dr. Bea will see no reason to alter it."

"Dr. Bea! Where's Dr. William?"

"You haven't heard? There was an ever-so-nice article about it in The Gazette. Dr. William has volunteered as a replacement medical missionary in Africa."

"When will he be back?"

"In a year."

"Actually, I'm in no hurry. Think I'll wait."

While the desk lady was in the middle of giving me a funny look, Dr Bea poked her head in.

"Whom do we have here? Ah! Sean. What can I do for you?"

"W-was wondering about an excuse for Gym—because of my asthma."

"Certainly. Quite justified in my opinion. No need for an examination; I listened to your chest not long ago. Come back in an hour, and it will be typed and ready for you."

This was one of those silver linings you hear sung about. Behind the office, I knelt in the dirt and poured thanksgivings to the Almighty. Putting myself in the hands of another female so soon after Elizabeth would've needed either the heart of a hero or the calm of a clam.

"A doctor's excuse? What a dope! Should've thought of it for you."

"God, Bryan! I'm so relieved! You don't know what it's like having something you dread hang over your head."

"Don't I now? Naturally, you wouldn't think so. The way you die the second you hit the pillow, you'd never notice that Great Nature's second course withholds its balm from Bryan, knits not his ravell'd sleave—in short, your favorite brother sleeps no more."

"Gosh, what's the problem?"

"September's the problem, time for Big Mouth Bryan to make good on his fancy words."

"September? What's September got to do with it?"

"Tell you in a minute. Close the bedroom door."

"Why? There's no one in the house."

"Humor me. I feel better that way. Be right back," he said, turning into the bathroom.

In two minutes he showed up naked with an erection.

"What do you think? Big enough for a ribbon at the County Fair? No? How about Honorable Mention?"

He held out a small jar, "Vaseline, a boy's best friend. On my 14th birthday, with the words, *Boys your age have a use for this,* Maman handed me a jar."

The fog was lifting, *Till fair September holds full her sway!*

"Bryan . . ." I whispered.

"First I lie down—I like my knees part way up—"

"Bryan . . ."

"Don't think I can get through this if you keep interrupting—"

"Bryan, I-I kn-know . . ."

"Know? You mean—when?—who?—not Joey!"

"At the doctor's . . ."

"The doctor himself?"

"The nurse . . . m-my f-father . . . s-saw . . ."

"Holy Mother! That explains a thing or three."

He took a seat next to me and put an arm across my shoulders.

"Don't hold back—I'll mop up afterwards. In time of trouble, we'll be father and brother to one another."

Bryan rocked me, softly crooning, "Hush little baby . . ."

He went through all the verses, ending at the beginning, ". . . Papa's gonna buy you a mocking bird."

"I'm all right," I said.

"All right! Of course, you're all right! You're Bryan O'Neill's brother! Begorra! Would you look at Johnnie! Limp as a wet noodle. Sure and what a turrible waste of a lovely boner."

# CHAPTER 61

**B**ryan knew the way of things, "I'm thinkin' we'll be havin' a small test. Who's always right?"

"Big Brother's always right," I answered.

"There's a smart lad. Now Big Brother says till he cuts the cord you'll be walkin' with him."

No hazing—that was the rule—but for two weeks teachers looked the other way, making it open season on freshman boys. Stories grew as they got told. Like the one about the frosh who the same afternoon got pantsed by seniors, pantsed by juniors, and pantsed by sophomores. Next time I heard the story, the seniors took off his pants, the juniors took off his pants and shirt, the sophomores took off the works; and after that the kid walked the rest of the way naked, figuring clothes were a waste of time. So far, I'd seen one initiation. At lunchtime where a circle of ninth-grade girls were eating, a boy was making the rounds in his boxers. He had to stop at each bunch and ask, "Wanna hold my weenie?" All he got was blushes. Lucky for him Janet was holding one down the road at the Dog and Bun.

Thursday afternoon when Bryan didn't show on time, I wandered off and got shoved into a line where freshmen had to play Dick Confessions. The guards were snickering; because no one laughed at his story, the last kid was bent over, holding his dropped pants, getting swatted on his bare behind.

"You're up!"

Here was the next boy's story: Early June I hitchhike out to the beach. It's a Tuesday and the place's empty. I find a spot to change, and carry my stuff a ways. It's sunny but cool, so I flop and hug the sand. Getting my nerve up, I run into the water, splash around for ten minutes with my teeth chattering, and come back freezing to where a girl—maybe 14—is standing by my clothes, which I'm anxious to get into.

"Yours, if you show me what a boy looks like," she says, holding out two bits.

This is easy money. I take the cash and put it in my swimsuit's little pocket; then spread my arms wide and say, "Here's what a boy looks like."

"Naked," she says.

This stops me.

"We're all alone," she says.

I do a 360 and have to admit she's got that right.

"Then give me back my quarter," she says.

You know I don't wanna do that, so I skin outa my suit and spread my arms like before, "This is the works."

She stares a while, which makes me kinda nervous, and says, "I thought it would be bigger."

I look down; my dick's a blueberry, somewhere between zero and size one. I look up; she's shaking her head.

"I'm never getting married," she says, and walks away.

Before the laughs died, I was pulled out of line by Bryan.

Friday we'd started home when he saw someone across the square and ran to meet him . . .

"We're going back."

"Why?"

"Because you went for a stroll yesterday. We still have another week to get through, and you better learn fast what happens to baby Pineapples who wander."

On the football field were four nervous freshmen holding tight to their unbuttoned boxers, along with a dozen older boys taking in the youngsters' pain. Happiness showed on the older faces; they knew what the freshmen didn't: one way or another those shorts were coming off.

"Hey Blondie! Pull the leg of yur underwear up and show yur balls."

"Ha, ha! What makes yuh think he has balls?"

"Hey Blondie! Yuh have balls?"

The undersized boy's fear was so thick I could taste it.

"Hey Doug! Yur in charge—pants the little twerp so we can see what he has."

"Wally's in charge, Jonesy, keep your pecker down—all in good time."

"Yeah, but shit, I gotta split."

Jonesy left, and Bryan turned to his friend, "Fill us in, Steve."

"Innocents—look like grade-schoolers. Wally put stakeouts six different places for kids leaving, asking if they took Gym. These four made boo-boo's—said they didn't. Had to choose between a gang shower and a water bucket—drank like camels. Wally loves to drag it out'n keep'em scared—plenty worried about their shorts—I'm sticking around to find out why. Shouldn't take long."

"Where is Wally?"

"Went to borrow some lipstick."

"OK, little frogs, here's your beauty operator," came from their keeper.

"You there, you there, you there, you there," Wally said, standing the freshmen so they faced the audience.

"Thought of something, you kids drank a creek; wanna take a break and go to the little boys' room?"

He got, *Y-yes*, four times.

"We'll wait a few minutes."

He painted their faces.

"S-sir—" came out of a boy.

"Have to go real bad?"

"Y-yes."

"How about some sexy red nipples? Damn good if I say so myself."

"P-please!"

"Real, real bad?"

"Y-y-yes."

"OK, Frogs, I'm going to give an order, and you're going to obey!"

Wally went to each of the four and shouted in his face,

"Understand!"

"Y-yessir."

". . . Put your hands on your heads!"

*Prob'ly in school under Mr. Stillwater.*

Blondie was small, smooth like the boy next to him; of the others, one had light brown fuzz, one had heavy dark fuzz, the only one who wasn't circumcised.

"Keep your hands on your heads! Pee!"

They went to it no-hands—peed and peed—wetting their fallen shorts—till they were peed out.

"Take your hands down! Didn't your fathers show you anything? Shake your dicks! . . . Call those shakes? Put some muscle in it!"

The boys didn't get bones, just dangles.

*Too scared,* I thought.

"Show 'em stiff!" came from the crowd.

"Soap'll take care o' that," Wally said.

"You four still alive?—what year is it?—what county you in? Doug, take the bares; I'll take the fuzzies."

Wally took them by the hand—"Step over your shorts—and smile if we meet any girls. To the showers! Everyone gets a crack at soaping. Who wants a leg?"

"Bryan, let's go."

He took me to where I'd be safe.

"You can make it from here. Knowing Wally, those kids need protection."

# CHAPTER 62

"How'd Blondie make out in the gym?"

"Better than the others—Jonesy's the only one queer for pre-pubescent boys—comprends?"

"As much as I want to."

"In case you're wondering, none of them lost their innocence, but unless you want to put in your autograph book about a dozen kids taking turns soaping your stalk and sliding your skin, you better stick to Big Brother like a tattoo next week."

I stuck to him like a tattoo.

The second Thursday after school Steve was coming toward us.

"Bryan! Behind the bleachers there must be 50 bare-ball freshmen getting The Treatment. For a nickel you get to pick a kid and work him stiff. If yours's the last one to pee his bone off, you win a buck, six bits for second, four bits for third. Ha, ha! There's one named Clarence with the smallest dick you ever seen. I'm betting it never goes up. Show starts in a few minutes. Meet you there!"

"Poor Clarence, he'll die."

"You know him?" Bryan asked.

"Went through most of grammar school together."

"I have six cents. What about you?"

I fished out a nickel.

"Let's go!"

We were behind the bleachers.

"I'll wait here."

"Not exactly. You bring Clarence after I've ransomed him. Big Brother has to wheel and deal."

One thing Dr. Reiter'd done for me, so long as I wasn't one of them, I could size up a field of naked boys coolly as a nurse. Close to equal numbers of smooth, fuzz, and hair; maybe ten uncircumcised; lot of half-bones; two circumcised smooths standing next to each other, skinny white poles all the way stiff, looking like they wanted to crawl under a rock—friends, I figured—elbow to elbow, hands on their heads—Wally again—a bettor studying them like slaves on the block.

"Ha, ha! Can I play with their peewees?"

"Balls are free, but touch a dick and you've bought it."

From Red Dirt School, I saw two of Joey's gang who were in on my pantsing by Outlaw Trail—half-bones, one with fuzz, one with hair—they blushed when they spotted me. And Peanuts—uncircumcised—Joey'd never mentioned it—showing a dark shadow—everyone was growing up. No Joey, no Bobby. For the first time, I looked at the face of the boy two feet in front of me; he sat across the aisle in Ancient History.

"Hi," he said, giving a sick smile—skin—bush—dangle.

A bettor came up, "You're mine, Kid. Hey, Wally, I'm taking this one!"

"Don't warm him up to soon, Barney!"

"I'll just start his engine! Watch this," he said. "Turn sideways, Kid. Wanna see his secret, Charlie?"

"Sure, teach'im to be friendly."

"Hear that, Kid, he wants your pecker peeled."

"Please don't!"

"How does that feel? Yuh like it, don't yuh . . . don't yuh?"

"No-o-o . . ."

"Well your dick likes it; I can feel it grow. Soon as Wally gives the signal, we'll stand it up tall."

I looked around for Clarence and saw Jonesy examining a boy's equipment—it belonged to a scared Blondie.

"Paid for yuh, but not to win—yuh'd never get off the blocks. Let's beat it—over there—other side of the bleachers—I'll show yuh a real one."

Jonesy led Blondie away and from nowhere Clarence was in front of me.

"All fixed. Got him for a penny. He's in shock. Get him out of here."

"Bryan, see if you can help Peanuts."

I took Clarence by the hand and went back the way I'd come. Steve was right; between the legs he could pass for 10.

"N-need to . . ."

"Well, don't mind me."

"H-here?"

"Close your eyes."

He held a lot of pee.

Afterwards he started to talk, "I don't take Gym. Never'd seen another boy till a month ago when I put my 9-year-old cousin to bed."

"Well, you saw plenty today."

"Being naked with all those naked boys—was awful! Remember the time Mr. Stillwater had us pee together?"

"You didn't peek did you?"

"No, but I saw your underwear—unbuttoned pretty far down. Remember?"

"No."

"Wondered when he got you back to his punishment room if he made you take them off. Did he?"

"'Course not."

"Well, the year after we left, a boy told me he was sent to the Principal with another kid. They had to stand naked together in front of Mr. Stillwater with their hands on their heads—just like today—while he preached. And they had to stay like that while he caned their bottoms . . . Could I ask you something? Back on the field I saw a kid with his—you know—all big and swollen. What does that feel like?"

I looked at Clarence sitting there showing his soft weenie—no way I could explain.

Interrupting us, Peanuts came past the bleachers with a full bone followed by Bryan, who caught my look.

"Don't blame me, Sean, he was peeled when I bought him. Go ahead, Peanuts, pee it off."

Like Gary at the Clinic, he spouted up. He was still spouting when Blondie came running naked into Bryan's arms, "Help me!"

Right after him came Jonesy, naked except for a shirt he was holding in front of himself.

"What'd you do to him?" Bryan asked.

"Nothin'—little runt freaked out when he saw my boner," Jonesy said, moving the shirt to show himself.

"You are some piece of garbage—get the hell out of here!" Bryan yelled.

"What about my money? Paid for him, yuh know."

"You got your nickel's worth. Am-scray!"

Jonesy am-scrayed

"Wow! What a big one," Clarence let out.

"Wait'll you see Sean's."

"Bryan!"

He turned to Peanuts, "Good job, now let's get everyone dressed."

The clothes of 50 boys made a pile.

"Too much to look through; just take anything that fits."

We were home alone.

"So guess you're wondering about the other nickel? I invested it."

"Invested it?"

"Did you notice that kid with the heavy dark fuzz and the foreskin? He was one of the four who peed on their shorts last week. I liked his form in the shower afterwards; soon as Wally pulled his skin back, he zinged like a spring. Stayed that way till he got dressed, so I put the nickel on his nose."

"You mean you . . ."

"Me or someone else—what difference did it make to him? Anyway I love to work skins—Little Brother, all you have to do is ask."

"Bryan!"

"Besides, he's in for a third of the take. By the time I left, a dozen starters'd already peed themselves limp, while our dog was still straining at the leash—I like our chances."

Friday, Bryan told me, "The winner was an outsider with no hair and a dick you wouldn't look twice at—we finished second by a neck—2 bits apiece. Next one of these, we'll enter you and bet the ranch."

# CHAPTER 63

Saturday. The two weeks of Hell were a bad dream; freshmen could worry about something besides their shorts and look forward to next year when they would do the hazing.

"Big Brother's cutting the cord; you can go where you want, do what you want."

"Thought I'd play tennis tonight—they put lights in at the town courts—want to come?"

"I'd cramp your style. Anyway, I've been asked over to listen to records. 'Course I dream of luring Lorna out to the swing—but no hope with her old man watching every move. How does he expect to become a grandfather?"

I came from showering wrapped in a towel, and noticing I was gathering up clean clothes, Bryan went to a drawer and took out a jockstrap, "Little Brother, you have it pat about the care of tennis balls, but you don't know diddly about the care of boy balls. Take it from an old gym rat, boxers don't cut it, you need this."

"I'd feel funny."

"Have I ever lied to you—about anything important, I mean?"

He took the boxers and handed me the jock, "On!"

"Not sure how it works."

"Drop the towel, and I'll show you."

"That's OK!" I said, backing into the bathroom, "I'll figure it out!"

So I got to the courts snug in my first-ever jockstrap. Janet was hitting with a married couple in their 30s.

"Sean! I need a partner!"

I'd half expected it—and good partners were hard to find—so I joined her.

"They have new balls and they're paying for the lights."

After the first set I whispered, "Janet, we ought to let them win a game."

"Why?"

"Because they're old."

"Well, we're young."

Sure it was luck we were handling his serve, the husband wanted a third set. I'd told him to lead off when a Model A with a full rumble seat came honking toward us. As the toss went up, a song came from the car.

"Pineapple Hi-igh, Pineapple Hi-igh, We'd live and die for you, There's nothin' else to do—"

The ball went off the server's frame into the net.

"Take two," I said.

"First I'll take a minute to settle those hoodlums' hash."

He went out to the car, had a few words, and came back.

"Can't get through to them—drinking hard liquor. Where are the cops when you need them?"

I'd planned to let the poor guy win his serve, but with Janet giving nothing away, and with more bellowing from the roadster, he served four balls into the net to me, and that was the game.

"Can't play in this bedlam; we're leaving. I'll put another quarter in the lights for you—keep the balls."

"Thanks!"

As the couple walked away, four older kids in yellow sweaters piled out of the Model A. Now soon as I saw all those red stripes, I should've yelled, "Wait for me!" and gone into my rabbit act, but like a dumb bunny I went to the other side of the net to hit with Janet.

The courts were surrounded by a 12-foot-high wire fence, and the lettermen came through the only gate, closed the latch, and took seats on a bench next to it. By the time I'd picked out Bob and Rob from the gym class, there wasn't a soul in sight except Janet and the four sweaters.

*Prob'ly won't recognize me.*

"Wanna see a match! . . . Com'ere, give yuh the rules!"

Trying to make like a cucumber, I went over to them, "We know the rules."

"Notour rules! Broad starts; firs' ta four wins."

Bob dropped his voice, keeping it private from Janet, "'portant rule, yuh lose, yuh get jacked."

"J-Jacked?"

"Ha, ha! Yuh know the joke—yur in the back seat with a broad an' her kid brother Jack, an' yuh yell, 'Stop the car! an' let her little brother Jack off.' Yuh get yur pickle pumped. She'll love watchin' yuh shoot."

My brain shut down.

"Hafta mak't fair—get his feet!"

And when they'd finished, I was facing Janet in nothing but a jockstrap.

"Minute rest each two games!"

"Win! Win! Win!" rattled around my head.

No breaks of serve. At three-all during the time-out, Janet put her hand on my leg and whispered, "I'll lose if you promise to neck afterwards."

"Don't know how."

"I'll show you. Nod if you want to neck."

Forty-thirty. It hit me—matchpoint—a movie starting with the jockstrap coming off ran in my head—I held up a hand, asking for time—nodded—kept nodding. She served a double. The game went another six points before Janet let me win. She walked around the net.

"They've gone."

". . . Clothes?"

"Gone."

The lights went off. She took me by the hand, led me outside, and sat me on the grass where she kissed me and pushed me onto my back.

Her tongue went crazy—licking my lips—going in and out my mouth—against my tongue—back in my throat—her hand on my belly—me jerking like she was 220—ran over my legs—back to my belly—landed hard on my bulge—a bone popped out the side—her fingers found it—squeezed and pulled—squeezed and pulled—squeezed and pulled—me one long moan—got to my bulb . . . I was falling down an elevator shaft . . .

She stopped in time—"Let's get rid of this thing"—unwrapped my pole—pulled the jock down so everything was out in the

open—examined me by what light there was—brushed my hair—stretched the curl—separated my eggs with her fingers—felt one at a time—weighed the pair in her palm—choked my shaft with both hands—"You're so big!"

She slid the jockstrap all the way off, "I love you naked!"

My brain went into gear. I sprang to my feet, and like when I was nine, ran naked into the dark. If anyone saw me, they saw a blur. Jeanne was asleep, and Bryan wasn't home—I fell into bed.

# CHAPTER 64

"... **S**ean! ... Sean!"

"... Bryan?"

"You'll never guess! Lorna let me kiss her goodnight! Got a big favor to ask. I'm booked solid for baby-sitting; could you be the best brother in the whole world and take over some for me? Could you, Sean?"

"... Sure."

In the morning I found my racquet and clothes on the front porch. *She knew where they were all the time!*

"You went to bed naked last night."

"How do you know?"

"Can I help where my hands land when I'm dreaming?"

"Bryan!"

"You didn't by any chance see Janet?"

"We played doubles."

"And afterwards?"

"Came right home."

"Next time you come right home, wipe the lipstick off."

My first baby-sitting job was a 10-year-old.

"Lights out at nine. Make sure he uses the bathroom, stops him wetting the bed."

"Bath?" I asked.

"Hadn't thought about it. He's shy."

"Take it from someone who knows, Ma'am—I used to be shy—
better get him over it sooner than later."
"You think so?"
"I know so."
"You'll be gentle with him?"
"Absolutely!"

It was time to start things rolling. I took him to the bedroom,
"Get your clothes off."
Nothing happened. I thought a little joke might help, "Ha, ha,
can't get our weenie washed with our clothes on, can we?"
That went over like a lead balloon. He was out of the box like a
greyhound at the buzzer—through the house and into the street—
he'd covered a block by the time I caught up. I carried him under
one arm, him twisting his neck, trying to bite anything he could
reach.
I dropped my package on the bed and was quick on top,
working things off—him kicking the whole time. Finally I had him
down to his BVDS, wondering how to do all those buttons with him
biting—*When I'm President, I'll pass a law against BVDs.*
"Stop or I'll spank!"
He wouldn't stop. I put a leg over his neck and worked on the
buttons—got his arms out—and yanked the BVDs free. What could
I do? I knew he'd run if I let go, so I carried him kicking to the
bathroom and held him up under his arms till he peed. Beat, I let
him off without a bath.

That taught me stuff. Don't ask, do—no use feeling sorry
for'em—Pineapple's just around the corner. A lot to be said for
Bryan's motto—*Strip'em, wash'em, hav'em pee, and tuck'em in.*
"The unwritten sitter's code is that boys get spanked bare-bottom,"
Bryan told me.
"What if the sitter's a girl?"
"Ha, ha! Especially if it's a girl. When I was 10, I had one who
spanked me bare everything, 'What are you supposed to do when
you're bad?' she'd ask.
"I'd take all my clothes off in front of her and feel my weenie go
funny—that'd make her laugh. Then she'd sit down, pull her dress
up, and lay me naked across her bare legs to get my spanking."

"Why didn't you tell Jeanne?"

"And spoil the fun? That white skin excited me like all get-out. And once—I call it up every time I'm looking to go horny—the sitter took me to the swim club where her family had a membership, stripped me in the girls' side right out in the open, and had me stand under the shower. Well, there I am, covering myself with my hands, my mop of curls making me look like a girl, when this gorgeous thing ends up next to me naked—tits just the right size—nipples tight—and a coal-black pussy to dream on."

"She took a cat into the shower? Why?"

"Ha, ha! Probably wanted to make it soft and fluffy."

I couldn't imagine a cat putting up with a shower.

# CHAPTER 65

There were three Pineapple girls who reminded me of Elizabeth, one for her red-gold hair hanging long, one for her high cheek bones, one for her green eyes. I didn't know what I'd end up with, but whenever I saw one of them, I tried to undress her in my head. What I'd end up with was a bone I hid with my binder.

A trip would be a relief from school and baby-sitting.

No one who didn't live through the time can understand what the Silver Screen meant to us in the '30s and '40s. Reruns give no clue. What curls a lip now had us rolling in the aisle then. We never complained that Bette always played Bette or Gary always played Gary. That's what we came for.

*They don't mak'em like they used to!*

Who would you want but Coop as Longfellow Deeds? Who could teach us passion like Heathcliffe? And what about those two cigarettes lit together in one mouth? And all those romantic comedies with Claudette Colbert, Clark Gable, Irene Dunne, Charles Boyer, Cary Grant, Jean Arthur, Jimmy Stewart, and Katherine Hepburn? Their innocence is as dead as the dodo. Was there a dry eye in the house when Charles Boyer finds out why Irene Dunne didn't show on the 102$^{nd}$ floor of the Empire State Building? And when will there be a second Marlene who could with a wink make us boys squirm in our seats? Or another Ingrid who taught us a purer kind of love? And who but Errol to split the arrow or stick Gisbourne? And who better to stick than Basil Rathbone? He had it coming for whipping little Freddie Bartholomew.

"A suit and tie! Ah! the Confirmation clothes your mother ordered. I will be the talk of the town with such an escort. Mon Dieu! How you have grown! I turn around, and just like that, you are as tall as Bryan."

It was early autumn, the most beautiful time of our year. The football coach who'd long been drooling over Bryan's speed had talked him into going out for left halfback; and though today was open on the varsity calendar, practice was scheduled. Taking advantage of our chance, as fellow schemers Jeanne and I set off alone, leaving a note, "Gone shopping."

Bryan's birthday was coming up, and I had in mind a surprise present, an Irish novel which—though he'd never held a copy in his hands—I'd heard him talk about with great excitement, James Joyce's Ulysses. Questions by a boy my age at the two local bookstores got head shakes and hard looks. Our county wasn't ready for Molly Bloom.

Jeanne, who'd been without a car, was driving us to the City in the Pontiac my father'd left behind. I opened the driver's door—"Merci, très gallant!"—closed it and got in the other side. I hadn't ridden with Jeanne. I wondered, would she be nervous like my mother, who always bucked us when she let the clutch out and never stopped worrying about her right fender? I shouldn't've wondered. Jeanne drove easily, with enjoyment.

"Want me to roll the windows up? Your hair's blowing," I asked.

"Let it! Makes me feel alive!"

I was in luck. City Books had a sale on Modern Library editions—$1.25 for Giants and 75 cents for Regulars. For two dollars—no sales tax—I was able to pick up freshly inked copies of both "Ulysses" and "A Portrait of the Artist as a Young Man," which Bryan'd read but didn't own. I'd planned to spend as much as three dollars on "Ulysses" alone, so I looked for a place to park the dollar burning a hole in my pocket.

We strolled past the plush Fox Palace where the sign said, "You Can't Take It With You." Without asking, I dashed to the box office

and laid down the dollar. "One adult and one student, please," taking the quarter in change—high school meant no more 10 cent movies.

We got in at the middle but thought nothing of that. Knowing how things came out wouldn't cut one bit into our enjoyment of the second showing—there was never a question of leaving before the end. It wasn't just the stars, Jimmy Stewart and Jean Arthur, who meant so much to us; it was also the supporting cast like Mischa Auer, Donald Meek, Edward Arnold, Spring Byington, and Lionel Barrymore—old friends all.

During the movie I laughed so hard I fell off the seat. While Jeanne would bury her face in my shoulder pad, clutch my sleeve, or take my hand to share the moment. We were still laughing as we left the theatre.

"Do you know what these people are thinking? They are thinking, *Look at that handsome young man with that ugly old hag.*"

"No," I said, "they are thinking, How lucky that clumsy boy is to be with that beautiful lady."

That was close to the truth; the eyes of the passers went from Jeanne's face to her legs. Then it hit me: her dress was at her knees; the dresses of the other women were halfway down their lower legs. Jeanne made her clothes to the latest Paris fashion, and in 1938 Paris said skirts should go up. The amount of silk stocking she was showing caused a stir; when you're not used to seeing them, it's surprising what a pair of shapely knees can do.

It was mid-afternoon by the time we finished feeding the crusts from our homemade sandwiches to the pigeons in Central Square.

"Now, we could start back, or we could go to the Art Museum to see the exhibit of famous paintings they have on special loan? What do you say?"

"Let's not go back."

"You wish to see the paintings, then?"

"Absolutely!"

I didn't want the day with Jeanne to end. Even if it meant tramping past fields at sunset dotted with cows, like the picture we'd voted to have hung in the hall of my first grammar school.

"When I was a girl in Paris, no older than you, I often visited the Louvre. This portrait of a young woman is by Renoir. Elle est jolie, n'est-ce pas?"

"Très jolie," I answered in my new-won French.

The girl wore an old-fashioned full-length dress. *No knees*, I thought. She was pretty, but measuring her against Jeanne, I knew who was La Belle. We were following a pair of ladies, expensively dressed but looking back 20 years on their prime. The voice of the one who did the talking drifted toward us.

"—nothing here can compare—she stands alone—the Mona Lisa of course—My Dear, let me tell you—I was so moved—the experience of a lifetime—seeing the original—Paris!—you can't imagine!—John actually forbade me—wouldn't hear of it—made me wait—I was simply too sensitive—*Rest a week between times*, he said—"

"Tell me, Sean, of those we have seen so far, which did you like best?"

"I think the one of the garden with all the colors."

"Ah! Claude Monet."

"What's amazing is that up close it looks like a bunch of paint splashes, but when you back away, it's beautiful. That must've been hard to do."

"It required technique, certainly, but perhaps the greater genius lay in the conception. Monet sought to paint light, light as it occurs in nature. Here is a question for you, mon Grand Penseur: Music can be divided into composition and performance; in painting, which role does the artist play, composer or performer?"

"Gosh, I see what you mean! He's both!"

The ladies ahead had climbed a stair, but the high voice carried.

"—Florence—My Dear, you really must go—one sees Michelangelo's David every day—I can tell you—ha, ha!—in two months—or was it three?—I never quite got used to it—I mean— well after all—that magnificent body—so very large—one really can't help—but a painting like this—Americans aren't Florentines—a masterpiece I'm sure—but I do think something might have been done—good heavens!—here comes that striking young woman with that very young man—I wonder?—too old to be her son, I

think—most awkward—he shouldn't be allowed—I really must say something—"

We caught up to the ladies.

"Forgive me—it's none of my business—I thought it my duty—it's quite unsuitable—Adam and Eve—don't you see—"

"That is thoughtful of you. You refer to the sixteenth-century Cranach?"

"Cranach? I'm not—possibly—yes, to be sure, the Cranach—a masterpiece, no doubt—quite unsuitable."

"You think it biblically incorrect?"

"No—I don't know—maybe not biblically—"

"If you will be so kind, perhaps we can decide together," Jeanne said, leading me toward the painting.

The work showed Adam and Eve fleeing The Garden. The view was straight on—no twining vines. Adam's parts were all present and accounted for, as for Eve's I had no way of knowing—to say the least, I was interested, so interested I didn't notice myself grow.

"I have always imagined Adam to be in the first blush of manhood. Do you ladies not agree that Sean here would have been the perfect model?"

Turning in my direction, the ladies fastened on my swelling pants.

"And what about you, Sean, do you think Eve's charms would make up for the loss of Eden?"

I looked down and took off, "Meet you by the Monet!"

MEN. Me going in and out three times to check the hall. I started taking things off so's not to ruin my new clothes—the undershorts came off with the rest. I splashed cold water on my naked body—kept splashing. An old gentleman dressed to the nines in a white suit looked in, took out his wallet, and dropped a dollar bill on my clothes.

"Buy yourself some rubbers," he said, as he backed out the door.

I didn't know whether he meant erasers or rain shoes.

As Bryan said, the second I hit the pillow—

. . . I am lying naked on a table . . . a girl is standing over me . . . she smiles in Technicolor with green eyes . . .

". . . retract the foreskin! . . ."

. . . I am running down a hall . . . there are paintings on the wall . . . I climb a stair . . . two ladies stare . . .

". . . he shouldn't be allowed . . . after all, it's not small . . ."

. . . I am walking in a garden with flowers of many colors . . . an ancient tree lies ahead . . . yellow apples splashed with red . . .

". . . you have eaten of The Tree! . . ."

. . . I am running down a hall . . . there is a portrait on the wall . . . a girl in a long dress . . .

. . . we are walking in the trees . . . I see her breasts . . . I see her legs . . . I see bare knees . . .

". . . would her charms . . . ?"

. . . she says my suit is new—her hair is blowing in the wind—her eyes are deepest blue . . .

". . . how you have grown . . ."

. . . I look down at my pounding nakedness . . . I look at her belly smooth and white . . . I look at her breasts . . . I look for places out of sight . . .

". . . eager to receive the thrust . . ."

I wake with a start—"Help me, God!" I whisper—turn onto my stomach—and moan into my pillow . . .

Early morning I wake to a sound next to me. Bryan is groaning in his sleep, uncovered and naked with a full bone moving under its own power.

*Why God? Why do you do it to us?*

# CHAPTER 66

**I** thought if I never saw another doctor it'd be too soon. But pain down below can change your mind. I didn't want to call Dr. Bea—I could picture my pajamas coming off with a drum roll—so I phoned semi-retired old Doc Brown who'd once served our family.

Bryan was there when he came, "Ha, ha! Want me to strip him before I leave, Doctor?"

It hit me why Cain killed Abel.

"That may not be necessary, and I can do my own stripping."

Bryan left, and Doc only did my belly—*Thank you very much*—but enough to see hair curling this way and that.

"Not appendicitis. By the way, did you ever get circumcised? Want me to check your foreskin?"

"No, it's fine! Perfect! Couldn't be better!"

"No problem with erections?"

"No problem at all!"

"You do get them?"

"Sometimes when I wake up, but they go away soon as I use the bathroom. Otherwise I never get them."

"What about girls?"

"Girls don't bother me."

"You're lucky."

Doc prescribed aspirin and bicarb.

"In addition—and this is important—I want you to have an enema [*O Jesus!*]. I gather you don't like the idea, but see here, Young Man, health is not something to gamble with. You are getting an enema! That much is settled. The only question is who will give it to you—what about Mrs. O'Neill?"

"Jeanne! Anybody but Jeanne!"

"Very well, tomorrow morning I will send someone who specializes in boys. Arrange with Mrs. O'Neill for the door to be left open."

Asleep in my bottoms—Jeanne and Bryan gone from the house—me shaken awake by the male nurse. I decided last night to keep my eyes closed throughout the unspeakable thing about to happen. It might be better to shuffle off the mortal coil like Bryan once recited to me. The covers pull back—*Thank God I'm decent*—I swing my feet to the floor—a strong hand on my shoulder guides me to the bathroom—pulls my cord . . .

The bottoms go down—I go up.

"You always liked showing yourself, didn't you! You think that great sausage between your legs makes you king of the world. Boys! Dirty bodies! Dirty minds!"

"Miss Adams!"

I open my eyes—it's true.

"Take your hands away! . . . Now! . . . You think I've never seen a penis?"

I take them away. My pole swinging side to side, she does the testicle thing—"Cough!"

"Into the shower!"

She turns it on full—and cold . . . five minutes . . .

Me gasping for breath—she pulls me out—turns off the water—pushes me to the toilet—"The doctor wants a specimen."

She takes me in her fingers—fixes it—picks up a jar—"Make wee-wee!"—I'm nine years old again . . . This time I pee . . .

Me on my hands and knees—my behind in her face—dying from shame—the nozzle sliding inside—filling . . . filling . . . filling—me ready to explode—screaming bloody murder . . .

In the end she puts me into a hot shower—dries me—smiling, she takes me in her hand, "If it were mine, I'd chop it off."

An hour later back in bed, I can't believe I lived through it.

For some reason the pain went away.

# CHAPTER 67

"**Y**our next job is a brother and sister."

"Who's oldest?"

"Hard to say."

"You mean twins? I don't like twins. But how can a boy and a girl be twins?"

"Little Brother, there's more to making babies than donating your milk; the girl has something to say in the matter."

"I don't want to hear about it!"

"OK, be ignorant—back to your job. Mother's dead; father has the ready. Jessie just turned eleven—tall for her age—slender as grass with long blonde hair—in a couple years she'll be a heartbreaker—Jamie . . . well Jamie doesn't say much. Oh, maybe I should mention you're spending the night."

"Why bother mentioning a small thing like that?"

"I assume Bryan filled you in about the servant being away, and of course the chauffeur is driving me. There's plenty of food—breakfast cereal—fruit—milk—all kinds of sandwich makings—cake and ice cream. Mrs. Bertoli fixed a large salad and a tub of spaghetti and meatballs to be heated up—can you manage that?"

"Yessir."

"Are you circumcised?"

"U-u-u-h."

"You don't understand *circumcised*?"

"I-I'm not."

"Good, you'll know how to handle Jamie. He gets a bath every night—helps him sleep. The time Bryan was here, he took one with him—you have a problem with that?"

"U-u-u-h."

"Tell you what, he gets company in his bath, you get an extra dollar. I'll put you on your honor. Fair enough? He's down past the pool in his sandbox. Get into a suit right away—you'll find one in the changing hut. I want you ready to go in the water. I'm buying a place in the City—see you tomorrow."

*Me a lifeguard?* But the pool turned out to be only 5 feet at the deep end—*maybe I can handle that.* I found the hut and changed into a white swimsuit that didn't cover enough and outlined what it did—reminded me of that new underwear in the Men's Shoppe.

Coming out, I caught my breath. The girl had the face of an angel with long blonde hair and long white legs—but more than that she was naked. At least I thought so till I took a closer look; she was wearing pink silk panties that you could almost see through, but not quite. Staring at her nipples, I couldn't be sure but there looked to be swelling.

"I'm Jessie."

"Sean," I said blushing, watching her eyes trace my suit, which moved a touch.

"I'll take you to the boys."

There were two, both wearing white suits like mine.

"That's Jamie," she said, pointing.

*Bryan!* Jamie was 14 if he was a day.

"He doesn't talk. And this is Timmy, our new neighbor. Just found out we have the same birthday, but he's two years older."

"How'd you like to stay for dinner, Timmy? Spaghetti and meatballs with cake and ice cream for dessert."

"Gee, thanks!"

"I'll ask you to help with Jamie afterwards. That a bargain?"

"Just tell me what to do, and I'll do it."

For the next few hours I switched my eyes from the sandbox to pink panties—Jessie was on her back sunning herself—*if she goes in the pool I'll see everything—God, I'd die to see her naked!*

"All right let's move it, time to get supper started."

"Should I change into my clothes?" Timmy asked.

"Wait till you leave. Run ahead and wash up. I'll bring Jamie."
I took him by the hand to the house.
"All washed," Timmy said, "now what?"
"You can set the table for four while I do Jamie."
I soaped his hands, pointed to the toilet, and touched his suit. He knew how to shake his head.

Supper was slow—Jamie needed help. I kept staring at Jessie's nipples; there was swelling for sure. Every time she got up, I went back to wondering how she'd look without the panties.
"Timmy, I'll do the dishes, you play with Jamie."
The dishes done, I went to the bathroom and ran the big tub— plenty hot water—*must have a jumbo heater.*
"Timmy, bring Jamie to the bathroom!"
He brought him, "Anything else?"
"Take your suit off."
"Wh-what?"
"You're taking a bath with him."
"Jamie's older than me."
"He doesn't mind. Take your suit off."
"I-I'm too embarrassed."
"Put your hands on your head . . ."
Circumcised with light fuzz and half a bone that quick went full.
"O Geez!"
"It's OK—all boys get them. Take his suit off."
Jamie was uncircumcised, behind his age, and soft as the supper spaghetti.
"I want you to take a long bath to relax him. Soap him twice all over. Got that?'
"Twice all over. What about his . . . ?"
"Just wash that part with clean water—soap burns. Call me when you can pee."
"P-pee?"
"You do know how?"
He blushed, "Sure, but—"
"Look, peeing with Jamie is like peeing with a dog. Jamie'll think it's a game."
"Yeah, but what about you?"

"Don't worry about me. I used to work for a doctor—helped many a boy pee. Anyway if Jamie pees, you get a quarter."

"I do?"

"Yes. Call me!"

It took 30 minutes.

"Th-think I'm ready!"

Timmy started, and me holding, Jamie followed.

"When you get to the hut, look in my slacks; the quarter's yours."

A six-bit profit—Bryan would be proud of me.

I put Jamie to bed, drained the tub, and ran a new one. The bathroom door'd been taken off so I went out to check—Jamie was asleep. I went back, had a pee, dropped my suit, sat in the tub, and closed my eyes.

"Do I get a bath too?"

That got me awake. She stepped out of her panties and tossed them—naked-naked—I looked her up—I looked her down—her belly, her??—I didn't have a word for it—her legs—so long and slim and white—her??—*how do you do it?*

Soon as her foot hit the water, my pole came up like a periscope. Using the tub side for a fence rail, I swung myself clear and dashed for the bed.

First light. I open my eyes—I'm spread out naked—Jessie with one leg over mine—she kisses my lips—I kiss her back—she puts her tongue in my mouth—she rolls me on top of her—rolls me off—runs her fingers down my belly—puts my hand on her nipple—touches my bulb all swollen—A-a-a-a-*h!* Keeps touching—touching—touching. *Don't stop!—don't stop!—my father!—swear on your immortal soul*—I jump up and run naked to the hut.

I stayed with Jamie the rest of the time so's not to be alone with her, but when I'd been paid and ready to leave, I went to the backyard to say goodbye. Jessie was in the pool with Jamie, her panties and his suit lying on the grass. She took him by the hand, led him out of the water, and whispered something he must've understood. He walked over bare like the baby he was and gave me a big hug.

Then she came—me hardly breathing—taking in her naked body—she kissed me full on the mouth—started unbuttoning my pants—"N-no," I whispered—but I couldn't make myself stop her—she put her hand inside—it was in her fingers.

"A-a-a-a-h!"

"I'm going to take it out."

"M-Mustn't."

"I want to see it in the light."

"Wh-What about Jamie?"

"He'll think it's funny."

It was out. "It's so big . . . Want me to . . . ?"

"O God! You mustn't."

She stuffed it in, buttoned me, kissed me again, and walked away.

It was hard not to think of her, hard to make conversation with Bryan.

"So how did it go with Lorna?"

"Left my fly open, but she never took the hint. Tried for a breast—got slapped—believe me, she packs a wallop. One lousy kiss—that was the evening. What did you think of Jessie?"

"Very nice girl."

"I mean her body."

"She has a pretty face."

"Pretty? She's a young goddess. What about those long white legs?"

"Didn't notice."

A week later I went back—there was a For Sale sign—and I ran into Timmy.

"She's gone," he said. "Can I ask you something? What do you think she'd look like without her panties?"

"Beautiful, she'd look beautiful."

In the day, I walked around school using the binder to cover myself as I undressed girls who reminded me of Jessie. In the night—the nights were bad.

# CHAPTER 68

**W**ith my body screaming for help—*what do priests do?*—*'fraid I'll find out*—when Mats brought up what any other time I'd've shut my ears to, I listened. He was a junior in my first-year French class; Mademoiselle Gilberte fussed with his hair; girls saw him as a blond Prince Valiant.

"I heard about a girl who does boys," he said. "Interested? We'd go together."

It was like he knew inside me.

"Think about it and say the word. My treat."

I'd imagined it—plenty—*as long as you don't touch yourself— can't be so bad if a girl does the touching—sort of like being married—what about Adam and Eve?—they weren't married.* I'd thought about asking Bryan whether there were such girls, but I was too embarrassed.

Friday I had my answer ready, "I'm interested."

He held out a folded paper, "Meet me at my house tomorrow afternoon; it's close to where we go. Afterwards you're staying for supper; my parents'll be away."

"What should I wear?"

"A pullover shirt and tennis shorts, all white; girls find white sexy. You have any Jockey shorts? I'll lend you some. Drives'em crazy— they love seeing your bulge."

I tried not to think about it; there was no other way it would happen. But soon as school was out I took the last of my clothes allowance and bought some Jockey shorts.

It was a relief when Bryan left before I dressed. The shorts were cut low and showed hair between the band and belly button; I wasn't sure if that was sexy or not.

Mats opened the door in a towel.

"Glad to see you! Just about to take a bath. You can talk to me in the tub; I'll bring a chair. This way!"

He set the chair between the toilet and the tub, which was starting to fill.

"Take a load off your feet."

As I sat, he dropped the towel—like Bryan with everything smaller.

"Oh, forgot!"

He left and came back with a pair of Jockey shorts.

"Try these."

"I'm wearing new ones."

"New ones? Are they different? Can I see?"

I must've blushed.

"I'm standing in front of you showing the family jewels, and you're embarrassed about showing underwear?"

*Do it!* I thought, standing up and unbuttoning.

"Not embarrassed; it's just there's not much to see," I said, dropping the tennis shorts."

"Wouldn't say that. Raise your shirt a little."

I pulled it up.

"Hey, you have hair all the way past the button, and that's some bulge!"

My shorts fixed, Mats turned off the water, climbed into the tub, and went to work.

"Could you do my back?"

I did his back; he did a rinse and got out of the tub.

We were on our way, both dressed the same.

"This is my first time," he said. "I'm nervous as a cat."

Not as nervous as me. *You're going to do it! No matter what, you're going to do it! If it means burning in Hell, you're going to do it!*

I turned and crossed myself.

"Here we are." Mats pointed to a falling-down cottage that gave my insides a twist.

An old man was rocking on the rickety porch, making a squeak with each rock.

"You wait here; I'll check things out."

He talked to the rocker, handed him something, and waved me onto the porch, "Have to wait a couple minutes."

It must've been 15 minutes before two boys—probably 16s— came out.

"From the enemy school," Mats whispered as heads down the two hurried by.

We went along a narrow hall—there were rags on the floor—one a pair of boxers with the buttons ripped off—and turned through the last doorway. There wasn't much light—the darker the better far as I was concerned. The main piece of furniture was a double bed covered with a faded blue spread.

"Sit on the bed."

"You go first," I said, "I'll wait outside."

"She does us together."

"D-did you say *together*?"

"Two boys at a time, that's the way she likes it, and that gets the bargain price. Sit down."

I more fell than sat.

"She'll be with us in a few minutes, name's Elsie. We're supposed to undress."

Mats did his feet, and seeing I hadn't started, did mine. Me no help, he did our shirts.

He dropped his tennis shorts—"Lie back," he said, pushing me flat.

"Always like the girl to do my pants and shorts," I got out fast.

"Oh, experienced, eh?"

Mats pulled his jockeys off and stretched out alongside.

"Oh, forgot, I have two rubbers in my pocket. Want one?"

The second time I'd heard the word, "What're they for?"

"To cover your dick so you don't cream all over yourself. Just a sec, I'll put one on you."

"Never use 'em."

"OK, then I won't either. When you go off, do you shoot much?"

"U-u-u-u-h."

"Ha, ha! Maybe I'm in for a shower."

She hadn't gotten through the door when I let out, "Him first!"

"That'll be a nickel extra."

I felt in my pocket for one.

She took it, laid it aside, and put her face into mine, "'Nother nickel if yuh wanna kiss me."

That gave me a good shot of her—nothing like Jessie—close enough to ugly to convince me, "No more money," I lied.

"How much for boobs?" Mats asked.

"Don't do boobs."

She went straight for his dick—it didn't do anything. She pulled out all the stops—it didn't do anything. Meantime mine made its way up my tennis shorts looking for a place to grow.

"Let's get yuh open—hafta warm up Softie here," she said, going for my buttons. "Gotta get inside—"

The thought of her hands on me—*Jessie!*

"Mats! Let's get outta here!"

"OK by me!"

We grabbed our stuff and ran.

"Yuh don't get yur money back!"

"Keep it!"

Mats dropped his clothes on the front porch to dress, and the old man came out with, "Your pecker looks soft enough, Boy, reckon she did a purty good job."

I turned my back and fixed my shirt to hide myself.

We'd finished a snack in Mats's house.

"Let's check the dames coming out of the Swim Club; it's not far from here. First I'll fix some pineapple juice. Ha, ha! Pineapple juice for Pineapples."

He came back with two tall glasses and handed me one.

"Bottoms up."

I drained it.

"It's warm out. We'll leave our shirts and show the girls some muscle."

The place was in sight when I started singing, "Pineapple High-igh, Pineapple High-igh . . ."

"You sound happy."

"Ver'happy."

"See that girl and that blond kid coming out the gate; he's bashful."

"Howd'yaknow?"

"She's dressed, but he's leaving in his swimsuit; means he was too bashful to come in his clothes and change in the dressing room. Want to help him get over it?"

"Mus'nbebassful."

"We'll take him behind those bushes."

"'Kay."

"Come here a minute, Kid, want to ask you something."

The boy came over, "What do you want to ask me?"

"Right through here."

He followed us and the girl followed him—Mats acting like she wasn't there.

"Get behind him, Sean."

"You an eighth-grader?"

"Yes."

"You're bashful, aren't you?"

"Wh-what do you mean?"

"You're bashful about showing it—Sean, hold him under the arms."

"'Kay."

"Step out of your suit."

The boy didn't move.

"Help me lay him on his back."

He shook as we lowered him.

"Let's see what you have."

Mats pulled the suit off. He was white where the suit'd been.

"Small for an eighth-grader. Let me work on him—don't fight it, Kid, just let yourself go . . . Don't hold back . . . Nothing doing, Kid? . . . Can't get it on? I have the same problem. Let's try something."

Mats used both hands.

"He's feeling it now. It's taking off! That's more like it. Look at your dick, Kid; bet it's never been that big. Seen freshmen do worse . . . Let's see how far he can go."

I looked in the boy's face and stopped being happy. I knew terror. I'd felt it. I'd seen it. I saw it in that face, "Let'imgo!"

"Why?"

"Let'imgo!"

"OK, I'll take my turn when he's a Pineapple—let's head on out o' here!"

Running, I yelled to the girl, "Get'imcovered!"

I stopped to see she did.

We'd had supper at the house.

"Drink this; it'll calm you down," Mats handed me another tall juice.

"All of it."

I emptied the glass.

"Do you want anything more to eat?"

"Couldn't."

"OK, you take it easy while I clean up the kitchen."

He came back. Me happy again.

"That's out of the way. Why didn't you want to finish the kid?"

"Tooyoung."

"Well, I'm not too young. Pants me."

"Why?"

"Just want to see if you're afraid to."

"Howzat?"

"Jockeys too."

"'Kay."

He stepped out of his fallen shorts.

"Now I'll pants you."

"Nopants! Nopants!"

"OK! Keep your pants on. I phoned Bryan's mother—you're spending the night."

"Can't."

"Yes you can. It's all fixed."

I tried to stand and fell back in the chair.

"N-needta . . ."

"I'll get a milk bottle. You can pee in that."

"Nobottle!"

"Yes bottle."

He went away and came back with a quart-size.

"I'll pull your dick out."

"Nodick!"

"Yes dick. You want to pee your pants? I'm pulling it out."

It was out.

"I'll take care of things," he said.

"OK, I've got you ready and pointed—go ahead and pee."

When I'd finished, he set the bottle aside, put my arm around his neck, walked me to the bed, and laid me on my back.

"Now let's get you all the way naked."

"Nonaked!"

"Yes naked," he said pulling everything off.

"You have the sexiest body in school. Want me to jack you?"

"Nojack!"

"I'm tempted, but your brother'd kill me. You know that freckle-faced kid Carlin in French class who looks like Innocence at Dawn? Ha-ha! Last Saturday I walked in on him at his place and got him out of bed. 'I'll help you get dressed,' I said, pulling his pajamas down. He got all red in the face because he had half a bone on—a measly half bone, can you imagine? 'Why does it do that?' he asked. Anyway, he has no big brother, so you can bet your new Jockeys that one of these days I'll get the other half on and show him what it's good for—nothing funnier than watching a first-timer. Sure you don't want me to jack you? You'll be sorry—I do a really good one. OK, I give up—go to sleep."

My head hurt. I cracked my eyelids—the light hurt. Mats was asleep on his back, his dick small, one arm reaching to a fist around my drooping stalk—*Just like Cousin Mary 'cept it was a long way from drooping that time.* I slid myself out of his fingers, dressed fast, and left the house.

# CHAPTER 69

It was Monday night in our bedroom when Bryan brought it up.

"So you going to tell me?"

"What are you talking about?"

"Talking about you and Mats; it's all over school."

"O God!"

"Tell me what happened—everything that happened."

I started at the beginning—he stopped me at Elsie.

"Was she good-looking?"

"Ugly as mud."

"Why didn't you throw a flag over her face and take a shot for Old Glory?"

"Bryan!"

I was too ashamed to tell him about the boy we pantsed.

"You said he gave you pineapple juice—sure it was pineapple juice?"

"Said it was pineapple juice; looked like pineapple juice; tasted like pineapple juice."

"So you let him take it out of your shorts?"

"Didn't let him! Couldn't do anything!"

"And he held it all the time you were peeing?"

"Don't know—guess he must've."

"And you didn't get it on?"

"No."

"What about Mats, did he get it on?"

"Not that I noticed."

"Very interesting. So what happened next?"

"He laid me on the bed, made me naked, and said I had a sexy body."

"He was right; you do have a sexy body—go on."

"He asked if I wanted him to jack me."

"And what did you say?"

"I said, *No*, of course, and he said I'd be sorry because he was good at it."

"You do know that's what happened to me with Joey in the barn, and what was going to happen to you by Outlaw Trail?"

"O God! Never thought of it. Joey brought up cats. Tell me about the cats."

"Don't mention cats! Well you might as well know the whole story; Joey rubbed fish all over my dick, and these two cats stood with their front paws on me licking—makes me shudder to think of it. Did you know cats have rough tongues? Every time they slowed down, Joey'd rub on more fish. Wonder if I'm the only boy who's been jacked by a pair of cats? Ha-ha! Let's hope they were girl cats."

"Bryan!"

"And here's the worst part, hot milk splattered my face, and the cats licked that too. Can you imagine cats licking hot milk off your face?"

"O Jesus!"

"After the cats, Joey took over the job—rather not think about it—let's get back to you and Mats. You sure he never did you?"

"I'd remember. I woke up naked with his fingers wrapped around me—that's all."

"You mean around your stalk, your very stiff stalk?"

"Actually it was more like a bag of Jell-O."

"Really? And what do you make of that?"

"Don't know."

"What I make of it is you better not drink on your honeymoon."

"Bryan!"

"The fact remains you let Mats hold it."

"Didn't let him!"

# CHAPTER 70

**I** prayed on my knees—*Forgive me, Lord!*—for helping with the pantsing, The Clinic was different—I had to—Dr. Reiter made me—what can you do when a doctor tells you to do something? But there was no excuse for terrifying that boy. A picture showed in my head of the girl chewing gum while he got handled—her never saying a word to stop it or help him. And at the end she stuffed his bone into his swimsuit like it was a loose shirttail. Girls don't understand that a boy's swollen bulb is a piece of his soul.

I knew there'd be punishment, but when and how was in the hands of God.

"Clarence is sleeping over with us."

"Clarence! Why!"

"Seems he has this tobacco-chewing grandfather who kisses him whenever he visits. Clarence's dad said if Clarence could stay with someone, he wouldn't have to go to the ranch. I thought it was the least we could do for an old friend. You ever been kissed by a tobacco chewer?"

"No I haven't! And where's he going to sleep?"

"Between us—he's small."

"Bryan, I'm sleeping on the rug."

"No, that would be an insult; you're sleeping in the bed. Big Brother has spoken; you can wait till the light's out to drop your drawers."

I turned down the offer of a 3-boy shower, an'd yet to touch a shoelace when the two of them came out naked and climbed into bed.

"We're sleeping as nature intended," Bryan said.

"Not me."

"Yes, you—if you can sleep in your skin with Mats, you can sleep in your skin with us."

Remembering the blond boy, I dowsed the light and waited till I heard Clarence breathe the breath of sleep. Then I pulled everything off, slipped under the covers, heard Clarence sigh and turn, and set my brain for dawn.

My brain went off; light was coming from the bathroom window. I slipped out of bed, snuck to the toilet, my pole in the air, and did what I had to. By the time my stream got going, I'd gone from pointing up to pointing out, and that's the way I was when Clarence joined me for a pee.

"Wowee! Bryan said I'd see something worth seeing!"

There was no way to stop—Clarence staring till the last drop. In too much of a hurry to shake, I grabbed a towel, wrapped myself—"Flush the toilet!"—and shut him in the bathroom.

"Bryan, why not invite the whole town in to see me pee!"

"Good idea. How much do you think we could charge?"

Something told me God wasn't satisfied.

The day with Mats'd done nothing for my body. I remembered my promise to my father about Confession, and I needed forgiveness for the blond boy and other things.

"Father, I have sinned."

"How have you sinned, my Son?"

I reeled off a list of small things, but when push came to shove, I couldn't get it out about Jessie or Elsie or the eighth-grader.

"I think you have more to confess."

"My body, Father, it won't leave me in peace."

"You abuse yourself?"

"No, Father!"

"You are 14?"

"Since Decoration Day."

"Your body is well-developed?"

"Yes, Father."

"You know what an erection is?"

"Yes, Father."

"How often do you get them? Morning? Night? When?"

"A-all the t-time."

"What I am going to say now is confidential; The Church does not officially recognize it. There is such a thing as possession, possession by a malignant spirit. Yours may be such a case; what you describe is not normal for a 14-year-old. Would you consider being treated for possession?"

"How, Father?"

"I have some Lourdes Water blessed by the Holy Father in Rome. This special water has documented curative powers; I propose sprinkling you with it while you pray. Are you willing to try?"

"I'll try."

An early morning time had been set in Father Terence's rooms. I was nervous, but seeing a priest beat seeing a doctor a country mile. A priest might have you bare-dick, but a doctor'd skin it and show it to your mother.

I knocked on the door—three times. Father Terence was in a bathrobe, his hair wet. I hadn't realized how young and small he was—under 30, thin, 5 foot 5 at the most.

"You caught me in my bath. I will just be a minute. Take your clothes off and lie faceup on the bed."

"You mean naked?"

"That is how it has to be done."

*What a dummy!* Hadn't thought of it, but I was desperate.

I waited till he left, took my clothes off, got out a clean handkerchief, lay down, unfolded the hanky to cover myself, and closed my eyes.

"This Holy Water is more precious than emeralds."

I flinched as the hanky came off,

"You have a beautiful body,"

"Forget my body, Father, get on with the cure!"

"I want you to join me in a Hail Mary."

The prayer over, I felt drops sprinkle . . . He took it in his fingers . . .

"Don't touch it!"

"This is the part that has to be treated."

"Father, I'll get an erection!"

"The better to work out the evil . . ."

He took it in his fist . . . "Come out, Satan!"

*O God, he's going to do me!*

I opened my eyes—Father was stark naked—the first grownup I'd ever seen—with a bone of his own.

I leapt off the bed, grabbed my clothes, and ran.


"Bryan, I think he meant to—"

"Maybe not. He's used to younger boys; every kid who tries out for CYO baseball has to strip for God and Father Terence—ask your friend Bobby."

"Really? But he was naked himself."

"He likes to take showers with the team."

"What about his—?"

"What about his boner? Most natural thing in the world. You can bet he's never seen anything like you; all the kids on the team have to be under 13 at the start of the season. Anyone—anyone except Mats—would get it on looking at your body. It's happened to me on more than one occasion."

"When!"

"I'll never tell. You should've let him finish—might've solved your problem. The worst that would've happened is you'd've gone off like Vesuvius, which if I may say so, you're long overdue for. Don't you know what your body's begging for when you wake up with a wet belly?"

"Bryan!"

"I've been putting the O'Neill brain on your problem; too bad you didn't finish your treatment with that doctor at the clinic. What was his name?"

"Dr. Reiter."

"I was thinking by now he'd probably have cured you."

"Cured me? He'd probably've killed me. You should go there sometime; those crazy doctors pull out dicks faster than magicians pull out rabbits. And the bigger the audience the better."

"Tell me again what he said about progressively stronger doses."

"Oh, he has this idea about getting stronger and stronger doses of the things you're most anxious to avoid."

"So what's your next dose?"

*That's what I'd like to know.*

# CHAPTER 71

**I** didn't go to the doctor; the doctor came to me. I'd never known pain till then—pain so strong that in the whole world that was all there was—pain that filled my body—pain that swirled in waves. I woke with it early Sunday morning, Jeanne away for her once-a-year week.

"Bryan," I whispered, "Bryan!"

"What is it?"

"Call Dr. Bea."

"What's the matter?"

"Call Dr. Bea."

Me in my bottoms, her hand found my belly. "Not appendicitis! That old fool! Positively tympanic! Bryan, do you think you could carry him to my car?"

"Little Brother's not so little any more, but I'll carry him."

Him staggering, Dr. Bea helping with my legs, they got me into the back seat. The three of us took off. Soon as we hit the boulevard, she hit the floorboard. It didn't take long for a siren to sound.

"Bryan, put your head out and wave him alongside—they all know me."

Next thing I heard was, "Emergency! On the way to the hospital!"

So with a black car ahead clearing the way, we went through town and stopped in front of some high steps.

The policeman was big. "I'll carry him," he said.

From then on I was in the hands of strangers. In the end I was lying on a wheeled thing, nobody around, me alone with my pain screaming inside with no sound coming out.

"Take care of you in a minute."

I couldn't miss the high voice—the junior salesman at Ye Olde Men's Shoppe where my mother'd ordered the Confirmation suit—he kept walking in on me in my undershorts. My new pants in place, his fingers between my legs—"On the snug side? All right, let's get them off"—his voice too like a girl's for me. Him doing the unbuttoning—*must be how it's done*—he didn't stop with the pants, went straight for my boxers—
"What're you doing!"
"We'll try some jockey shorts—you'll love'em! Fit like a glove."
It was all I could do to fight him off.

He came back with a tray, Dr. Bea right behind him.
"I have to prep him, Madam."
"Well get on with it."
"Not allowed, Madam, you'll have to leave."
"Sean, tell him who I am."
"Sh-she's my doctor."
"Doctor Palmerston to you."
"Sorry, Madam—Doctor Palmerston. This is my first week."
"It could be your last. Get on with it."
His hands were nervous while he pulled my cord and made me naked. It didn't get there fast . . . but it never stopped till it went the distance . . .
His fingers shaking as he fixed to do me, he dropped the razor.
"Give me that! He is to be shaved not castrated."
My pole in one hand, the razor in the other, she did me—me moaning with pain.

Dr. Bea went away and came back with one of those needles they stick in you.

Nobody covered me—naked—alone again—now and then someone looking in—lady nurse—janitor—another doctor.

The pain went away—me floating in my favorite place next to the ceiling—happy as a python that'd swallowed a pig.

Just before they put me under, "I'm prepared to die," I told the surgeon.
"You won't die. We got you in time."
"Too bad. I may never be this ready again."

I wake up in a bed. A second bed is empty, a third bed is in use. A naked boy is getting a wash from the salesman. Half asleep I see a hand slide up and down a penis—I close my eyes.

I opened my eyes. The boy was covered—probably 12.
"You didn't see did you?" he asked.
"See what?"
"My bath—never had one like that! After three days they give you one."

"Bryan, you have to get me home on Tuesday—you have to!"
"Why?"
"Do I need to ask my best friend?"
"That bad?"
"That bad."

Next day a houseboy who worked for a rich lady was laid down between us. He didn't speak much English, but he smiled a lot. The male nurse stripped him, got him erect, and shaved around his pole, giving the 12-year-old a free education.

The older boy's operation wasn't as serious as mine, so we were able to get to our feet about the same time, which with the 12-year-old gone, meant we saw a lot of each other.

. . . When the male nurse had us in his power, he'd help us across the hall and pull our gowns off, "I'll give you a quick wash."
. . . What he'd quick wash'd quick go up . . .

. . . At the bowl together, naked and erect . . . the salesman taking us in with a look on his face . . . Nature finally showing pity, letting us pee . . .

. . . Too weak to complain, I'd suffer in silence, but the houseboy thinking it a great joke, would never stopped smiling . . .

My roomies gone except for a new one still under the anaesthetic, Dr. Bea came to drive me home in clean pajamas. But I didn't get away without a pound of flesh. Spread out naked I went big as it gets while she checked me out. "That's what I want for Christmas," she said, taking her sweet time stuffing me into the pj's.

The next morning—me in bed—Bryan came out with, "Suppose I have to play nurse and wash your willie. I smelled a rat and cornered your first roommate on his way out—Dr. Bea's been told—that fruitcake's going back to fitting jockstraps. How come you let him strip you?"

I had no fight in me.

"If you let him, you'll let me . . . As Clarence would say, *Wow what a big one!*"

No fight at all.

"This may tickle. Have to do your foreskin."

*He wouldn't.*

He would.

"I do it for Sean. Sure as the sun lights Galway Bay, Big Brother'll live to see the day Little Brother's cured all the way."

# CHAPTER 72

**I** was up and about, back to school, waiting for my hair to grow. It was part of me now—part of who Sean Lacey was.

Jeanne had me alone, "In this parish 14 is the age for Confirmation; so as one says, there's no time like the present. Do I have the words right, Cheri?"

"You have them right."

"I have put your name on the list as I promised ton papa I would do. It is important that Confirmation take place before you grow out of your suit. The big June induction is past, but they are holding a small one for latecomers. The ceremony will be a week from Sunday at Mass, but the preliminaries will take place tomorrow at the Catholic High School Gymnasium. Your father will throw me into the street if I fail him."

"He won't throw you into the street; you won't fail him."

"Is that a promise?"

"That's a promise. I swear on all the Laceys, whoever they were—probably pig raisers and spud growers."

I waited behind a tree till they were ready to close up. A blond boy an' me made it by shouting, "Wait!"

Brother Thomas was in charge, "You're late. Strip off!"

"I have my own suit," I said.

"Me too," from the blond.

"You have to shower to see Doctor Day—Strip!"

*O God!*

You didn't say *no* twice to Brother Thomas.

Me naked, Brother Thomas said, "I never forget a boy; I know you, don't I?"

"Don't think so," I lied.

"I remember, you play with this," he said, taking it in his hand.

He let go and looked at the other boy.

"Do you two know each other?"

"No," I said.

"Yes," said the blond.

"You do it together, don't you? And you'll burn in Hell for it."

We stood in the showers till things calmed down . . . After we dried, Brother Thomas left us at a door. When it opened we saw a boy sitting on a table with it out of its skin.

"I'm not going in there," my partner said.

He convinced me.

Father Arne took us. He'd gotten used to naked boys—hardly did a second take—and was now the final word on foreskins. Father O'Connor was gone with no one saying why, and the blond priest was put in charge of boy activities to the relief of all concerned.

He told us the purpose of marriage: To have children who will be brought up as faithful Catholics and have children who will be brought up as faithful Catholics. From an answer to the other boy's question I found out what Kotex was for and wished I hadn't.

"Tell us about the wedding night, Father, will we both be naked?"

"That's not something I can answer."

"I'd want her to see what I was going to stick in her. Wouldn't you, Father?"

"Enough questions. Go get dressed."

"You don't recognize me—l'il ol' Scooter, half a foot taller. From the first time I saw you naked, I knew you'd end up with the biggest one in town."

"You never saw me naked."

"Oh, no? Remember the time Mr. Stillwater whipped you? That was the week his building was getting painted. The workmen left a ladder outside his two high windows."

"*You didn't.*"

"Of course I did—stayed after school on purpose . . . Let's take a pee for old time's sake."

"Nothing I'd like better, but I've got a job to get to."

Scooter was now a Dog, a mortal enemy. Bryan'd told me that each year on Halloween night the Dogs made a raid to pee on the Big P, and it was the duty of every yellow-blooded Pineapple to shut off their water or fall down drunk trying.

When Big P Night came and went, I asked what'd happened.

"And how should I be knowin'? Me out cold on the cold cold ground drunk as a sailor home from the sea."

It turned out that Bryan'd never made his Confirmation—he didn't say why—and wouldn't set foot in Church. But with Jeanne sitting proud in the audience, mine went by smooth as the silk of my tie.

# CHAPTER 73

**E**verything was back, hair, modesty, nights.

Bryan and a senior'd been picked to represent Pineapple at a Boys' State thing in the Capitol Building.

"The Principal's going with us, and that worries me."

"Why?" I asked.

"When the cat's away, the mice will play."

"What do you mean?"

"Shouldn't've brought it up. Well better mention that Wally's got it in for me 'cause he thinks I did him out of going on this trip. I didn't, but that's what he thinks. Anyway, keep away from him, understand?"

"Darn! I was planning to ask him to take your place in bed. Never fear, if he comes within a parsec of me, I'll do a Flash Gordon and turn on the blasters."

"Make sure you do. Ming the Merciless could pick up a few pointers from Wally."

"How long will you be gone?"

"It lasts a week, and the day after there's a dinner with the Governor and other bigwigs to wind things up. We'll leave soon as that's over; I should be ridin' Old Paint into the Circle L Saturday night in time to get all sexed up soaping you in the shower."

"Bryan!"

Monday after 7th period I was talking to Bobby, Peanuts, and Clarence in the hall when Joey showed up.

"Haven't seen much of yuh lately, Sean, keeping busy?"

I'd no sooner got out, "Busy beating the girls off," when upperclassmen came from all sides, boxing us in.

"You Bryan's kid brother?"

"Follows big brother around like a puppy dog," Joey grinned.

"And you're all his buddies?"

"Oh, we go *way* back."

"Should be more careful picking your friends. Could get you into a heap of trouble. But this is no time to talk of unpleasant things; you're all invited to a party."

"Sorry," Joey said, "Got stuff to do."

"Yeah, and the stuff you got to do is by the bleachers. Wouldn't want to spoil the fun and games Wally's gone to so much trouble over."

*O God!*

"You guys take the others to Wally. We'll take the kid brother to Mr. Winter."

I'd handed Bryan my class schedule.

"See you got Winter for English; that was a smart move."

"Why?"

"You can cinch an A like Big Brother."

"How'd you do it?"

"Cornered him at his desk after classes—'What do I have to do to get an get an A,' I asked. 'Pull up a chair,' he answered. 'I like to compare modern boys with ancient Greek boys.' Me innocent as spring rain, sitting like a dummy while he unbuttoned my pants—'Greek boys were never circumcised. What about you?' he asked, putting his hand inside my shorts and pulling Johnnie out— easiest A I ever got."

"Bryan!"

"Anyhow, there's no way to avoid Winter; he not only teaches English, he got himself appointed Official Pool Tester—supposed to be an expert on the subject. Means he has the right to go through the boys' locker room anytime he wants. Whenever freshmen are swimming bare-weenie you'll find Winter testing the water—gets away by giving his class a reading assignment. When there's no swimming, he'll show up just as the boys are stripping for the showers and strike up a conversation with a student from one of his classes. He's outlasted many a boy in his jock—eventually the kid

has to throw in the strap and show Winter what he's got—no jocks in the showers, that's a school rule. There was one kid who went airborne every time Winter stalked him—ha, ha!—stalked his stalk, you might say. You'd be a big hit with Winter."

"Thanks all the same, but a B'll do me fine."

"Get his shoes and socks off . . . You don't want to know what's going to happen if you don't do exactly as I say, but I'll tell you this, there'll be girls, oodles and poodles of girls watching and touching and giggling."

He told me what to do, pushed me into Mr. Winter's room, leaving the door open a couple inches so he could follow the goings-on.

The teacher was alone, walking back and forth, reading aloud.

"Sophocles, Sean, what can I do for you?"

"U-u-u-h . . ."

"Are you all right? Why are you barefoot?"

"S-supposed to give you a s-sample."

"A sample of what?"

". . . U-u-u-h . . . S-Sample of the Greek Games c-coming up by the bleachers."

"Greek Games sound interesting. Who'll be in them?"

"M-me and s-some other freshmen."

I did the first button of my shirt—slow like I'd been told—felt my face go hot—glanced at Mr. Winter—he looked interested—did button after button. I pulled my shirt wide to show my chest—let it hang loose for a few seconds—slipped my arms out—watched it fall to the floor.

It hit me—I'd gotten used to the feel of Jockey shorts—was wearing them now—wished I wasn't—I'd feel more comfortable showing boxers.

I did the top button of my pants—waited—next button—waited—last button—waited—pulled my fly open wide—showing the Y of my underwear—took my hands away—let the pants slip slow down my legs—kicked them aside.

Mr. Winter said nothing.

"L-like what you see?" I said, following orders.

"Let's hope you're not circumcised. Do you need help with the undershorts?"

I turned my back on him—quick stepped out of my Jockeys—just as quick stepped into them—scooped up my clothes—turned to face him—"Come to the Games and see it all!"—and ran for the door.

I was back in the hall.
"Ha, ha! Winter'll show all right."

They marched me to the other side of the gym and past the bleachers. A couple dozen lookers were already there, and more joined up as I waited in a tight pack—all in our undershorts—with the others. Here and there I picked out a freshman I'd gotten to know—the last thing I wanted to see was a friend. Mats and Carlin—the freckle-face from my French class—were out front.
Wally showed up carrying Big Bertha. He pointed to me, "Any of you friends of his?"
Carlin waved his arm.
"Bring him here! . . . Everything off!"
It took a swat from Bertha to get him to drop his boxers.
"Any more friends out there? . . . Seems you just ran out o' friends."
Wally took care of my jockeys with his own hands; the others did themselves with encouragement from Bertha. Bobby'd sprouted a sprinkle of dark hairs since I'd seen him—Peanuts's shadow had turned to fuzz. Anyone who didn't get a bone on his own got help—I didn't need any—Clarence couldn't make it—Carlin's was skinny. Three jugs of water traveled around the circle and kept going, bottoms getting whacked to make us drink.
With Bertha poised to strike if they came down, our hands stayed on our heads. The six of us ran a race that way, once around the track with a crowd of boys cheering us on—think I won.
Then they made us wrassle, Joey and me, Bobby and Peanuts, Carlin and Clarence. Joey and me twisting and turning, our poles pressing against each other—he treated mine like a hot potato—made sure not to touch it with his hands. They called it a draw. I'd gotten as strong as Joey—the only good thing I'd remember from that day. Bobby pinned Peanuts and peeled his dick as a prize. Carlin pinned Clarence and worked up half a bone on him—probably his first.

Our hands went back on our heads, and the boys who'd cheered before examined now—hands all over me—I didn't look at faces—I was paying triple for the eighth-grader, and my friends and Joey were paying with me.

"I brought some string," one of the lookers said. "Hav'em do a roll race."

"How does it go?"

"Pair'em up in teams of two, tie each team's dicks together, and make'em roll over each other on the ground from the starting line to the finish."

They tied mine to Carlin's, Joey's to Bobby's, and Peanuts's to Clarence's. I couldn't tell who won.

"Ha, ha! That was fun. Any more ideas?"

"How about a horse race. Take the same teams, have the biggest kid carry the other kid on his back, the rider reaching around to hold the horse's dick."

Carlin had my stalk in a vise the whole way 'round. I closed my eyes, stumbled, and threw him, but they put him back on. Joey and Bobby won.

"Over here, Mr. Winter!"

Carlin and Clarence were ready to let loose, facing each other two feet apart. A volunteer fireman on each dick pointing his stream at the opposite belly—the crowd giggling like crazy as streams crossed and spattered. Bobby and Peanuts got the same treatment with different volunteers.

Mr. Winter watched all that, then turned to me, "You look uncomfortable, Sean. No need to be embarrassed; you have an exceptional body, uncircumcised as a boy should be. Anyway, an initiation never killed anyone. In ancient Greece sporting events always took place in the nude; naked boys were commonplace in Athens—although I must say in your case boy is perhaps not the correct term."

Right at the start, I made up my mind to hold it or pop trying. I was about to pop.

Wally whispered, "Later for a special audience including our girl friends to warm them up, I'm gonna have Freckles jack you upside down and sideways . . .

"Think he's ready; would you like to skin him, Mr. Winter?"

I opened my eyes—looking at Mr. Winter I saw Mr. Stillwater's blurry face . . .

. . . His fingers were doing my foreskin—I'd cinched an A in English . . .

. . . no holding back . . . pee came a gusher . . . I passed out . . . fell to the ground . . .

That scared Wally and broke up the party. Bobby dressed me and guided me to my room.

Tuesday Jeanne gave me two aspirin before leaving for the library.
Bobby stopped in after school, "Know what happened to Peanuts and Carlin? Mats took them home—you can guess the rest."

I'd made a doctor appointment—*maybe there's some medicine.*

Thursday I got back in the saddle—*have to sooner or later.* Mats gave a wink and pointing to Carlin a seat ahead, whispered, "You should've seen his face."

After school I kept my appointment, not Doc Brown but the other old doctor.
"You look healthy enough. What's the trouble?"
"My body—it won't leave me alone."
"Drop your pants and I'll take a look."
"My pants are fine. Just want to know if there's some medicine."
"How often do you masturbate?"
"Masturbate?"
"Choke the chicken, stroke the weasel."
"W-weasel?"
"Pump your pickle."
"Don't"
"Never?"
"Never."
His hands went to my fly, "I'll just open you."
"No! Don't touch me! Don't want anyone to touch me!"
"Calm down! Do yourself."
"Don't want you to look at me! Just tell me about the medicine."
"Swimming. Best medicine in the world—there'll be no charge."

Bryan'd mentioned that the YMCA pool was deserted weekday afternoons, so Friday morning I set out with a few butterflies flopping around my belly and his swimsuit in my lunch bag—no room for a towel. After school I hitched a ride from a lady in a new silver Buick—some car—*Things are looking good—must be my lucky day.*

No one was at the desk, so I signed the book, went through to an empty locker room, and on guard for strollers, took my time with shoes, socks, and shirt; then with a quick look both ways, skinned out of the rest and pulled on the suit.

Like the Sparta Club, the sign said NUDE SHOWERS REQUIRED BEFORE SWIMMING—nothing about soap—*prob'ly too cheap to buy it.* I stepped under the shower in Bryan's suit. In a few minutes, I was turning off the water when a young man came through the archway and said in a squeaky voice, "You have to shower in the nude."

"I did."

"You did not; what's that if it's not a suit?"

"First I showered without the suit; then I thought I should wash off the suit, so I showered again."

"I don't believe you. Hand me the suit!"

"No! You just want to see my dick!"

"I do not! Drop the suit!"

"The only way you see mine is if I see yours—deal?"

"Certainly not!"

*Thank God for that.*

"Then go away, and I'll take another shower without the suit."

"How do I know I can trust you?"

"Because I'm an altar boy, and it's a sin to tell a lie."

He went away, and I took another shower in the suit.

The swimming went good as could be expected, but my muscles were asking for a break. No towel, so to dry some before dressing I sat on a bench in my damp suit. Five minutes later when I was ready to pull it off, a big boot came down on the opposite bench. Looking up, the man was tall with dark glasses and a torn felt hat. There was nothing to do but wait.

He unlaced the boot and laced it up again. *That should be it,* but he went on to the second boot. *That's it for sure,* but he sat down straight across from me, so close he could've touched my bare legs.

*Something's wrong.* The thought came to me that the building might be closing and we'd be the last ones left. In a panic I scooped up my things and ran. The front door was still open, so I stayed just inside, dressed over the swimsuit, fastened my wristwatch, and stuffed the undershorts into my pocket.

# CHAPTER 74

I spent a few minutes looking over some chipmunks in a pet shop window as they took turns running inside a wire wheel . . . *How do they decide when to change places?* I watched them switch off a couple times—couldn't figure out how they talked to each other—and went to the other window to check some kittens. They didn't do anything, just stayed curled up fast asleep. Nothing more to see, I moseyed my way three blocks to the first good corner to thumb.

The car that stopped was an old black Tin Lizzy. I'd gotten spoiled by the new silver Buick and wanted to wait for something better, but when the driver put his head out the passenger window and said, "Get in." I got in.

"Have to go back to the crick to load up with water for the radiator. That OK or you in some kind of rush?"

"No rush at all; I'll help carry the water."

He drove to the main intersection, made an against-the-law turn around the button, and went in the opposite direction.

"Need to get out o' town to a place where we can stop."

I closed my eyes; the swimming'd made me sleepy.

When I came to, we were on a dirt road.

"Where are we?"

"Almost there."

He stopped by some trees and cut the engine.

"Should I get out?"

"Just a minute, want to show you something."

He reached under the seat and came up with a six-shooter—I'd seen plenty come out of their holsters at the Saturday Matinee.

"You like games? Has one bullet. I'll give it a spin."

He put the gun to my head and pulled the trigger.

"A-am I d-dead!"

"Next time you might be. Throw your clothes in the back seat."

I turned and saw dark glasses and a torn felt hat. *O God!*

"Please, Mister!"

"You have one minute."

My pullover shirt was gone in two seconds, but I had trouble with the double-tied sneakers—at last they went over my shoulder—sox—pants. The knot inside the trunks wasted more time, and when it came undone, I was so nervous I threw the suit out the window.

"You're built; let's see if it works."

He did everything you could one-handed. My brain went back and forth between the gun at my head and *Don't fail me now! God can't blame you! Give him what he wants!*

He was rough, real rough—*The pain doesn't matter—in the end he'll kill you anyway.*

The pain stopped. He had as much luck with me as Elsie'd had with Mats.

"Take mine out! . . . Do it you little cocksucker!"

Even with the practice from the Clinic—those were boys, this was a man—I didn't think I could make myself . . . the gun barrel pressed hard against my head . . . I made myself . . .

"Skin it!"

Looked like it had some bad disease—made me go sick all over . . .

"Do me!"

I threw up on him.

"I'll kill you!"

The gun hammer hit metal—I jerked back—went hard against the door—knocked the rickety latch open—fell out of the Lizzy—jumped up—ran—kept running till I heard the engine start and the car go.

Me trembling behind a big tree, it took a long time before I could get my nerve up to sneak back and check on the swimsuit. Sure enough it was there on the ground.

I hadn't paid attention to directions—didn't know which way to walk when I got to the highway—*one way's good as another*—didn't

put my thumb out—hadn't had much luck last time. Car after car whizzed by; three or four slowed to take a closer look, but no one stopped. I'd gone a fair distance when a police car pulled over in front of me. The officer got out and opened the back door.

"Get in!"

Two boys were already there.

"What're you doin' out here in a bathin' suit?"

"I-I w-was—"

"Never mind; we'll check on it."

"I-I—"

"Said we'll check on it. Till we do you'll be at Happy Valley Boys' Home."

"S-Sir—"

"Keep you mouth shut! I've had a long week."

It hit me quick—*why didn't I use the tree?*

"Need to pee," I whispered.

He stopped the car and came around to the door.

"Out!"

I stumbled out. The boy next to me—maybe 15—followed; the officer followed him.

"You need to piss too?"

"Jus' wanna watch."

"It's a free country. You! Drop your suit!"

Me behind the trunk. Cars going by—a big bunch in a row—a short break—my brain gone dead. I dropped my suit facing square to the road and peed toward the pavement while the boy, the policeman, and the passers watched.

Wherever we were going, we didn't get there soon—*better remember the way.* I thought of Hansel and Gretel—but I had no white pebbles, not even bread crumbs—*have to study stuff as we pass it*—but my brain wouldn't work. The only thing that sank in was a small creek as we turned off the pavement. It wasn't a whole lot further.

The younger boy—13 but no more—asked, "Why do they have bars all over the place?"

"Ha, ha!" the policeman chuckled, "Should have a sign saying, *Abandon Hope All Ye Who Enter Here.*"

He pulled a rope and a bell clanged. It took a while till we heard a lock click, an inner door open, another lock click, and the outer bars swing wide.

"Inside!"

"Brought you three, Stony."

"No paper?"

"No one seen or heard o' them in this county. My guess is they drowned."

Stony smiled, "This one might be fun."

"Hung like a horse, but—"

He used a finger to make a circle by his head.

Stony felt my bulge.

"The dummy's a skin," the policeman said.

Stony took his hand away, "Be mine soon enough."

The officer started to go, "Sam gets credit for one—don't forget to mark us down."

Stony closed things and did the locks.

Then he turned to us, "Too bad yuh missed supper, but runaways take what comes."

He led us to where three boys were squatting on the floor, an older kid in a chair next to them.

"I'll do guard, Gus, fetch a pair o' the General's silkies—better make it two, small'n medium."

In a minute Gus came back, "Hav'em in my pocket."

"OK, we'll close up now. That'll be it fer the week. Good haul no? General'll be pleased."

We went down a dark hall to an inside room. Stony switched on a light that showed brown walls and a brown floor. To cheer it up there were four wooden benches, some shelves, two buckets, and a big round tub filled with smelly water.

"All right, let's see some cocks! Down ta yur skin!"

Me empty inside. I'd given myself up for dead in the Lizzy—whatever happened after that was borrowed time. I put my watch on a shelf and covered it with the swimsuit. When I turned around everyone was looking at me—didn't matter—the me they were looking at wasn't the me that was me.

"Like Big Cock there!"

When the third oldest kid—probably 14—dropped his shorts, he had half a bone.

Stony and Gus went away. The cook didn't see much difference between a naked boy and a plucked chicken. She never let out a sound, just grabbed us one by one and shoved. In the end she had us all sitting the way she wanted and went to work on our heads with electric clippers like Jerry the barber used, these on a long cord plugged into the wall. After the clippers came soapy water and a straight razor that made us into cue balls.

Heads finished, she went around checking under arms, and took care of anything she didn't like with more soapy water and a safety razor. The three of us who needed work between the legs got stretched out on the benches where we were shaved clean. When something got in the way, she picked it up and moved it.

Me done last. She had trouble but kept at it. I gave myself up for lost—God'd turned his back on Sean Lacey and I'd run out of prayers. She could do what she liked with me; if she'd taken it in her head to lop things off, I wouldn't've stopped her. The blade never got changed, and I ended up scraped. She did my new growth to the button and past—even the six hairs on my chest bit the dust. At the end, eyebrows were the only cover any kid was left with.

The two buckets were brought to the center of the floor; she stood us three to a bucket, touched here and there to get her meaning across. The other uncircumcised boy couldn't get started. No one was fast, and though I'd peed earlier by the highway, my brain somewhere between dead and asleep, but closer to dead, I started first. The 13-year-old came last with time to spare.

Then with the help of some wooden steps she got us all into the round tub. I thought she'd soap, but she didn't. Taking one boy at a time she closed eyes, held noses, and like we were dogs being dipped, ducked heads under the smelly water till the heads forced themselves up, choking for air.

# CHAPTER 75

**W**e were done dripping when Gus came back. The cook took off and Stony showed up, "Gimme the small pair."

Gus handed him what turned out to be white silk panties. Stony put them on the young uncircumcised boy; they fit tight.

"I'll take this one an' set things up fer the General—should be back from town soon. Take the others—put the little blond in my bed—rest go in yur section."

Stony left with the kid in panties and Gus took charge.

"Grab yur stuff!"

We dropped the blond boy off at a double bed. "Clothes on the floor! Under the covers!"

And went to another room with a single bed.

"Big Cock, what's yur name?"

"Sean."

"OK, yur comin' with me—rest o'yuh stay here—in yur skin!"

"Yuh got class—c'n always tell class—Stony don't care 'bout class, but I do. We never had no class—when Ma died, Pa took in this no-good—jus' a year older'n me. Pa'd leave mornin's an' she'd walk in on me showin' her snatch, 'Oh, didn' know yuh was here,' she'd say.

"I'd run like hell—knew Pa'd beat the livin' shit out o' me. One time she tole 'im I got fresh with'er. Pa took me outside an' stripped me clean right in front of the no-good—she loved that—tied my hands ta this tree branch an' took his belt ta me. Left me that way fer her ta whip my ass some more. She went back'n forth 'tween

whippin' an' jerkin' me off. Decided that was enough shit—ran away an' ended up here."

"What I wanna tell yuh is there's a chance I c'n get yuh out o' this place if yuh do jus' like I say an' make it worth my while. Yuh know don' yuh that cop gets paid fer bringin' kids—the more kids, the more dough the General gets from the State. No one'll ever find out 'bout yuh—yur folks'll give yuh up fer dead. The General's got his ass covered all the way up the line. 'Course if yuh get caught runnin', Stony'll have yur balls fer breakfast. That's why I gotta show yuh how it's gonna be if yuh stay—so yuh c'n decide. I'll show yuh right now. Wha'd'yuh say?"

My brain was in a thick black cloud—I couldn't think—nothing made sense—this wasn't any world I knew. If it wasn't Hell itself, it was a place made by the Devil to get some practice in. I said the first thing that came into my head, "How old're you?"

"Me? 16 I think, not sure—in this place yuh don' even know what year it is, let alone when yur birthday comes. Stony's prob'ly 17, mean, bad-mean. His idea of a vacation'd be cuttin' weenies off babies. I seen the way he looked at yuh, Shan; he's jealous o' big cocks. When he finally gets yuh, he'll have yuh crawlin' an' beggin' an' squealin' like a hog gettin' butchered. Yuh wouldn' believe the things I seen'im do ta kids an' the things I seen'im make kids do. So yuh want me ta show yuh?"

"Sh-show me."

"OK, put yur suit on, an' never leave yur watch out o' yur sight. Come on, gotta move ass."

We were on our way.

"The reason yuh didn' get jerked is yur a skin."

"You mean because I'm not circumcised. Why?"

"Easier ta tell yuh after yuh've seen."

I thought of something, "Why can't a boy run away when he goes to school?"

"This's home, school, church, hospital'n cemetery. 'Less yuh get yur hands on a key ring, got 'bout much chance breakin' out o' here as breakin' off The Rock. The General hires teachers that come days. State pays the General and the General pays peanuts 'cause he finds homos that like the work. If a teacher keeps yuh after class an' pulls yur pants down, yuh keep yur mouth shut if yuh know

what's good fer yuh. Jus' this mornin' I walk in on a teacher with a naked 12-year-old. An' there's this priest—likes kids with good-size cocks—I made a peephole ta watch. Think I'm makin' it up?"

I didn't want to think about it.

"Here's where we climb."

We went up some steep stairs that ended in an attic.

"Nobody knows 'bout this place we're headed fer 'cept me. Comin' soon ta a long crawl through the dark, spider webs an' stuff."

"What kind of spiders?"

"Nothin' that c'n kill yuh I don't think; never been bit—least not bad—just 'nuff ta make yuh scratch yurself. Sorta hang onta me. When we get there, gotta be quiet, but we c'n whisper."

I was ready to scream when Gus whispered, "We're there. Think they had one o' those windows that come through the roof an' took it out. Didn' fix where it went inta the room, jus' put in this piece o' glass—lucky fer us. Look down."

The 13-year-old from the police car was sitting on a bed in his silk panties.

Gus whispered, "The General goes back'n forth from hair to no hair; right now he likes kids that're smooth. He's always lookin' fer new skins—gets first crack—Stony'd be in deep shit if he touched a skin before the General had'im."

My legs told me it was half an hour before a male with a shaved head showed up in a Japanese Kimono. There was something familiar about him, but it wouldn't come to me.

"That's the General. Likes young boys best—12 or 13—that's Stony's orders 'bout what ta line up fer'im. Stony never goes 'gainst orders. But the General takes 14s and 15s when there's no new young ones. He'll keep a boy till he's tired of'im before he goes on ta the next. Today wasn't usual—we could go months without gettin' a new skin that's 12 or 13. Jus' a matter o' time till yuh'll be wearin' silk panties.

This bounced off without sinking in—I was busy trying to place the General.

The boy in the panties got off the bed and circled around showing himself off.

"The General's tellin'im what ta do."

This went on for a few minutes like a bird doing some kind of nesting dance. Then as the dancer came near, an arm went out fast as a snake and ripped away the panties.

"What's the General's name!"

"Lacey, General Lacey."

I needn't've asked because right then he threw off his kimono, showing a green crocodile and a pole big as mine—a folded towel on a bureau flashed in my head—*O God!*.

"I'll do anything you say!"

"Shhh! Jus' what I wanted ta hear, but don' yuh wanna see what's gonna happen?"

Crawling away, I whispered, "Th-think I kn-know."

# CHAPTER 76

**W**e picked up the three newcomers and went to a sleeping room.

"'Tenshun!"

Maybe 40 boys stopped like they were playing statues. All but a few had a head of hair.

"Cock time!"

They stripped fast, stuffing their clothes under their beds.

"Piss!"

Buckets lined one wall, and they ended up 3 or 4 to a bucket.

"Places!"

They stood with their hands at their sides in front of the beds—single-size. There were more boys than beds, and half the beds had two boys in front of them.

Gus pointed to the 14-year-old, "Who wants'im?"

A boy smooth between the legs walked up to the newcomer.

"Show it hard! . . . Don't yuh know nothin'? Show it hard an' I'll do yuh."

Tears started down the 14-year-old's face. *God have mercy on him.*

"Under the covers!" from Gus.

The younger boy led the older boy away, "I'll milk yuh dry."

Gus pushed the oldest boy forward, "Good meat here."

An older boy came toward us, pulling his foreskin back.

"Guess what yur havin' for breakfast."

*God in Heaven!*—I crossed myself twice.

"Under the covers!"

Gus got to the last boy, "He's tight."

A hairy kid come forward, "I'll do yuh like a bitch-dog."

*Jesus help us! Hail Mary full of Grace* . . . I crossed myself—kept crossing myself.

"Everyone in bed!"

When Gus talked, kids hopped.

"Let's go, Shan!"

We were on our way, "Late Friday's when that priest comes, but he'll be through by now. Let me check."

We went around a corner and Gus looked through a small hole,

"Take a peek . . . Go ahead!—fer yur own good yuh gotta see this."

. . . A naked Father O'Connor was kissing a naked boy on the lips . . .

I quick pulled away . . .

"When the General's through with yuh, he'll turn yuh over to that priest."

I went down on my knees, "Please help me!"

We were back in his room.

"Only fair I get somethin' out o' this. Get rid o' the suit."

"Kill me, Gus! Please kill me! C-can't d-do th-those things!"

"Easy, Shan! Yuh don' have ta do nothin' like that."

"Wh-what do you want me to do?"

"Jus' take the suit off—nothin' bad'll happen—yuh got my word."

I stepped out of it.

"Yuh really do somethin' fer me all shaved like that, but I don' wanna do nothing bad ta yuh. Don' even wanna jerk yuh. Any idea how many cocks Stony's made me jerk? Yuh think I like it? Yuh think I like puttin' little kids in Stony's bed? Shit no, I don' like it. But I gotta live same as anybody—they'd bury me quick as they'd bury a cat. I ain't mean like Stony, but I got this notion o' sharin' like pals with a classy kid—make me feel I was more'n a dog turd. So what I want us ta do is lie down next to each other—maybe hol' hands—while we jerk ourselves off—I'll jerk left-handed—good as right fer me—we do it slow, real slow. How does that sound?"

"O God!"

"What's a matter?"

"I-I swore to my f-father—swore on my immortal soul—I'd never do it."

"Geez! Never heard o' nothin' like that—but I wasn't raised classy. OK, I'll help yuh out. How about yuh jus' do me—like it better that way? Far as I c'n go—take yur pick."

*. . . you have to do it—understand!—you have to do it . . .*

"I-I've never done it."

"I'll tell yuh what ta do—jus' like the General—OK?"

*. . . you have to or you'll die in this place . . . or you'll wish you'd die . . .*

"Strip me, Shan—anyway yuh want—pull my cock out first if yuh want or do me slow—whatever yuh like."

I did him slow . . . his undershorts fell . . .

"Yeah, I'm a skin too. It's goin' on two years, but I've danced in silk panties fer the General."

"Wh-what do you want m-me to do n-next?"

"Ha, ha! Like I said, nothing bad—yuh got too much class. I'll settle fer cummin' on a classy kid's belly—that's not much ta ask."

He knelt on the floor. "Kneel close as yuh c'n get. Take my meat an' jus' hol' it a while. When yuh move yur fingers, do it slow, real slow . . . Open yur eyes. Won't work fer me if yuh don' watch. Jus' go ahead an' think o' things ta do."

*. . . get it through your head, Sean Lacey—you have to . . .*

"That's good—do some more . . . When yuh feel me start ta cum, don' let go—hol' on tight. But till then take it slow . . ."

"O-o-o sh-sh-i-it! H-h-ho-o-old o-o-o-on!"

He shot all over me—I didn't feel so good.

"That was great!—little somethin' ta remember me by. Go ahead, put yur suit on."

"C-can I w-wash?"

"No water here, an' we don' wanna make noise—ole pipes sound all over the buildin'. Put the suit on—I'll grab my shorts. One more thing, I take the watch—that's what I get outa it—notice it's gold. Where'd yuh get it?"

"M-my step uncle—sort o' rich—sent it for graduation—i-it's 18 carat."

I handed him the watch—it was my pride and joy.

"Thanks, Shan. Here's the plan. No way ta get keys ta the outside locks, but—an' Stony don' know this—the guy before him hid an extra key ta the exercise yard an' I found it. The place has a big high wall, but I'll boost yuh an' yuh c'n stan' on my shoulders."

"W-won't you get in trouble?"

"Stony won' fill the General in till tomorrow."

"What about the cook?"

"She don' know one cock from another; all look the same ta her, an' she only talks somethin' nobody unnerstan's. Early mornin' I'll tell Stony yur gone—searched high'n low but yur nowhere to be found. He'll patch things—wouldn' report a missin' kid 'cause he's ta blame fer whatever happens. I'll jus' play dumb—say yuh must be some kinda Houdini. Anyway, nothin' Stony c'n do ta me he ain't already done. The watch'll be my secret—come in handy if I ever get the balls ta break outa this place."

It'd been circling in my head, "Could I ask you something?"

"Hell yes, ask away—I owe yuh."

"Did you ever hear of a boy called Damon?"

"In Stoney's bunch, 'bout yur age, the General's favorite once. Damon Harry somethin'."

"Harrington. Is there any way I could take him with me?"

"Wouldn' go."

"Why not?"

"Cock-crazy. Where else'd'e get the pick o' so many cocks?"

It was a prison yard. Me going from Gus's shoulders to the top of a high grey wall.

"Good luck, Shan—yur on yur own—thanks fer the watch—keep clear o' cops!"

# CHAPTER 77

**I** ran fast as I could . . . I slowed to a walk. It was dark and I wasn't sure of the way. I remembered seeing a shallow creek near the turn-off from the highway; if I went in a straight line, I should come to it . . .

There it was, just ahead; next to it was a small fire where an old man with a white beard was cooking what looked like a skinned rabbit. The idea of eating bunny would've make me sick any other time, but right then it made my juices start. A sharp bark sounded and a prayer that the dog wouldn't come after me wiped away thoughts of food.

"Stay!" the old man commanded.

I was able to go my way without the tramp getting a look at me, and in less than a mile I came to the main road where the traffic'd thinned to a car every few minutes. This time I knew which way to go. I'd never thumbed in the dark, and I worked out that for a driver to spot me, I'd have to stand on the pavement and jump back if he didn't slow down. I was set to flag a distant car when I noticed the spotlight—*police!* That sent me scurrying off the road and under a barbed-wire fence.

For a good 15 minutes I lay there shivering from fear and a night too windy to be out in a swimsuit—*What if it rains? The season's ripe for it.* There was no choice, I'd have to take my chances. The first cars gave me a whoosh of air and a sinking heart. Maybe I'd have to go back and beg the tramp for a place by his fire—*but remember the dog.*

A movie from when I was 10 came into my head: an old rattletrap screeching to a halt when Claudette Colbert pulled up her skirt to

show her leg. My body wasn't mine; anyone in charge could order it stripped, shaved, and shamed—might as well get the good of it. A pair of headlights showed up the road—no time to think—I stepped out of the suit, and waving it hard over my head, raced naked to the center of the lane.

Like the old man in the rattletrap, the driver hit the brakes. The car stopped just ahead of me, and as I ran toward it, a strong gust of wind came up and ripped the suit out of my hand. I started to chase it, but the door of the car opened, "No time for that. Get in!"

I got in.

"Just us boys," the man said.

He was old enough to be my father—*Better naked here than naked in Happy Town.*

"You have an interesting way of hitching a ride."

He spoke well, dressed well, looked normal—*Thank God.*

"Any particular destination?"

"The next county—at least I think so—up the main boulevard near Red Dirt School, if you're going that way."

"Depending on the time we make, should be able to get you close."

He didn't mention my bald head or shaved body, and he asked no more questions, for which I was thankful. What he did do was steer one-handed with the other hand on the inside of my bare leg—close to things—real close—but he got no rise out o' me. *Keep your mouth shut—could be worse—lots worse,* I thought, calling up what happened to Happy Valley kids. We drove the better part of an hour before he pulled over to a late-night stand at a crossroad.

"Wait here," he said.

Twenty minutes later he came back holding a paper plate with two fat hot dogs in buns, not to mention pickles and slices of onion—my stomach churned. He put them on the seat next to me.

"Hungry?"

"Yessir."

"These are yours—but I'll expect something in return."

*So what else is new?* Didn't surprise me—*no free lunch—the world's turned its back on Sean Lacey.* What I'd waked up to and what I'd go to sleep to were different as cake and sawdust. I wasted no time grabbing a hot dog and going to work on it. The first one

with its trimmings knocked off, he started driving. I was taking a bite into the second wiener when I felt his hand on my leg again.

Something told me I wouldn't get it on. *Probably never get another long as I live.*

We'd been driving. We stopped. I opened my eyes and recognized where I was, less than three miles from home, a place off the highway with a nightlight, trees, and a picnic table. His hand was still on my leg. *Let him think you'll do what he wants.*

"I've never masturbated anyone—what's the going rate?"

How I found the answer, Jesus only knows, "No need for money, the hotdogs will cover it. Would work best to do me on that picnic table."

"All right, get out and lie down on the table."

I got out, but I didn't lie down. I ran like a deer.

The trip home was a blur—feet sorer by the minute. I went through alleys and backyards, over lawns, down sidewalks, past barking dogs, and at one point I had to dash under a streetlight in view of some people sitting out late on their porch. Finally I saw the house—half a block ahead—*Thank God!* I skirted the side to the back and tried our bedroom window—locked—I tried the living room windows—locked—I tried all the windows—locked. Since Bryan was away there was nothing for it—I had to ring the bell.

Jeanne opened the door in a white silk nightgown all lacy on top.

"Cheri! How worried I have been!"

I pressed my nakedness against her, put my head on her breasts, and broke down sobbing.

"No need to talk about it. Are you hungry?"

"N-no. C-can I have a b-bath?"

She walked me to her room where I flopped face down on the bed while she ran the water in the bathroom.

"Do you want me to leave?"

"N-no."

"Then let me help you into the tub."

Once in the water, I closed my eyes and lay back to soak.

"Comme tu es beau!" she whispered.

# CHAPTER 78

**S**omething should be done about Happy Valley Boys' Home—I knew it—knew it in my heart—but not by me—not by Sean Lacey— let someone else do it—*never want to think about it again*—I put Happy Town—the General—Stony—Gus—the cook—Damon— everything—out of my head—and kept it out—except there'd be dreams—a kimono coming off—a green crocodile—a towel folded on a bureau . . .

The story I told Bryan was I'd been captured by boys from another high school. Saturday night he grilled me, "Which high school?"

"Don't know."

"Tell me everything they did."

"Don't remember—passed out—went blank—"

"I can guess which school. Since you came home naked, it's pretty clear what they did. Don't worry, Little Brother, vengeance will be ours! There's a clergyman's son a couple miles down the road who's a freshman at Pricksville. Suppose we capture him and have Elsie do her stuff with him at the Lettermen's Bust; that'll put him on the road to Hell. Or maybe we should have Mats do him; that'd freak out an Orangeman. Come to think of it, why not have Elsie *and* Mats do him. A man-of-the-cloth's son should have enough saved up for a second go-round. Now tell me everything from the beginning."

"I'm too tired. Bryan, I'm asking you as my best friend—no vengeance!—let it go. Please, Bryan! Don't make me talk about it—don't make me think about it—I'd just like to forget. Anyway, thought you wanted to shower after you rode Old Paint into the Circle L?"

"You mean—?"

I was already undressing, "You want to shower? Let's shower."
He watched me strip.
"Will wonders never cease! Never thought I'd see the day! Jesus!
You really are sexy all shaved like that! Not sure Johnnie'll stay down."

We scrubbed each others' backs—Johnnie stayed down.

He'd promised as my best friend—*Thank God*—I wouldn't have a
clergyman's son on my conscience. I didn't want another Confession
ending up dosed with Lourdes water or whatever else a priest might
come up with.

Monday Bryan found out about the Greek Games. Tuesday after
7th period there was a boxing match in the Gym, the fighters barefoot
in undershorts, a bucket of water, a pair of scissors, shaving stuff,
and Big Bertha nearby for the pleasure of the winner.
The first two rounds the Irish Kid used his speed, backed away,
came in, peppered his opponent with left jabs, bloodied his nose.
Wally took some loop-the-loop swings, but never landed a solid
blow.
The third bell. More jabs, then out of nowhere a right cross—
Wally went flat on his back. Bryan pulled off both sets of gloves,
threw half the bucket of water in the loser's face, bringing him to,
yanked Wally's shorts off, and tossed them to the crowd.
"Who wants to shave him?"
"I'll do it!" Clarence yelled.
"We'll take turns," Carlin joined in.
Clarence got there first.
"Sean, take the scissors to his head and see how much hair you
can get off before we use the razor."

Wally was shaved clean.
"On your hands and knees! . . . Crawl! . . . All the way around the
locker room!"
Bryan followed him with Bertha, giving him one every few feet.
Mr. Winter came up to me, "Good-looking boy, but not as
good-looking as someone I know."

# CHAPTER 79

**S**ubject: Physical Education Excuses.
Report to Room 2 at the Boys' Gymnasium at 3:45 p.m. Friday.

Two dozen or so freshmen had gotten the notice.
"Let's see if we have any males! Clothes off!"
I started undressing, Clarence and Gran—the dog who'd won us six bits—huddling next to me.
"You bunch over there! Drop your shorts! . . . Line up backs to the wall! . . . Give the helper your name, so he can enter your vitals! . . . Hands at your sides! . . . Hands at your sides!!"
"And do they call you Bald Eagle, Young Man?" the helper asked.
"Big Cock, they call me Big Cock, and wouldn't you like to swap," I answered Joey.
The teacher—he taught Boys' Biology—playing doctor, got a quick bone from Gran.
When he moved to me I said, "My father's a G-Man, and if you touch my cock I'll get you put on J Edgar Hoover's Black List."

He didn't touch my cock.

It was my first week of gym class. I climbed naked out of the pool; Mr. Winter was waiting for me. I didn't cover myself. *Let him look, it's no skin off my dick. Takes all kinds to make a world.*

Saturday night after the lights went out on the tennis court—my shirt already off—I led Janet to the grass with one hand, while I unbuttoned my shorts with the other . . .

". . . Don't stop! . . . Don't stop! . . . Don't stop! . . ."

She didn't stop.

"I'll take my bra off next time if you promise to marry me?"
"Can't."
"Why not?"
"Going to be a priest."

# EPILOGUE

We had no bodies to bury, Jeanne and I. First my mother and father—they never came back for a visit. The war in Europe was going strong when they left Arabia. The second leg of their trip home, the light plane they'd boarded was shot out of the sky over Greece by a Messerschmitt. No survivors.

The Western Union boy came on a bicycle.
"Jeanne, do you have a dime!"
"No dime," the boy said, "it's bordered in black."
She got into bed with me that night—no sinning—just me sobbing, pressed against her silkiness.

Then Bryan. A cadet at West Point, he was champing at the bit to get into the action. So the week of my birthday he resigned and signed up for the Marines. The day I turned 18 was our last time together.
"You're Big Brother now—taller by three inches. There's something we have to talk about; remember how Maman went away one week every year? Know why?"
"Wanted to break the monotony, I suppose."
"She went to see an old boyfriend who died a year and a half ago. Maman is a young woman with a young body—she needs a male. Understand what I'm saying? You've been living alone together for almost two years—you're that male. You kiss goodnight, don't you?"
"It's a mother-son thing."
"Oh yeah? You mean you've never thought about her body?"

"I try not to. Besides, you don't go to bed with your best friend's mother."

"You've never been in bed with her?"

"U-u-u-h."

"Fess up—how many times?"

"Just once."

"Just once? What about that vacation you took together last year?"

"They didn't have twin beds—and we couldn't afford two rooms—but we didn't do anything."

"How many erections did you get?"

"Bryan, you're embarrassing me!"

"Thought you'd outgrown that. So what's the answer?"

"One a night."

"Yeah, one that lasted all night long. Did Maman notice?"

"She didn't say anything."

"Starting as of now, your best friend gives you permission to go to bed with his mother."

"But you've forgotten—I'm going to be a priest."

"You can't be a priest; you're too highly sexed. Remember, I'm the guy who slept in the same bed. You have no idea how close I'd come to taking things into my own hands to put you out of your misery."

"Bryan!"

"And what do you think will happen when you're a priest?"

"Don't know, but that's the last thing my father asked of me."

"Your father didn't become a priest. Remember the story you told me about your mother saying there'd be no Saturday night for a month? Your father needed his sex regular as clockwork; you've got his genes and probably his dick . . . Getting back to Maman, she has to love somebody, and right now that somebody is a boy named Sean who just turned legal. You really haven't noticed how she looks at you? I have."

"God, I'm stupid! Never thought I had a chance. Can't imagine not being around her—we eat together—read together—listen to music together—laugh together—walk together—tell each other things—do everything together. I could never leave her and marry someone else. I love her. It's as simple as that, I love her."

"All right, so let's forget all this nonsense about becoming a priest. I've never asked you anything as my best friend, but I'm asking you now: When the time's ripe, offer Maman Olympic Gold. Ha, ha! And not just Honorable Mention—get what I mean? You can be the father I never had . . . One last thing, no matter what happens, I want no priest."

"Was it Father O'Connor?"

"Little Brother's gotten too smart by half. I cannot tell a lie—at least not another one. Actually they weren't lies because I made myself forget. It happened the summer before I turned 14. Never having known my dad, and late in getting my growth, I was green as grass and easy pickin's. It started with a bath. Is that how you want to end up, washing little boys like Father O'Connor?"

"O Jesus! God help me—not that!"

"See that you don't."

Then Bryan gave me a hard hug and began to walk . . . "Remember! Olympic Gold! Not Silver or Bronze, mind! I'm asking you as my best friend!"

That was the last I saw of the best brother a boy ever had—on my side through good and bad.

Private O'Neill gave his life on an island in the South Pacific; he'd never be able to come from halfway round the world to keep his oath to Joey. It wouldn't be necessary—Joey died in the war too—like many of my classmates. Bobby and Peanuts made it through—Clarence too—but not Carlin, not Gran, not Mats.

They didn't even tell us the name of the island.

"Shall we have a priest perform a ceremony?" Jeanne asked.

"No priest. Bryan wanted no priest. He told me that before he left. If you don't mind, we'll have a stone made with all three names on it and two short lines Bryan was fond of."

> *Fear no more the heat o' the sun*
> *Nor the furious winter's rages.*

"That is a fine idea."

I couldn't pop the question right away because the Army wanted first crack at my body. There must've been 200 of us at the City Induction Center—all strangers to me.

A soldier was giving orders, "Get in one of the lines, take a paper bag, and use the pencil to write your name on it."

The boy alongside me was small, "Can I stay next to you?" he whispered. "I-I'm s-scared,"

"Sure, let's keep together."

"You all got bags with your names on'em? . . . Everyone? . . . All right, take your clothes off and put'em in the bag."

Fast as you could peck out *The quick red fox jumps over the lazy brown dog,* 200 of us were naked. My companion with one leg short and bony—skin but no flesh to speak of—a little-boy penis, and a face red with embarrassment.

I signaled the soldier with the most stripes on his sleeve.

"Why put him through this? Let him get dressed and go home. Even the Army should see he's not cut out to carry a gun."

"Better learn ta keep yur mouth shut, Big Balls. If they take'im, reckon he c'n stop a bullet good as the next Joe."

A two-stripe soldier took charge of 20 of us and handed out paper cups. My Clinic know-how told me the cups were useless—no names on them—didn't make sense. I pointed this out to the two-striper.

"Listen, Smart Guy, I don't give the orders, I just follow'em, and that's what you better learn ta do."

He had us take our penises in both hands and squeeze downwards to clear them out before peeing into the no-name cups—the small boy couldn't.

"He's busy showing that kid at the far end—let me give you half of mine," I whispered.

The cups set down, we had to get into one of four lines. When it came the small boy's turn, the doctor asked, "Can you get any fun out of that thing?"

A red face got redder.

A group of us were put into a half-circle. There was a blond boy—all but hairless below—who looked like a high school freshman. The psychiatrist asked him, "You're a virgin, right?"

"Y-yessir."

"I can usually tell. First chance you get, ask a newsboy for the nearest Cathouse—they always know—and get yourself laid. Afterwards go straight to a Pro Station."

All the boys were lily white, all except one who was brown—looked Polynesian. "Which is heavier a pound of feathers or a pound of lead?" the psychiatrist asked.

The kid never had a chance—the doctor had a barrel of questions ready to spring.

"Mental incompetence." There'd be no browns mixed with whites.

One of our group wanted out, "I'm a homo, Doctor—I go down on men."

"Show me."

"Show you?"

"Show me on the virgin."

Everyone looked at the blond boy—he popped a 5-incher—nobody laughed.

"Well he's ready."

The shirker went over to the blond, knelt in front of him—the rest of the group holding their breaths—took the erect penis in his hand—the blond boy shaking . . .

"C-can't."

"You're in the army, Soldier."

There's no telling what happened to the lame boy—me ending up in the Deep South for training. The sergeant in charge watched us take showers—didn't bother me—I'd made it through four years of Mr. Winter.

My nearest thing to a friend was a skinny kid from back East—he could talk a mile a minute—never ran out of jokes. Every few days the sergeant would call him to his private room.

"What's going on?" I asked.

"Don't ask," he said.

"OK, I won't ask."

"OK, so I'll tell. Afraid to say no. He can get you killed."

I decided a young ranch hand from Texas—tall and freckled—reminded me of Carlin—was more my speed. Slow talker—a good buddy to have a beer with—when they finally let us off the base.

"Let's rent a room and find some chicks," he said.

The girls held their liquor better than us, and by the time we hit the hotel we were out of it.

I woke up naked in bed with the Texan and checked my wallet on the night table—empty. My buddy woke up and checked his—empty.
"Did we at least get laid?" he asked.
"What does your dick tell you?"
"That it's ready for action—what about yours?"
"Double in spades. They played us for suckers. Lucky we didn't have much money."
"Yeah, and now we got none."
"Look on the bright side."
"What's the bright side?"
"Don't know, but there's always a bright side."
"Guess the bright side is money or no money the Army has to feed us."
"Yeah, and the other side is morning, noon, and night we have to eat grits—like to get my hands on whoever invented 'em . . . Let's grab a shower."
"I'm embarrassed."
"Why?"
"Got the grandfather of all bones."
"Should've had my big brother; he'd've scrubbed embarrassed out o' you. Come on, mine'll keep it company."

Monday we lined up naked for a short-arm inspection.
There was nothing delicate about the two corporals doing the inspecting. One of them had a penis in his hand. It tried to get away.
"You queer, Boy?"
"Nosir."
"Yuh call me *Corporal*, I ain't *Sir*—got that?"
"Yessir, Corporal."
"Yuh get fucked yesterday?"

"My buddy said I got pussy."

"First time?"

"Yessir, Corporal."

"Use a rubber?"

"Used my dick."

"Yuh know what you done, Boy? Yuh jus' went an' got yurself all clapped up. Gotta treat yuh."

The other corporal picked up a giant hypodermic with a thick needle.

"Hold yur piss long as yuh can—then use the bucket."

"Don't need to piss."

"Yuh will—pull your sheath back."

"What?"

"Get your pecker ready, Boy!"

The kid watched that needle coming at him, and seeing where it was going, collapsed against a table. The corporals picked him up, laid him out, filled him, and clamped him with a clothespin.

The needle and the clothespin set off a run on condoms. They rook the place of dimes in barrack crap games.

I almost made it through—almost—till we had an all-day march through rain and swamps. My asthma did me in. The Texan packed me out on his back—me struggling for air. Strong kid—said he'd practiced lifting calves—lucky for me, me being no small package.

"Double pneumonia," the doctor in the ward said.

Sean Lacey, the proud possessor of a medical discharge.

Bryan'd told me what to do when the time came—made me promise as his best friend—and as far as I was concerned the time was long overdue.

"Put on that Wagner I like, will you?"

"You want the Liebeslied, Cheri?"

"Right through the death part."

I went to the bedroom, took my clothes off—thought about Jeanne's body—sewed up Olympic Gold, and went out to her.

"Will you have me? Will you have me from this day forward? Think I loved you from the moment I set eyes on you. I offer you this body for as long as you'll have it."

"Let me slip into something more comfortable," she said.

"No, don't do that. Pack a bag. We're driving to where we can get married by a Justice of the Peace. Before he left, Bryan gave us his blessing; how you see me now is how he told me to propose."

"Cheri, merci beaucoup, but I am too old; I doubt I could give you so much as a single son."

"You're only 38. Anyway, the last thing I want is to supply the Church with altar boys."

The first sign said *The Biggest Little City in the World.* Our eyes were looking for a second sign—"There's one!"

*Marriages Performed 24 Hours a Day—Ring the Night Bell.*

The judge came out in a tasseled cap and a long nightgown—no nightwear for Jeanne and me.

I couldn't believe it as I signed the register: *Mr. and Mrs. Sean Lacey.*

"Thank you, Sir!" the bellboy said after I tipped him a silver dollar.

The two of us alone, I had to tell her, "I'm not a virgin."

"Dieu merci! Neither am I."

There was nothing fancy about the room, but there was all we needed—a mattress.

Naked, she was everything I'd dreamed of—*so beautiful!* We made love . . . again . . . and again . . . and again . . .

"I wonder what the first-night record is?"

"Whatever it is, Cheri, I think you will break it."

Holding my newborn son for the first time, I thought, *If Dad could see him, he'd forgive me for not becoming a priest.*

"Do you want to call him Michael after his grandfather?"

"No—there's only one name I'd consider—we'll call him Bryan after our big brother."

"Do you want him circumcised?"

"That's a tough one. God knows it hasn't been easy—there have been times—tons of times—Cherie, I leave it to you."

"I like my husband as he is, and a boy should be like his father."

"Settled. He'll go through life as I have."

"As Big Brother would say, *Have mercy on me for I am about to sin!* Is it too soon to make love?"

"Can you wait encore un peu?"

"If I learned anything growing up, it was how to wait—I can wait."

"Would you like me to bathe you, Cheri?"

"I'd be embarrassed."

"Bryan said you were beyond that."

"Not completely. I'll wait, and when it's time we'll set a new record."

Little Bryan didn't grow up bashful—he didn't get the chance. From the week he could stand till the week he graduated from Pineapple, he took showers with his father.

And many a bath our Bryan shared with Cousin Mary's little girl Maggie—and her with no panties—I made sure of that.